SURVIVES

Written By: **Jennifer Foor**

Marketing: INKSLINGER PR

Beta Readers
Georgette Geras
Kayla Kennedy, Emma Clifton, Kristy Davidson, Catherine
Roberts, Lara Petterson , Danielle Sanchez, Jennifer Harried, Teresa
Coleman

Acknowledgements:
This book is dedicated to all of my family members
who have served in the Armed Forces.
Carl T Meyers
Owen Schultz SR
Owen Schultz JR
Owen Schultz III
Adam Schultz
Gregory Scott Thomas SR
Gregory Scott Thomas JR
Kathy Thomas
William Freed
Michael Freed
Mike Jones SR
Lee Rosser
Edward Zimmerman

Intro

Love isn't always something we learn to feel or experience through years of heartbreak and personal endeavors. Though it can grow stronger, people aren't able to choose when it will happen. Sometimes, in rare instances, it becomes the only thing we live for; the reason we keep striving to move in a forward direction. In other circumstances, it can be the whole reason we exist in this world. That kind of rarity isn't one to boast about. Loving someone with extreme compassion comes with great agony, and even more patience. Feeling as if you can't breathe is only the beginning of what could occur when your emotions play a part in the existence of such a powerful word. There have been days where I've woken up and wished it wasn't there, hounding me from the depths of my core. I've always considered myself a strong man; one that could withstand extreme amounts of despair without breaking down. I felt like I could get beyond it, however, learned quickly that it doesn't work that way.

Imagine being in love with the same person since you were a young child, only to have them fall for your twin instead. This story I'm about to tell you is rocky.

It will rip you apart and possibly put you back together again.

I know this because it's my story.

The pain and anguish in this story is what it was like to hold onto hope that some day we'd find each other again. I won't sugar coat the details of what I went through to have her, nor will I apologize for any actions that led me right back into Kat's life.

There is one thing I've learned from all of this.

Sometimes love isn't enough.

Sometimes it takes a little fate, some bad experiences, and a lot of time.

Chapter 1

My story starts from as early as I can recall my first memories of knowing she was everything to me. It was back when life was easy, and the only thing we cared about was how long we could stay outside to play at night. Katy Michaels wasn't just a girl I met on the streets when I was out playing as a child. She was our next door neighbor, the only child of my parent's best friends, and the most beautiful thing I'd ever laid eyes on.

Even when we were small, young enough to be bathed in the same tub, or dressed in similar coordinating outfits for pictures, we'd formed a sacred bond. It wasn't just the two of us either. My twin brother Branch was the third member of our elite group, and although we'd shared other friends, none would ever compare to the relationship that the three of us had. While young, we displayed different personalities. Branch was a jokester, always using ridiculous mockeries to grab Kat's attention. I, on the other hand, was somewhat of a protector. I made it my life's mission to make sure I was always around when she was sad, which gave me the benefit of learning to read her early on.

It wasn't hard to stay close when we lived only feet away from one another. We shared meals, holidays, and every memorable occasion. We were inseparable by fault.

Back when we were too young to realize how complicated life could be, my feelings for Kat began to change. Her hair grew longer, her eyes were brighter, and when she smiled I did the same right back. There was nothing she could do to change my mind either. I felt like she was my angel and assumed someday she'd be mine forever.

Unfortunately, I wasn't the only one who had those same aspirations. My brother Branch also found interest in Kat.

As we grew older, we found ourselves falling into the pressures of being accepted by our classmates. At the age of twelve it was easy to admit that my plans of becoming Kat's boyfriend were quite obvious.

While Branch used his cockiness to get under her skin, I was always the person who had her back. I wanted her to feel like she could count on me for anything.

One night we all agreed that we'd practice kissing though admittedly my intentions weren't only to master the craft. I'd been dying to press my lips against hers, and with that anticipation came a lot of nervousness. She wasn't just some friend; this was *my* Kat.

Right before my brother and I headed out to meet her in the tree house, he stopped me, acting weird and irrational. He didn't make it known that he was claiming first dibs, but I could tell from the way he was acting that something was clearly up with him. Being twins gave me that ability. "Don't get bent out of shape if after tonight she only wants me." Branch announced.

"Did you practice on your pillow?" Banter was normal between the two of us. It was something my brother enjoyed, and in a way it had become how he'd learned to communicate when he was nervous or afraid. This gave me an advantage from the get-go.

Lucky for me Branch was in fact a pussy. He couldn't bring himself to kiss her, which gave me an added benefit.

At first I was shaking profusely. Our lips met and the shock of it all made me lose control. I was unhinged, forgetting what I was supposed to be doing with my tongue. The utter disgust in myself made me pull away.

Branch laughed at us. "I knew you wouldn't do it right."

That was all the motivation I needed to give it another go. "Come on, Kat, let's try it again."

I leaned forward, only closing my eyes after I looked into hers, hidden behind long strands of hair that were always in her face, back then. I had no idea how this very moment would seal the deal for me, utterly and completely. I took my time, memorizing, savoring, and trying not to become embarrassingly aroused. Being this close to her was too much for me to handle. Even as our bodies remained parted while we embraced, it was still enough to make it difficult, to say the least.

After a few long seconds Branch had seen enough. He made a snarky comment, announcing that my time was up. "Let me show you both how it's done."

Opening my eyes to see her pulling away was unbearable. My brother shoved himself between us to get his own fix. I'd never in my life been jealous of him. We'd learned to share before we came out of the womb, yet this circumstance introduced us to what it felt like to want something completely for ourselves. While they took their moment together I could feel myself turning; the disgust of it all hitting me like a deer in headlights. I hated that he was kissing those perfect lips, wiping away remnants of mine. He was distorting our perfect moment, damaging how innocent it all was.

While stewing in anger, I heard our mother calling out to us. It was time to go inside for the night, and a part of me was relieved. It meant that Branch had to get his grabby hands off of Kat.

While I stood there watching him running inside, I turned to see Kat doing the same. An instant reaction caused me to reach out and take her by the hand. "Thanks for being my first kiss, Kat." She looked down with a huge smile across her face as if I'd embarrassed her by talking about it.

She responded in a whisper. "Thanks for being mine, Brooks."

I looked down at the ground and kicked some rocks, feeling overwhelmed by how close we were to each other. Those lips, so sweet, were calling my name. I was experiencing many emotions, but mostly an intense need to feel them again. "So can we try it one more time, so we'll be sure we got it right?"

Kat shrugged before leaning her body close to mine. As soon as our lips touched, our tongues played together. A jolt of unexpected pleasure rushed through me, causing me to react by continuing our embrace.

Then I heard my mother's voice, calling out to me for a second time. We broke apart and looked at one another for a single moment.

"I gotta go."

"Okay. I'll see you tomorrow." She turned to begin running away from me. Even though I started to do the same, I couldn't help but freeze and look back to watch her.

It was in that moment when I knew she'd be my future. "Bye, Kat."

Once inside I had to hear a bunch of crap from my twin. It began as soon as my foot hit the top step in our two-story home. Branch was standing in the hallway, waiting with his arms folded across his chest. "What took you so long?"

The look in his eyes was discerning. I could tell he already knew exactly what had went on when he left. Because I didn't want to hurt my brother, I gritted my teeth and looked away. "It was nothing."

"It looked like more than nothing. We agreed to one kiss."

"It's Katy, Branch. It's not like it's some girl you like. We're all friends. Leave it alone." I needed to go to my room before he saw right through me. Unlike my brother, it was impossible for me to stand before someone and lie.

"Maybe I do like her. I'd appreciate it if you didn't kiss her again, and if you do it behind my back I'll make sure to tell her things so she hates you."

"Stop being such a jerk, Branch."

"I'm not being a jerk. She told me herself. She said she only likes you as a friend. She said she'd never be interested in you that way. The chances of her ever picking you were slim anyway, not when she has me. Just because you act like a pussy and kiss up her ass doesn't mean she likes you more. Girls aren't like that. They want the tough guy, who makes them laugh. They like the ones that are hard to get, not the guys who follow them around like a lost puppy."

As I turned to walk away I closed my eyes, wishing I hadn't heard that. She didn't feel the way I did about her. She liked him more. There was nothing left to say. We'd been taught to be respectful of each other. Our parents had instilled values that I appreciated. Even at twelve, I couldn't see anything, including Kat, coming between us. If I didn't know how fickle my brother was perhaps it would have bothered me more. Maybe I would have stood my ground and fought for Kat back then. I couldn't have seen that it was the first step in my demise; what would lead me to break and eventually have to flee. I should have known he was full of crap, saying whatever he had to in order to get under my skin. Back then I was too naïve to fathom that he could be blowing smoke just to have an advantage. Up until this point I didn't think he had it in him.

None of us could have known that the next day would change us forever.

The ride to school was obviously quiet. I was unable to even glance at her without wanting to kiss those lips again. Looking back, I know it wasn't just puberty beckoning me to explore. It was something deeper that came from my heart, not the muscle between my legs. Even after hearing she wasn't interested, something kept telling me not to give up. If there was some slim chance that she could change her mind I'd be there waiting for her.

Once inside of the classroom it was obvious that the teacher was upset about something. We'd done fire drills, and even discussed circumstances such as shootings, but this seemed worse. As she delivered us the first bout of news, I looked back to find Kat worried. I stuck out my tongue to make her smile, knowing it was only temporary. Out of the corner of my eye I could see my brother staring at the two of us. I turned quickly to prevent him from thinking there was more to it.

As the minutes passed, we were all sent to wait for our parents. The three of us expected Kat's mother to walk in and rescue us from another dreadful day full of lessons, but unfortunately she never stepped foot in our school again.

It was a day that would live in America's hearts forever; a day that we lost so many of our own from terrorism. My mom said nothing on the ride home, but it was obvious she was frantic for answers. Once my dad came home it was clear that they were desperate to find Kat's mom. We all assumed it was only her dad that we needed to fear the worst for. Hours passed, with my parents clung to each other, watching the news for a glimmer of hope, while we stayed back keeping Kat far away from seeing the aftermath.

It wasn't like any of us, including the adults, could prepare for something so tragic. We didn't know what to say, or how to act. Her pain could be heard as she flooded a river's worth of tears. It got even worse when the truth was revealed.

On that day, September 11th 2001, Kat not only lost her mother, but also her father to the attacks on the Pentagon. We didn't know the reason, not that it even mattered why. All any of my family cared about was protecting Kat from the extreme amount of pain she was going through. As the days passed, and the horrors became her own reality, I watched my best friend, and the girl I'd fallen in love with, lose herself. She put up walls and seemed lost in the truth of it all. It didn't help that every channel on the television had coverage of the events that took her parents lives. Seeing the videos playing out, watching the building crumble, it was inevitably difficult. Her parents had been our family too. We'd called them aunt and uncle. We'd loved them our entire lives.

A day or so had gone by before my mom was able to obtain the recordings from their home voicemail. It was then that Kat heard her parent's voices for the very last time. In their last moments alive they sent her a desperate plea to be strong and know they loved her more than anything else in the world. In my honest opinion it only made matters worse. Kat was destroyed, and I don't know if she'd ever be able to forget what they sounded like in those last seconds they were with us on this earth. It was obvious that she'd lived with that memory, dwelled on it, until she lost herself completely.

From the very beginning our parents both pulled us aside one night to talk about it. My mother carried a tissue in her hands while she paced the small study. Dad sat back in his chair watching her with concern. "Boys, what's happened is tragic. We still don't know all the details, but Katy needs us to stay strong for her. It's imperative that she not see us crying or upset." My dad wasn't always outspoken, but it was very obvious they considered Kat family. In his own way he was hurting too.

"What happens if they're dead?" Branch asked.

"Don't talk that way," our mother interrupted with more sniffles.

"She's right, Branch. Don't say that. Think of Kat. She needs them to be okay." Even though I was wondering the same thing, I couldn't bring myself to admit it like my brother.

"Sorry, but it could happen. What then?"

"Then we take care of Katy. We give her support and love." Our dad folded his hands as he spoke, looking over at both of us the whole time. "Do you understand, boys? It's necessary to stay positive. We can't give up hope." It was weird, but I watched him turn to my mother when he said it, as if he was sending some kind of innuendo just for her.

Branch and I watched our mother march out of the room, seemingly disgusted.

When we turned to our dad for answers he faked a smile. "You're mother is just upset. She'll be fine."

In those days following the death of her parents I put my personal feelings for Kat aside. She needed her two best friends, so that's what Branch and I provided her with. We stayed by her side, even when we had nothing left to talk about. I held her hand when I knew she needed an extra amount of comfort. I cried when I knew she wasn't around to see it, and come the day of the funeral, I held it all in to be the rock she needed me to be.

It wasn't just Kat that was suffering though. I couldn't remember ever seeing my mother so heartbroken before. Her tears were genuine, and I knew why. I'd been keeping a secret of my own for a long time, hoping that maybe my eyes had been playing tricks on me that night. I couldn't believe that it was more than a friendly embrace. Yet, somehow I now knew it had to have been. Something had been going on with my mother and Kat's dad; something taboo that could tear our families apart. There was no need to bring it up to my father, or even mention to my mother that I knew why she was having such a tough time. Mr. Michaels was dead, and whatever was going on between the two of them was irrelevant. I couldn't shame my mother even though for a while I kept my distance. Now, more than ever, we had to become one family. Kat's future depended on it. I depended on it. We needed my parents to stay together, so we wouldn't be ripped apart anymore.

I'll never forget the day they found her parent's remains. Kat had to be comforted by adults while Branch and myself were left to prepare for what we would say when we got our chance. In the tree house, where we'd shared so many good memories, the two of us discussed what we could say to Kat.

"I'm going to tell her a joke, not a bad one either. I'll find the funniest thing I can, and make sure she smiles," Branch announced.

"She doesn't need to smile right now, you idiot. She needs to cry. Put yourself in her shoes." It annoyed me how Branch thought he knew what Kat needed. "She's falling apart. Both of her parents are gone. They're never coming back. A joke isn't going to solve anything."

"It will make her smile. I'm no good at the other stuff."

That's where he was right. Being supportive was my specialty, and I was fully aware of how much he hated that quality in me. "We need to be there, even if we say nothing. She needs to know she's not alone, Branch. Kat needs to know that she's loved."

His eyes opened wide, as if he knew my love for her was stronger than a family type of bond. Though he didn't argue, I could tell when he walked away that he was still stewing over it. With no time to address the elephant in the room, we parted ways, avoiding the topic all together.

The next few days were pretty hectic. My parents scrambled to get in touch with lawyers, and important people handling the estate of the Michaels. Having only one aunt as her next of kin, both Branch and I worried that Kat would be sent away. We listened to our parents making calls while reassuring us that our lifelong friend wouldn't be going anywhere. It wasn't until her aunt left to go back to England that we could rest assured.

The next couple of months everyone walked on eggshells. The news hadn't let up, yet we'd all learned to keep the television time to a minimum. My mother did everything in her power to transition Kat over to our house without causing her extra grief.

She'd pulled Branch and I aside to prepare us for the transition. "Boy's, I need you to be gentlemen. You'll be sharing your bathroom with a lady. That means you need to keep the toilet seat down, and always flush when you're done going to the bathroom. If she needs to go, you let her in there first, and please give her privacy."

We both nodded to agree.

My mom was falling apart. Dark circles were under her eyes, and at night I'd heard her downstairs crying when we were all supposed to be asleep.

If my mother wasn't hard enough to watch, my beautiful friend also struggled. It was obvious she was broken. The once charismatic girl was quiet and withdrawn. She didn't initiate a conversation, or activity. The more she pushed us away, the harder I tried to be the shoulder she needed to cry on. There were a few moments we shared that were intense. Several times, when we were alone in the tree house, I wanted to hold her; to kiss her and tell her she'd be okay. Yet I couldn't bring myself to chance it. She needed a friend, not a horny pre-teen. Being her boyfriend could wait. After all, we had our whole lives to work that out. Back then I didn't have doubts that she'd pick me. I'd been the one to wipe away her tears, to hold her hand, and to silently reassure her that she'd someday be happy again.

Chapter 2

About a year after the death of her parents, Kat finally began to open up. She'd been seeing a doctor, who seemed to help her on the outside. I don't even know if my parents were aware that inside she was still a disaster. Only someone who knew her would see the brutal truth firsthand. At night, while my family slept so silently, I'd creep toward her bedroom door and listen to her crying. Every sob was like tiny shards of glass being driven into my heart. At thirteen I knew I'd be in big trouble if I opened that door and got caught in her bed. Though it would have been innocent, I wasn't going to risk any reason for them to want to send her away.

Kat belonged with us, no matter how hard it got sometimes. On good days it was obvious she was happy to be with our family.

My brother Branch had his own way of handling Kat. He'd wait on her, going above and beyond to cater to her every need. While I connected with her on a more emotional level, his actions were all physical. Our bonds were still strong, but clearly changed.

One night, after I'd been out in the tree house with Kat alone, doing nothing wrong, Branch pulled me aside in his room. He kept tapping on the post at the foot of his bed while staring me down. "What is your problem?" I finally asked.

"I want you to back off."

"Huh?"

"Katy."

"I don't know what you're talking about, Branch. We're friends, that's all." At the time it was the truth. We couldn't be more. It was still too soon to take it to another level. She wasn't emotionally ready to sneak around behind my parent's backs.

"She says you're smothering her. I told you before that she didn't like you that way."

Feeling defeated, and pathetic for holding onto hope, I walked away from my brother. It was obvious that all my efforts were for nothing.

For the next year I watched my brother pick on Kat, not in a rude way, but one that would indicate he was attempting to get under her skin for the attention. I became the one she turned to, but only for the support I'd always offered her. For a while I was certain we were on the same page. I kept telling myself that she was interested, and if we waited it out we'd be able to be together without causing problems with the family. After all, she lived in our house, and unless I wanted her to be shipped off to England with an aunt she barely knew, I had to keep the peace.

Then it happened.

The choice was made before I had a chance to grasp it was taking place. Sure, I'd seen my brother interacting with her. He'd warned me that she'd chosen him, yet I needed to see it with my own eyes. It was obvious he was still interested as well. We'd all begun to change, physically and mentally into young adults. Kat was blossoming into a beautiful woman. Her curves were pronounced, and she was who everyone at school wanted to have a piece of.

I'm sure our classmates knew they never had a chance. There was no way Branch or I would allow for them to. We'd already laid claim to her, not understanding that one day she'd have to choose one of us. Never in a million years could I have accepted that she chose Branch if I hadn't seen it with my own eyes.

I'd like to say her decision came out of left field. I think I wouldn't have as many regrets if I didn't feel as if it were my fault that it happened. Certainly there was a reason why she chose him over me. I mean, it made no sense at all. He'd picked on her until she lost it and came running to me more times than I could count. I'd waited my whole life to make her mine, only to have my own brother step forward and take her away.

The first time I saw them sneaking off to be together I felt my heart being ripped from my chest. I hadn't confessed my love, yet knew my brother was fully aware of my feelings. Our secret hide-out in the tree house became unbearable to visit. I couldn't sit opposite them and see them having their own first time experiences without me. I couldn't pretend that every little touch didn't make my stomach turn and fuel my anger.

No longer could I look Kat in the eyes and not feel anguish because I'd missed my opportunity. For a while I wanted to tell on them, to get them into trouble so they couldn't be together. Then I went through a phase where I presumed she'd dump my brother and realize it was me she was in love with. Day after day I watched them desperately falling in love, and there was nothing I could do to make it go away. I was stuck living with it; with their secret because it would never be as bad as Kat having to live somewhere else.

Burying my feelings deep inside was my only option, but even that came with consequences. Branch could see right through me, and one night he let me know that I wasn't going to get my chance.

We were sixteen, and they'd been secretly a couple for quite some time. He didn't knock when he came into my room full of smiles. I could tell something monumental had happened, even before he confessed it.

He started tossing up a ball as he spoke, probably because he couldn't bear to look me in the eyes and watch me hating him. "I never thought I'd gloat, Brooks. I told myself that I'd keep it a secret, but I've got to tell you this. I have to tell someone how awesome it was."

I sat up in my bed, already knowing what he was going to say. I'd watched them making out, groping, and everything else that comes before the actual deed. "What are you going on about?"

"We did it, me and Katy. She finally let me get into those panties. It was scary at first. She bled, and seemed to be in a lot of pain, but I'm sure the next time will be even better, because we'll know what to expect."

How was I supposed to sit there and listen to him bragging? "Congrats to you, I guess."

"You're probably pissed she picked me, aren't you?"

"No." I shook my head and looked away, unable to lie to his face. "It's great. I'm happy for you. She obviously made the right choice." The bile was rising in my throat as I began fighting back the agonizing jealousy. This was bitter, ugly, and it was destroying me from the inside out.

We heard someone walking into the bathroom, and I could tell Branch was worried our parents were awake and listening. "I better get back to bed. Don't tell Katy I told you. She made me promise to keep it a secret, especially from you."

I don't even know if I held in my first tear until my door shut. I lost control, over not just my emotions, but also my heart. For so long I'd assured myself she'd come running to me. I could feel our connection, knowing that there was still something between us. How could I have been so mistaken? Was I blind? Had Branch been right all along? Was I only a dear friend to Kat, and nothing more?

Like a little child, I bawled myself to sleep, with images of my brother screwing the love of my life.

After that night it became even more difficult to hang out with them. I could feel myself withdrawing, but they didn't seem to care. Even though they attempted to include me, I knew it was only to cover up the fact that they were a couple to our parents. I hated being used for their benefit and knew I had to make a change to rectify the situation. I was inadequate.

For a few months I was good about keeping my distance. I started talking to other girls, but only to attempt to get Kat out of my head. It was quite ridiculous since she lived in the same house as me. How was one to forget someone they saw every single day, sat across from at the table, and brushed their teeth alongside of?

Reluctantly I turned my pain into something else. Fueled by jealousy and regret, I distanced myself more from the two lovebirds, becoming troublesome to hide the brutal truth of what I knew I'd never have.

It was hard to imagine loathing both of them, but with each day came the hope of being able to finally rid myself of the constant ache I had in my heart.

It wasn't always bad though. On occasion Kat and my mom would go out for hours, shopping and doing what females liked to do. In those instances Branch and I were cool. I didn't hate him for loving her. I hated myself for not being brave enough to tell her first. For that reason I'd be forever envious of his life, hoping someday to replace my feelings for Kat with someone that I could have wholeheartedly. Until that day came I'd continue wishing she was mine; and just hoping for the moment when she'd realize that she'd made the wrong choice.

Chapter 3

On the anniversary of her parent's death, at the age of sixteen, something broke in me. I'd been doing so well, portraying someone who pretended not to care that the other half of my heart was bedding my brother.

On this particular evening Kat was a wreck. My parents had started a tradition with making her favorite meal; one her mother used to make. Each time, since their death, it would start out nice and end up with everyone sad, reminiscing about what could have been.

When Kat headed up to bed I watched my brother giving her a look, but he didn't follow behind her. Silently I sat there next to him, playing a video game and acting like everything was well in the world. All the while I wondered how he could be so insensitive. She clearly needed him to reassure her that everything would be okay, yet he was in his own little world, ignoring the fact that his girlfriend was falling apart.

"I think Kat's upset."

"She's always upset about something," Branch replied.

"Yeah, but tonight is the anniversary."

"She told me she was fine, Brooks. Let it go. It's not your problem. Honestly, I don't know why you still care. Can't you take a hint?"

I ignored his comment, unable to accept that Kat would ever want me to leave her alone. When we were together she was content, almost blissful. That wasn't how someone acted when they were annoyed. This wasn't the first time my brother had mentioned it to me, nor was it going to prevent me from being there for my best friend. Until she told me from her own mouth to steer clear, I'd be by her side, offering her anything she needed.

By the time we headed up to bed all I could think about was Kat. After the house got quiet I could hear her sobbing through the walls. Something happened that night. It was like I snapped. I couldn't fathom being so far away from her when she needed someone to wipe away her tears and comfort her until the pain subsided. I considered waking up my brother, but refused to allow myself to let him take credit for my concerns. She needed the love that I had to give her because it was effortless.

Before I could rationalize with my teenage self, I was already opening her door. The room was silent, but I knew exactly where to walk. I crouched down on the side of her bed, following the direction of her sniffles to place exactly where she was on the mattress.

A hand reached out and touched mine, leading me closer to her. Her cries beckoned me to hold her, to take the pain away, even if only for a few moments. I could do this without getting overwhelmed. This was my Kat. I was put on this earth to take care of her. I knew it more than anything else.

Eventually, I began to relax. Being so near gave me this feeling of empowerment. As her lips narrowed toward mine I realized she thought I was Branch, but I refused to stop her. I couldn't prevent something so tremendous and unrehearsed from happening. In that moment right from wrong didn't exist. I had to cross the line because spending another second without her in my arms seemed unbearable.

I never intended to take it so far. From the second her lips pressed against mine I felt myself losing control. Her body was like a wonderland, welcoming me to explore. I'd dreamed of this moment, even prayed for it to happen.

This wasn't just some girl that I was about to be intimate with. This was Kat, the girl I'd loved my whole life. She kept crying, pulling me closer. Her kisses were desperate, and I needed to save her from the pain. I wanted to be the one who could take it away, not because I wanted to, but because she desired it to be me. In my head I convinced myself that she knew the difference. I told my body to proceed.

From that first kiss, with every touch, I knew I couldn't hold back. I'd love to be able to blame immaturity on my decision making, or perhaps my lack of control came from pent up anxiety of wanting her. Whatever the case, I couldn't refrain.

"It hurts so much. Please just make the pain go away. Make me forget about it for just a little while. I can't feel this way," she continued sobbing.

I tried to talk my way out of it as a final desperate plea. "This won't solve anything," I whispered.

Her lips were back on mine, her tongue immediately taunting me to participate. She only pulled away to beg some more while reaching her hands up my sides underneath of my shirt. I should have pulled away, but her touch awakened parts of me that I didn't know how to control. I became carried away, lost in the perpetual moment of having her all to myself. She hadn't said my brother's name, nor had she pushed me away. Denying her would be like refusing to breathe.

I took my time, kissing her soft skin, and savoring each and every kiss. I caressed her tender areas, making sure she knew I appreciated this opportunity. Her tears were silenced once our clothes were removed, and we lay there overtop of one another. Though shaky, I entered her with little effort, sending my body into an uncontrolled euphoria. I began to shake, hiding it with my movements as I set out for an unpracticed pace. Kat wasn't just my first love, she was my first everything, and knowing that caused my senses to go awry.

When the moment was over we laid there in each other's arms in silence. Out of breath, and still frazzled from what we'd just done, I knew I had to leave the room. It took everything in me to separate our bodies, kiss her, and then walk away.

Once I reached my room I closed the door and plopped down on my bed, first to celebrate silently to myself, but then to punish myself for the sins that I'd allowed myself to commit.

I'd just lost my virginity to the girl I loved, yet felt as if my heart had vacated my body and been replaced with utter guilt. I'd disrespected my brother, my parents, and most of all the one person I cared the most for.

When she awoke the next morning, clearly giving all of her attention to my brother, I knew what I feared was true. Kat hadn't made love to me. She'd thought I was Branch, and I hadn't corrected her.

For the next week I steered clear of them the best I could, in fear that they'd both approach me after discovering my secret. When a month passed I started to question if Kat was keeping it a secret, yet nothing had changed between us. I was still the third wheel, the person who kept them from being alone.

Deciding to let it go, I buried my pain by hooking up with random chicks from school. They'd never be Kat, but I couldn't let it keep breaking me down. If she wasn't meant to be mine, I had to move on, before the pain consumed me.

Each time we were together, every second I spent close to her, reminded me of that special night. When I rested my head to sleep, I spent countless hours thinking about her, drawing her in my sketchbook, and even writing letters that I knew I'd never give her. It was the only way to cope with what I'd done, and how I still felt.

The more I attempted to move on, the harder it became. Kat was relentlessly picking on every girl I talked to. She felt she was being a friend while I saw it as something else. It got her attention, which only made me do it more frequently. By the time the anniversary of her parent's death came back around, I'd given myself a terrible reputation. No matter how hard I tried, she still wouldn't stop giving me that look; the one that always left me hoping there was something between us.

It wasn't until I brought someone home with me to her special dinner that everything became apparent. It was the breaking point; the one that would send me as far away as I could get.

After meeting Kat and my brother at the cemetery to pay our annual respects to her parent's lost lives, I parted ways with them. While they went to catch a movie, I ran into someone from school that had been trying to get with me for months. Her name was Natalie Chambers. She was blonde, bodacious, and could probably get any guy she wanted. From the moment we were alone, I could tell she was willing to take things as far as I wanted. In this case, I'd only set out to get a rise out of Kat. She and Branch had been up each other's asses, and since it wasn't just the anniversary of her parents anymore, but also the one year mark since we'd last been together, I wasn't handling it very well. It didn't help that my parents had both been questioning my reasons for acting mischievous. At one point, they'd both asked me about my feelings for Kat, but since my brother and her had finally come out with their relationship, I knew I couldn't make it any harder to live under the same roof as them.

Branch, on the other hand, had been adamant about his intentions with Kat. He'd basically used the excuse that he deserved her more. Had it not been for my guilt, I probably would have fought harder, but living with the knowledge that I pretended to be my brother in the bedroom was still too heavy on my heart. I couldn't look at my mirror image and not feel like hell over my actions.

My only hope was that he would one day screw up, and I'd be there to pick up the pieces, because after all, good things come to those who wait.

Destined to fail, I decided to use my energy on something more constructive, like proving I could get over Kat.

The moment she set eyes on Natalie it was obvious I'd gotten under her skin. She threw me a dirty look from across the table, only making me want to keep at it. I wasn't always interested in making her mad, but this was different. She was becoming unhinged with jealousy. It caused me to wonder why. If she was so in love with my brother, why would she react this way?

Since I'd clearly gotten a good rise out of her, I took the next moments to test my theory. With a witty smile across my face, I reached down beneath the tabletop to stroke Natalie's leg. While taking notice to Kat's expression, I witnessed her dropping a utensil. Had I really gotten her undivided attention, and if so, how far was I willing to take it to prove my theory?

I let my hand slip in between Natalie's thighs, knowing that Kat was under the table getting an eye full. When she sat back up in her chair I could tell I'd hit a nerve. Her eyes were beading out of her head, and she looked like she was about to get ill. Then I saw something I hadn't noticed before. It wasn't jealousy, like I'd assumed.

It was pain.

All of a sudden my demeanor changed. I'd hurt her. I'd caused her pain for no reason but my own benefit. How could I have assumed it was a good idea? Was I really willing to mess with her feelings to make myself feel better about her being with Branch? Was I that cold of a person?

When Kat got up from the table Branch looked toward me as if he knew I was the culprit. I wondered if it bothered him knowing that I could get to Kat that way. Didn't he get curious as to why she cared what I was doing?

At any rate, I took it as my cue to get the hell out of there. Kat clearly wanted to be away from me. When we finished our food I led Natalie out of the house. For a while we drove around. She kept reaching for me, tucking her hands between my legs and rubbing where she knew she'd get a reaction.

I could have nailed her. In fact, I could have done anything with her that night, if I'd wanted to. Except I didn't. The only person I wanted to be with was Kat. She needed to know that I was sorry for ruining her special dinner. She had to be told why I couldn't stand being in the same room as her and Branch, and I didn't care what I had to do to convince her of it. I was ready to tell her the truth because I couldn't keep it locked inside any longer.

Chapter 4

It took me a while to drop off Natalie and clear my head. I'd taken her to a fast food place to grab an ice-cream, but knew that the longer we were in the vehicle the harder it was going to be for me to kick her to the curb. My anger was rising, and with that came the pain of knowing I'd shoved Kat even further out of my reach.

All the lashing out, the terrible choices I'd made, had only left a bigger mess to deal with. Kat needed to know once and for all why I couldn't handle it any longer. She needed to know that I was being ridiculous in order to hide my true feelings.

As soon as the vehicle came to a stop in front of Natalie's house I expected her to hop out. Instead, she unbuckled her seatbelt and leaned over to my side. "My parents aren't home. You should come inside. We have liquor." Her lips coursed over the skin of my neck. Had I not been so consumed with rage, perhaps I would have taken her up on the offer.

"Not tonight. I've got something I need to take care of."

Seemingly confused, she climbed out of the car. I didn't wait for her to get inside like a gentleman would do. Instead I pulled away as soon as the door slammed shut. There was someone I had to see.

When I entered the house I could hear the television on in the family room. I found Kat and Branch passed out on the couch, so I took the remote and started flipping through channels while avoiding watching how close they were.

From where I was sitting I noticed she'd sat up, leaving Branch to remain sleeping. Before I was able to react she was right up in my face, slapping me hard across the cheek. I didn't waste any time scooping her up onto my lap and keeping her close. "What was that for?"

"Let me go," she angrily whispered while squirming to free herself.

I chuckled, releasing my hold and watching as she sunk to the floor beneath me. "You look better down there anyway." With my brother in the room I couldn't react the way I wanted to. It was important to keep the peace even if hurting her was the only option.

Kat gave me a quick glare before standing and kicking me directly in the shin. A rush of pain overwhelmed me, so I reached down to sooth the area.

"What is wrong with you?" She asked.

"You wouldn't understand even if I told you." If I could only look her in those blue eyes and confess my love for her. If she only understood what it was like for me to live under the same roof as her, to see her loving on my twin as if I didn't exist. How could all of our years being so close end up like this? I'd been the one to love her, to comfort, and protect her. Yet she'd picked my brother, the guy who only cared about himself. I'd had it with them.

"Is this about me and Branch?" Her inquiry was a day late and dollar short. I was done fighting.

I shrugged and let out an air-filled laugh. "Kat, why don't you go back over there with your boyfriend, and stay out of my shit? You want to ask me if I'm jealous, but you're the one that got all hot and bothered at the table, wishing it was your pussy my fingers were touching. Stop acting like it's not true. I know you, and I can tell it got to you."

She froze. I recognized the look and was fully aware I'd hit a nerve. Kat turned to look at Branch before responding to my rude comment. "I hate you!" Even as a whisper I could hear her loud and clear.

When she began to walk away I captured her arm. "Kat, wait. I was kidding."

She did what anyone in her situation would have done. She walked over and woke my brother, before pulling him out of the room, leaving me to sulk in my own misery.

It took me a while to come to grips with what had just occurred between us. Snapping wasn't exactly how I should have responded to her, yet the situation was something I could no longer take back. This wasn't just a breaking point for me. Kat needed to hear me out, once and for all.

Entering her dark room was like walking in front of a locked and loaded firing squad. I knew she was angry, and possibly even hurt. The moment I closed the door behind me I rushed to her bedside. "Please don't cry," I took her hands, pulling her close to me, while my lips instantly pressed against her face. I could tell from the way she stayed still that she thought I was Branch. Her sobs quieted, and my next comment was only spoken to test the waters. "Don't be upset because of that asshole."

"I just want to forget about this whole day. Please, make me forget," She begged.

I'd waited three hundred and sixty five days to be in this situation again. I had a whole year to kick myself for pretending to be my brother, but I couldn't keep from touching her. Once again I was right back in this predicament, yearning to have what I knew I wasn't allowed to grasp.

Kat made the next move, pulling me down on the mattress with her. Our kisses were in sync, and I couldn't understand how perfect it felt to experience it again. I was patient, taking my time as I ventured over her skin with my gentle hands. Though I tried to fight my fears, I couldn't deny that my shaking wasn't from being scared. There were so many reasons I should have pulled away and walked out of the room. I was risking my family once more.

Restricting myself from this for the past year had only intensified my need. Nothing could have stopped me, not even Branch himself. The more she reacted, the less worrying I did. I'd succumb to the pleasure, and when it was over I'd come clean. I had to because I hated the terrible person that I'd let myself become.

After we'd made love for the second time, I held her close to me, kissing her on the head. My heart was beating rapidly, and I knew I couldn't puss out. I'd been living with a lie for far too long. "I love you so much," I whispered.

It felt so good to say it that I had to hold back my emotions. For a while I kept my arms around her, unable to rationalize with those words. Kat deserved the truth, but what would it get me? I was kidding myself if I thought we could be together. She'd made her choice, and as much as it pained me to accept, I was aware that I didn't have a choice. When I climbed out of that bed and went to my room I knew I had to get away from them. I'm not talking about dating other people. I literally needed to walk away from my family so that they could be happy. It was the only way; the only choice I could make. I loved her enough to let her go; to give up hope on us ever being together.

It took a while for me to fall asleep, and even longer to find the courage to head to her room that next morning. Once again I feared that my brother and parents would be waiting to tear me down to nothing, and once more I was surprised when I found Kat all alone instead.

She was on her way to the bathroom, bedhead and all. As she came toward the doorway I blocked her from continuing. "Still mad at me?" I had to break the ice in order to feel her out. She wasn't exactly a morning person.

"I'm not in the mood for you. My head hurts too bad."

When she pushed past me I grabbed her by the waist, pulling her back before she could make it down the stairs. "Go get back in bed. I'll get you some Tylenol and water."

Kat looked at me for only a moment before rolling her eyes and turning to head back into her room. "Whatever."

When I went downstairs, I found that I was alone. This was the perfect time to come clean and beg her to forgive me. After I'd obtained some medicine, and a fresh glass of water, I headed back up to confess the truth to the other half of my heart. She didn't have to forgive me, or even understand why I'd done it, as long as when I walked away from her she knew that I loved her, more than any man had ever loved a woman.

"Thanks," she mumbled as I handed her the pills.

I sat down beside her, trying my best not to think about what we'd done the night before, when she thought I was Branch. I closed my eyes and pushed the thought away. "So, are you still mad?"

"Are you going to ask me this until I answer?" It was obvious that she was still bitter.

I placed my hand on her leg. "I can't have my sister mad at me." Calling her that made me want to cringe.

"Get off. I don't feel good, I told you."

I laughed it off, refusing to let her see how much it hurt. "Branch isn't here, you know. You don't have to pretend to not care, Kat. Natalie was fun, but that's it."

Kat put her pillow over her head and let out a growl. "Seriously, I don't want to talk about this."

"I'm staying until we talk it out." If she only knew how hard this was for me, maybe she'd understand why I refused to walk away. I'd come this far.

"I guess you'll be here all day then. I'm going back to sleep." She rolled over, literally giving me the cold shoulder. I felt defeated.

"I didn't sleep with her, Kat." It wasn't as if I was trying to earn brownie points. I just felt like she needed to know that. "I really need to talk to you about something. Please, just hear me out?"

She refused to reply.

Several times I tried to come out with the truth. Each instance I knew what I was about to say was wrong. Kat deserved to live without regret. She'd lost so much already. I couldn't ruin her, not again.

Then I had to consider my brother, and our already struggling relationship. I'd put on a brave face, but it was quite obvious his relationship with Kat was coming between us. Without admitting my feelings, I was forced to pretend to be happy for them, at the cost of losing myself each and every night. I hated the sound of them laughing, the sucking noises when they kissed, and even the times when I knew he was sneaking into her room.

I tried so hard not to listen to their conversations, especially when my brother made her promises I knew he wouldn't keep. What hurt me worst was knowing that Branch was fully aware of my feelings for Kat. I hadn't hidden them. He was my twin, yet acted out of his own selfishness to win her heart. What I'd done in her room was wrong, but it wasn't in vain. Kat needed to feel loved, and that's exactly what I'd provided her with. If I couldn't have her forever, at least we'd part on good terms. I'd know what it was like to hold her in my arms and make love to her with all the passion I had in me. Life was about to rip us apart, but I wouldn't let it cause me to forget.

With a ton of regret, I left her alone in the room, convinced that leaving was my only option, and I knew exactly how I had to go about it so that no one was able to change my mind. There was no other way to keep the peace. Kat needed my family, probably more than I did. Out of us three kids, I was the strongest. I could handle being out on my own when I knew the two of them wouldn't be able to.

My only concern then would be to look her in the eyes and say goodbye, without the whole world seeing right through me.

Chapter 5

"Mom, Dad, there's something I need to talk to you about."

My mom played with her hands while my dad sat back in his chair trying to figure me out. "Did you get a girl pregnant?" He asked.

I focused my gaze elsewhere and shook my head, wishing that were the case. "No. It's not that." I looked down at the tan carpet, unable to face their reactions. "I've enlisted in the Army."

"You what?" My mother stood up, grabbing my attention immediately. Tears filled her eyes as she covered her mouth in a natural reaction. "Why?"

I shrugged. "For a lot of reasons. It doesn't matter. It's happening."

"Brooks, you're seventeen." My father was already trying to find a loophole to get me out of it.

"By the time I go to boot camp I'll be eighteen. This is what I want." For the record it wasn't what I'd always set out to do, but it was the only way I knew I'd be able to stay away from Kat. "Please don't fight me on this. I need your support." With tears in my eyes I watched both of my parents face the hard facts. They couldn't change what was done. I was going away, taking myself out of the equation before I lost control.

After our chat, I had to give my brother the news. Honestly, he took it better than anyone, making me upset. His reaction only proved that he still felt threatened by my presence.

It wasn't hard to deal with Branch until Kat entered the room. Then I could feel my heart being tugged in a different way.

"So, I told Mom and Dad earlier. They know I leave right after graduation." It was the easiest way to break the ice with Kat; to get a feel of how she would take it.

"Where are you going?" Her curiosity made the hair on my arms stand up.

"He enlisted," Branch announced.

"What? When?" Kat sat up and stared right into my eyes as if she was having a bad dream. I wasn't certain, but I sensed more than a friendly concern on her face.

"Last week, like you care." I'd been playing a video game with Branch while we talked, and unpaused the game to avoid looking at her for a long period of time. Besides, it made it easier to hide my emotions when I stayed occupied with something else.

She was quiet for a minute, but I refused to look in her direction. She couldn't know how much it hurt me to imagine being away from her. She'd never know what it was like to be so close, but feel as if she were miles away. I couldn't take the agonizing truth anymore. I had to free myself from this hell. It was the only way to stay sane. She was with Branch, who she obviously loved. She'd made her choice, so I had to make mine.

"We all care. What made you want to do that?"

"I want to be able to give back to our country, Kat. You've got until June to make amends with me," I said with a snicker.

"Whether it's June or next week, it wouldn't change my opinion of you."

I couldn't handle the truth. Kat didn't care if I left. She acted like she did, but it was obvious she and Branch wanted me out of their hair. I was holding them back, being the third wheel.

While standing just outside the room I listened to what they were saying. "That wasn't nice, babe." At least my brother had the decency to notice she'd been cold.

"I meant that we'd miss him the same." Kat's argument didn't make me feel better.

"It wasn't how it came out. All I heard was you telling him to get lost."

"Well, I didn't mean it that way. Maybe if he wasn't being such a jerk lately he would have known."

"Go apologize. Mom is already freaking out on him. He needs our support. I know he pissed you off last night, but maybe he's scared and wants to occupy his time. He can't be up our asses every second. Since we share the same DNA I'd say that he's probably horny constantly."

"Fine, I'll go talk to him."

I ran up the stairs after hearing her agree to come talk to me. The last thing I needed was her finding out I was still listening to the two of them talking.

When she came into my room I was tossing a ball against the wall. Even out of breath, I pretending to act annoyed when she spoke.

"Can we talk? I think you misunderstood me back there."

"I didn't misunderstand anything, Kat. I get that you want me out of the way. Trust me, I want to get the fuck away from you and my brother too." It was important to push her away, so she wouldn't hurt when I was gone. I didn't want her to miss me because it would make me want to come home to comfort her.

"That's not true and you know it. Why are you saying things like that? We would never cut you out of our lives. How could you even think that?"

I captured the ball and held it tight in my fist. "Do you love my brother?"

"What? Why would you ask me that? You know I do."

"Yeah. He loves you, too. Don't you get it? I can't sit around here while you two are planning this fantastic life together. I'm drowning in your fucking happiness." That was the first true statement I'd made all night.

"Don't say it like that. We'd never push you away. It isn't like we're broadcasting ourselves. We hang out just like we used to."

"It's different even if you don't see it. As far as pushing me away, well, you don't have to, Kat. I'm the one walking away."

"I don't want you to go." Her face was distraught, and as much as I wanted to look away I couldn't. My heart was beating fast, beckoning me to keep staring.

"Did my brother send you up here, or did you come by yourself?"

She shrugged. "Both."

"Just go back downstairs. I'm not going to waste my time explaining and I've already signed everything. I'll be eighteen and able to leave on my own free will. You and Branch can go off to college and ride into the sunset on your white stallion for all I care."

"That's not fair. Why are you being so mean to me?" She'd begun to sob. I couldn't get over how it made me feel inside.

I leaned forward and pointed toward the door. "Kat, we're friends, even family. I didn't do this to hurt you. Get it through your head and get out of my room."

"You're hurting me right now, Brooks. I don't understand what I ever did to you to make you treat me this way. You used to protect me."

"I used to do a lot of things and it got me nowhere."

As I stood to be near her I couldn't help watch as she closed the distance between us, leaning forward so no one else could hear what she was about to say. "I don't want to lose you."

I grabbed her arm at the wrist, causing her eyes to stare into mine. "Why? Say it, Kat. Tell me what we both already know."

Her lips parted, but nothing came out. For a second she just looked at me, another bout of tears fell down her cheeks. "I'm not saying anything."

It wasn't until she began walking away that I responded. "Yeah, that's what I figured."

It was obvious that I'd hurt her. I could hear her clear across the hall sobbing. What caught my attention was that Branch didn't check on her. He was probably still playing his video game while she laid in her room falling apart.

I had to admit that a part of me, the one that wanted to go inside and comfort her, felt terrible. The idea of hurting her crushed me though I knew I couldn't cave. I had to stand my ground and put distance between us. It was the only way out of this mess I'd made. If Kat knew the truth she'd never forgive me.

The next few months went by too quickly, as did the growing tension between Kat and myself. By the time graduation came around, I could tell she was hiding something from me, though I didn't know if I had the energy to figure out what it was.

"Congratulations you three. How about you all stand together for a picture?" If it hadn't meant so much to my mother I wouldn't have been open minded about the slew of photographs she was determined to take. While Kat and Branch posed happily together, my mind was in other places. This was going to be our last moments together. As much as I tried to convince myself that it was the right decision, I was suddenly having extreme doubts.

It didn't matter though. Kat and Branch were going to attend Salisbury University. They'd be on the opposite side of the state, while I was on the other side of the country. Our lives were headed in different directions.

Chapter 6

During our large graduation party, where Branch clung to Kat for dear life, my dad pulled me to the side. He led us into the house before turning to face me. "Brooks, we need to talk."

"What about?" If he wanted to give me one last ultimatum about joining the military he was too late.

"About Katy."

This shocked me. "What about her? I think you have me confused with Branch."

He shook his head and poured himself a vodka tonic. "That's where you're mistaken. I'm sure I have the right son." My dad leaned against the countertop, sipping on his drink while narrowing his gaze on my reaction.

"I don't understand." Playing stupid was only going to get me so far.

"You're leaving because of her aren't you?" He held up his hand. "Before you deny it, hear me out. For years I've watched you around Katy. It's not like I could avoid it. Her living under the same roof makes it hard to ignore. Your brother may walk around with blinders on, but it's pretty obvious to me."

"Dad, don't do this. Nothing can change my decision. It's set in stone."

"That's not why I'm asking."

I didn't understand why he wanted me to admit my feelings for Kat, not when it wouldn't make any bit of a difference. I'd never be with Kat. She'd made her choice, and as much as it crushed me, I knew I had to move on. "You already know the answer."

"You know, Brooks, some things aren't so set in stone."

"What's that supposed to imply, Dad? Everything is set in stone. Look, I appreciate whatever you're trying to do, but Kat's with Branch. He'll be good to her. They'll have a great life together. I'm sure they'll marry and have a couple kids. Maybe eventually I'll be okay with it."

My dad shook his head and looked out the window at the party going on. "There are things I think you should know about your brother, Brooks."

This time I was the one putting up my hand. "It doesn't matter. It will change nothing. I've done and said things I can't take back. Spending time away is what we all need."

After the talk with my father, I retreated to my room. I couldn't stand around communicating with the family while pretending I didn't care what the girl of my dreams was doing with my brother.

A little while later I heard someone knocking on the door before coming into my room. I was still in my swimming trunks without a shirt, and it was clear that was the first thing she noticed. "Hey, I brought you food."

I leaned up to face her. "Thanks. I wasn't that hungry." She sat down beside me and put the tray to the side. "I like when you don't hide your face."

Kat looked away, but I could tell she was blushing. "I'm going to miss you, Brooks. Promise you'll visit?"

I couldn't take my eyes off of her. There was something about the moment, or perhaps it was the fact that we were completely alone in the house. "Yeah. I'll come see you." I didn't know when, but I knew I couldn't stay away forever.

"I better get back downstairs."

I took her hand before she could get up. Her body came down against mine, and all I could see was how close her lips were. With one hand I stroked her cheek. "Don't slap me, Kat. Please, just let me have a few seconds of this." Then I kissed her, softly on the lips.

When she didn't pull away or freak out, I took it upon myself to add some tongue. Far be it from me to deny her my skills. After at least a minute of full-blown making out, she pulled away and covered her mouth, as if she was ashamed.

"I'm sorry. I need to go back downstairs."

It only took me a second to see the truth across her face. For so long I'd felt terrible for wishing for it. Now it all made sense. "Does he know you're in love with me?"

She couldn't look at me. "Please don't do this, Brooks."

I had to laugh. I'd been a fool for too long. My own conscience had prevented me from seeing what was right in front of me the whole time, and now I didn't know what to do. "Kat, have you asked yourself how long you're going to go on with my brother before you realize you picked the wrong guy?"

She stood and put her hands on her hips. "Don't go there. You know I love Branch."

I sat on my knees, staring directly into her eyes. My hands were trembling, but this was important. I couldn't ignore it anymore. "When I'm on that bus tomorrow and you're done waving goodbye to me, I want you to do me one favor."

"What?" She asked in a whisper.

"I want you to think about being without Branch for a few months. Then switch it around and think about being without me. When you have your answer, you'll know why I had to leave."

Her tear-filled eyes allowed me to see that I'd gotten to her. "That makes no sense. You already know I'll miss you."

I cackled and plopped backwards on my mattress. "Kat, this ain't even about missing me. This is about you living with a lie. It's about my brother getting everything he wants and never considering that you were never his to have."

Kat stood and turned her back to me. The moment was too intense. Maybe I shouldn't have come on so strong.

"Please stop." She said.

"Stop what? Stop feeling sorry for myself because I wasn't man enough to fight for what I wanted?" I wanted to hear it from her lips.

Kat started pacing around my room, going in one direction, only to turn and head in another. She was waving her hands around as if she were having a private conversation with herself. "What are you talking about?"

Just then the door opened. Branch was standing there, and it was obvious he was surprised to see us in the middle of a heated discussion. "Hey, I was wondering where you two were. Mom needs us to get the grill going. Dad had to run out for the cake."

"I'll give you a hand, bro." I didn't look at Kat when I left the room, nor did I mention what we were discussing to my brother. It wouldn't have made a difference. I had my answer even if she was too ashamed to admit it.

When I came back into my room, probably about fifteen minutes later, I found Kat sitting on my bed. She'd obviously been crying the whole time and prying through my things. In her hands was my art book, and she was flipped to a page that revealed one of my most exquisite pieces. I didn't need to take a picture into class to copy from, and I certainly hadn't asked her to model. I had her memorized. It was even possible that I could draw the woman with my eyes closed.

As soon as she noticed me entering the room she came at me, shoving the drawing against my chest, "How long have you been in love with me, Brooks?"

I smiled. "That question isn't going to get answered."

Not knowing where my brother could be, I tried to walk away from her. She grabbed me, pulling me back to be facing her. From the look in her eyes I knew it was about to get very serious, but I couldn't have predicted what she was going to tell me. Once again she'd left me speechless. "I would have picked you, and you know it. So I need an answer. How long?"

It was gut-wrenching, hearing her truthfully coming to grips with what could have been. The burning in my eyes let me know that I couldn't keep holding my feelings from her. I'd waited all this time, protected her, because I thought it's what she needed. This was my chance to come clean. "I've loved you for as long as I could remember."

Kat's face scrunched up as she began to cry heavily. "Why didn't you tell me?"

"It doesn't matter anymore. You're going to be happy with Branch. He loves you. I'll be out of the picture and it will get easier. The distance between us will help." I was attempting to convince myself.

Kat kept shaking her head, as if she was in denial.

I couldn't resist. My lips were on her forehead, leaving her with a reminder that even space couldn't make me forget about her. "Just remember that you were my first."

Kat looked into my eyes and grinned. "I'll never forget our first kiss, Brooks."

It wasn't until she began to leave the room that caused me to clarify exactly what I meant. "I wasn't just talking about a kiss, Kat."

Her body spun around. "Huh?"

"September 11th, for the past two years. I'm surprised you didn't know, being as I've always been there for you on that day, because unlike my brother, I never could sleep that night knowing you were so upset."

It took a couple seconds for it to all sink in. Then I watched her composure change. I knew what was coming, so I prepared myself for the blow. "You...oh God. You."

She covered her mouth and started backing away, but I refused to let her. I closed in on her, breaking the distance between us, while whispering so no one else could hear. "I waited until the perfect moment to have you for myself. You had to be my first Kat, and I knew it was the only way it could happen."

I watched her haul ass out of my room. She slammed her bedroom door shut, and I didn't bother going after her. The noise alone would have caught everyone's attention. Not wanting to draw the curiosity to the both of us, I closed my own door and retreated back to my bed.

Nearly twenty minutes later she came barging back inside without knocking. Her finger pointed in my direction, and I'd honestly never seen her so pissed. "Don't come visit me in college, Brooks. You're right, I need to be away from you so that I can be happy with Branch. We don't need you trying to push us apart. And as far as those two nights go, that goes to your grave with you. I won't lose Branch over this."

I spent my last night at home all alone. I think my parents assumed that I wanted space. Perhaps they thought I was packing, or resting. In reality I was a freaking mess. Kat hated me, and I felt like I couldn't live with myself. I'd known the repercussions before acting out, and overlooked them anyway.

With nothing left in me to lose, I sat down at my desk and wrote her an explanation. I wasn't going to give it to her before I left, but hopefully when I returned she'd be willing to read it.

Dear Kat,

If you're reading this letter then I've already left for the Army. Which also probably means that I was too chicken shit to tell you how I really feel about you.

I don't even know why I'm writing this because you'll probably never come up into this tree house again. In the chance that you do, I need to set things straight, once and for all.

The first thing you need to know is that from the first day we met, as infants even, I loved you. I can't remember one day where I didn't, so it has to mean it's since birth.

The second thing you need to know is that I wanted to tell you when we were twelve and had shared our first kiss. I know you remember that night. I pulled you aside and asked you to do it again. I was going to tell you, but I got called in for dinner. That next day you lost your parents and being your friend was more important than any horny kids' feelings.

So I waited.

The thing was, I accidentally told Branch all about it. He told me that you secretly confided in him that you liked him, but didn't want to hurt my feelings. It was a shitty move, but well played by him. He knew that if I thought you wanted him, I'd back off.

I waited for the day that you would break up with him, hoping that one day you'd want me instead. After time, I knew it wouldn't happen.

Our family was too close, and my parents wouldn't tolerate a scandal like that, besides the fact that I couldn't destroy the whole family over it.

I stepped aside and let him have you. I watched him hold you and kiss you, day after day, until I finally couldn't take it anymore.

One night, I snuck into your room. You thought I was Branch, and I didn't correct you. You asked me to make the pain go away and so I did. I wanted to be that guy that you needed.

That was when I lost my virginity.

I'm not sorry about it either because *I know it is something I will never regret.*

You'll probably hate me now, but that wasn't the only time it happened. I snuck into your room the next year, on the anniversary of your parent's death, again. I wanted to be the one to make your tears go away.

Now that you know the truth, you'll understand why I had to leave. I want you to be happy with my brother. He'll treat you right and give you everything you want.

Maybe when we're older, with gray hair and lots of children, we can be friends again.

Until then, know I love you.

I always have and I always will.

Love, Brooks

Chapter 7

I always thought that the tragic death of the Michaels was the most brutal thing I'd ever experienced, when in fact looking into Kat's eyes as I said goodbye was just as horrible, maybe even worse. The idea of not being able to see her, to touch her, to know that she was okay, was killing me inside. I wasn't just riding off into the sunset to start a new life. The real Brooks was still somewhere close to her, clinging to hope that someway we still had a chance. What was left of me was an empty shell; one that longed for some sort of resolution that didn't involve pain, or being alone.

I think I would have felt better if my last words were about love, but instead I'd only reassured her that her secret was safe with me. I didn't plan on ever telling my brother, or anyone else that I'd slept with Kat. She didn't deserve to suffer because of my actions.

After a whole day of traveling, I'd arrived at intake. So many men and women my age stood around waiting to be called and assigned. One by one we were taken to areas to start the long process. During the first week I said goodbye to civilian clothes, lost all of my hair to a buzz-cut, and prepared for the physical aspects of the following week. Testing mental and physical endurance would have been easier if the drill sergeant wasn't such a hard ass. I swear that there was no possible way someone should be able to yell as much as this guy did. No matter what he was talking about, it was in a piercing announcement. For the most part, I was thankful that he pushed us to the limit because if I wasn't so exhausted I don't know if I would have been able to sleep. My last thought every night before I closed my eyes was of Kat, and how I'd left things so unhinged. Thinking that she hated me made me work harder. I couldn't fail at this too because I'd have nothing left of my own.

During the fourth week we practiced and learned marksmanship. I never knew that there was so much to learn about a weapon. We were taught how to hold each gun, how to breathe, and even how to break it down to clean it.

The fifth and sixth week forced us to work together with our fellow members. It wasn't always a success, and I say that with a grain of salt, because sometimes I felt as if I was the weakest link. It was there that I started to get close with two fellow trainees. Mullins, or Trevor Mullins that is, was from Kentucky. He'd just gotten married, and they were expecting their first child. Amanda Taylor was also someone I found interesting. It was obvious that she'd been raised by her father. The girl could bench press a large man, and she didn't hold back her opinions. Nothing about her reminded me of Kat, making it easier for me. Her blonder hair was always tied back, so I'm not very sure how long it actually was, but her huge brown eyes were what really stood out. I read once that a person's eyes stayed the same size since birth. If that was the case than as a baby she must have looked like an alien. Now, it had become a good feature, not that I'd ever bring it up in conversation.

For the next four weeks the three of us teamed up during our drills and helped each other as much as we were able to. After the tenth and final week we graduated basic training, but that was only the beginning for me.

I'd found a liking to weapons and wanted to pursue a position that would enable me to get out on the battlefield.

You have to understand that at this point I was only fueled by motivation to keep trucking forward. My aspirations of ever being happy were replaced with taking risks because honestly I felt as if I had nothing to go home to.

I hooked up with Amanda after a month of us being friends. I didn't do it to erase Kat, or forget all the feelings that I clearly still had for her. I did it because I was tired of feeling so alone. I could tell she was in the same boat. We both needed reprieve, so one night, after a lot of drinks, we decided to go at it like rabbits. Admittedly it helped for a short while. That first night I slept like a rock, so we continued doing it, sneaking around at night when everyone was asleep. There were no feelings on my part. I'd made that clear from the beginning. Amanda, on the other hand, had gotten carried away, reading too much into it.

When I knew it was time to stop, she agreed. We were headed in different directions, and I used that as my excuse to let her down easy.

Mullins watched his child being born from an internet video chat box. I sat next to him, staring in shock as his wife labored and struggled to birth his daughter. I honestly had to close my eyes when it began to happen. It felt too intrusive, like I didn't have a right to witness it. As they pulled the crying baby out, cleaned her off and stuck her in the mother's arms, I watched my friend fall apart. He wanted nothing more than to be there for them. He'd become a father in that moment, and I was grateful he wanted me there to experience it with him.

In the next few weeks, I watched him break down too many times to count. We were supposed to be strong soldiers, rangers, but inside we all had our demons.

One night after doing drills, we found Amanda passed out in the bathroom. She was unresponsive at first. Mullins and I watched them carting her out, not knowing what was going on with our friend. Come to find out she'd taken a bunch of pills and left a note on her pillow. She said she couldn't handle it anymore, and that going home was never going to be an option.

We never saw her after that night, not even when we graduated.

The longer I was away, the easier it got to pretend that I hadn't left my heart back at home. Honestly, I'd learned to shove all of my emotions to the farthest place in my mind. I experienced loss, life, and brutality. It made me strong on the outside, but unlike how I pictured,

I could see that every person around me had their own personal flaws.

I learned to hide my feelings, to stay distracted, and distance myself from the things that hurt too much to think about.

Even my calls to my parents were quick. I could tell they were worried, but also knew they were trying to prepare for Kat and Branch to move to Salisbury to start college. Soon they'd be home alone, without any of us kids. I just hoped they'd remain together, because after all this time, I still worried my parents had stayed together for the three of us kids.

It took me about a year to come to grips with being able to communicate with Kat again. In that time I'd trained to be a ranger, and parts of me were obviously changed. She'd been sending me letters, never saying much on a personal level. I think she felt like she was including me in her day-to-day as if we still lived under the same roof. At least once a week I'd been getting mail for the past several months. Sitting down to write her back, after all the time that had passed, was so difficult.

I was a different person than the young man that walked onto that bus. Even though I'd seen my parents when I graduated boot camp, I hadn't seen Kat or my brother since that day in June when I left.

I think I wrote five letters before settling on something simple. I wanted her to know I was okay, but couldn't lead on that I missed her. I was a soldier. I was strong, and brave, but when it came to Kat, I was weak.

Dear Kat,

Thanks for writing me all those letters. Sorry it's taken me so long to respond. My life's been busy and I know yours has too. I hear you and Branch are doing well from Mom's letters. Tell him I said hi.
I will try to write more.

Love, Brooks

Her return letter was just as boring.

Dear Brooks,
I can't believe you finally wrote me back. I was beginning to think that you'd forgotten all about me. Yesterday I tried snails for the first time. The texture grossed me out, but I managed to swallow them without barfing. I'll write to you again soon. Please keep in touch as we all miss you.
Love, Katy

We kept in contact up until Christmas. That's when I got the news that reminded me of still having feelings.

I'd called home to wish my parents a happy holiday and hung up after hearing about the engagement of Kat and Branch. Aside from feeling sick to my stomach, I couldn't understand how I'd ever be able to be around them. I'd thought I'd been strong enough to let her have a happy life with Branch, but that wasn't the case. Hearing that news made every single painful emotion come right back into play. I was a nervous wreck, who refused to respond to something that would forever destroy me. Even though I'd known this day would come, I wasn't able to grasp the fact that she'd never be mine.

I realize that made no sense. She was never actually mine to begin with, not since we were little, but this was like a forever kind of commitment. If she married Branch I'd never have my chance.

That night I had a burger for Christmas dinner and shared my table with the one friend who had spent the last year at my side. It wasn't fancy, or even something memorable, and it certainly wasn't as cozy as looking across the table and seeing Kat smiling back at me, but it would suffice. It would keep from wanting to high tail it to Mexico and drown my sorrows in tequila.

In the next year, I fought with myself over staying in contact with Kat. There wasn't a single day that passed where I didn't miss her sweet voice, but I knew calling or writing would only drudge up old memories, while she was busy making new ones with my brother. That's why, for a while, I refused to keep in contact with Kat, or anyone else. To keep them convinced that I was fine, I'd randomly mail a short note to each of them.

Much to my surprise I received a message to contact my brother because it was apparently an emergency. In that moment I pictured Kat injured, or even worse. I closed my eyes and attempted to erase the image, unsuccessfully. The phone rang three times before he answered. "Brooks, is that you?"

"Yeah, what's wrong? Is Kat okay?"

"Of course you'd be worried about her," he said rudely.

"What is it then? Are mom and dad okay?"

"The only person who isn't okay is me, brother. You see, I just found a letter for my bride to be, from my so-called best man. What I want to know is how my own brother could sneak into my girlfriend's room and fuck her? How could you, Brooks? You could have any girl you wanted in high school, why would you go after mine?"

I clenched my jaw to prevent from saying what would clearly end our relationship. "Does she know you found the letter?"

"You're not going to answer me?"

"Whatever I say won't make a difference. Yeah, I went into her room those nights, and yeah things became heated, but you have to know that she thought I was you, both times. In fact," this was only for his benefit, and I was obviously lying through my teeth. "She doesn't even know it happened. Branch, I never told her."

"What?"

"You heard me. Those nights she was a mess. I only went in there because I heard her crying, and it was keeping me awake. Both times she practically begged me to be with her. When she called me by your name I didn't correct her. This is all my fault."

"Consider yourself uninvited to the wedding. No brother of mine would be so vindictive. Just so you know, I'm still marrying Katy. Hell, I'd marry her just so you can't."

"For the record, Branch, you knew all along how I felt about her. Did you really expect me to hold in my feelings forever?"

"Fuck you! We're done."

I wanted nothing more than to hang up on him, but knew I was in the wrong. No matter how much I loved Kat, I'd stepped over the line that was never to be crossed. "Branch, I'm sorry. You don't know how many times I've wished I could take it back."

The line was silent, and then I finally realized he'd hung up on me. That evening, while I was lying on my bunk, I heard my phone vibrate. When I checked the message I saw that it was from my brother. "She's not going to marry me unless you're a part of it."

"Tell her I've been shipped overseas. Tell her they are deploying me. Tell everyone for all I care."

"If I find out she knows, all hell is going to break loose. I'm warning you now."

I wasn't afraid of my brother, or his threats. He could shove them up his ass and twirl around for all I cared.

I wished that phone call had been the end of it, but a letter from Kat told me I was wrong.

Dear Brooks,
I hate to be the bearer of bad news, and maybe I should have told you a long time ago, but I found your letter in the tree house. Before I make you hate me, I want you to know that your words touched my heart. I don't hate you for

being there for me. I was mad, but I didn't hate you.

Look, I took the note to your room and put it under your pillow so you'd find it when you visited. I didn't know someone else would go in there.

Now it's missing and I'm freaking out. Someone knows your secret; our secret.

Please don't hate me, Brooks.

Love, Kat

PS: Please come home for the wedding. Whatever happens we can explain that it was all in the past. We're a family and we'll work through it.

At first I didn't know how to respond. Obviously she didn't know Branch had been the one to find the letter, and she certainly hadn't suspected that he'd already called to rip me a new ass. What bothered me the most was the secrets being kept between two people that were about to marry.

Figuring that I should leave well enough alone, I refused to write her back at first. Then, after two weeks of letting it all simmer, I decided she need not worry about the letter, so she could focus on everything else that was more important to her.

Dear Kat,

I can see how you're freaking out right now. You don't need to be. The person that found the letter isn't going to say anything, I can assure you of that.

Maybe if you weren't always going into my room when you visited, they wouldn't have went looking.

Anyway, it doesn't even matter now. All is good and you can calm down.

As far as me coming home for the wedding, that may be a problem. I'm being deployed in January to Afghanistan and I've signed on to stay for two years.

By the time you get this letter Mom and Dad will already know and I will have made them promise to let me call Branch to tell him the bad news.

I'm really sorry I can't be there to see you walk down the aisle. I know you'll be the most beautiful woman that this world has ever seen.

Take care of my brother and yourself.
Love, Brooks

That next day I volunteered myself to be shipped to Afghanistan. Nothing else mattered. I had no reason to be optimistic about a future. My life had ended the day I signed it away to the Armed Forces. I knew what I was getting into, proving only that going home would never be an option. They'd all be better off if I never returned.

Chapter 8

I'll never forget the July morning when my cell phone rang with a familiar number displayed across it. By the time I got the nerve to answer she'd already hung up. My reaction wasn't well thought though it didn't need to be. Talking to Kat came natural. I redialed her number and listened to her answering. Suddenly everything I'd worked so hard to forget was right back as if it had only been pretending to be dormant.

Her voice filled my senses, making the hairs stand up on my skin. I could feel my body shaking, reminding me that after so long I was really hearing her talk.

"Hello?"

"What, did you change your mind or something? Is my voice not as sexy as it was before?" I wasn't sure if breaking the ice with humor was a good idea, but I did it anyway, out of my own uncomfortableness. I hadn't practiced this because I swore it would never happen. Even though I'd spoke to my brother, it was obvious he didn't want the two of us communicating.

Her laughter allowed me to know that she was in good spirits. "Your voice is fine. I just... I had to sneak to get your number, and I don't really know why I'm calling. I guess I just wanted to hear your voice."

"Is it everything you wanted it to be?" I teased.

"All that and then some." God, I missed her so much. A constant ache was tugging my heart, forcing me to face the truth, and it was very clear. No matter how much space I put between us, it would never change the amount of love I felt for her.

"I miss you, Kat. It gets real lonely sometimes. On nights like that, I wish I could call you and talk about damn near anything to pass the time. You and I never ran out of things to talk about, did we?" I could hear her sniffling. "Please don't cry."

"I can't help it. I think Branch is keeping us from each other and I don't get it. We're family, and he knows how important you've always been to me. You're thousands of miles away. I don't understand why he wouldn't want us talking."

So I'd been right. "Kat, Branch found the letter. He went into my room after you fell asleep and read it. He called me that morning before you woke up." I couldn't believe he hadn't mentioned it to her. If she was my girlfriend, I'd want answers. I would have gone to her immediately and let her have it. The fact that he hadn't mentioned it was like a red flag. Something was up with Branch. It was as if he couldn't bring me up in conversation to Kat, and I wanted to know why.

"What?"

"Yeah. Do you really think that I would talk to everyone else on the phone and not you? If I had to pick anyone to call, you'd be my first choice."

"He knows about what we did?"

"Yup. He knows."

"What did he say to you? Did he threaten you? Do your parents know?"

I could almost see her expression clearly as she questioned me. Kat was freaking out, and

I couldn't blame her. This was her livelihood on the line. She'd never be able to face my parents if they knew the truth. Kat was too good of a person to live with that kind of guilt. "Kat, he doesn't blame you. You didn't even know, which I'm just going to put it out there, it's sort of weird. I know I'm a way better lover than my brother, but that's beside the point."

She giggled, reassuring me that she was okay.

"Anyway, we had words, and he made threats. It's why I wasn't going to come to the wedding."

She interrupted. "You have to come, Brooks. I want you there."

"Yeah, I heard. When he called to tell me the date had been moved up, I was shocked I was invited again. He's pretty much said that if I come within ten feet of you and he isn't around he's going to kill me with his bare hands. Honestly, I'd like to see that fucker try it. After all this time, I'm pretty sure I'd rip him apart."

"Okay, I don't need to know all that. Forgive me for saying that, but I find it hard to believe that he's never confronted me about us being together."

"Kat, you're innocent in all of this. Don't you get it? He doesn't even know you saw the letter. He thinks I left it under my pillow and you never found it. At least, that's what I convinced him happened. As far as you know, we've never done anything. It's all on me."

"Why would you do that?"

"I think you know why." The line got quiet, and I knew I'd crossed a boundary again.

"Brooks, I want you at the wedding, and Branch isn't going to touch you. I appreciate that you kept me out of it, but it doesn't change anything either way. I'm marrying Branch because I love him and we have a life together. I hope you understand that."

As impossible as I knew it would be, I had to be there for her. Sure, I'd support my brother as well, but it wasn't the same. I was coming home for Kat, and she needed to know that.

"I get it, Kat. I'll be there for you on your special day and I won't cause problems. I'd never do anything to hurt you."

"Thank you."

"Listen, I need to go."

"Wait. Can I call you again?"

"You can, but you may want to use someone else's phone. Branch may act all innocent, but I guarantee he checks your phone bill for my number. You've got a month to come up with a good excuse as to what we talked about and why you called me today."

"I'll handle it."

"Bye, Kat."

"Bye, Brooks."

Our short conversation left me vulnerable, and fearful of how far I'd go to speak to her again. I imagined talking her out of marrying Branch, and what other extremes I was willing to go to save her from being committed to him. Still in my heart she was meant to be mine. Nothing had changed. There was something in her voice reassuring me.

With only five months until they tied the knot, I was running out of ideas. All I could hope was that she'd wake up one day and realize that she'd made the wrong choice. Thankfully, Kat started calling on a regular basis, brightening my days with her comforting voice. She didn't know that her talking about a clogged drain, or being stuck in traffic calmed my nerves. It reminded me of being home with the family. She wasn't the only person I'd missed. Somewhere along the line I'd pushed my parents away. In the back of my mind I figured it was the right decision, but yearned to make things right, somehow, someway.

From October until the beginning of November Kat's calls stopped. I was okay the first week, moody the second, and then a complete mess the third. It made no sense. We hadn't discussed private affairs or being together. Our mundane conversations would have bored everyone else. We were being friends, like we were before love got in the way.

Finally, I couldn't take it anymore. I didn't care if my brother was standing in the same room, or even if they were in bed. I had to know she was okay because worrying about her prevented me from being able to keep my head in the game at work.

"Brooks, now isn't a good time."

"Why haven't you called me, Kat? What's wrong?"

"Nothing." Her short answer allowed me to tell she wasn't being honest.

"I know you better than that. Did I say or do something that made you mad?"

"No. It's not you. It's me."

"So, I guess we're breaking up?" I was desperately attempting to make her laugh, even though the idea of her pushing me away was tearing me apart, weakening me yet again. "You can tell me anything."

"I'm scared."

"Has he hurt you?" I'd be on the first plane to kick some ass if he had.

"No. Of course not. I guess how I'm feeling is normal." She may have seen it that way, but I had other opinions. Could she finally be waking up to realize that Branch wasn't right for her?

"When's the last time you ate? You know you have to take care of yourself, and you forget to eat when you're stressed."

"I'm fine, Brooks. I've just been busy and nervous."

"I worry when you don't call."

"I'm sorry."

"Kat, you know you don't have to go through with this. You have a choice. You always have. If you aren't sure about being with Branch for the rest of your life, then don't do it." I needed confirmation.

"Why would you think that?" She snapped.

"Isn't it true?"

"No!" Her quick response only made it more obvious.

"Okay. Whatever you say. I'm just telling you that you're allowed to change your mind."

"Why would I change my mind? Do you honestly think I'm in love with you?"

I closed my eyes and imagined that kiss in my bedroom, her tear-filled eyes when we said goodbye, and how desperate she was to get back in touch with me. Something inside of me may have been broken, unrepairable, but I refused to deny what I knew was true. "Yeah. I do."

After I said it the line went silent. Perhaps I should have dialed her back, but I knew Kat needed to simmer for a while on our conversation. If anything, it had given me hope when I thought all was lost. She was having doubts. Even though some have pre-wedding jitters. I knew Kat's concerns had more to do with me than Branch. That only verified that the bond between us still existed, and I hadn't been imagining it all this time. I knew Katy Michaels, obviously better than she knew herself. She chose my brother because at the time, he made her feel safe. I was a rebel, acting out of jealousy, though I couldn't admit that to her, not back then, and certainly not now.

My mind traveled back to all the times my brother had filled my head with the idea that Kat never wanted me. I wondered if he'd gone to extremes to make sure I didn't pursue her. Had he lied so that we couldn't be together because he knew I'd be her first choice?

As the questions began to pile up in my head, so did the fact that I was about to see them after years of being apart. I was going to be able to look into her eyes, to touch her skin, and feel her close to me.

I may have been going there to watch her walk down the aisle with Branch, but I was going to make sure she knew exactly where I stood before that happened. She was going to tell me the truth, once and for all. Best man or not, I couldn't let my brother win, not if he hadn't played fair from the beginning. That saying, "cheaters never win," was true. If he'd lied, he didn't deserve her.

I realized that I may have been getting excited for nothing. Perhaps my own desperation was making me imagine things that were never there, but if for some reason I was onto something, I had to find out, one way or another.

Chapter 9

Since I was going to be heading overseas after my trip home, my friends threw me a going away party. It wasn't anything fancy, just beer and the company of my bunk group. I didn't know why, but my sergeant handed me a journal. When I gave him a curious look, he simply patted me on the shoulder. "Trust me, you're going to need it. You should prepare yourself. There are things that no person should ever have to see. When I did my three tours in Desert Storm, writing my feelings down was the only thing that helped. I suggest you do the same."

As much as I appreciated the gesture, I couldn't understand how I would ever want to write down my feelings.

Then, the day before I was to fly home for the wedding of my brother and Kat, I sat down on my bed and stared at the journal. I think it took me longer to locate a pen, then it did to find words to express how I felt.

I started with the date, hoping that someday I could look back and appreciate that it was in chronological order of when I'd hit rock bottom to when I finally figured out how to move on without Kat.

December 20th 2010

I'm about to embark on a trip home, not knowing if I'll be able to keep my shit together. It's been years since I laid eyes on Katy Michaels, but a day hasn't gone by where I didn't miss, think about, or wish she was preparing to marry me instead of my brother.

The Army has taught me to be strong, tough, and in control. I know when our eyes meet for the first time I'll lose all of that. She's my only weakness.

I'm getting ready to head to the airport and then be on my way to the hotel where they'll wed. I keep thinking that if I tell her how I've felt for so long, she'll choose me instead, but I know it's not true.

Kat made her decision years ago. What's done is done. I can daydream all I want, but she's not going to change her mind, not this close to her wedding day. It isn't like we can run off into the sunset together. I don't even know why I'm writing this down. It's only going to piss me off more when I read it later.

After confessing my feelings to a ridiculous book, I laid awake staring at the ceiling. There was no way I was going to be able to sleep knowing I was about to see her. My heart was already on edge and facing my brother was going to be an even harder challenge. He'd known we'd slept together. He didn't even want me at the wedding to begin with. I'm sure he was only doing it for Kat. All I could imagine was getting into a brawl in front of everyone who'd be a part of our lives. My parents would never forgive me, and if they found out what I'd done under their roof I would never be able to justify the repercussions.

I'd already lost so much, actually I'd given up. Was I really willing to show up just to rehash what couldn't be changed?

By six the next morning I was awake and dressed. I got a ride to the airport and watched the driver pulling away, wondering if I should call him back and forget about the trip. What good would it bring anyone if I showed up. Sure, Kat would be angry, and probably hurt, but it was better than having her wedding ruined because I couldn't be near my brother.

Since all of this was my fault I knew there was only one thing I could do. It was better he hear it from me first anyway. I dialed my dad's number, hoping he wasn't close to my mom when he answered. This was one thing I never wanted her to find out about. The thought of disappointing my mom got under my skin. It would bother me forever if she thought she hadn't taught me right from wrong.

"Brooks, I hope you're not calling because your flight is delayed."

"No. The flight is fine." I honestly hadn't checked. I hadn't even stepped foot in the airport yet.

"Are you calling to confirm when you'll arrive at the hotel? Your mom gave you the address, didn't she?"

This was going to be harder than I thought. "I have the address. I'm just not sure I should come at all."

"What do you mean, son? Why wouldn't you be here for Branch and Katy? You're the best man."

"You wouldn't be saying that if you knew what I've done, dad." I watched a woman leading her child into the airport. They were each pulling matching luggage, and it was cute seeing the little girl pretending to be grown up. It made me think about Kat and Branch having a child. I wondered if she'd have a daughter that looked just like her. Would she call me uncle, or would I be kept away from her because of what I'd done behind my brother's back?

"Brooks, you're not making any sense. Can we talk about this when you get here? Your mom has me running all over the place today."

"Actually we can't. There's no way I can show up tonight without you hearing what I have to tell you. It's important."

I could tell my dad was reconsidering what he'd said. He cleared his throat before responding. "Sure. What's going on? Are you okay?"

I scrunched up my face even though I realized he couldn't see me. "Yeah, I'm fine. I'm just worried. I've been holding something in for a while now. Honestly, I hoped you'd never have to find out it happened, but since Branch knows there's no telling what he'll say or do."

"This is about your brother?" He inquired.

"No. I guess, maybe indirectly. It's more about me, and something that I did years ago...with Kat."

"Oh. Please don't tell me that you...Brooks, how far did it go?"

I closed my eyes. This wasn't like writing it in a letter and mailing it off. I could hear my father's breathing change. I knew he was going to be repulsed that I'd done something so heinous under his roof. I was a disgrace, and he'd seen it that way. "Dad, you need to know it wasn't planned."

"When did it happen? How did your brother find out?"

I pinched the bridge of my nose. "Kat didn't know it was me."

"How is that possible?"

"It was dark. She was crying. She thought I was Branch, and I didn't tell her differently. She didn't find out until after I'd left. Branch found a letter I'd left for her in the tree house. Look, it doesn't even matter now. What's important is knowing why I can't come to that ceremony and stand up for him, not now, maybe not ever. I'm not a good brother. I've been in love with Kat my whole life. There's no way I can watch her promising to love him forever, not when I'm wishing it was me instead."

"Son, why are you telling me this? Did you call for advice because honestly, I don't know what to say."

"I guess I'm calling because I want you to tell me that it's okay if I don't come to the wedding. Say that someday you'll forgive me.

Tell me I'm not ruining the ceremony by showing my face."

"I spoke to your brother this morning. He's looking forward to seeing you. He picked up your tux already. Whatever happened in the past, he's obviously either gotten over it, or he's letting it go for the family. It would break your mother's heart if you didn't show up. Son, I can't tell you how to feel, but you've got to suck it up, at least for the next two nights. We're all excited about seeing you. Things have changed. They're happy now. We've all made mistakes. It's part of the learning process."

"It's not just that, Dad. I still care about, Kat. I still love her."

"Brooks, you're a grown man now. The choice is yours, but I do hope you make it for the right reason. I'll be looking for you at the hotel, but if I don't see you, at least know that your mom and I love you no matter what. It couldn't have been easy being in the same room as them. I'll never understand how she chose Branch, but that's another story for a different time. Whatever you decide, I'll be proud of you."

"I appreciate that, sir."

"We'll be seeing you soon. I know you'll make the right choice."

When we hung up I looked at the double doors opening and closing as people entered and exited the airport. I was one flight way from seeing the love of my life again. Was I really going to be scared about my brother? What more could he throw at me that I hadn't already experienced a million times before? He already had what I wanted. He'd won, I'd lost. The truth was sleeping next to him every night, wearing the ring that he'd saved up to buy. If he knew her any at all, he would have presented her with her mother's ring, which she'd mentioned using again and again.

As much as Branch irked me, I recognized there was little I could do. My job was to stand by his side while he promised to love and cherish Kat. It was going to be the most important day of their lives, and they'd invited me to stand beside them. As a brother I understood I couldn't let them down. As much as it was going to sting, it was paramount to all the guests, but mostly our parents. Kat was finally taking the Valentine name. I'd dreamed of the moment that she'd become my wife, I just never suspected she'd be his instead.

There was no right decision. In my eyes it was all wrong.

I made one more phone call before checking in for my flight. I didn't know how he'd react to me contacting him, but I at least had to attempt to keep the peace.

"Hello, brother. Are you calling to tell me you're not going to show?"

"Is that what you want to hear?"

"I don't know, Brooks. In a way, yeah, it would make it less weird, but it's not just my wedding. If I had it my way we would have eloped a long time ago. This ceremony is for Katy. It's what she wants, and I promised to make sure it's perfect."

"That's the reason for my call. Are you going to be okay if I'm there?"

"As long as you keep your hands off my soon-to-be wife, I don't care. We're still brothers even if I want to rip out your throat."

I wasn't sorry for what happened. I could have said no at any time. I slept with Kat because I wanted to. It was selfish, and I deserved to lose her forever because of it. "I want to get past this. I'm sorry, Branch. I know you hate me. Can we try to be friends while I'm there? It's the only way I'll be able to get on the plane today."

"Fine. I'll be nice. Maybe I'll even give you a hug, but don't think for a second that I'm letting my guard down. What you did can never be forgiven."

"I understand. I guess it's final then. I'm getting on a plane to come home."

"I guess so."

When we hung up I didn't feel anymore excited about seeing Branch. I half expected him to tell me to stay away. Nothing was more clear to me than knowing this was Kat's idea. For some reason it made me smile. I just had to be on my best behavior.

Chapter 10

While on the plane ride to Washington, DC, I had a ton going through my mind. My first initial gut feeling was telling me to avoid eye contact with Kat. If I didn't reconnect with her in person then everyone would assume I'd moved on and gotten over it. I was certain Branch would have a skeptical watch over me, but actions speak louder than words. I had to make it seem like I held no interest in Katy Michaels. My family depended on it.

I think my nerves were at extreme levels when I climbed into the cab that was taking me to the hotel. I was about to come face to face with the woman that I'd put on a pedestal. I knew she was going to take my breath away. Hiding that sort of excitement wouldn't come without effort. I might be able to fool half the people in the room, but none of the ones who truly knew me. I wondered how I could hide the only thing I'd never been able to deny. How could I look into her eyes and not want to hold her; to make up for all the time we'd spent apart, from all the mistakes I made that pushed her into my brother's arms? How could I face what breaks me down, lowering me until I'm riddled with pain?

As we pulled up to the entrance of the lavish hotel I wondered if I'd be able to will myself inside. That's when I saw her, standing right in the lobby. As far away as she was, I knew it was her. Waves of heat overwhelmed me as I handed the driver some cash and stepped out of the vehicle with my bag thrown over my shoulder and my eyes still fixated on the prize. She couldn't see me checking her out, finding all the things that had changed about her in a matter of seconds.

Her beauty had only accentuated with time. I worried she wouldn't feel the same about me. In that moment, when I walked into the building, nothing else mattered in the world. I'd forgotten about the promise I'd made to my brother, or the fact that anyone could have seen this reaction as a threat. My only focus was to get to her, hold her, and contemplate never letting her go.

I never would have expected her to react the way she did, and it only made our connection more consuming. My arms wrapped tightly around her body, while I took in the fragrance of her hair, remembering back when we still lived under the same roof. I had to keep holding her there to prevent her from seeing the tears that I was fighting back. She'd never understand how much I'd wished for this. For as many nights as I could count, I dreamed of this moment with her; one that was mutual and more endearing than any letter or phone call could provide. "I missed you so much," I whispered, barely able to get words out.

She backed away and took in my appearance. I wondered if she liked me being in my fatigues. Did she notice any changes in me?

"It's been a long time."

What did that mean? Was she disappointed? Couldn't she come back into my arms for a little while longer?

I had to remain calm. This was much harder than I expected it to be. "You look great, Kat."

"Can I help you, sir?" The lady behind the desk interrupted.

For a second I had to look away even though I didn't want to let her out of my sight. "I'm here to check in. The name is Valentine, Brooks Valentine."

Before I had the chance to hug her again, or even consider what else we could talk about without me losing my cool, I heard my brother's voice. He was in the room with us, and it was the first time we'd seen each other since he'd found out I'd slept with Kat.

"Well look at what the cat dragged in." Branch came walking in with his arms full of boxes. He sat them down in a chair and walked over to greet me. I knew right away that this was all an act. "It's real good to see you, bro," He said loud enough for everyone to hear. Then, in a low whisper he spoke only to me. "If I see you putting your hands on her again it's going to get ugly fast."

I pulled away and faked a smile, realizing he'd seen how uncontrolled I already was around Kat. I couldn't help it. For some reason I felt like I loved her even more, as if the distance between us had only made it stronger, instead of helping me to forget. "Yeah, you too," I finally replied to Branch. He may have been fooling everyone in the room, but I was on high alert, as if he was my sworn enemy.

It felt great to see my parents again. I'd missed them and noticed right away how well they both appeared. I'd worried that they'd fall apart, but perhaps being forced together because they were all that was left had made them stronger. It was strange to me how that could happen, but it also gave me hope that sometimes love conquers all. Now, I'm the farthest you can get from a sap, but it was definitely a nice feeling to see my parents this way.

Before I'd even noticed what was going on, Kat was walking away from us. I tried not to let my brother notice that I was watching her, but it was too late. His expression left me wondering if he was going to kill me while I slept. I'd been there for less than ten minutes and already had a hit out on me because I couldn't keep my shit together when I was with Kat. Coming to the wedding had been a terrible idea. I already knew it wasn't going to end well.

While trying nonchalantly to search for Kat without being obvious, a cute red-head bounced over to greet me. It took me a second to realize that this must have been Kat's friend Melissa. She stared into my eyes as she grabbed my hand to shake. I'd seen this look before, but found it hard not to laugh at how she was acting like a teenager who was flustered at the sight of me. "Hey, you must be Melissa. I'm Brooks."

"I know. Kat told me all about you," she responded with a smile. "Branch said you were single. I just wanted to introduce myself and let you know that we're in this together."

"Come again? In what?" I had no idea what she was talking about. Was she implying that being single was something to celebrate?

"The duties of the being the best man and maid of honor, of course. What did you think I was saying?"

"I don't know. Sorry, I've been traveling all day. My mind's in a million places."

"That can be resolved. There's a bar right over there. After a couple drinks I'm sure you'll feel more comfortable."

I'm pretty sure she was hitting on me, and for some reason it was disturbing. I wondered if Kat had put her up to it, or possibly Branch. At any rate I had to be cordial because my brother and his accusing eyes were fixated on my every move.

Since I didn't feel like carrying on a long conversation with this chick, I decided to head to my room. "I'm just going to go get changed. If you'll excuse me?" I moved her body to the side, picked up my bag and headed for the elevators. Once inside I leaned back and took a few deep breaths. I didn't know where Kat was, or even if she was thinking about me, but I couldn't get my mind off of her to save my life.

I'd no sooner sat my things down on the bed when someone knocked on my door. I turned hoping and praying that it was her. To be behind closed doors and hold her again would have been fantastic, unfortunately that's not who was waiting when I opened it up.

"Branch? What's up?"

He punched me in the gut, sending me back to the bed. While I tried to catch my breath he started to speak. "You were here for a few seconds and already went back on your word. What the fuck is wrong with you? I told you to stay away from her."

I shook my head. "You've got it all wrong," I lied. "I was simply saying hi. If I didn't hug her she would have suspected something. Get over yourself Branch. It was just a hug."

He pointed directly at me. "Keep your hands off of my girl, Brooks. This is my last warning."

"Or what?" I peered him right in the eyes while I stood to be level with his face. "What will you do? Will you send me away? Will you attempt to beat my ass because we both know how that will end. I'm almost double the size of you and have been trained to take down the enemy. There's no way you could handle me. Take your threats and get the fuck out of my room. I'm here because I was asked to attend. Like it or not, SHE wants me here, and there's not a damn thing you can do about it."

My brother just stood there, searching for something he could say that would bring me down. He looked away as he replied. "She feels sorry for you. That's why you're here. Kat's like that. We're the only family she has left. She thinks of you like a brother and nothing more. You're fooling yourself if you thought you could come back here and be friends again. If she only knew what you did to her. You should be in jail."

"She wouldn't do that to me," I whispered under my breath.

"Oh really? You think she'd ever forgive you?" He shook his head and began to chuckle. "Just remember who she's marrying, brother. You weren't her first choice. You lost. Say whatever you want, but I never had to sneak my way into her bed."

It took everything in me to not plummet my brother to the ground. It was a low blow, one that I'd lived with since the first night I'd been intimate with Kat. He'd taken what I'd done and used it as a weapon against me, knowing there was nothing I could say or do to defend my actions. He had every right to be angry with me, but at the end of the day he was correct. She'd chosen him, and I couldn't change that.

"Get out of my room!" I gritted my teeth and clenched my fists as I said it.

Branch stood with the door half-open. "If you can't act right don't bother coming downstairs later. It's going to be hard enough pretending that I like you during the service. I'd hate to have to strain myself this early on."

When the door shut I buried my face into my hands. This couldn't be happening already. This mess was mine to clean up, but I didn't even know how to begin making it happen, not when I knew she was the only reason I was there in the first place.

Chapter 11

My father rapped on the door until I answered. Dressed casually, he placed his hands in his pockets, like he frequently did. "Everyone is meeting downstairs for cocktails. Do you think you might want to join us? I'd hate for you to spend your whole visit alone in this room."

I leaned on the door frame. "Yeah, well I'm better off steering clear of Branch. He hates having to put on a show when I'm around."

"I'm not going to take no for an answer."

I hated disappointing my dad, so I realized I didn't have much of a choice. I slipped on a pair of shoes and followed him down to the lounge, where I found everyone there except for Kat. Since I knew I couldn't ask about her, or make it obvious that I was scanning the area to locate where she was hiding, I ordered a drink.

Melissa approached me immediately. It was obvious this girl was going to be a thorn in my side; one that I could use to distract everyone from the fact that I was infatuated with being close to Kat. "What will you be drinking tonight, Brooks?"

I stepped up to the bar. "A draft beer is fine. I'm taking it easy tonight. We've got a big day tomorrow." I looked at my brother and nodded.

He raised his brows, giving a sarcastic smirk then downed a shot. Without making it obvious, I turned my attention back to Melissa. She sipped her drink through her straw while staring at me. Since I was still wondering where Kat was, I decided to walk toward my parents, until I saw her coming into the room. Then everything around me stopped. As excited as I was it was important not to make a scene.

We all sat down at a nearby table. When Melissa and Branch stood back up to get drinks for everyone, I couldn't help but lean over and speak. "Are you feeling better?"

I could tell she was looking around to see who was watching. "Yes, thanks."

"Nerves got the best of you, I assume." As I said it I stared at the television as if I wasn't paying attention to her.

For a while everyone chatted about mundane things, mostly the guests that were coming to the event. I kept my focus off of Kat, but didn't check to see if my brother was watching my back. By the time our seats were ready for dinner, I was starting to unwind. I'd had a few beers, and the focus turned to an interest in what I'd been through so far in the military.

"Are you nervous about being deployed?" Melissa asked.

I shrugged and played with the rim of my glass. "Not really. I'm as prepared as I'll ever be, I suppose. I mean, it's nothing you can be one-hundred percent sure of."

"I don't know why someone would ever sign up to risk their lives. It's so dangerous." Her response made me feel tough.

I swished my beer around. "I'm proud of my choices," I lied. Sure, I was happy how I'd been brave, but walking away from Kat was definitely not something I'd ever forgive myself for.

"Our son has dedicated himself to serving this beautiful country. That's something to be proud of." My father was the first to make me feel at ease.

"Dad, as much as I appreciate that, I've been taught to fend my own battles. Now, as far as going overseas, I'll take it day by day. We have one life, and I plan on making the best of it. It's my job, and I take pride in that."

"What was it like at first?" Kat asked. "When you left for basic was it difficult? I don't think I ever asked."

I wished I could tell her that my struggles weren't because of joining the military. What I fought daily with was the decision to walk away from not only my family, but most of all from her. It didn't matter that she was with Branch. I should have stayed, because just maybe they wouldn't be tying the knot, putting me through more pain and suffering. "It wasn't all that bad. I was learning something new every day. I made a couple friends, and we leaned on each other when times got tough. I'll never forget the first week when we all had to get our haircuts. There was this guy who kept making fun of people with weird shaped heads. Well, let me just tell you, as soon as they shaved the first half of his scalp it was like looking at an egg. From that moment on he was known as Humpty. I guess you had to be there to get the full gist of it."

A couple people smiled while Kat seemed to be pleased.

"What are the girls like in the Army? Are they all butchy?" Branch asked. Leave it to him to open his mouth about other women as if I didn't know it was purposely to get under Kat's skin.

"Much to my surprise there are plenty of beautiful women in the armed forces. In fact, it's a lot like college. We just walk around in camouflage and work out way more. We go out for drinks, play games, and lack sleep."

Kat giggled and said something under her breath to Melissa. "It sounds just like college."

"Yeah, if every day was like rush week," Branch rudely commented, while waving down the waiter for another drink.

While I sat there looking at my brother I noticed how the years had changed him. Maybe I just didn't recall ever feeling scrawny, or perhaps it was the fact that I was so much bigger than he was now. "I'm hoping to eventually work in a recovery unit. My sarge thinks I should focus on marksmanship, but I don't know if that's all I want to do. I think I'd rather help people, instead of focusing on destruction."

None of the people at the table could respond to my statement. It was like they were shell-shocked. They couldn't have understood what I was preparing to walk into. There was a good chance that I wouldn't be coming home. I had to be realistic. Bad things were happening overseas, and I was about to be right smack in the center of it all.

"Can we talk about something else now? It's my wedding eve." Branch was all about himself, just like he'd always been. Every statement he made caused me to wonder what the hell Kat saw in him.

"Yeah, sure. I was simply answering a question."

"Wait," Melissa interrupted. "I'd like to hear more. My cousin is in the Navy. He always has the best tales to tell."

"I don't know if I have anything worthwhile to talk about. I mean, I've lived on a base for quite some time. My day is like anyone else's with a job. I wake up and put in the time, and then I'm done." Explaining what it was like for me seemed so boring, but Kat's friend was staring at me like I made millions of dollars selling paperclips. She was whacked.

"Maybe we should order dessert," My mother stated. "The pastor will be here soon for the rehearsal."

Out of the corner of my eye I saw Kat looking at me. Quickly, she turned away, I suppose because she was embarrassed I'd caught her. For the next several minutes it kept happening, each time one of us would turn away before we were discovered. It made no sense to me. She was acting like a teenager does when they're crushing on someone. Obviously that wasn't happening between us. She was about to get married.

After dinner, we all made our way into the hall where the ceremony was to be held. The pastor waited for us to come forward before beginning to explain what would happen. I know it was by accident, but instead of positioning my brother across from Kat, he grabbed me by the arm and stood me right in front of her. I could hear gasps around the room while Kat and I stood still staring at one another.

As fast as he was able, Branch shoved me to the side. The look on his face made me want to laugh, but I held it together, even as everyone else in the room laughed at the discrepancy. The whole time I kept turning back to meet eyes with Kat. I couldn't understand why, but I felt like she was upset about something. I wanted to pull her aside and ask her what was going on, but understood it wasn't the time or place. After the wedding I figured things would be easier. Branch would let his guard down and I could make sense out of everything that I was feeling.

When the rehearsal was over, we all went back to the bar, except for my parents, who retreated to their room early. Even though I don't think my brother needed another drop of alcohol, he kept pouring them down. Meanwhile, Melissa also continued binge drinking, as well as throwing herself at me in front of everyone. She kept smiling at me, sticking her chest out, I assume to get me to look at her cleavage. Honestly, I tried. I thought that if I put all of my attention on her, I would get by with little peeks of Kat. Sure, it was terribly wrong, but it was all I could do to prevent from walking over to her and ruining my life some more.

Then Branch went too far. "So, what room did you say you were in again?" He inquired.

"I didn't. It's seven zero two. Why?" I expected him to say he was kicking my ass later, but that was far from what came out of his mouth next.

"You hear that, Mel? Write it down for later. I'm sure it's been a while since he's had a ginger."

I faced him, ready to throw down. He'd taken things too far. I figured Melissa would get angry for him making a joke out of her having red hair, but instead she seemed even more convinced that she had a chance. "Don't speak for me, Branch. You have no idea what I do with my free time."

I refused to look at Kat. The first reason was because I didn't want to see her disappointed face. The second was because I did. I wanted to know that she was offended, so much that she didn't want to marry him. This guy, the one that was acting a fool, was the true identity of my brother. He may not present it all the time, but behind closed doors he was selfish, heartless, and out to make sure he won at whatever he'd set out to do.

Melissa came over, wrapped her arm into mine. "So, should I join you in your room?"

I stared directly at Kat when I replied. "Maybe later."

I had no intentions of sleeping with her, but needed my brother off my back, at least until the service was over. It was a good plan if I could just put up with Branch for a little while longer.

It was obvious that Kat was becoming frustrated with my brother. She and Melissa went into the bathroom together, and when she came back out she had a disgusted look on her face.

Only a short time later Branch started cursing and giving other people at the bar a hard time. He was out of control.

Kat tried to grab him, but his weight knocked them both down. I managed to help her before he could crush her anymore.

"Alright, bro. It's time for you to call it a night, man."

Kat told Melissa that she'd see her back in the room as we started to exit the bar.

While in the elevator, Branch began singing at the top of his lungs. *"Going to the chapel and I'm gonna get married."*

We managed to lead him to his room, and Kat opened the door. Branch started on her again. "Don't leave me baby. Give me some love before you go."

She swatted his hands away. "I can't stay, Branch. It's bad luck."

My brother pointed to the door. "Then get the fuck out. I knew I should have gotten strippers."

That was the last straw. I wouldn't let him disrespect her in front of me. I slapped him hard on the back of the head. "Be respectful, you drunk piece of shit. That woman is going to be your wife tomorrow. Don't talk to her like that."

Branch rolled over on his back. He pulled his knees up and started laughing. "Listen to you, standing up for her still. Do you know how many times I've been inside of her? She's never going to be yours now. I marked her."

This wasn't just an attempt to get to me. He was hurting her too.

I pointed toward the door while looking at Kat. "Go outside and wait for me."

"But I-"

"Kat, go outside. Now!"

She looked back at Branch, who was watching her exit the room. "In twenty-four hours you'll be my wife, Katy. Don't forget it!"

I waited for it to shut before giving him a piece of my mind. "What the hell is wrong with you? She's not some punching bag."

He covered his head with a pillow like my words meant nothing. "Go away. Who invited you here anyway?"

I stood over the bed, looking down at him in such a terrible predicament. "I don't care how much I've had to drink. I'd never talk to her that way. You don't do that to people you love."

Branch started laughing. "Fuck you! You think I care how you feel? You're just pissed that she wants me. I could beat the shit out of her and she still wouldn't go running to you. Just get out of here, Brooks."

"You know, it doesn't matter what you say to me. You'll never deserve her. I hope you oversleep, so she doesn't make the worst mistake of her life. You're pathetic. She may not see it now, but it's only a matter of time."

When I went out into the hallway I saw her sitting there on floor, her hands covering her face. All it took was for her to look at me, and I could feel myself becoming weak. This was my best friend, and she needed me.

"I'm really sorry about that. He didn't mean it." Even if he had, she didn't deserve to have her heart broken. She may not have wanted me, but I'd never give up on her.

Chapter 12

I was leading Kat down the hallway towards her room. I'd waited to be alone with her, but after what had occurred I knew it wasn't the right time or place to catch up. If things were different I would have been willing to stay up all night reminiscing about our memories together. After all, Kat wasn't just the woman of my dreams, she was my everything.

She broke my concentration when she stammered out a comment. "People say the truth when they're drunk."

"Not all the time. His issues are with me." I clenched my jaw and hoped she'd believe me.

Someway or another my brother would pin this on me in the morning.

Kat halted and looked up at me. Her eyes were full of unreleased tears. "Maybe I shouldn't go through with it?"

It was unbearable to hear. I'd waited so long for her to wise up, but now it was too late. "Don't say things like that."

"No. I mean it. I've been having all these feelings and I can't shake them."

We ended up stopping at my room first. It was time to end the conversation and get behind closed doors before I said something I'd regret later. "This is me." I stared at my keycard to prevent from allowing her to see how conflicted I was. "Listen, get some sleep and things will be all better tomorrow. You can marry Branch and start your happy lives together."

I'd unfastened the door and attempted to step inside, only to be thrown a loop by her next statement. "Do you still love me, Brooks?"

I leaned my head on the door and closed my eyes, still refusing to turn around. "Don't do this, Kat. You've been drinking and you're upset at Branch."

"It's a yes or no answer."

I was losing control. We were back at this point already, just like before I'd left for boot camp. I already knew how this would end; how it had to end. "It changes nothing."

She hugged her own body, and I watched her trembling. As much as she attempted to look away, our gaze was fixed. It was then that I started to break down my walls. Was it really too late? Was this her final plea to get out of her impending nuptials? Was I willing to lose my family over it?

Her next question made me weak in the knees. "What if I don't know how to stop loving you?" I held onto the door in hopes to elude from falling to my knees before her. She'd just admitted out loud to loving me. It was confirmed, after all this time, after hoping and praying, it was happening.

I could feel the burning in my eyes, letting me know that I had zero control over my own emotions. At this point I longed to pull her into my arms and never let go, but the repercussions were too hard to bear. We couldn't take that route. The damage was too extensive. "You have to."

She sobbed and shook her head. "I can't."

I lifted her chin as I spoke words I never thought I'd say. It wasn't how I felt at all, but I wouldn't be that guy who fell right into things with her after a fight. I'd already stooped too low to be with her in the past. Love wasn't enough at this point. "You have to, Kat. You can't do this now. Your future is already determined. The choice was made years ago. There's no going back."

She closed her eyes as she requested something out of me I knew I wasn't strong enough to give. It wasn't the act that was scaring me; it was everything that came with it.

"Fine. If it has to be that way, kiss me goodbye. Kiss me for all the years we've lost and all the ones we'll never have together. Kiss me and make me forget that every moment without you in my life crushes me."

"No!" I had to push her away because she was becoming impossible to resist. It was like God was punishing me, sending me one last test to redeem myself. I had to be strong and do the right thing, no matter how much pain it inflicted on my soul. "Please don't do this." I started walking around, hoping that if I couldn't see the look in her eyes, I'd be able to avoid the burning desire to take her into my room. "We can't go there."

She was sniffling, begging with her whole heart, but I refused to listen. I wouldn't let myself fall, not again, not when I knew she'd run right back to him. Kat was talking, she was saying things I'd always wanted to hear, but they were coming out after an argument with Branch. She'd been drinking, and so had I. The combination was dangerous. I'd be a terrible man if I allowed anything to happen, and she'd probably never forgive me in the morning. "Please, Brooks. I don't care if it's wrong. I need to feel it one last time. Just make this pain go away because I'm suffocating in it."

I furrowed my brow and looked down at the floral designed carpet. "And you think I'm not? My God, Kat, I left the state because I couldn't watch you with him for another second. You think it's hurting you? How do you think I felt when that pastor put me in his place? Do you know how hard it was for me to not announce to everyone in the room that I belonged there and it wasn't a mistake?"

She continued crying, making it hard to make out what she was saying. "What am I supposed to do, Brooks? It's too late. You should have fought for me back then. You should have told me how you felt. Branch said you didn't like me that way. How could I have known?"

"Because you felt it in here." I pointed to her heart and kept my hand there. "Because deep inside you knew how I felt about you. It was never a secret. I worshipped the ground you walked on. When you were sad, I was there. Not him! I was the one to wipe away your tears. You should be wearing that God damn dress for me, not my brother!" My anger was coming out with my words, and although I didn't mean them, it was helping to be able to say what needed to be addressed. "You broke my heart, Kat. You pushed me away, like an old toy. That's why I stopped hanging out with you. It's why I stopped wanting to do things and stayed by myself. Do you know what it was like to hear you and him sneaking around together? How do you think it made me feel?"

She sobbed and moved her head around, as if she was trying so hard to understand, but couldn't grasp exactly what was happening. "I'm so sorry, I didn't know."

I threw my arms in the air. "You didn't know? How could you not know? Even my fucking parents knew. Don't tell me that you lived in the same house with me and saw me every single day, but were oblivious to how I felt about you?"

"I swear, it's true."

I tugged my key card out of my pocket and stuck it in the slot as I spoke. "You know what? It doesn't even matter now. There *is* no us. You've never really been mine and I've spent the last few years being okay with that." I opened the door, but didn't go inside. "I'm not going to kiss you, because it won't get us anywhere, and you'd be cheating on my brother. No matter how much of an asshole he is, you're marrying him in less than twenty-four hours. I can't go back there again. It hurt too fucking much the first time, and it's going to take everything I have in me to get through tomorrow." By this time my tears were drying. I was willing them to vacate so I could get through this without her arguing about it. "I think we should just call it a night and start over in the morning."

When I went into that hotel room and closed the door I knew she was standing on the other side, waiting for me change my mind. I pressed my head against the other side before crumbling down to the floor. That's where I began to weep, like I never had in my life.

Kat was in love with me. Her words repeated in my mind like a broken record. She'd always been in love with me, which meant Branch lied to win her. He'd lied to both of us to prevent us from being together because even back then he knew she wanted me.

It took every ounce of energy I had to not bust through his door and beat the living shit out of him. He'd ruined my life. He'd purposely destroyed me for his own gain. What kind of brother does that? For the past twenty years he'd done nothing but lie to make sure I never had a chance.

It was too unbearable to fathom.

After a few minutes of losing my shit, I headed into the bathroom to wash off my face. I was prepared to sleep it off, in order to get through the next day with composure.

Then I began to regret my decision. This was my last chance. Did I really care what anyone else thought? Even if my parents were pissed, they'd know before anyone that I'd acted out of love. Kat wasn't just my weakness. She was my reason for existing.

When a knock came from the door I was sure she'd come back. In that moment nothing else mattered. This time I would pull her inside and never let go unless she asked me to. This time I'd act on impulse alone.

Except it wasn't Kat at the door. It was Melissa. She's freshened up her makeup, hair, and even her clothes. Her what I'd call reddish, hair looked brighter in the hallway lights. Her smile was probably tantalizing to some, but not to me. Unlike what my brother had assumed, I wasn't into 'gingers' or any other type of woman. In fact, I didn't have a type, because there was only one particular woman for me. On a planet full of options, my heart yearned for Kat.

"Melissa. What're you doing here?"

"You told me to come."

"Where's Kat, err Katy? Have you seen her?"

"She's a wreck over some falling out with Branch. She left me in the room to go pout about it somewhere. I'm sure by now she's gone after him to make amends, she's got some rule about not going to bed angry. Katy can be irrational at times." Her flip comment made me want to cringe. If my brother wasn't such a pompous asshole than maybe she'd be a happier person. "So, are you going to let me in?"

I leaned on the doorframe, sighing before giving her the bad news. "No, I'm not. To be honest, I'm just not in the mood. I know what my brother said, but he doesn't know a thing about me. I'm already taken."

"I didn't realize. I feel like a fool."

She started to turn to walk away, and I touched her arm. "Don't. I'm a private person, who considers himself loyal. I'm sure you're a good time, but I promised myself that I'd never let my cock make the decisions for me. It got me in heaps of trouble in the past. Now I think with my brain." It was a sappy response that made her smile immediately. She'd gained respect for me, which was something I hadn't felt in a long time.

"Thanks for telling me. I guess I'll just head back to my room then." She turned around one more time. "Whoever she is, she's a lucky woman."

If she only knew that the person I was referring to wasn't even mine to begin with. She'd never been mine to claim, so why did I feel the need to run after her again? Why was my heart pulling me right to her when I knew it wasn't going to end well?

I knew the reason as I stood there questioning myself.

It was love.

I'd finally gotten the confirmation that I needed. Katy Michaels was in love with me. She'd admitted it without regret. That alone caused me to let my guard down and go after what I'd wanted for so long; what I felt should have been mine from the very beginning.

Chapter 13

This could be all my imagination, but there was also a chance this was happening the way I was seeing it play out. It took me no time at all to head out of my room, determined to get the answers that I desperately needed. Before she said her vows to my brother, we needed to get things straight with us. I couldn't live like this for the rest of my life. Slowly she was killing me whether she meant it or not.

At first I searched downstairs in the lobby, and even outside where the front entrance was located. While riding the elevator back up to the floor I was on, I had an idea. It was a long shot, but when we were kids she'd always run to the tree house. Without further thought, I made my way up to the roof, praying she hadn't run back to my brother so soon.

As soon as I opened the door leading out to the frigid temperatures that December blessed the state with, I saw her there, laying on the cold, hard pavement ground. She didn't notice me heading in her direction, or even when I squatted down in front of her. Finally, after a few seconds went by, she lifted her head.

Never in my life had I ever seen her so wrecked, not even when her parents were killed. She wasn't just sad, or worried. She was tormented, even tortured with grief. I knew it because I'd experienced the same hell for years.

"How did you find me?"

I peered around at the empty area. "Well, it's not exactly a tree house, but I figured you'd run to high ground. You always did."

After wrapping my jacket around her cold body, I answered. "It's freezing up here, Kat."

"I know. I don't care." Her gaze moved away from me as if she were ashamed. "Where's Melissa? I figured you'd be all over that."

I rubbed my hands on my knees to keep warm, wondering if she really thought I'd hook up with her friend so easily. I assume that years of flaunting slutty girls around to get her attention had backfired. She obviously considered me a player. "You would assume that. Look, I never said I wanted to sleep with her. I told her that maybe we could hang out. Honestly, I figured she'd get so drunk that she'd pass out and forget I said it."

"So where is she?"

"I don't know. She showed up and knocked and I thought it was you. When I saw her standing there, talking about how much of a mess you were, I told her to get lost; in a nice way, of course."

"She's probably looking for me."

"She thinks you ran to Branch to make amends because you have that motto where you never go to bed angry."

She shrugged like she didn't know what I was talking about. "Yeah, I don't really care about that anymore. In fact, I don't really care about anything anymore."

Kat put her head between her knees. I wasn't sure if it was to increase her body heat, or hide me from seeing her expressions.

"You look like shit." I wanted her to smile at me, not turn the other way.

"Thanks. I appreciate that."

"No, I mean I've never seen you look so upset. Is it because of me? I didn't mean to be so harsh with you. I just couldn't let things happen between us. You understand, right?"

She shrugged, also avoiding eye contact. "Yeah, I know."

"Branch will make you happy." I hated saying that. I didn't even know why I had. Helping her makeup with my brother was the last thing I wanted.

"You don't know that."

"Yeah, I do. It's his life's mission to love you more than I do. So I figure that as long as I still love you, he'll worship the ground you walk on."

This time I had her attention, and she wasn't even blinking. "You just admitted that you still loved me."

I reached for her hand, hoping, pleading, that she wouldn't pull away. "I will never stop loving you, Kat. For as long as I am breathing I will love you with everything I have in me, not because I hope someday to have you, but because nothing could ever make me stop, even you marrying my brother."

"You know, you have everyone fooled. They all think you're the son that they could never count on. It turns out that you're the most beautiful soul they've ever known."

We sat there looking at each other for couple seconds, not saying anything.

I expected her to tell to me leave, but it hadn't happened so far. "Don't go calling me a saint just yet. I've been reconsidering that kiss since I let you walk away earlier."

Each word that came out of my mouth was like a test. I wanted her to push me away; to tell me that us being alone was all wrong. It was important that I keep my guard up. At any time someone could walk out and find us in this compromising situation. They'd see the truth immediately because it was written on both of our faces.

"Please don't hate me for saying this. I'm probably already going to Hell anyway. The thing is, I'm not married to your brother, not yet at least. If I had one wish in the world, besides seeing my parents one more time, I know what it would be."

I smiled, but only because she was insane if she thought it was a good idea. "We can't, Kat."

I hated seeing her react like she was disappointed. I understood how mixed feelings and distance had made our time together so intense, but I wasn't sure if I was willing to let myself fall, not here, not now. "We shouldn't," she whispered as she inched toward me.

"It's wrong on so many levels." This was impossible to resist. I needed this to happen as much as I needed air to breathe.

"We should probably call it a night then." Her lips were right there. I could feel her words as they came out of her mouth. This was going to happen, and I wasn't going to be able to stop things once it did.

I inched closer until I felt her soft skin grazing over mine. "Yeah, we should." I couldn't back away, or stop myself. I wasn't going to restrain, because not only did I need this to happen, but I'd wished for this my whole life.

"It's just one kiss, Brooks," she whispered against my mouth.

The insatiable desire I had for her was overwhelming. I'd been with other women, but just a kiss from Kat opened up senses I never knew how to control. She consumed me, so much that I craved more. This wasn't going to end well, and I was done caring. As our tongues played together, the vicious truth was apparent. I needed to make her mine even if we had to drive away from the hotel and never look back again.

It was impossible to stop once we'd gotten started. I didn't have an urge to continue; it was a necessity. The fact that she wasn't pushing me away was enough incentive to press on. This woman, who I'd clearly loved my whole life, was finally letting me in. I realize at this point we were only making out, but something told me it wasn't going to end there.

I nuzzled my nose on the inside of her neck, savoring the way her soft skin smelled. My tongue drug over it, lapping up the salty flavor while the vibration of her first moans sent me into a frenzy.

I picked her up and made sure she was then on my lap, where I could be more in control. The way I was touching her, the feel of her body against my palms, there was no way ever to be able to describe it as being anything other than perfect.

Kat's lip were meant for me to kiss, and as she matched my movements I started thinking about the next step. Our first line of business was to get off the roof. I needed her to be warm, so that I could remove her clothes. I knew just how to heat up her chilled body.

My hands traveled over her ass, and explored other areas of her body, while I took my time, respecting that she could stop this at any moment. She ran her hands up my shirt, kissing me again. "We should stop."

With ease my shirt was removed. I didn't even mind the brutal temperature. "Five more minutes." Our tongues raced to a combined tempo again.

I shoved her dress up over each hip, tracing her panties with my fingertips. When I slide them over to the side I felt the smoothest pussy beckoning me to keep exploring. This was all too much. I wanted her naked, immediately.

I got so caught up that I had to peer down and watch what I was doing because every other time I'd touched her had been in the dark. This was a pivotal moment for me, like a teenager learning the female anatomy for the first time.

I practiced a pattern on her tantalizing clit while gradually working my finger inside of her. She was so warm and welcoming, giving off a vibe that this was just the beginning. I was hot for her, steaming with the thrill of what we were doing. I didn't care who found us, or what was going to happen next. We were living in the moment, taking everything else in our lives for granted.

Kat reached down and started unfastening the buttons to my pants. "We need to stop," I announced abruptly.

She leaned in for a chaste kiss. "Don't you want me?"

If she only knew how much. "I've got two fingers inside of you while on the roof of a building. My dick is going to rip out of my pants, and you're asking me if I want you." Our next kiss was ravenous, giving her more proof of what was going to happen if we didn't stop. "You're all I've ever wanted." In that moment the button to my trousers popped open. I felt her chilled fingers sliding down under my boxers. In that moment her hand took ahold of my cock and immediately got to stroking it. I sucked in a deep breath, trying so hard not to lose control.

Before I knew what was happening, I grabbed her arm. "How far are we going to take this, Kat?"

Kat let go of me, only to remove her panties and fling them away. "That was the only thing standing between you being inside of me. You can sit there and think of a million reasons why we shouldn't be together, or you can take me in that stairwell and fuck me like we both know you want to."

A jolt awakened my cock. I'd never been so turned on, not by any other woman in my life. She was my kryptonite, and I was desperate. I wanted to shout out to the world that I loved her more than life itself. Perhaps she already knew it, but I'd held it in for so long that it felt trivial to not say constantly.

Kat had told me what she wanted me to do, but I wasn't about to waste it in a dirty stairwell. I stood up, quickly putting my shirt back on. "I'm not fucking you in that hallway."

I took her hand and started leading her back inside. "You're coming back to my room and I'm making love to you, and this time, you're going to know it's me you're in bed with."

I peeked out of the door to make sure nobody was around before we made a mad dash to my room. Once inside, we both leaned against the door and started laughing. This was so bad, but I almost like the naughty side of her; a part I knew she'd probably never revealed to anyone else before.

This was it. Nothing could stop us, because I wasn't opening the door until she knew, without a doubt, that we were supposed to be together all along. Our clothes began to come off quickly with one intention on our minds. When her nipple became exposed I lowered my mouth and lapped it up, then sucked on it hard. I shoved her against the door. Our lips were almost touching. I kissed her softly and then pulled away just enough to speak. "Are you sure?"

She nodded. "Are you?"

"Baby, I've never been more sure about anything."

While carrying her to my bed my thoughts were of how I was going to be able to keep her, because now that I had her, I knew I'd never let go.

Chapter 14

Our hunger to be together was constricting our ability to understand what we were doing and how all of this would change our lives. I knew there would be no going back, but I was too scared that I'd lose her again if I brought it up. This was something I had to be selfish about. She'd never be able to understand that being alone with her on that roof had altered my decision to keep the peace. I was done sitting back and letting her get away from me. After my brother's actions, it was obvious that she'd made a huge mistake. Branch would never be able to give her the life that I knew I could. I'd love her through good, bad, and even the ugly. I'd make sure she was never taken for granted, and if we had to flee the country to keep me from being court marshaled, I'd do it. All she had to do was say she wanted to be with me forever, and I'd drop everything in my life to make it happen.

Clearly we had a ton to discuss, but for right now, we needed to take it one moment at a time.

While she lay naked next to me, I traced over her exposed skin around her mouth, and then down the rest of her body. I moved slow, making sure to watch every inch that I was exploring. This was all new for me. Before, I never had time to spare on little details. I wasn't letting any of her out of my sight until I'd seen every single square inch. This wasn't just a spontaneous decision between two people. I'd had years to imagine what it would be like if we could be together.

While tears fell down her cheeks I wasn't afraid she was changing her mind. It was obvious that us finally being together was making her over-emotional. I, myself, had the same feelings. I'd just been trained to hold them in better.

Our kisses were slow, managed and full of intent. Each time her tongue brushed over mine it reminded me that the best was yet to come.

I couldn't be so close to her and not want more. Without breaking our embrace, I let my hand slide down between her legs. As soon as my palm slid over her pussy I was losing control. While keeping my eyes closed, my lips traveled down her neck, then further to her breasts. I teased her nipples with my breath and chin, noticing how excited she seemed to get from it. Right away I could feel how turned on she was, making it even harder to take my time.

When I'd gotten low enough to kiss her thigh, I was fully aware what was in store next. I then traced my tongue around her hip, becoming more aroused when her body reacted to being touched there. While her prize beckoned me to proceed, I took in the moment, realizing that I had to take my time, making sure it was everything we'd both ever dreamed it to be.

It was very obvious that Kat was enjoying this. As I looked up I saw her eyes gazing down at me. Even without words I could tell she wasn't going to get up and leave me alone in the room. This was her finally giving in to what was always there between us. She had to know that I'd tortured myself for so long because I wanted something I thought I'd never have. In this moment, I'd become inundated with sentiment. I wanted her more than any man had ever desired. She was my heaven, my light at the end of a dark, gloomy tunnel.

My finger skimmed over her pussy while my mouth watered. There was no need to haste. I craved a taste, yearned to have it stuck in my memory, reminding me of where I'd finally been.

The second my lips grazed over her smooth skin, I watched Kat's head fall back on a pillow. A tiny moan escaped her when I used my chin hair to tickle her clit. She was already wet, letting me know that foreplay wasn't needed to heighten the mood. This act was my pleasure and as much as it was hers. This was something I refused to skip. She needed to have all of me, and I was prepared to give it to her.

The taste of her musky arousal filled my inner senses, causing a chain reaction straight to my engorged erection. Being with her like this, bringing her such a personal jubilation, left me wide-open to experience every bit of ecstasy that I was providing her with. We shared in the elation as I licked her to no end, savoring her flavor, while striving for the highest of praise. I didn't only want to be the best so far, it was important to be the best she'd ever have. I needed to make sure she'd never desire another man again. Kat lost control, not just once, but several times due to the skills of my maneuvering tongue. By the time I brought my lips up to kiss her, we were both famished, ready to seal the deal once and for all, finally together. This wasn't going to be one-sided. She knew it was me bringing her pleasure, and with that came a sense of security, because she was fully aware that I had no plans to stop.

Kat took control of the situation. She began rocking her body against mine, torturing me until I broke down and entered her. Being a man, it was hard to find something that could break me. I'd like to think I was tough, although I knew my weakness far too well. The moment I slid inside of those tight walls I could sense my body becoming vulnerable. She was giving off vibes, divulging on her own rapture, while I fought to stay composed. With every touch, each kiss, and all of our movements, we were discovering each other, perhaps for the first time in many ways. What I couldn't understand was how in sync we were. This wasn't like feeling someone out for their special spots. Both Kat and I knew exactly where to touch, tease, and pleasure. In this moment we were simultaneously reaching euphoria.

Then I lost myself, utterly and completely. My teeth clamped onto her shoulder as I climaxed. I couldn't move, breathe, or rationalize with what was happening to me, while I was overcome by waves of gratifying pleasure.

Sweaty, panting for air, and never wanting to move, I looked into her eyes, finally accepting that she was mine. There was so much we'd need to talk about, but in this instance it was just us.

"Don't stop, Brooks." It was the first words she'd spoken since this started and hearing them caused me to get carried away again. I did my best to oblige, taking her to the highest peaks.

As we both began to come down from our perpetual bliss, I press my lips against hers, pulling away to express my gratitude. "I love you so much."

She reached one hand up and ran it through my hair. I couldn't stop. My body rocked over hers again while we watched each other breaking free of all our fears. Our high took us to new places while we remained connected. Never in my life had I ever climaxed twice, but as I filled her with pent up years of heartache, I knew it was possible. This was the utmost perfect moment of my entire life. We both lay there, connected and trembling. I held her tightly, stroking her hair, and remaining high on life. It was as if nothing could take this moment away from me. I had everything I wanted in life, I just needed to make sure I could keep it.

We stayed up until the sun started to rise, making love, and satiating our desires, until there was nothing left but exhaustion. I felt whole, and with that came a sense of worry. I was concerned how we'd escape together, and more so how it would all play out once our secret was revealed.

Kat abruptly began crying, and it broke my heart. I knew she had a lot on her plate, but I longed for her to share in this happiness for as long as possible. I wanted to distract her so she didn't have to be concerned, not yet.

I wiped away her tears on either side of her face. "Please don't do that."

"I can't help it," she sobbed. "It was a mistake. It was all a mistake."

I quickly sat up and looked at her like she'd driven a dagger through my heart. "Us? This?"

"No. Branch. Being with him was a mistake and if I'd just admitted that a long time ago, I wouldn't have to say goodbye to you."

My eyes began to burn. She wasn't going to let him go. "What are you saying, Kat? Are you still marrying my brother today?"

"No. I can't marry Branch. I couldn't live with myself and how I feel about you. He deserves to be with someone that isn't hiding the fact that they're in love with someone else. I know it doesn't make what we did any better, but he should have known this would happen, eventually. I mean, did he really think this would never happen? Is this why he kept us apart? Did he do this to us, Brooks?"

I straightened my grimace and bit my tongue. In all honesty I wanted to explode with frustration. This wasn't how I saw this all playing out. "I'm sorry, but all I heard from that was you saying we couldn't be together."

"You know it isn't possible. What we did will destroy the family."

"Last night was the best night of my life. I won't regret it, and I won't let you walk away from this. I'm tired of letting him have you. He doesn't deserve you. I deserve you, Kat. You've always been mine and you know it. How could you lay there saying you can't be with me?" The brutal truth was tearing me apart, piece by piece.

Kat shook her head and cried harder as if she knew what this was doing to me. "I'm sorry. I can't look at your parents knowing what I've done. All these people are here to see me marry your brother and I'm in bed with you."

"I don't give a fuck who's here." Wasn't it obvious?

"Brooks, please don't get angry."

It was entirely too late for that. I was livid, beyond being able to rationalize. I stood and started walking around the room, desperate to find a solution. "Do you know how long I've waited for this to happen? Kat, wake up! I want you. How people feel about it doesn't matter to me. I don't give a shit about anyone else. You're all that matters."

Just as she opened her mouth to respond we heard someone knocking on the door. I had a terrible feeling in the pit of stomach, but said nothing as I pulled on a pair of boxers and headed to answer it. I was prepared to face whoever was on the other side, so long as when they left, she'd still be in my bed, waiting for me to help her figure everything out.

Chapter 15

"Where is she?" It was Branch, and he wasn't happy. Before I was able to prevent it, he came ambling into the room, discovering exactly what he was looking for.

I didn't know how he'd react. I mean, I knew he was destroyed, and probably irrational, but I couldn't predict how he'd treat her. "Branch, don't hurt her. It was my idea. I made her do it," I lied. I wanted Kat to be safe. I'd say or do anything for that reason.

While I stood behind him, Branch peered down at Kat. His eyes were glossed over, and it was obvious he was about to explode with animosity. She wouldn't be able to rationalize with him because he was beyond the point of being able to accept the truth. "The night before our wedding, Katy? How could you do this to me?"

I refused to let her answer his question. "You did this, bro. You kept her from me for all these years. I told her everything. She knows you kept us apart to have her for yourself."

Branch turned around and shoved me against the other bed. "Get the fuck out of my face, Brooks."

I jumped up and got right up in his face, challenging him to push me a second time. Kat climbed off the bed and threw herself between us as if that would prevent a war.

Her naked body was like a beacon, and I could tell it only fueled his need to decapitate me. "Please don't do this. We all need to talk this through," she was pleading, while new tears trickled from her eyes.

When my brother reached forward, taking her by the neck something snapped. I refused to allow him to put a hand on her even if I had to take him down the way I'd been trained to do. I threw him away from her with one hand. "If you ever touch her like that again, I'll kill you."

While I anticipated my next stroke, by keeping my grip fastened to his neck, I felt her gentle hands grabbing me from behind, as if she was begging me to stop. Then I heard her reiterate. "Please, don't do this." I felt my body relaxing, giving in to her request as if she had magical calming powers. Kat spoke from behind me, making sure it was loud enough for both of us to hear. "Branch, we need to talk."

"Bullshit. You need to get dressed and go get ready. This shit never happened, do you hear me?" I couldn't believe my ears. Was he really going to let this go? Did he not see that we'd spent the night together? What could he possibly do to rid himself of the image of walking in and finding us together? Then it hit me. He didn't care about what she'd done as long as I didn't get to be with her. It made the bile rise to my throat. He was the epitome of desperate.

Kat refused to let him win this battle. "No! I'm not marrying you. I can't. I don't love you like you need me to. I've never loved you like I love him, and you've always known it, haven't you? Why did you tell me he never wanted me? How could you do that to your own brother, and to me?"

Branch pushed me out of the way to be facing Kat. She put her finger up to make me wait for a second. I could tell she was prepared for whatever he was about to do or say, in her own way showing me that she could be strong and fight for what she cared about.

Branch responded, spitting as his spoke with such aggression. "Are you really going to bring up shit from when we were teenagers to justify you fucking my brother the night before our wedding? I should have known you'd whore yourself out to him. You always did want things that were beneath you."

Like slow motion, I watched her hand slap against his cheek. "Get out! Get out of my face!"

He grabbed her arms, and I'd finally seen enough. I placed my hand on my brother's back. "Let go of her, Branch."

"Screw you. You two make me sick. If I never see you again it will be too soon. Get your shit out of my apartment before I get home, Katy. After I'm done telling my parents about the two of you, I'll be the only child that this family has. You just ruined your lives. I hope that pussy was worth it." The last part was for me. Though I didn't intentionally set out to hurt my brother, I knew in his own way he was hurting, but I couldn't feel sorry for him, not when I knew he'd done everything in his power to keep us apart. All this time he'd known that we were in love with each other, yet he fed us lies to prevent us from being happy together. Even jealousy wouldn't make me do that to my own brother. I didn't have that kind of deceit in me.

I hit my brother, sending him falling down to the floor. Then I lifted him by the collar of his shirt and shoved him outside of my door. When it was shut, I turned to see her collapsing on the floor, struggling to breathe. She was fighting to control her emotions, and I didn't know how to soothe her.

When she looked at me I saw what I feared the most. This couldn't be happening. Kat was about to push me away. I may have been away for a long time, but I knew her every expression. Her conflicted mind wasn't going to allow her to be happy, not even if it broke her into a million pieces.

She started dressing before I could come up with something logical to say. I approached her, feeling as if I was losing everything I'd gained. "What are you doing? You don't have to leave. We can do this together. Did you think I'd expect you to face them by yourself?" I couldn't let her leave me. It wasn't an option. We hadn't just made love, I'd given her all that I had left. She'd brought me to life, only to shock me back to death. This was unbearably hard to watch.

"I need to get my bag out of my room before they all come looking to kill me. I'll be right back, I promise. You don't have to worry."

Somehow, as her words were meant to be reassuring, I knew they were a lie.

Before she could step foot out of the door, I reached for her, taking ahold of her arm. "Kat, you are going to come back so we can talk, right? You're not just saying you are?" I wanted her to look me in the eyes even if it broke my heart. I wanted to remember how she looked when she walked away from our future once again.

She tried to put on a brave face, but I saw right through her. "Of course. Stop worrying. I'll be right back."

I leaned down and kissed her, fighting back the tears as I pulled away. "Hurry back to me. We've got forever to spend together."

Perhaps I should have stopped her, or pleaded for reasons why she should stay. Maybe I could have followed her to assure she'd come back to me. I think in my mind I pictured her realizing that walking away was a mistake. I kept telling myself that I was imagining the worst because we were so close to having it all.

I didn't want to be right, not this time. I refused to accept that she was about to walk away from me, not when she knew what it was like to experience what we'd shared. I wasn't alone in what happened between us. Everything was mutual, and I was sure she loved me, yet couldn't begin to fathom how she could run from the idea of us having a future.

The longer I waited, the more I knew she wasn't going to return. After nearly twenty minutes I knew I had to go find her, to talk some sense into her and show her we could deal with my parents together, as a team. She'd never have to be alone. I'd stand by her, protect her, and make sure she never needed a reason to fear anything ever again. I was determined to make her concerns dissipate. I was prepared to face my brother again, and anyone else that was going to try to stop me.

By the time I made it to her room a group of people were already standing there. Branch, my parents, and a hotel employee looked at me while I approached. I thought about turning around to avoid the look on their faces. It would have been easier to hide my uncertainties, not that it would make it any better.

"What's going on?"

Branch pointed in my direction. "Where is she, Brooks?"

I tried to keep composure as I imagined where else she could be beside her room. "I don't know. She left after you did."

"Yeah right. If you're planning on coming here to get her things, you're too late. The room is empty."

I turned to look at both of my parents, who were clearly devastated that I'd had a part in this happening. "I'm sorry," escaped my lips. Feeling their disappointment was a burden I'd live with forever. On top of Kat missing, I had to deal with the fact that they'd be left to pick up the pieces. They'd have to make the announcement and send everyone packing.

"Brooks, maybe you should just go," my mother suggested, while she sobbed against my father's shirt. "You can't be here when everyone finds out. Just go find Katy. We can all talk about it tonight at the house." The fact that she was asking me to find Kat struck me as peculiar. Why wasn't Branch designated to locate her?

I nodded, refusing to look at my brother as I turned with intentions of checking the roof. She had to be up there, hiding until she knew everyone was gone. What she didn't realize was that my parents loved her too. Even without a marriage certificate, she'd always be family. They wouldn't push her away for making a mistake, or realizing the truth before it was too late. Sure, they'd be angry, and hurt, but they were forgiving people, and I was their son too. Even if Branch was hurting, they'd want to make sure to help us find resolution.

I think I'd built up the possibility of walking out onto that roof and seeing her there. I thought about what I would say, and how long it would take me to pull her into my welcoming arms. I prepared to tell her we'd be okay, and I'd find a way to make my trip to Afghanistan as short as possible, just so I could get back to her. I wanted her to know that this was going to be a new beginning for the both of us. We could make it work because our love had stood the test of time.

Except Kat wasn't on the roof. I checked every corner, calling out her name to have it echo off the neighboring buildings. She was nowhere in sight. Just as I'd feared when she'd left my room, Kat was gone. Kat had run from the pain, and the truth. She'd ripped me apart, leaving me to face the facts that I wasn't worth the fight. Love wasn't enough for Kat to want to be with me and that alone shattered me.

By the time I made it back to my room I'd busted my fists, cried until my throat was numb, and lost all sense of reality. I'd tried to call her, getting the voicemail every single time. Nothing mattered. For the longest time, I peered over the edge of the building, wondering if my demise would take away the pain. I couldn't handle being without her, wondering where she was, or the fact that she didn't want me.

On the floor was an envelope addressed to my name with my room number. I picked it up and pulled out a letter, recognizing the handwriting immediately.

Dear Brooks,
This letter means that I broke my promise to you. I had to walk away from this before I had to look them all in the eye and admit what I've done. I couldn't stay and face the consequences. I know I'm a coward and that a part of you will never forgive me for this.

Not only have I destroyed the bond that you and your brother once shared, but I've disrespected your parents and all the generosity that they've given me for so many years.

This letter isn't something that my heart takes lightly. I know what I'm giving up, and it hurts more now knowing how absolutely perfect it felt to be in your arms and feel your love radiating through me.

I will cherish the night we spent together and remember it every day for the rest of my life.

Please don't look for me. I've decided to finally go out and make my own decisions for once. I want to move forward and start fresh where I won't be judged for loving you. Just know that no matter where I end up, you will always have a piece of me.

Some people say that love never dies. If that's true then I hope you can forgive me for walking away from it. I know I'll never be able to forgive myself for this.

I would do anything to take back the last few years and be with you, instead. If I had known what I know now, there would never have been a question as to who I wanted to spend the rest of my life with. It's always been you, Brooks. I've known that I loved you since our first kiss. Maybe even before it. Denying it will always be my biggest regret. I know what we could have had together, and it kills me inside.

This is my goodbye. It will be the last time you ever hear from me again. Please tell your family that I'm sorry for what I've done. I hope in time they can forgive you. After all, you're the son they should be praising, not your brother. In fact, you're the most brave, beautiful man I've ever known. Don't let my actions change that.

I'm sorry and I love you,
Katy

It only took me seconds to pack up my things and take a cab to the airport. I couldn't say goodbye to anyone, because I didn't know if I'd ever be returning, not when there was nothing left for me.

Chapter 16

Loving her was effortless, but trying to forget about how much she'd destroyed me was impossible. Time slipped away from me, and before I could make sense of anything, I was on my way to Afghanistan to experience another kind of heartache.

I was fixated on my demise, determined that it was better than suffering. It wasn't courage leading me to danger, it was stupidity. I'd given up hope, not just with being happy, but with being forgiven. At this point in my life I didn't care what killed me. Inside I was already dead, dwelling in an empty shell of pain. I forgot how to laugh. I even kept to myself, not letting my friends know what had happened to change me so quickly. Nothing they said could bring her back into my life. Her kiss goodbye was meant to be forever. I knew it then and still did. Silence wasn't just my answer. It was my enemy. Kat may not have meant it, but she'd killed me that morning. She'd taken away my ability to be optimistic, to have hope, and to strive for a better life. I simply didn't care.

Feeling overwhelmed with guilt, I sent my parents my new address for correspondence. None of this was their fault, and I couldn't allow myself to blame them by making them worry.

I enclosed a letter even though writing it drudged up everything I'd been through since she walked out of my hotel room.

Dear Mom and Dad,

I wanted you to know that I've arrived overseas and have settled in the best I'm able to. I owe you both an apology. Never in a million years did I see things playing out the way they have. I didn't show up at the wedding to ruin everyone's lives. The truth is that I couldn't help myself. I had to pursue her because I've loved that girl since we were children. She's everything to me.

I know I made a mess of things. I screwed up and embarrassed you. I ruined my relationship with Branch, but I think you deserve to know why. All this time, all the years since they started dating, he'd been feeding Kat and I lies, keeping us apart. From the age of twelve he told me Kat wasn't interested. I trusted him.

Apparently he was doing the same to Kat, telling her that I didn't like her that way. All this time we could have been together, but instead he weaseled his way into her heart, making her feel bad for ever having feelings for me.

I'm not saying that what I did wasn't wrong. I know right from wrong. Two people went into my hotel room that night, and what happened was mutual. We knew the risks, but took them anyway. I honestly couldn't stop myself. Once the truth was revealed nothing could have kept me from her. I snapped.

You may never be able to understand what it's been like for me, watching her with him, year after year, as if I was a punching bag. I've got thick skin, but even the toughest person would have broken down at some point. I've been trained to replace pain with power, but this doesn't apply. I'm on a path of destruction because I simply don't care anymore. Branch ruined my life. He was the reason I had to get away. Joining the military was my way out. I knew it would keep me from coming home and *bearing the burden of watching them happy. I punished myself for loving her and attempted to move on with no result. No matter how hard I try I can't stop loving her, that's why I know I can't come home. There's nothing left there for me except pain. I'll never regret being able to live under the same roof as my two best friends, but I will hate myself for not going after what I wanted sooner. I could have prevented all of this. We could be sharing our lives together, having children, and waking up to knowing nothing will tear us apart. Instead I'm on the other side of the world, throwing myself into defending my country, because it's the only thing keeping me going.*

I can't promise that I'll write back all the time. It's hard for me to sit down and put my feelings on paper. I've already been warned that what I'm about to see over here will haunt me forever. I'm used to living in hell, so I've got every reason to believe that I'll get through it. For what it's worth, I'm sorry that I was such a disappointment. I was acting out because I couldn't have what I wanted. Jealousy took control, forcing my hand to make irrational decisions. At the end of the day I deserve to be here, in the middle of this battle zone. If something happens to me and I don't return please don't dwell on my death. Just know I'm no longer in any pain. Nothing will ever hurt me again.

Thank you for bringing me up right and teaching me what love was. As much as it hurts, I don't regret experiencing it. How I feel about Kat is something special. Not everyone finds their true love so early in life. Perhaps that's why I couldn't keep her. Maybe I had enough time with her when we were younger. No matter the case, I'm appreciative.

Take care of her and Branch. Help them to make amends. We'll always be family.

Until next time with love,
Brooks

Before I sent the letter home I needed to take a couple seconds to come to grips with everything I'd expressed. It was as if I was sending away a suicide letter because I knew I wouldn't keep in touch. My old life was over, and I had no plans of ever returning to it. Branch could consider himself an only child from now on. The damage was irreconcilable.

After I regained enough courage, I placed the pen down to another fresh piece of paper.

Branch,

I'm not writing this to apologize. You don't deserve that.

All of this could have been avoided had you told us the truth from the beginning. What kind of brother purposely keeps the two people he cares the most about apart? How could you look yourself in the mirror after that? Didn't you know that one day we'd talk about it? Did you think she'd never tell me?

You can be mad at me forever, I frankly don't give a damn. You took everything from me. You ruined my life. I hope that helps you sleep at night because I can't close my eyes for a second without thinking about her. I'm not going to argue about loving her more than you do. It's obviously the truth, because I'd never lie to her, not even for my own benefit. I love her enough to lose her.

Live with that, Branch. Dwell on the fact that you alone made this happen. I'll never forgive you for making me believe that she never loved me and taking my future that I could have shared with her and destroying it.

Until you take your last breath I hope you suffer because I know it won't even compare to the pain that I've already endured.

Brooks

After I'd mailed out both letters, I found refuge back in my bunk. I laid there, staring at the ceiling, replaying every part of my life that led me to this point. I was a ticking bomb, just waiting to detonate. Kat may as well have decapitated me in that hotel room because I came out of there in pieces.

Two weeks later my group had gotten their first assignment. We were doing recon in a dilapidated little town. Concrete buildings had been blown to smithereens. Remnants of humanity were scarce, and even the sight of a stray dog couldn't make it any less surreal. It was the first time I'd ever experienced the silence of death. It terrified me, snapping me back to a new world; one that existed without love.

The unnerving feeling that overwhelmed me would stick with me. Seeing my first dead body did me in.

We'd entered a standing building. Though rubble surrounded the area, this place was intact. It was obvious that the person had been ambushed. The female was holding a basket full of rotten fruit. Her arms were clung to it as if she was trying hard to scrape up enough means to survive until help came. Shot point blank in the temple, her head was leaning to one side. Behind was another body. At first we assumed it was also a deceased victim. Just as another ranger turned to check our surroundings, it moved. We rushed over to the little body, more bone than skin. Her little eyes were sunken in, and she was unconscious. I watched that soldier carry her back to the vehicle to get her medical attention. She couldn't have been more than ten. While my adrenaline kept me on my feet, I watched the medic struggling to revive her. By the time we returned to base, she was gone. That little girl never had a chance. God only knows how long the child had been without food. I'd come to the conclusion that her mother must have stolen it for them to eat. Just as they prepared to give their bodies nutrients, someone came in and murdered her. The child, an innocent victim, was left to starve to death, next to her mother's corpse.

It made me appreciate my life, my family, and the safe roof over my head. It also helped me to see that even though I'd never be able to bring back her parents, I'd be able to give Kat a reason to sleep at night, at least in theory. I needed her to know that they hadn't died in vain. One way or another, I was going to bust my ass to get revenge for all the lives lost. I was determined to save as many people as I could because watching a child die was unbearable.

That night I found a quiet area in the sand and crouched down to pay my respects. I lost it, there alone, on the cold hard ground. My pain wasn't just for the deceased women. It was for everything I'd been through up until this point. It was for a love that was so strong that it couldn't die. No matter how bad I had it, there was still someone worse off than me. That's when I knew I had to get my ass up and make something out of my life. I had to fight because it was all that was keeping me from letting go. I was determined to be a hero, to make up for the pain I'd caused my parents, the mistakes I'd made with Kat, and the fact that love wasn't enough to keep us together. In that instant I was going to live like tomorrow wouldn't come. I'd bury what was left of my heart and live solely to help others. It was the only way I could see that light at the end of the tunnel again; the only way I could breathe without wanting to break.

Chapter 17

"Are you sure you want to do this?" The Corporal asked as he put the ink in his custom tattoo gun. He'd been lucky to have a hobby while we were overseas. Some of us were too busy moping around in misery. As far as his question went, I'd never been more sure about anything before. This was a symbol of something I knew would never die. Every day I could wake up and have a reminder of her; a memory of what could have been.

The makeshift room was only secured by thick plastic walls. Instead of having a custom table, he'd constructed one out of scraps around the base. His light was also something he'd scavenged. It was an extension cord with a light bulb attached with electrical tape. I was certain at any moment it would catch and burn the place to ash.

A couple other soldiers were standing around, waiting for their turn. Apparently this guy had a lucrative business. I heard them talking about getting matching tats for their unit. Maybe if I was close to the people in mine, I would have been included if they decided to get one. Instead I ignored their playful bantering. I knew they did it to pass the time and disguise their fears. I just chose to live within my own bubble.

"Yeah, I'm sure."

"Where do you want it?"

I placed my hand on my heart, but then moved it just underneath where my ribs sat. "Here. Where my lungs are."

I wasn't going to explain why I was putting it there. No man wants to tell another that he can't breathe fully without the woman he loves even if they've experienced that kind of pain before. It's just a code that men stick to. We aren't open books, waiting to be read. For me, I wanted my business to stay buried.

While the gun dug into my skin, dragging over each bone, I thought about Kat. I imagine her hands tracing the letter, and how she'd feel about me marking my skin with her initial. In that moment I wanted to cry, but not because of the constant stinging I was adhering to. My pain was so intense. Losing my grip on life was even harder. I sat there imagining my dead body being returned to the states, and somehow her discovering my tattoo. I pictured the pain she'd been in, and a part of me felt good about it. I wanted her to know that I'd spent my whole life loving her, only to lose in the end. I needed Kat to remember the times we'd shared, good and bad. She deserved to know how she'd broken me to pieces, and why I'd never forget it. It was obvious we'd never be together again. We were through. Forever and always we'd be separated by life's path. Nothing could bring us together again, not even prayers.

Day after day I watched soldiers come and go, some in body bags. I wondered when my time would come, and who would be there when it did happen. I started running in my spare time, using it as therapy. I'd run until my legs got weak, or I couldn't breathe.

Nothing helped alleviate the pain.

Easter morning I awoke to the sound of a siren. Like everyone in my bunk, I jumped out of bed and began putting on my fatigues. This could have been a drill, but I wasn't taking any chances. By the time we were all dressed our orders were delivered. Another street had been ambushed by terrorists. It was an hour helicopter ride to the location, which was enough time to get my adrenaline pumping. Who knew if this would be the last moments of my life? This could have been the plan all along. They'd attack another area and then shoot the helicopter down with all of us in it. I held my gun tightly against my body, closing my eyes and leaning back against the hard metal shell of the transporter.

Silently I prayed for a safe return, hoping that this wasn't a suicide mission. I refused to look around at the other soldiers because I knew that it would force me to think about their lives. Were they all running from something, or did they have something to live for? Were the women mothers? Were the men husbands, father's even? Could their families survive without them?

We landed safely about a mile outside of the target location. We all took a second to fill up with water since we didn't know when we'd be able to stop again. One by one we got into position and began our blind venture into danger.

It was obvious when we reached the city limits that there wouldn't be much to salvage. The buildings that weren't still burning were nothing but rubble, but that wasn't the worst part. Randomly, positioned to where they couldn't be missed, were posts with beheaded victims placed at the tops. Pools of blood covered the ground beneath them. I watched a female ranger get out of line and begin puking. It wasn't the visual of it that disturbed me. It was the silence. Something was wrong. I could feel it in every bone of my body. All of a sudden before I was able to speak my concerns I felt the ground shaking.

I woke up in a haze of sand. The familiar smell of fire filled my lungs. People were yelling, but the sounds were muffled. As I opened my eyes I saw someone standing over me. It was obvious they were yelling though it appeared like they were calling me through a long tunnel. My ears rang as I sat up and looked around me. We'd obviously either hit a landmine, or been fired at. The explosion had put everyone on the ground, and some of us weren't getting back up.

Without being able to hear properly, I started checking the soldiers around me. The third person I came to had half of his face blown off. He was gasping for air while blood trickled out of the corners of his mouth. I lifted his head, watching as his eyes rolled in the back of his head. "Hang in there, ranger. Help is on the way." It was the reassuring thing to say. "You'll be okay." After checking for a pulse I knew there was nothing we could do. His internal organs had shut down, probably because he'd had severe trauma. I sat his head back down and headed over to the next body as if he'd been just a shell of a man. I had to treat these people like objects because the moment I thought of them as my equals I knew I'd care too much.

That day we lost two people from our unit. The ride back to base was even quieter because it included the dead. This time I kept my eyes open, watching as the people around me cried to themselves, as if their pain would bring the soldiers back to life. Crying didn't solve anything, and it certainly didn't contain magical healing powers. It was a human reaction; one I'd taught myself to avoid.

Our mission had been a failure. We hadn't been able to finish what we'd set out to do. The same helicopter had turned back around to retrieve us, or what was left of our group.

I helped others carry one of the bodies out of the helicopter. The ranger's name had been Carter. He'd always been cordial to me when necessary, so I owed him this type of respect. I could only hope that when my time came my peers would do the same for me. Then I began to think about my family, and who would carry my casket to my burial spot. Would my brother be there? Would he even care if I was gone?

Then there was Kat. I wondered if she'd be there, sitting in the front row with my parents. Would she stick around after everyone was gone, and talk to what was left of me? Would she have put something inside of my casket to be buried with me? The idea of her hurting crushed me. I wanted there to be another way out of this hell, but knew there wasn't. This was what my life was worth. I was a soldier, with nothing to look forward to. If I died, I'd become a memory. It was as simple as that. I'd trained for this, taken the oath, and known what it meant.

A statement was required for each case. We took turns explaining the entire situation from start to finish. I noticed a few people wiping their faces; the ones that had personal connections to the deceased. I wanted to reach out to them to tell them that it was easier to get through if they stayed to themselves. They were just bodies to me. I didn't know the people. Sure, we slept in the same room. We showered in the same open area, ate our meals, and risked our lives together, but I didn't know any of them, and I had no intentions of changing that. I was safer this way.

Later that night we stood out by a fire and paid our respects. Nothing would bring those people back, and I was thankful I hadn't gotten to know them. It was less I had to feel. While I watched everyone else reminiscing I sat down and stayed to myself, thinking about loss in general. Everywhere I turned was tragedy. I was beginning to wonder if I was the problem. Maybe I was doomed from the start. Maybe nothing good was ever meant to happen to me.

Chapter 18

I'd been in Afghanistan for nearly five months. Just when I thought I'd seen it all, I would witness something horrendous, leaving me wondering if a God existed, because if there was one, how could such devastation keep taking place? How could innocent families, little children, continue losing their lives?

One night, while I was staring up at the ceiling, unable to sleep, I began thinking about my old unit and the friends that I missed. I remembered what the sarge had said when he'd given me the journal, and how everything so far had been spot on. The next day, after duty, I sat down outside with a pen and the empty journal, and started writing down some of the events that I'd experienced. Since I wasn't reading, or responding to any mail that my family was sending, I wanted them to have something, in case I never returned.

July 1st 2011

I've avoided writing in this thing until now, mostly because I was afraid of what I'd reveal to myself. My demons are real, and no matter how hard I try to bury them, I know they won't hide for long. Everything is a reminder of what I lost. Even waking up every morning makes me wish I was back home, right across the hall from the woman I loved. By now she could have reconciled with my brother. It pains me to think about it, but what other choice did she have? They've spent years together, planning a future around both of their dreams. With me out of the equation they have plenty of time to get past what happened in the hotel. Knowing my brother he'd take her to Vegas so they could elope without drama.

I want her to be happy. More than anything else, it's what I need to know. I couldn't bear to think she's somewhere alone, wishing she could take back our last moments together. I wondered if she regretted it. Did she feel like she'd ruined her life being with me? Was I her greatest mistake?

"This is stupid." I said as I shut the journal and prepared to throw it across a field. Something wouldn't let me though. It was like that little notebook was my only friend. Sure, I had a unit that was with me every day, but I didn't have the energy to get close to them, not when I knew that we could perish at any moment. This book was my last link to humanity. My sarge had been right all along. I'd need this bit of normalcy if I wanted to survive mentally. It wasn't like I could get a shrink on the line and have an hour long session. This was as good as it would get because if I walked into the medical center and requested a shrink there's no telling how they would diagnose me. I already knew I was borderline losing it. Not being afraid of dying was a good sign of that. I certainly wasn't at peace. In fact, I couldn't come to grips with one reason that they would find me fit to do my daily routines. I'd withdrawn from socialization, and even from finding the ability to open my correspondence from home. There's no telling what my parents had written in their letters, so I just assume not read them. I didn't want to hear about Branch or Kat. I honestly didn't want to hear about any of them. Anything in those sealed envelopes could trigger more pain for me, and at this point even death wasn't something I wanted to know about.

I realize that I was being irrational, but to be in my situation one couldn't begin to grasp what it was like to wake up to random sounds of gunfire or explosions, or even military helicopters landing to either bring in more troops, supplies, or even fly out the dead.

A couple things happened to me in the next several days. I was being transferred to a different unit. At first I thought it was for my lack of group participation. Perhaps someone had complained about my being withdrawn. It wasn't until I saw him turn around that I knew it was for another reason. Trevor Mullins spread his arms out and welcomed my manly hug. "Did you miss me, pretty boy?"

"What the hell are you doing here?" It had been months since I'd seen him, but in that time he'd changed. His face was scruffy, and his eyes looked tired. "You look like shit."

"It's been a hard few months, man. I guess you haven't heard what happened." He pulled me to the side, away from all the other soldiers standing around. From the way he hesitated I could tell it was something bad. "They're gone, Brooks. My girls are gone."

"Gone? Did you separate?" I thought maybe his wife left him. She hated what he did for a living.

He shook his head and looked down, only coming back up with pools of anguish in his eyes. "First I lost my little girl. She'd been up crying for hours, and neither Amanda nor I could keep our eyes open any longer. We put her in bed with us to soothe her. When we woke up the next morning she was cold." He turned away and scrunched his face up. I placed my hand on his shoulder, absorbing some of the same pain as it rushed through him. "There was nothing the paramedics could do. She was already too far gone."

"I'm sorry," was all I could manage to say.

"My little girl died inches away from me and I couldn't do anything to prevent it. While we selfishly slept she suffered. The doctors said it was SIDS, but who knows for sure. At any point we could have rolled on top of her. I hate thinking about it, but the thought never leaves my mind. It tortures me, man. I missed being there was she was born, only to be so close when she took her last breath."

"What about Amanda?" He loved his wife, so it made no sense why they weren't together. He was entitled to bereavement, so they'd obviously been together when it all occurred.

"She left. We'd started going to counseling, but it was too much. She couldn't handle talking about it. The more we sought out help the harder it got at home. One night she never came home. I got a call a week later that she'd met someone else; someone who didn't remind her of our little girl. I figured it was just a stage in her recovery. I would have taken her back, Brooks. I get that she needed to cope differently than I did, but I was alone. I couldn't even go into my bedroom without thinking of them. One night I ripped my mattress into the backyard and burned it. The neighbors called the fire department, and then the fucking military cops showed up. Even though I knew I had a choice, they gave me a few options with how to make the problem go away."

"Don't tell me you came here on your own free will."

"Okay, I won't," he laughed out.

"Trev, seriously, this ain't the answer. It's bad. It's ugly. You wouldn't believe the shit that I've seen."

He put his hand on my shoulder and looked directly at me. "I have nowhere else to go, brother. I've got nothing. I can't look at what's left for another second. My parent's can't even speak to me without passing judgment for what's happened. Amanda's not coming back. She served me with papers three days before I

184

shipped out. I've lost everything except for this."

He'd never be able to understand how I could relate to his pain. Sure, I knew Kat was somewhere living her life, but she was alive.

Then it all hit me.

How did I know she was okay? Something could have happened while I was busy being stubborn.

I spent the rest of the afternoon transferring my things over to my new unit, happy to bunk with Trevor again. We never brought up his baby, or his pending divorce. I could tell he wanted to avoid it, just as much as I needed to do the same with my problems.

July 4th 2011

"Mom, it's me."

"Brooks? Is it really you?" I could hear her tears clearly as if she wasn't on another continent.

"Yeah, don't cry."

"Just let me get your father. Hang on." I could hear her calling out his name. Her excitement made all of my reservations about getting in touch with them go away.

My father picked up another line in the house and cleared his voice before answering. "Brooks?"

"Hi, dad."

"We've been worried, son. Have you not been getting our letters?"

"I write once a week. Do you think we have the wrong address?" my mom asked.

It hurt to tell them the truth. "We've been away from the command center for a few months. I just got back," I lied.

"Are you okay? Is it safe there?" She questioned. I couldn't blame her. They watched way too much news to sweeten the conditions.

"I'm fine. How about you? Is everything okay at home?" I couldn't say her name out loud, and I wasn't about to ask how Branch was.

"It's as good as can be expected. Your brother graduated. He's still living in Salisbury."

Why hadn't they mentioned Kat? Immediately I began to worry about her. "I'm sorry for the mess I left."

"We're not angry at you, Brooks. You need to know that."

"Still, my being there ruined everything."

"It was for the best, son. Your brother has already started seeing someone new."

I don't know why this excited me. I was too far away to do anything about it, and they still hadn't mentioned Kat. I wondered if they'd shut her out. Why else wouldn't they let me know she was getting by? I decided to approach the situation like I was concerned for my

brother. "It's probably a rouse to get Kat back."
My sarcasm was obvious. If they knew me at all
they'd be able to sense how annoyed I was to
bring it up.

"Brooks, Katy's gone. She left the day of
the wedding and we haven't heard from her."

"What? Where did she go?" I started
wondering where someone, with little family,
could run to. "Did she go to England?"

"We really don't know," my father
answered. "She turned off her phone and
emptied her accounts. We hired someone to
look for her. She used her credit cards the day
she left, but never again. We pray for her,
Brooks. We don't blame her for what happened.
We just want her to come home."

"I need to go," I said abruptly. I couldn't
stay on the phone with them when all I wanted
to do was get on a plane and find her. I was
desperate to know if she was okay.

"Please keep it touch, Brooks. We worry
about you. Write us. Find some way to let us
know you're okay." My mom was trying to keep
me on the phone longer, but our chat was over.
In some ways it had been a mistake.

"We love you," my dad cut her off.

"I love you too. Goodbye."

That night I waited in line to use a laptop
with a satellite internet signal. I searched for
her, on every social media site possible, with no

result. My parents were right. She'd dropped off the face of the earth, and there wasn't a damn thing I could do about it, especially being so far away.

Chapter 19
July 5th, 2011

Kat's out there somewhere, all alone, and it's killing me inside, just like the moment I knew she'd left me in that hotel room. I would have followed her anywhere. All she had to do was ask me to be a part of her life. Since she hadn't given me that option I'm stuck wondering if she ever loved me the way I clearly love her. I don't know why I'm writing in this damn journal.

I guess after hearing about my friend's child and wife, I can't help but wonder about my *own broken heart. Why am I holding onto some hope that I'll have her in my arms again? It makes no sense, and that's the reason I won't share my feelings about it with anyone. They'll just laugh at me for loving her so much. When I close my eyes we're together. She's running through a field of tall grasses, while beams of sun are shining down, highlighting her brown wavy hair. The smile on her face makes me beam, and I stand there, arms open, waiting to catch her when she comes into my reach. I want to lay there in that field with her until the sun sets, and even after. It's no longer about making love. In that moment I know she's mine, and nothing can tear us apart again.*

I just wish I could talk to her. I want to tell her that I miss her. I need to know she's okay.

I need to know she's still alive.

That next evening I was faced with the scariest situation of my existence. We could hear the gunfire while proceeding toward the danger zone. The Taliban had attacked this particular location, leaving a path for us to follow. In this instance, the military had gotten to the area in time to corner some of those involved. While units surrounded the vicinity, we were approaching from the northern side, armed and prepared to do whatever it took to free some hostages that had been seized during earlier gun fire.

I'd been trained for this. I'd had years to prepare, but nothing could stop my hands from shaking. Each step I took toward the enemy made me think harder about my decisions. If I died on this battleground, I'd be flown back to the states and buried as a hero, but I wouldn't see myself that way. I was a coward, one that had run and hid, instead of standing up for what I wanted so long ago. I hadn't done all that I could have to be with Kat, or to make my life something other than it was.

I couldn't have anticipated to see boys, no more than fourteen, standing there firing weapons almost as big as they were. Even through binoculars, I could see the hate in their eyes, knowing they'd been taught this way of life. Then I watched them falling to the ground, simultaneously, while gunfire continued to shoot from their weapons. Down they fell, taking their last breaths, dying for what they'd been told was right.

I don't recall aiming my weapon, or even firing my first shot. Once I saw the man in the window pointing his gun at a soldier, I reacted. I held onto that trigger until I watched him fall two stories to the hard ground. The noise around me ceased to exist. I'd killed for the first time, and with that came confusing, and brutal guilt. That person had been fighting for what they believed in. He was someone's son. He bled the same color as me.

My thoughts overwhelmed me until my name snapped me out of it. "Valentine, cover me," Mullins yelled.

I nodded and held my weapon still, scoping out anyone or anything that would cause my friend harm. When he ducked down behind a building, positioning to watch as I followed, he started firing. I ran fast, shooting the entire time. Like slow motion I was willing to take down anything in front of me. Behind Mullins, I saw a shadow peering around the corner. With nothing but a large knife in his hand, an older man came at him. I shot one time, clipping him in the temple. He fell to the ground, the blade landing right in front of where Mullins stood speechless. There was no time to check on each other. We were directly in the line of fire, and if we didn't keep our focus, we weren't making it out alive.

On our radios, we were being directed to a safe area. Resources were on the way, but with the amount of smoke in the air we couldn't see or hear helicopters or even fighter jets.

Two more members of our unit reached our location, panting for air from running so fast. A female named Anders had been shot in the thigh. She sunk down to the ground, screaming in agony. We rushed to her side, ripping some fabric, forming a tourniquet in order to stop the excess bleeding. In that moment I pretended she was Kat. My mission was to get her to safety, no matter if my life was taken in doing so. If we could make it to the safe house, she'd survive. I was pretty sure it hadn't hit an artery. If I had to drag her, I would.

Anders hopped back to a standing position. She reloaded her weapon and looked directly into my eyes. It was the first real connection I'd had and thinking it could be my last moments breathing changed me. "You can do this. Stay behind me. No matter what happens, keep going. Do you hear me, soldier?"

When I turned around, I saw Mullins standing over the other ranger. He shook his head when our eyes met. While I'd been attending to Anders, he'd been shot in the neck. It was obvious he was gone. Mullins picked him up over his shoulder, prepared to carry him out anyway. "We need to get moving. The bullets are getting too close."

I turned to look at Anders. She was cocked and ready. Since I had to cover both of them, I took in the surrounding area and started firing where I saw bright lights from weapons unloading. Structure by structure we traveled together, at this point we were fighting to stay alive.

Finally, we were greeted by soldiers waving us down. I recognized our lieutenant as the three of us jumped into a large vehicle. While a medic assessed the damage to Anderson's leg, I turned back to watch something exploding into the air. The noise of fighter jets broke the sound barrier as they flew away from the cloud of fire.

The ground rumbled, but the vehicle didn't let up.

We were told that they'd recovered the hostages. The ambush wasn't expected, so they said. It didn't matter if it was. Lives were lost. I'd killed at least two people, and I'd never be able to forget it.

Since I refused to let anyone see me shaken up, I went over to check on Anders after being debriefed. She was sitting up when I entered the facility. Her face was so filthy that it made her teeth glow when she saw me coming her way. "You forgot flowers," she teased.

I stood over her bed, appreciated the humor after something so terrible. "How's the leg?"

She shrugged. "I'm out of commission for a while. If I'm lucky, I'll get to go home to recover. They're going to operate to remove the bullet. It's stuck in my bone."

"Ouch."

"Thanks for covering me out there, Valentine. I know they prepare us for that, but it's..."

I cut her off. "I killed today." It was like I needed to confess even though she'd been there to see it.

"Me too," she sadly replied. "I don't think I want to do this anymore. I don't want to die."

I sat down on the edge of the bed, shocking her. "Neither do I."

I stared at the far wall, avoiding eye contact with the girl. It had been a long time since I'd interacted with someone of the opposite sex, and I was too messed up to act accordingly. "Thanks for coming by and checking on me. Maybe you could stop by tomorrow and check on me again. I'm bored already."

I smiled while I stood up. "Yeah, maybe. Keep your chin up, soldier."

When I left the room I thought about a lot of things, but mostly the fact that I was in another country, fighting for freedom, while Kat was busy hiding from everyone that cared about her. I needed reprieve even if it was an innocent conversation with someone. It sure beat pretending that my heart was made of steel when it was obvious it wasn't.

The next day I visited Anders. Due to the severity of her injury, her surgery was going to be done back in the states. She had one more night of hell before getting to go back home safely. "You've come twice now without flowers, Valentine. I'm starting to think I'm not your type."

I shrugged and pulled a deck of cards from my pocket. "I thought you might like these better."

She smiled and scooted over on the bed to make room for a game. "Hmm, you might be right. Good call."

We started playing a simple game while the woman in her came out full force. "So, Valentine, what's your first name?" She reached for my dog tags as I answered anyway. "Brooks."

"I like that. It's different. Where are you from?"

"Near D.C., you?"

"Utah." She laughed. "I know, it's not as exciting as being neighbors with the president."

"I'm from the burbs. The city is about thirty minutes away. Traffic sucks, and taxes are higher." I was attempting to keep her smiling. For the first time in months it brightened my mood.

"How come you transferred to our unit? It's obvious you know Mullins."

"We went through boot camp together. He's one of my closest friends. I don't know why

I got transferred. I either didn't do something right, or I accomplished more than I should have. Either way I haven't got a clue. I didn't know he'd become a ranger until he showed up."

"I thought when I came here I could do some good. I knew it was bad, but this is like standing in front of a firing squad. I've never wanted to be back home so bad. This isn't what I signed up for. I'm all about defending our country, but why are we even over here fighting? It's like our country picks fight to keep the military active. I'm done with it. The sooner I get home the better. I don't even care if people think I failed. I'm just done."

"You'll be a hero. You were shot in the line of duty. You were brave." If she only knew my demons, then she'd think her problems were minimal.

"A hero doesn't murder people, Brooks. That's what I feel like I am. A murderer. I killed a child. How can I live with that?" She began to cry, making me reach out and hold her hand.

"I'm struggling too. It sucks. I've got to keep telling myself that it was the right decision even if they were forced to be those people. They were prepared to kill us. If we didn't fight back we'd be in a wooden box right now."

I started to pull away, but she tightened her hold. "Please don't let go. It's fine if you're not interested in me romantically. I know that's not what this is. I just don't want to be alone, not tonight. I didn't sleep at all last night, and I know tonight's not going to be any different. Just stay a little while longer. Please, Brooks."

When she said my first name it touched me. A little spark flashed as if to remind me that somewhere deep inside I still had a longing to feel connected to someone. I reassured her by squeezing her hand. "I'll stay as long as you need me to."

People came and went around us, but I remained on that small bed next to her. We held hands and talked about the previous day. She told me about her family, and how they hadn't had money to send her to college. I talked about my parents, what it was like to be a teenager, but never mentioned being a twin, or Katy Michaels.

Before getting up to head to my bunk, Anders leaned forward and pressed her lips against mine. It wasn't sexual, but more about her being appreciative. "Thank you. I'll never forget what you've done for me."

Just as I started to get up and walk away, she called out to me. "Hey, Valentine, maybe you could look me up when you get home?"

"Yeah, maybe I can show you around the nation's capital."

I didn't know when I walked out of that medical facility that it would be the last time I saw Anders. During her transport to the airport her convoy was attacked. All three travelers were slaughtered and left on the road to be discovered at a later time.

We weren't even notified until two days after it happened, and even then I found it impossible to fathom. She was so close to going home, only to lose her life in such a horrendous way. How cruel life had been to her.

July 9th
There are no words to express how I feel tonight. It seems that my path of destruction has claimed the life of another innocent victim. I've relinquished all hope on humanity. Death is eminent. I can't avoid the road that I'm on, nor can I understand how I got to this point voluntarily. I've killed. I've taken someone's child, ending their life. I aimed my weapon at them and pulled the trigger. I'll never forgive myself, just like I don't think the image will ever leave my mind. At this point I don't think I deserve to return home. There's nothing there for someone like me.

I've been trained to kill people.

I just found out that a new friend lost her life tragically. Given my luck, it's probably all my fault. She was on her way back to the states. She had hope. I wondered what she felt in her last few minutes on this earth. Did she suffer?

I don't know who I can talk to about this. It's too hard imagining that this could also be my fate. I just want to go back to a time when life was carefree, and the biggest thing I had to worry about was making Katy Michaels smile. God, I miss her so much. I miss everything about the life I used to live.

Chapter 20
September 11th

I wish I could talk to her. I know, of all days, she was thinking about her parents, wishing there was some way to change the past. I wished she could because I know I wouldn't let her slip away from me if I got a second chance to do it all again. I would have told her after our first kiss that she was going to be my future. I would have held her hands that night when she pressed her lips against mine, and when we *pulled away she'd know that I was already in love with her. I would have reminded her every morning when she woke, and then before she closed her eyes at night. I would have made her so happy. I hope wherever she is she knows that's the truth.*

That next week I took it upon myself to write to Kat, hoping that eventually my parents would find her, or at least an address I could send it to. Until then, it would stay in my journal.

Dear Kat,
There isn't a day that goes by where I don't think about you. All my life I've been waiting for us to be together. I know it's not possible anymore, but that doesn't mean that I love you less. Being away from you, even though it was my choice, is the worst mistake I've ever made. I should have fought harder, proving to you that I was the right choice all along. I guess it doesn't matter now. You've left everything behind, in some ways taking my same route. If I'd known this would happen, I could have warned you about how lonely it would be without the love of your family. I struggle daily with my choices. It pains me that you're out there somewhere doing the same thing. I wonder if

you're okay. I hope you are. God, I pray for it every night.

I'm finding it hard to write to you tonight after so many nights of trying to convince myself that it's time to let go. For some reason I'm unable to do that. You have a hold on me that I've never been able to explain. It's not just about the love I hold for you, but more the way we're connected, maybe in some sort of spiritual way. Perhaps it's your parents sending me reasons to always look out for you. I'd like to think that they're watching you while I'm away, making sure you're not biting your nails, or forgetting to eat.

I keep wondering if you'd want me to apologize. Would it make you feel like I didn't want to be with you, or that I regretted it? For the record I don't, and I never will. My heart will forever belong to you even if you don't want it. I've come to realize that I have no control of that. It's always been yours.

I wish I could scream across the ocean and let you know how much you mean to me. As I'm writing this, I know it's unlikely you'll ever see it. I can't give up hope because it's the only thing keeping me sane. The truth is that I need you. I'm losing myself over here, Kat. I feel like it's ripping my soul away, day by day. This world we live in is so messed up. What keeps me strong is knowing that you'll never have to see what I've *experienced. It wouldn't just break your heart. It would destroy your livelihood.*

I'm going to keep writing you. It's what lets me have hope. Someday we'll meet again, and when that happens, I know I'll never let you slip away. I'll make you mine forever even if I have to put you over my shoulder and carry you all the way to Vegas.

Until then know I love you, with every part of me.

Brooks

My unit was called to do another ground sweeping that following month. We'd set out through a small village. Children were running around together as we delivered resources to the people that had survived the most recent attacks. I was carrying some bottled water into a house that could be compared to a shed back at home. Inside I found a small women sitting on a bed in the far corner. She was running a soiled rag across a child's face. As soon as she saw me she stood up. Even with most of her face hidden behind fabric I could see that she'd been crying. It was obvious the child was sick. I sat down the carton and pulled out a fresh bottle of water, offering it to her. She snatched it up, rushing over to the child. While tilting his head upward she helped the boy take a few sips.

As I began to leave she ran toward me. Grabbing my hands and thanking me the best she could without knowing English. The simple gesture left me with a glimmer of hope.

After running back to the vehicle, I was able to scrounge up some Tylenol and other medications. They wouldn't heal the child's illness, but certainly break his fever and manage any other pain symptoms. Once again the woman was thankful. She started offering me bread, insisting that I take it with me. Since I didn't want to offend her I nodded and walked back out to keep moving with my group.

All day long I thought about that woman, and her sick child.

A week later we were traveling to another area, passing through that one. After seeking permission from my superior, we stopped so that I could check on the mother and child. This time the father was home as well. The boy was sitting up in bed and managed to smile. I could tell he was feeling better. The father walked up and shook my hand, saying something I couldn't make out. He kept repeating it, like it was important I understood. I pretended to, feeling as if whatever he was saying meant they were grateful.

I was far from being a saint, but somehow this family made me feel better about my life's choices. I couldn't know for sure if the water or medicine had helped to start healing their sick son, but I felt like it was important. Helping people made me want to be a better man.

October 2nd

Last week a new troop came into camp. Mullins noticed the two women first, insisting that I need to get laid. In some ways maybe he's right. I definitely want to be able to unwind from the tension I put myself through daily. I still don't know if getting involved in anything sexual would alleviate the aggravation I carried with me. For me, Kat will always be the one, even if I never see her again. Since I'm not an idiot, it's obvious I can't go forever without physical contact. Just because she isn't with Branch doesn't mean she won't move on. I get it. I even understand it in some ways. She's living in another country. We can't be together even if it was possible. I guess it's time to stop punishing myself for what I couldn't change. I can't keep living in daydreams and fantasies about the life we're never going to have. I can't allow myself to continue to hope that we have a chance. Kat's gone, and there's not a damn thing I can do about it.

I let Mullins take the lead, watching him hit on the first woman. She was curvier than her friend and reminded me a lot of his ex-wife. It made me sad seeing him go after someone that resembled her though the selections on base were slim. Most women were married or batted for the opposite team, not that I was scoping it out, but people talk.

The first night we hung out in the rec room getting to know each other. Allison Anderson was a California native, who had a love for surfing and cappuccinos. She'd also been fourth generation military, choosing the Army over Navy at the last minute. Right away Mullins was in awe over her, minus the drool. For me, Hilary Spencer, who liked to be called Spence, was someone to pass the time with. She was from North Carolina, grew up without knowing who her parents were, and joined the military for their education program. She had short brown hair that was straight as a needle, and she had dark brown eyes that seemed to appear endless.

"Do you have a girlfriend or a wife back home?" I'd answered her questions up until this one. Suddenly I found my ability to reply difficult. While I struggled to come to terms that I was alone, she spoke for me. "It's not a hard answer. I'll take that as a yes."

"It's not like that," I replied. "We were never together."

She crossed her legs while giving me a curious stare. "Don't tell me you're holding out for someone. Have you not looked outside lately? Life is too short."

"What about you?" I changed the subject.

A half-smile formed across her face. "There's someone back home. We've been together for three years on and off. When I go home I'm sure we'll hook back up, but neither of us are a fool to what being apart does to some relationships. We agreed that while I was away we'd do our own thing." I must have seemed shocked. She released an air-filled laugh and shook her head. "Judge away. My family thinks I'm stupid. At the end of the day it all comes down to reality. It wouldn't be fair to string each other along. He knows I'm going to be here for a while. We'll talk when we can, but I can't expect him to live alone without daily contact. We're not married."

"No, it takes a strong woman to be so confident."

"So back to this girl. Does she even know you exist?"

My brow furrowed, and I think right away she knew I was uncomfortable. "Yes. I've known her my whole life. If it's okay with you, I'd rather not get into it."

For the rest of the evening we talked about the Army; the fun, scary, and everything else. While Mullins and his new friend disappeared for a little while, I took my time, feeling this girl out. I still wasn't sold on the idea of hooking up, but it passed the time. Unfortunately, it also made me miss Kat.

After a month of hanging out, the four of us became inseparable on the base. Sure, we each had jobs to do, but when they were over we spent our down-time together. Mullins and Anderson were tied at the hip. They'd been sleeping together since three days after they met while I still hadn't even kissed Spence. I could tell she was anxious, and maybe a bit reluctant. I refused to share my feelings about Kat. It hurt too much to think that I had to move on; that my chances of ever being with her again were never going to happen.

On a chilly night, outside, while the wind was whipping the sand around, I laid next to Spence on the ground, holding her hand. We were staring up at the stars in the sky, both imagining that we were somewhere else. I didn't try to ask about her ex, but it was obvious she still loved him.

"Sometimes I like to pretend he's out there somewhere looking at the same bright sky. Do you ever do that, Valentine?"

"Yeah. I guess."

She rolled over to be facing me and placed her hand on my chest. We were both in fatigues, so there was nothing sexy about her touch. "I'm not a shrink, but it's obvious you have it bad for this woman. You never talk about it, albeit you don't even have to. The truth is written across your heartbroken face. What happened to you, Brooks?" She never called me by my first name. This made the conversation more serious.

"Kat was my first love. Our parents were best friends, and we lived next door to them. They were both killed on 9-11."

"Oh my god," she interrupted.

"Kat came to live with us when we were twelve. The three of us were inseparable back then."

"Wait? Three of you?"

"My brother." I cleared my voice. "My twin brother, Branch. He was the third musketeer."

"You have a twin?" She smirked that it was interesting.

"An evil twin. A brother that would stop at nothing to steal her away from me. For years he told the both of us lies so we wouldn't attempt to be together. When she chose him I stepped aside. I joined the military and moved away."

"That's so sad. Are they still together?"

210

I let out a chuckle. This was going to either make her get up and never talk to me again, or maybe laugh in my face. "We slept together the night before they were supposed to get married. That's the last time I've seen her."

She sat up abruptly. "What? You're kidding?"

"No, I'm not. It wasn't planned. A lot of truths came out, and it happened. You may think I'm an asshole, but I don't regret it. I wouldn't change anything about that night with her."

"Did they still get married?"

I looked away. "No. She ran away from everything. Even a private investigator can't track her down. I just found out about it when I finally called home. It happened last Christmas, and nobody has heard from her since. I don't even know if she's alive."

"That's terrible. You don't think she hurt herself do you?"

I shook my head. "No. This might sound stupid, but I'd feel it if she were gone. Wherever Kat is, she doesn't want to be found."

"Wow, I'm sorry. I get why you never want to talk about it."

"Nothing numbs the pain, Spence. It's always there, reminding me of my mistakes."

She leaned forward and pressed her lips against mine. Feeling that type of connection while discussing something so personal, opened me to the possibility of drowning everything for as long as possible. I was hungry to survive, no matter what I had to do to make it happen.

I pulled Spence on top of me, appreciating her kisses more than she'd ever know. This wasn't someone who wanted to win my heart. She was a friend, trying to comfort the hell out of me. Her hat slipped off when I reached up and ran my hands through her hair, pulling it out of the tiny bun. Her kisses were ravening, taking me away from the constant ache. I needed this to keep going; to stay sane. After making out until I was ready to explode, we snuck into a small building for supplies. In there we removed our clothes. I picked her up, sitting her on a stacked piled of armor cases. Her legs wrapped around my ass while more ravenous kisses consumed me. She only stopped me right before I was ready to take it to the next level, pushing me back so that she could fetch something from her jacket. I heard the familiar sound of a plastic wrapper. "Why are you carrying that around?"

"Mullins gave it to me a few weeks ago. I told him he was crazy." She ripped it open with her teeth, grabbing at me like we'd done this a million times. "Even in the middle of war we should practice safe sex."

I lifted her chin up to be even with my approaching lips. "Stop talking."

This wasn't love. We weren't out to lay claim on each other. Our adulterated encounter was for stress relief. We were friends, trying to find something good in the mist of a terrible situation. Fueled on the hunger of physical contact, we shared our first rendezvous of many to come.

That didn't help me feel better about what I'd done. As soon as I was redressed my mind went to Kat. I started imagining the roles reversed, and how hurt I'd be if she'd found someone else to share her time with. The thought made me disgruntled, so much so that I walked outside and punched a wooden post, causing my knuckles to bleed.

Once I was in my bunk I pulled out my journal, thinking of ways to make myself feel better for being so selfish.

Chapter 21

It was November. Weeks had turned into months, but nothing changed. I'd seen so much death and destruction, people tortured, cities destroyed. Communities had been evacuated, and families were separated. I carried screaming children that had been left behind when troops came in and took their parents while they were out playing. I'd seen fathers fighting because they didn't want to leave. I'd watched elderly couples wave goodbye because they wouldn't survive the trip.

Never in my life had I ever been taught about how terrible it was to live in other places.

Bound by their faith, these people kept forging forward, even when they had nothing left to be thankful for. They were putting their trust in us; people who didn't even understand their language or religions. It was horrid.

That kind of environment takes a toll on someone. Even though I had Mullins, and even Spence to keep me occupied, it still didn't help when the lights went out at night; it didn't keep the demons from haunting me.

There were a lot of nights where I dreamed of Kat or other family members. Most of the time it was like memories, but on occasion I'd dream that I was on a mission and discovered their dead bodies. I'd wake up in a pool of sweat, searching the room to make sure it hadn't been real. There was nothing like going through the motions of a regular day while still seeing the images of my decapitated loved ones.

It was very rare to dream something refreshing, that woke me with a smile on my face, but when it did happen I thrived on it. It was much like going without food and water, and then magically a double cheeseburger and fries shows up in front of you.

Because of those special dreams, I knew I couldn't give up hope of finding Kat. I had to keep searching, praying that I would be able to know for sure that she was okay.

I'll never forget the November afternoon that took more from me then I knew I had. We'd been dropped off by a helicopter near a zone that we hadn't been before. Details weren't really something we were privy to. Basically we'd suit up and be on our way. During the ride they'd tell us what we were doing, I guess, so it was fresh in our heads. Like every time, we exited the chopper with caution and proceeded to the coordinates we'd been given.

There wasn't a ton of coverage in this location, given that we were near an area of dessert. For as far as we could see there was dried vegetation and sand. After walking a ways we spotted a few buildings, realizing right away that it was our target location. The job was simple. We were to extract the four families and arrange for transportation to a safe house. Since it appeared that we were safe, everyone had their guard down.

Mullins started whistling Christmas carols, getting everyone to chime in with him. For once we were all smiling. Some of the people in our group were planning on taking leave. I envied them being able to have welcoming homes to return to.

I don't think anyone could have suspected that we were in danger, or that in a matter of seconds some of us were going to lose our lives. I don't even think the soldier first in line had a clue he'd stepped on an active land mine.

Everyone was thrown in the air as the explosive device was triggered. With the wind knocked out of me, and my ears ringing loudly, I managed to sit up and look around. Sand made it difficult to see, even with safety gear on my face. When I pulled off my helmet I could hear moaning, and people calling out. After a few seconds I stood and searched for Mullins. I expected him to say something sarcastic, or be looking for me at the same time, but what I discovered was much worse.

He'd been second in line that day, and I wasn't even sure which body parts were his, or the soldier in front of him. Strewn across the area were the remnants of my unit, closest to the mine. As it became harder to breathe, I crouched down in front of what was left of my dear friend. His eyes were still open beneath his goggles, but there was no life remaining. Both of his legs were half gone, one arm was dangling, and the impact had obviously caused severe trauma all around. In an instant my friend's life was over. I fought to hold back the tears as I touched his bloodied chest. He'd been through so much. He's lost everything that mattered to him. This was the beginning of the end for me. It was the point when I knew I'd reached my limit.

Aside from a helicopter coming to pick us up, much of the rest is blurry. While in the shower alone, I cried for my friend, enough so that when I had to tell Anderson, I'd be able to hold back the tears. While Spence comforted her friend, I went off on my own to a spot where Mullins and I used to hang out. For a few moments everything was so quiet. It was as if I was being granted a minute of peace before hell broke loose again.

Nothing I did would bring him back.

November 11th

I lost my friend today. He's the only person who knew what it was like for me when I first left home. We'd taken this ride together, and I don't really know if I can continue on this journey without him. If he'd only been in the back of the line near me, he'd be sitting next to me right now, still whistling his annoying carols. Instead he's going back to the states in pieces. I wondered if he'd requested to be stationed with me. Had he died because he wanted to be with me again? It was more proof that every person who gets close to me is cursed.

I don't know how I'm going to get over this, or how I'm expected to go back out there again. I don't want to die, but I also have no idea how to stay alive.

November 24th

It's Thanksgiving, but I'm not real sure what to be thankful for this year. I've seen too much death to be able to appreciate that we stopped to have a semi-nice meal. I mean, I'm not really sure we ate turkey, and if it was it certainly wasn't freshly plucked. The instant potatoes were nothing like my mother made, and I don't even want to get started on the stuffing. For entertainment, a couple of people sang and told jokes. I sat across from Anderson and Spence, saying nothing as they seemed to be enjoying themselves.

Later, after we left the makeshift mess hall, I found Spence sitting out at my special place. She was alone, obviously waiting for me.

"I don't really feel like having company tonight, Spence."

"Well I don't feel like hearing that. Come on Valentine, I know you're upset, but you can't shut me out. It's like you're with us, but you're not. Mullins wouldn't want you to act this way. He told Anderson what you've been through. We both know you're hiding a huge heart behind that wall. Valentine, let me in. Talking to someone will help."

I turned to face her. "It won't bring him back. Nothing will. He's dead, Spence. I watched him being blown to pieces. I was there."

"I'm not arguing about that."

"Look, I get that you're trying to help me. I don't need you reminding me of everything that's wrong in my life. It's fucked up as it is. Just go enjoy the night with your other friends."

She reached for my arm. "I'm not leaving you, Brooks." Using my first name wasn't going to make me cave.

"Can't you take a hint? I don't want you here. Just go away!" I had to be rude. Spence was stubborn. She'd fight me.

She crossed her arms over her chest. "No! I'm not going anywhere."

I buried my face in my hands and closed my eyes. If she wanted to sit there all night so be it, but I wasn't going to keep her company.

I felt her hand on my arm again. "Do you have any idea how special you are? He loved you like a brother, Brooks." She paused when I didn't respond. "What we do, how we risk our lives, it's our job. He died defending our country even if it wasn't during an attack. Mullins was brave. Two weeks ago we lost our friend too. You know, I told myself that when I got over here I was going to keep to myself, that I didn't want to be attached to something temporary. I didn't even make it to land before I met

Anderson. You might be strong enough to hold it all in, but I'm not."

"I'm not strong," I whispered.

When our eyes met she could see what I'd been hiding. In that instant I broke down right in front of her. Spence leaned on me while I let go of the pain, accepting that our fallen friend was in a better place. "He's with his daughter now," I said quietly.

"He's happy then. I know it's where he'd want to be."

After that, we started talking about the good times we'd shared in the past month with the women, and even before that. I told her about times when we were back in boot camp, and how he'd always tried to talk me out of being so hung up on Kat.

We ended the night back in the storage shed, taking out our frustrations on each other. Instead of using a punching bag, we found solace in sex. Time after time I felt nothing when it was over, just that empty hole coming right back into my mind, reminding me that I was alone.

When I laid down in my twin-sized bed at night I couldn't remember what it felt like to hold someone in my arms or spread out on an extra large mattress. I'd forgotten what breakfast cooking while still being in bed smelled like. The one thing that I knew I could never let go of was Kat. I could close my eyes and smell her shampoo. I could touch my own skin and recall what it was like to feel hers. Every single detail of that woman was etched into my mind.

Spence was right. I couldn't dwell on what we were unable to change. We had to keep going because if we stopped we lose ourselves completely. We weren't just physically fighting to survive. We were battling to keep from losing ourselves.

November 28th

I don't know if I can do this anymore. I miss him. I miss everyone. It's like life won't give me a break. I'm fucking dying in misery. What did I ever do to deserve this kind of outcome? Am I really cursed? Is there a target on the back of my head? If so, I wish the bullet would come sooner than later. I can't take this torture much longer. I've woken up for the past week wishing I was dead. Anything is better than living this way. The monotony of this tour is brutal. Each day I wake up praying not to go out into the field. I don't want to see anymore death. I can't handle it. Every time I close my eyes I see Mullins on the ground in pieces. I don't want that fate. I'd rather put a bullet to my head and end it quickly. I can't be one of those soldiers that hangs on. I think I've suffered enough already.

If this is the last entry I make, I hope it doesn't go unread. I want everyone to know what it was like for me to walk away from everything I love only to come here and die. I'm better off gone, because another day, week or month in this place is going to rip me apart until there's nothing left.

Chapter 22
December 24th, 2011

I woke up to mail being delivered. There were two packages from my parent's address, and a red envelope with my brother's name as the return sender. I figured that since it was Christmas Eve, I could at least open this bunch of mail, instead of sticking it with the other's I'd never bothered to read.

The Christmas card from my brother was signed by not only him, but also a Melissa. I couldn't help wonder if it was the same Melissa that had been Kat's friend, and maid of honor. It was definitely something I'd like to hear about for entertainment purposes. Included in the card was a note from my brother, simply stating he wanted to get past our issues. I rolled my eyes and put the card to the side, focusing on one of the two boxes.

Wrapped in smaller, individual packages were three presents. I smiled as I pulled them out and opened them. The first box contained chocolate truffles. I'd been getting them in my stocking since I was a child. My parents knew they were my favorite. I popped one in my mouth, savoring the familiar flavor. It was like heaven, almost bringing me back home for just a moment in time.

The next box contained a pair of gloves. Even though I had military grade ones, these were a newer version, and much more versatile for the weather conditions I was currently experiencing. I could use my weapon without having to remove them.

The third package was a photo. It was one I recognized immediately. I had a copy of it in my room. Branch, Kat and I stood outback under the tree house. We were all about eight at the time. They'd obviously blown up the original to a larger size and included a note with it.

Brooks: I thought that maybe you'd like to have something to remind you of what home is all about. We'll always be

family, no matter how far you all go. There's no place like home.

Love: Mom & Dad

I sat there holding that picture for the longest time, hoping one day I'd be able to return to that yard. Even though they weren't pictured, I appreciated my parents more than they'd ever know.

The second box addressed to me contained books and magazines. They must have known how boring it might get. Once I was done with them I'd leave them in the rec area for everyone to be able read also.

Before I could change my mind, I grabbed some paper and started writing my parents back. They wouldn't get it right away, but at least they'd know I was grateful. Just as I began to write their names down I felt a burning in my eyes. This wasn't how I saw my future when I was a kid. I'd never pictured being away from my family, missing out on traditions, and sharing moments together. I missed them all so much, but knew there was nothing I could do about it.

I crumbled up the paper and headed to where the phones were located. After waiting in a line, I finally had the opportunity to dial their number.

Hearing my mother's voice was so relieving.

"Hello?"

"Mom, it's me, Brooks."

"Oh, honey, it's so good to hear from you. We've been so worried."

"I miss you." I could barely get the words out. "It's getting hard to keep it together, mom. I think I made a huge mistake."

I could hear her beginning to cry on the other end of the connection. "I pray for you every day. We watch the news, hoping you're okay over there."

"I'm trying to be. I lost a friend last month. We were in basic together." I fought back the burning in my throat. She didn't need to hear me upset. "I watched him die right in front of me."

"I can't imagine what that was like for you."

I decided to change the subject, to keep from losing my shit and wasting the call. "How is everyone at home? Are you ready for the holidays?"

"We're getting there. Did you get your packages yet? We mailed it two weeks ago."

"Yes, I got them this morning. They're awesome. Thanks for sending them. It was nice to wake up to presents."

"I wish we could fit more in the boxes. Your father thought I was silly for wrapping them all individually, but I wanted them to be special."

"It was sweet, mom. Thanks."

The line was quiet for a couple seconds. "Brooks, there's something I want you to know. Katy called a while back. She didn't say much, but she asked if you were okay. I think it was the fourth of July. She seemed upset."

"Why didn't you tell me this sooner?"

"She hung up after that. I didn't have anything to tell. The call couldn't have lasted more than thirty seconds. I told her to come home. I pleaded."

"It's okay, mom. You don't have to be upset about it. Kat obviously needs more time. I'm sure it's hard for her to face you and dad after what happened."

"I love her as if she were my own child. We'd never turn our backs on that girl."

"Maybe it had to do with pride. I don't know. Not a day goes by where I don't think about her, but there's nothing I can do. Until she wants to be found, we just have to sit back and wait."

"You're right. Though her presents keep piling up. We still include her, expecting she'll come home one day. I can't give up hope."

"I can't either."

Once again the line was quiet. I'd said too much about Kat.

"I hope you have a good day tomorrow, Brooks. Your father and I love you so much. He's going to be upset he missed this call. Please keep your chin up. You're stronger than you know."

"I love you, mom. Tell everyone I'm okay. I'll talk to you soon. I promise."

For a few minutes I stood outside trying to calm down. Kat had reached out to make sure I was okay. She still cared. Even though it was temporary, I was happy for the first time in months.

Feeling the sentiment of the holidays I headed to grab something to eat early so that I'd be able to see Anderson and Spence. Like always, the girls were sitting at a table having their coffee. Spence smiled when she saw me approaching. I pulled the box of truffles from behind my back and sat them on the table. "Merry Christmas, ladies. My parents sent these. I've been trying to watch my figure, so I thought I'd share the calories around."

Spence picked one up and began unwrapping it. "How thoughtful of you," she said sarcastically.

"I've been stress eating for weeks. If that hits my mouth it'll go straight to my ass."

I popped another one in my mouth and looked around at the people in the room. For once everyone seemed to be in good spirits. "It's weird seeing everyone in a good mood."

"I wouldn't call it a good mood, Valentine. We're all stuck here instead of being home. If we're lucky none of us will have to go out into the field for a couple days, but Muslims don't care about Christian religions. If they're smart, they'll use it to their advantage." Anderson's comment made me lose my appetite. I'd never talked to her about Mullins death, or at least her feelings about it. My own feelings kept me from talking about things that hurt. I knew better than to drudge up parts of my life I needed to keep buried, for my own sanity.

"How about we try to remain positive?" Spence had a point. Thinking about the negative was only going to put us in bad moods.

"If we don't do something we're all going to end up in the ground. Our heads need to stay on."

Anderson waved her arms around, pointing at the two of us. "I don't know why you aren't taking advantage of this time off. Shouldn't you be in a shed somewhere, naked and consumed?"

I tried to laugh it off, but when I turned to see the look on Spence's face I realized she thought it was a good idea too. I stood up and nudged my head for her to follow me. "Come on."

She giggled. "Seriously, right now?"

"We're going on an adventure. See you later, Anderson. Thanks for the push."

Instead of the shed, which was getting pretty old, I borrowed a vehicle, and we set out into a deserted area. Once I had the vehicle in park, Spence and I looked around to make sure we were alone. She then climbed over to my side. When she was on top of me, with her arms around my neck, we kissed. I opened my eyes to be staring into hers. "Valentine, you sure do help the time pass."

"Yeah, you too."

"I talked to my ex today. I know he's been dating, but he swears he's waiting for me to come home. He says he wants to get married."

I wondered if I should push her off of me. Was this some kind of end to our arrangement? "What are you telling me this for?"

"I just wanted to talk about it. Is that off limits?"

"No. It's just weird."

"Have you heard from your girl? What's her name again?"

She was killing the mood. "Katy."

When I looked away she could already tell I hadn't been in contact with her. "I admire your devotion, Brooks."

"Yeah, well I think it's a joke. What good will it do?"

"Don't give up on her. When we're all home safe I want to hear about the two of you finding each other again."

I started to push her off me. "We should go back to base."

She stopped me. "Wait. I didn't mean to upset you."

"Kat and I won't be together in the future, Spence. We don't even know where she is."

She sighed and unfastened the door before climbing out of the truck. When she disappeared toward the back I got out and followed her. "Where are you going?"

She plopped down on the sand and closed her eyes, dragging her hands in the sand. "Sometimes I like pretending I'm on sandy beach. I'm sweating because the hot rays are beating down on my exposed skin."

I sat down next to her and looked around. There was nothing but dead plants and dirt mounds. "You have a vivid imagination."

"Just close your eyes and hold my hand. Go with the flow."

I did as she requested, only because I knew she wouldn't let up. When my head hit the sand I found her awaiting grip as her fingers laced with mine. My eyes closed, and I did my best to focus on being at a beach.

"Can you feel it?" She asked.

"What?"

"The mist of the water."

"No."

She didn't budge. "Fine. What if I was your Katy? Can you imagine holding her hand on a beach?"

I focused on Kat, realizing how easy it was to fantasize about being close to her. "Yes."

"What would you talk about?"

"Anything. Everything. She was my best friend."

"So let's talk. You're on a beach and you're together. What would you say to her?"

"This is stupid."

"Shut the hell up and go with it, Valentine. It's just us. I won't tell if you don't."

I kept my eyes closed and focused again, imagining that I was holding onto Kat. "I'd tell her I missed her."

"Talk to her. Try again."

"Fine." I waited a second to think about what I'd say if I were on that beach with the love of my life. "I missed you while I was away."

She squeezed my hand tighter. "I missed you too, Brooks."

I wanted this to be happening so much that I finally let myself fall into the game. "I've thought about you every day, imagining holding you in my arms again."

"We're here now."

"Marry me."

Spence sat up and leaned on her elbow as I looked over at her. "You'd ask her to marry you with your eyes closed?"

"I don't know." She was so confusing. "You said to pretend you were Kat."

"When you ask her to marry you, look her in the eyes." She got closer to my face while climbing on my lap. Her fingers traced my mouth. "Speak from your heart, but never take your eyes off of hers. Make sure she knows that nothing else matters to you. She's everything." When she kissed me I felt carried away in her words. "Show her how much you missed her in the way you hold her. Promise to keep her safe forever."

I couldn't hold back any longer. I kissed Spence, pretending she was Kat, and she was letting me do it. I tossed her hat to the ground and dug my hands into her hair, pulling her against my mouth. Her tongue teased mine, just enough to force me to reciprocate. She started unbuttoning my fatigues, one at a time. We spent the next hour pretending we were other people, making love in the hot sand of the desert. I couldn't remember a time when I hadn't thought about the negative around me. With each touch, stroke, or connection, I imagined I was on that beach with Kat.

Spence laid next to me when we were finished. Our bodies were covered in sweat, and it was hard to not want a gallon of water to quench my thirst. She looked up into my eyes and giggled. "So that's what it's like to be with the real Brooks Valentine."

I reached forward and kissed her on the head. "You made me do it."

She tapped on my chest. "She's a lucky girl."

"I wouldn't say that. I've pretty much ruined her life."

"When you get home, make sure you don't stop looking for her. Don't give up. No matter how much it hurts, keep searching for her." I was shocked when I heard her starting to cry. I lifted her and held her close against my chest. "What's wrong?"

"I want to go home, Brooks. I miss my boyfriend. No offense to you. I'm glad I have you in my life right now. It's not the same though. I need to feel him holding me."

"Yeah. I get it. Don't cry though. You'll make me feel like shit."

She laughed through her tears, but before she could respond we heard an approaching vehicle. Since we'd taken the vehicle without permission, and were only in our underwear, we both stood and began scrounging for our fatigues. At first I had her jacket, and she had mine. We tossed them to each other and continued rushing. By the time the vehicle stopped behind us we were at the front, both ducked down checking under the truck.

"Everything alright, soldiers?"

"Yeah, we hit something a while back. I was just checking it out."

"Okay. I only stopped to make sure you weren't broken down."

I came out from under the truck and avoided eye contact with Spence. "Thanks. We're good. I'm headed back now."

Once we were both back inside of the truck we began to laugh. "That was close."

"I'm sure he knew what we were doing."

"Who cares. He's just jealous." I started the truck. "Thanks for today, Spence. It was nice to be on that beach with you."

"With Katy, you mean?"

"No," I looked in her direction. "With you. I mean, yeah I imagined you were Kat, but I knew you weren't. You're a good friend. For a while I was convinced that I didn't need anyone while I was over here. I figured if I wasn't connected to anything I couldn't get hurt."

"Yeah, it makes sense, but we're all feeling the same thing. When I signed on the dotted line I never expected this. I'm holding on for dear life here, too. It's not easy."

"Yeah, I just wanted to get away from home. I didn't think far enough into the future to see this. Don't get me wrong. I won't regret defending my country, but I'm spent."

"You're a good soldier."

I tried hard to be the best, even when I doubted myself. "I appreciate that."

"We should get back."

I looked at her one more time, wishing we were back on that sand, pretending that life wasn't falling apart around us. "Yeah, I guess we should."

December 25th

It's Christmas.

My mom is making her annual dinner, and I'm sure my brother's there. An empty space will be left for me and Kat. I wonder where she'll be eating. Has she made friends? Does she have any presents to open? Is someone else holding her?

I'm trying not to be upset today, but it's difficult. Yesterday I spent time with a friend, who gave me a nice present. She helped me pretend I was with Kat on a beach. It also broke my heart. More than anything I wanted it to be real.

Wherever Kat is, I hope she's okay. I don't want her to be sad. She needs to live her life without regret. I want her to be happy, above everything else, even if that means she's found another to hold her at night.

Chapter 23

Another year had come and gone, leaving me with more loss. Each day I woke up wondering if it would be my last. I thought about Mullins every day, sometimes I even talked out loud to him, as if he was out there somewhere watching down on me. I knew I'd lost my sanity, and frankly I didn't care. Life was redundant. I wasn't where I wanted to be, and I certainly had nothing to look forward to. I was going with the flow.

Being a ranger was tough. Almost weekly I'd been sent out with some mission that required me to take a life. So far I know I'd killed at least ten people; ten people who may have had children, wives, or even living parents. I didn't know what they'd done before this, and it didn't matter. If I put thought into it I'd be weak when I knew I had to remain strong. I'd become bitter, lonely, and a man of few words. Even Spence noticed the change, but knew she could do little to change me. She too was going through the motions of figuring it out for herself. The first time she'd shot her gun she came back to base and cried for two days. That's when I knew it was time to turn off my feelings. I couldn't have them if I wanted to get through this. I had to be numb.

Then something happened that would change me. In an instant it snapped me back to reality. I almost couldn't believe that I wasn't dreaming.

It was mail time. I was sitting on my bed reading one of the books my parents had sent. When they called my name I grabbed the envelope and stuck it to the side until I could finish the chapter I was on. Had I peeked at the return address I would have known right away that the next few pages could have waited.

The moment I picked that letter back up and saw her name I had to do a double take. My stomach knotted up as I ripped it open, eager to see her handwriting that was meant just for me.

Dear Brooks,

I hope this letter finds you in good health. I know it's been a long time and you may not even want to hear from me. I don't blame you for hating me. I hate myself for what I did to you.

I walked away from everything because I wasn't willing to fight. I was a coward.

I'm not writing this letter to beg you for forgiveness. I don't deserve that. I'm writing to you because I know it's time to move on. I've held onto some crazy idea that one day you'll be back in my life again.

So, that brings me to the reason that I'm writing you this letter.

Tell me that I shouldn't hold onto you.

Tell me we're definitely over, so that I can finally let go.

Katy

I didn't know what to do. After reading her words nearly twenty times I contemplated what I could do to tell her how long I'd waited for this moment. She was okay, and reaching out to me, but only because she was ready to move on. Asking my permission was like a knife to my heart. Is this what she wanted? After all this time, was she ready to let it go?

I quickly grabbed a piece of paper and began to reply.

Dear Kat,
I hope this letter finds you.

I considered not writing you and letting it be, but I've kept things bottled up for so long and I don't know where to begin.

I'll start by asking you the one question that has been on my mind for two years now. Why did you run?
Please tell me it wasn't because you regretted being with me. Still, to this day, nothing has ever compared to feeling you in my arms that night.

My life hasn't been easy the past two years. I've seen things that I wish I could wipe out of my memory and just when I think it can't get any worse, I see something even more devastating. I've seen children slaughtered and fathers being shot by their own sons and brothers.
I'm sorry for sharing that. It's just so hard, living here.
I still miss you every day Kat, so I guess that finally brings me to answer your question.

If you think it's time to let go, I will understand. Just know that I've thought about you every day since you walked out of my life. I'll never give up on you.

Take care of yourself in whatever you decide.

Love always,
Brooks

When I saw Spence it was hard to contain myself. Right away she knew something was up. "Who are you, and what did you do with Valentine?"

"She wrote me."

"What?" Seeing the excitement on her face only made it better. She hugged me in front of a ton of people. "Oh my god, that's awesome. You must be so happy."

"You could say that." I pulled the letter out and handed it to her. "Do you want to read it?"

We found a place to sit down, and I watched as she began reading the words Kat had written to me. When she looked up I saw a worried look in her eyes. "Please tell me you wrote her back?"

"Yeah, I mailed it already."

"What did you say?"

"I told her I was glad to hear from her and if she wanted to move on with her life I would be okay with it."

She slapped me on the back of the head. "You idiot! Are you crazy? She was reaching out to you. You weren't supposed to let her go. She wrote that so you'd tell her to hold on."

"What?" I was immediately concerned.

"When a woman writes this it's because she needs to see you haven't given up hope. You just basically told her to go out and find someone else."

"Oh shit. What do I do? The mail has already gone out."

I stood up, but she pulled me back down. "Wait. Just see if she writes back. If she doesn't, send her another letter."

"I can't sit here wondering."

"Then write her back now. Whatever you do, don't freak out. If she wants to move on there's nothing you can do anyway. I think she needed to know you still love her. Hopefully that will be enough to keep her from doing something she'll regret."

"This sucks. What if I lost her again?"

"Calm down. You have to be patient. Promise me you won't go all psycho on the girl? You've waited all this time. A couple more days won't hurt you."

As much as I appreciated having Spence to keep me in check, I feared she'd been wrong. For weeks I anticipated to get something back from her, but nothing came. Since I was about to head to another area for a few weeks, I knew I had to reach out to her beforehand. After twelve days with no response I wrote her another letter.

Dear Kat,

Okay, I lied when I said that it was okay with me if you let go. It's not okay.

I'm miserable over here and feel like I have nothing to come home for. I don't want to see my brother and visiting my parents only reminds me of you.

You're still everywhere I turn.

God, I miss you so much. I miss the way you smell and the way you twirl your hair when you're nervous. Most of all, I miss my best friend.

Please Kat. Write me back.

Tell me to go to Hell.

Say something.

I have to go away for a few days, but I'll check the mail when I get back.

All my love, Brooks

While I was away for work purposely my mind was focused on one thing alone.

Katy Michaels

Thankfully, we weren't ambushed or held at gunpoint while we were out delivering parcels to the needy. Day after day I found a place to sit and write to her. My first letter during that time flowed so easily, almost like we hadn't skipped a day from seeing each other. Even though it was about missing her, she was close to my heart again, which made every second of life worth living.

Dear Kat,

I can't even explain how happy it made me to get your letter. Now, it seems like I can't stop writing you. Every day I sit down and think of all the things that I want to tell you.

If you saw the pile of paper bundled in my trash can, you'd understand.

While this place lacks the feeling of home, I find peace knowing that you're out there somewhere thinking about me too. I can only hope that one day, when I'm finally done with this tour, I can see you again. Would you be opposed to that? I understand if I'm being too forward. I just feel like we've missed so much time together.

Please write me back as getting your letters is the happiest I've felt in a very long time.

Love, Brooks

When I returned to base I was greeted with mail on my bed. I didn't waste time opening the envelope and reading her words.

Dear Brooks,

I'm happy too. For so long I felt like you hated me. I've kept so much pain bottled up inside of me for what I did. I want you to know that walking away from you that day was still the hardest thing I've ever had to do. It was harder than losing my parents, because I knew I could have changed it, if I'd just been brave enough.

It's taken me a long time to be able to accept that there are things I could have done to prevent what happened to us. It all starts with admitting that I should have known Branch had lied to me about your feelings.

About your brother...

I almost don't want to know when he and Melissa hooked up. It isn't like I care if it happened the day after I left. I knew I didn't want him. In fact, if I never see him again it will be too soon. Your brother is the reason that we are worlds apart. He's the reason that we've lived in Hell for two years. I will never forgive him for that.

Looking back now, I can actually see how he was full of shit most of the time. It makes me sick knowing I was that naïve.

I should be the one begging you to write me back because I sure as hell don't deserve your heart after what I did to you and have still been doing to you.

Getting our friendship back would mean everything to me.

I hope to hear from you soon.

Love always,

Katy

I wasn't surprised to hear that Branch was with her friend. I'd suspected it for a while. A part of me was elated that she could see him for what he was. Finally!

None of that mattered to me anymore though. I had one goal, and that was to have Kat in my arms again. Even though I still had plenty of time overseas, I could now see a future for myself for when I returned.

Kat's letters explained all about her new life in South Carolina. She seemed like she struggled at first, but had made good friends who'd helped her along the way. Her letters were cheerful and kept me positive while being in the midst of chaos.

I wrote her every single day, sometimes even twice if I had extra time. When responses would come in from her I'd stop what I was doing to read them. It was as if we were dating, but from afar.

I'd been reluctant to call her for a lot of reasons. Mostly it was because I couldn't hear her voice and not want more. The letters were a good start. They were enough to make the pain go away. For me that was all I could give her, not because I didn't want to hear her voice telling me she missed me. It was obvious I did. It was more to the point of wanting something special to have to look forward to.

By March I had a whole bag full of her letters; each one of them giving me hope that we were finally going to have our happily ever after. I was optimistic, so much that Spence and Anderson made fun of me.

Then, out of nowhere, I was told that my unit was moving to another location. I can't say that I was sad about losing my friends. Aside from the occasional sex, I'd grown close to Spence especially. She took the news as hard as I did.

The night before I was set out to leave we met in our secret spot. She cuddled her body up against mine and held it there. "I'm going to miss you, Valentine."

"Yeah, I'm going to miss you too."

"I need you to do me a favor."

"Anything." She couldn't know how grateful I was to have had her when I lost Mullins.

"Don't you dare give up on getting home to Katy. Once you have her, don't ever let her go."

"I promise."

She kissed me on the cheek. "Seize the day, my friend. Godspeed to you."

Those were the last words that Spence ever said to me.

For a while we were going to be without a way to send mail home. As much as I hated the idea, I knew when I returned there would be letters for me waiting.

Chapter 24

What happened in the next couple days would change my life drastically. This would prove to be the hardest mission as a ranger that I'd ever performed. My job was to kill, and I was mentally and physically prepared to do it, because I knew it would get me back to safety, and a day closer to going home.

My mindset was in order, and as direct orders were being delivered to us I stared down at my weapon, making sure it was loaded and I had enough supply of ammo on me to reload accordingly. My heart was racing, fueled by adrenaline and fear. I wasn't scared of what I had to do. I was scared the aftermath would haunt me forever.

We waited until nightfall to enter into the small city. The quiet of the night was only a camouflage to what awaited us. One by one we crept through the streets, guarded and alert.

The first shots came from the high end of a western point. We all turned around unloaded a few rounds as we ducked for cover. Separated by the situation, I took in my surroundings, located a building to set up and scope out where the enemy was.

The building was clearly vacant since only half of it was still remaining. Once I'd cleared an area near a window I knelt down and set my weapon for better aim. The only way to tell where the shots were coming from was to listen and watch the sky light up.

Out of the corner of my eye I saw someone running across a street, dressed in white. I knew it wasn't one of our guys. A second was all it took for me to aim at the moving target and take him down. His body flailed for the few minutes it took for him to die. I reset my weapon and took a few deep breaths before the next target came in sight. From where I was positioned I could see the rest of my unit ducked down in an adjacent building. They signaled me with a flashlight, and I did the same back, giving them confirmation that it was just me. They then used Morse code to let me know that there was a group to my left. I no sooner turned to look to that side of the building when I heard someone running nearby. I turned off my flashlight and hid behind some debris until I could figure out where they were. Shots ricocheted off the stone walls around me and I knew that if I wanted to get out alive I was going to have to face this person head on.

Without regard for his proximity, I turned and started firing a full clip. When my gun was empty I looked around the room, turning my light on to reveal the man was very dead.

I could hear a few more speaking in their language. I crept closer to that area, peering out the window where they couldn't see. One was on the roof, aiming his gun near the location of my unit. I took him out easily with my gun, but only to signal to his companions where I was squatting.

They ran after me, chasing me into another building. At the same time I heard more shots fired as my group was trying to cover for me.

By the time I made it inside of another building and secured the door, the shots had ended. I clicked on my light to make sure I hadn't just ran inside of a building full of the enemy. In the far corner I spotted a man who was clearly dead. A small girl. She was crying softly. I ran to her side. "It's going to be okay." She couldn't understand what I was saying. I held out my hand for her. "Come, please."

Slowly she squirmed out from behind the man and took my hand. I held her close as we made our way to the exit of the building.

I could see my unit in the clear. They thought they'd gotten everyone. Then I heard the sound of the grenade. I tried to shine my light to find it, but there was too much on the ground, and I was running out of time. I pulled the child along, counting the seconds until I knew there was no time left. I threw my body over that little girl, shielding her from what was about to come.

Nothing could ever compare to the feeling of hot metal shrapnel digging into the skin. I couldn't hear, and everything seemed to be spinning. While it was all happening I clung to that little girl, praying she'd be safe. If this was my last few moments on this earth I wanted to die knowing I'd saved her.

Then everything went black.

I woke up in a hospital bed, the lights were dim and I could hear people talking around me. That's when I knew my eyes had been covered. I went to reach up to remove the bandages and realized I was hooked to an IV. I started calling out for someone to help me, praying that I wasn't going to be blind when they did.

I could hear someone approaching. "Calm down. You're in the hospital."

"Get this thing off my face," I ordered.

"Calm down, sir. It's just to protect your head wound. It seems to have slipped down while you were sleeping."

The room brightened as she adjusted the bandage. I was immediately able to see. Relief swept over me as I looked around the room at the other occupied beds. "Where am I?"

"You're in the military hospital on base." The nurse replied.

"How long have I been here?"

"Two days."

"That's impossible," I argued. "How did I get here?"

She looked at my chart. "I wasn't here when you were brought in. According to this you were flown in. If you give me a couple minutes I can figure out more."

"Yeah, I'd like that. Thank you."

I watched her walk away before sitting up and accessing the damage to the rest of my body. When I couldn't feel my left hand I knew something was very wrong. It was casted and had pins sticking out of it.

Up until that point I'd forgotten what had happened to me. The rush of it all hit me like a ton of bricks. My head began to pound, sending me back down on my pillow.

The nurse ran back up to me. "What's going on? Your blood pressure is rising."

"My head. It's killing me. Make it stop."

Ten minutes later I was dosed with something through my IV. I closed my eyes, appreciating the ease it brought me.

Later, I was visited by my commanding officer, who informed me that I'd managed to save the little girl. He also let me know that my concussion was so severe that they feared I had bleeding in my brain. The fact that I'd woken up was a good sign. While he talked about how I was recovered and flown to the medical center, I thought about what my injuries meant for me. With no regard for interrupting I said what was on my mind. "This means I'm going back to the states doesn't it?"

He nodded. "You're no good to us in your current condition. A ranger needs to be able to handle a weapon."

All I could think about was going home and seeing Kat again.

While I was waiting for all of my paperwork to go through I asked a nurse if she could write Kat for me since I had no use of my hand. I had to wait until everyone was taken care of before she could give me enough time to do it. It was obvious she'd done this sort of thing before for others who were injured.

With a pen and paper she sat there ready. "Who am I sending this to?"

"Katy, uh, address it to Kat with K."

I watched her write down her name and add the comma. "Okay I'm ready for the message."

I took a few deeps breaths to calm myself down. I was so damn excited to be sending this type of message that I didn't want to leave out any details.

I took my time reciting the words, making sure she had time to keep up. Every once in a while I'd get a dirty look, but she kept going with it, so I refused to stop.

"Sorry it's been a couple weeks since I wrote you and I know you're probably wondering why my handwriting sucks so bad. I will first start by saying that I'm alright. You can stop worrying about me.

My left hand, the trusty one that I've done everything with my whole life, is out of commission.

It was a late night call and none of us had gotten much sleep. My lieutenant had us running into a building that had been attacked, retrieving any living bodies we could find. I came across this father, holding a little girl tight in his arms. As I approached, I realized that he'd shielded the impact and lost his life protecting her.

After prying her out of his rigged hold, she started to scream, as if I was there to harm her. Everything happened so fast after that. I started running, holding her in one arm and my gun with the other. I got to the corner of the building when I heard the grenade being thrown. The only problem was that it was so dark I couldn't see the direction that it had rolled. Knowing that any second it was going to blow, I threw myself over her, blocking her with my arm and hands from injury.

The impact was insane, shoving shards of metal and debris into my arm. I could smell my flesh burning, but knew saving her was still a top priority.

Then my body gave out on me; unable to withstand the amount of pain I was under any longer. I collapsed out on the road, with the girl still in my arms.

When I woke up, I was in the hospital. I had no recollection of the day it was, or how I'd gotten there. One thing I did know was that my hand and arm was casted and I had no feeling in my fingertips. I found out that I suffered from a concussion and messed up my arm pretty bad. They think it will get better, but for now, I can't perform my Ranger duties. So, that's the bad news. Now for the good. Kat, I hope you're sitting down. I'm coming home. Well, not exactly home. I've been re-assigned to a new base and you're never going to guess where. Fort Jackson. I can imagine that you're probably in tears and wondering how long you have to wait to see my handsome face again. It's going to be soon, but I'm not exactly sure when they'll give me the go-ahead. It's just a bunch of ridiculous paperwork really.

At some point, I'm sure I will have to have surgery in Bethesda at Walter Reid, so that will be a joy. Seeing the family hasn't been the highest of my priorities.

None of that matters right now. My temporary profile for now will allow me to assist with combat training and since it's what I do best, I know I'll enjoy it. So, I want you to know, I'm coming home for you, Katy. We're going to start over and be together. This time there won't be anything standing in our way. We can make our own lives now. I can't tell you how excited I am to hold you in my arms. I feel like it's been forever. I'll let you know when I'm in town, by probably stopping by unannounced to surprise the hell out of you. Be on the lookout for me. I love you so much. See you soon, Brooks"

When we were finished the nurse folded the paper and stuck it in an envelope. I recited her the address and watched as she filled it out on the front. Then she assured me that she'd send it right away.

With that in order, all I had to do was convince my superiors to send me somewhere on the east coast, preferably close to where Kat lived.

Chapter 25

Three weeks went by before I was transferred to the U.S., and I wasn't even taken to the east coast. Back at my original base in Texas, I met with surgeons regarding my injury. In between appointments I spent time researching locations that I could be sent to where my skill set could be essential. Even though I was ranked as a Sergeant, there were plenty of other higher ranking officials with better titles. For instance, I was sent to meet with my staff Sergeant regarding a transfer.

Since I was being given a temporary profile due to my injury, there was limited jobs

I'd be able to do. Lucky for me, Fort Jackson in South Carolina offered training programs that I was well qualified for. Getting in would serve as the hard part.

Being on medical leave with the military isn't like a regular civilian would have. Sometimes appointments took weeks, and then I'd have to wait for that paperwork to go through to see the next doctor. I didn't have my choice of physicians, or where I could go. The Army was in total control of my life at this point.

By the end of March I called my parents to let them know that I was still in Texas. They offered to fly in to see me, but I was hoping for a transfer to a closer location, so asked them to hold off. Day after day I waited to be given the go-ahead to move to South Carolina. I didn't care what my job would be. All that mattered was getting to Kat.

I'd like to say that I kept her letters close when I boarded a plane to come back to the U.S., but that's not what happened. I packed all my things up and loaded them into my military gray travel gear. When I got off the plane it didn't arrive with me. I'd filled out more paperwork three times, but they still had been unable to locate my gear.

While I was freaking out about not having all of Kat's letters, and the rest of my belongings, I used my spare time to internet search for her number. I needed her to know that I'd arrived and was waiting for orders to transfer. I didn't want to go for months without communicating. I knew she'd be worried, even after I'd sent her a letter explaining how time consuming the military could be.

Unfortunately, there was no listing for a Katy Michaels anywhere in South Carolina, not anywhere near the town I'd been mailing to. It made no sense. She didn't have to hide. She wasn't in danger.

I tried her old number, but someone else answered, claiming they'd had it for a year. Nothing made sense.

I wondered if she moved. She could have lost her job and needed a cheaper place. Perhaps she was living with friends, but finally started to do well enough to live by herself. Maybe she'd told me she'd built a house because she didn't want me thinking she was struggling? Maybe she'd changed her mind about me? Surely she'd gotten my letter saying that I was coming home. Why would she make it so hard for me to find her?

Chalking it up to bad luck, I decided to wait it out. My bag was finally located back in Afghanistan. After a ton of calls it was being shipped to me.

It was April before I got approval to transfer. I'd already had one procedure on my hand, but there was little improvement. Still, nothing, and I mean nothing, could have prevented me from taking that job and moving to be close to Kat.

There was never a doubt in my mind that we wouldn't be together. I'd played it all out in my head a million times. First I'd get settled on base. I'd buy a cheap vehicle to get around in and then show up at her door. I could almost feel the way my arms would wrap around her body. All I hoped was that I could keep it together when our eyes met for the first time.

I'd waited years to be with her again; to see her in the flesh. Nothing was going to stop us; not my brother, and certainly not the military. This was our chance after praying it would happen. I'd been patient, understanding, and as brave as I could be.

I deserved this new chance at life, especially after thinking for so long that it would never happen.

It took me until the middle of April to get situated. I'd wanted to rush over to Kat's house that first day, but life got in the way. I knew I needed all my ducks in a row before dragging her into chaos.

I also needed to get my work situation managed. I couldn't keep wondering what would happen with my hand.

On the day that I was finally going to get my girl, I bought a bouquet of flowers, got a haircut, slapped on some cologne, and headed to the address of her letters. My palms were sweaty against the old leather steering wheel as I turned off the highway onto a country road. This all seemed so surreal, almost as if I couldn't believe it was about to happen. My stomach was in knots, and I felt like my head was spinning as the numbers on the mailboxes got closer. Then I was sitting right in front of the house, her house.

I put the truck in park and looked over at the property, taking in the surroundings of where my girl was living. The house was new, and it seemed so nice. In the back yard I saw a swing. I wondered if she was a babysitter, or maybe she had friends living with her that had small children. Since I'd pulled past the driveway, I climbed out and prepared to walk to her front door.

Just as my feet hit the pavement I saw someone coming out of the home. I would have thought my mind was playing tricks on me if I didn't wipe them and recheck for the same result. A man, looking to be around my age, who walked with a limp, was leaving the house. A female, who much resembled my Kat was kissing him goodbye. He turned to walk away and went back for another kiss.

I clung to my truck door to keep from falling to my knees in the middle of the street. This wasn't possible. I know I hadn't talked to her in months, but I'd sent word that I was coming home to be with her. How could she get involved with someone so quickly?

Before I could make sense of it, I caught the man looking my way. To avoid her from seeing me distraught, I climbed back in the truck and drove away. It wasn't until I was about five miles from her place that I pulled over and lost it.

How could she do this me? Did Kat not care that I'd come across an ocean to be with her?

That night I laid in my bed wondering what was going on. I kept trying to rationalize with who the guy was, and what he was doing there. With no sleep at all, I visited the house again the next morning.

Around the same time as before, I saw the man leaving for work. This time a little girl was waving. Then it hit me. The man had a child. Maybe Kat was the babysitter, and they'd been seeing each other. Maybe he was just someone like Spence was to me; a friend with a little on the side. I didn't expect her to be a saint.

Even though I assumed it was just that, it took me a couple days to calm down. I didn't want to appear at her door looking jealous. She obviously didn't know I was in town, and I had to respect that if I'd just called her beforehand maybe things would have been different.

The next week I decided to try again, but this time with a different approach. I waited until my shift was over and then journeyed to her address. Much like a stalker, I sat in my truck waiting to catch a glimpse of her. It took a while, but I saw her and the little girl walking outside to hang some clothes. As I prepared to step out and greet her, I paid attention to the items she was hanging on the line. It was obvious that, not only the man lived there, but also the little girl.

This got me so hot that I had to leave. I beat on the steering wheel, wondering if in the time I'd not communicated with her she'd met someone and invited them to take my place. I felt as if maybe she never loved me to the extent that I cared for her. If she had, then nothing would have prevented her from waiting for me.

This time I stayed away for a month.

For those four weeks, I tried to stay occupied. My new training position kept me busy during the day, and as new recruits continued to come in, I kept my schedule full. It was the nights that tore me apart.

Finally, one evening, my superior invited me to have dinner with his family. While we sat there exchanging war stories like old buddies, his wife asked a question about my love life. "Since you're back have you thought about finding someone to settle down with?"

I smiled and wiped my face with a napkin before responding. "As a matter of fact, I did. Unfortunately, I arrived too late. It seems that the woman I wanted to marry is shacked up with someone else."

"Oh no. How did you find out?" She asked curiously.

"I drove to her a couple times. I saw him coming outside, they were together."

"Have you spoke to her?"

"No. I thought about writing her a letter, but I can't bring myself to do it. She's moved on."

"Were you involved before you left?"

I nodded. "I've loved her since we were kids. That's why it's so hard. I asked to be transferred here so we could be together."

"Then I say you shouldn't give up. Call her. Stop by again."

"Forgive my wife, Valentine. She's a bit of a romantic. All those novels put crazy ideas in her head."

"It's okay," I laughed. "She's right. I should have tried harder."

"It's never too late," she said as she stood to clear the table. "It doesn't hurt to keep trying."

She was right. Had I come this far to give up so easily? Had I risked my life, been through, and lost myself, only to come home and not fight for what was mine?

I needed a new approach because avoiding her now was becoming impossible. She was going to give me answers even if they weren't the ones I wanted to hear.

Chapter 26

That next evening I drove over to Kat's house again. She wasn't home, but ended up pulling in while I was sitting there. I watched her climb out of the vehicle and fetch the child from the back. She kissed her a few times before letting her walk alongside of her. That's when it really sunk in. This little girl was her child. Kat had gone away and had a kid. She was a freaking mother, which meant there was obviously a father.

While I sat there trying to do the math with how soon she got pregnant after she'd left, the male pulled into the driveway. As soon as he got out the child ran toward him and threw her arms up. He lifted her, kissing her whole face. This was the dad. It was all very clear.

I couldn't have been sure, but I swear Kat noticed my truck sitting on the road. I quickly pulled away before she said something to whoever the guy was.

That night, after I knew everyone was probably asleep, I left the barracks and headed back to Kat's address. I climbed out of my truck and looked in the mailbox, hoping to find the guy's name. When it was empty I looked back at the house and saw the curtain folding.

As fast as I could move, I got back on the road, hoping they didn't call the authorities.

Since I had no luck, a few days later I went back during the day when I figured nobody would be home. I'd climbed out of my truck and opened the mailbox, hoping to get a name to put to the guy's face. Once I had it I planned on writing her a letter, hoping she could at least explain why she'd given up on me.

The answer was as plain as day.

The first envelope was addressed to Mr. and Mrs. Robert Parsons. The second was made out to Katy Michaels Parsons.

They were married.

They had a child together.

The letters came out of my hands, falling to the ground at my feet. As I dropped to pick them up a police car pulled behind me. An officer climbed out and approached with caution. "Can I help you, soldier?"

It was impossible to keep the burning tears from pouring out of my eyes. This wasn't just heartbreaking. It made me wish I was back on the battlefield. This was a nightmare.

I shoved the mail back in the box. "Sorry. It's not what it looks like. I was trying to see if this was the address of my friend. I've been away for a couple years, and I'm just trying to locate her."

"The owners of the home have reported a suspicious vehicle sitting outside the property. You can't be going through their mail. It's a federal offense."

"I'm sorry. I won't come back again. I assure you."

I went to get back into my truck before he spoke again. "So is it your friend's address?"

It was hard to answer him. I didn't know what to consider Kat because she'd obviously lied to me. "Yes. I know Mrs. Parsons. Well, I knew her a long time ago, before she was married. I'm sorry you had to come back out here. I assure you it won't happen again."

"I'm going to need your name for assurance. If I get the report I'll have to write something up."

Since I knew I wouldn't be returning, I was fine with giving him my information. We shook hands before I got into my truck and pulled away from the residence.

I ended up in a bar a mile from the barracks. It was a dive, not that I paid attention. To keep from losing my shit, I poured alcohol down my throat until everything felt numb.

Kat had destroyed me. There was nothing left to hope for. The last few months of correspondence had been lies. She was married with a child, who was obviously around each time she wrote about still having feelings for me. I wondered if she waited until her husband left for work to send me those lies, or did he know she was giving me false hope?

Thinking about it made me cringe. I'd gone through hell to get stationed close to her, only to find out we never had a chance. Yet again something was coming between us, but this time I wouldn't push my way back into her life. I couldn't do that knowing she had a child; a family.

I'd never be able to compete with that, and so I decided to walk away.

April 21st

I came all this way for nothing. Everything I've done was a waste. She never wanted me. It was all some sick game she was playing, probably to make herself feel better about what happened in the past. How could she rip my heart out again and again? I'm starting to wonder if she knew I loved her all along. Maybe she was just evil. It would make more sense than assuming she up and married the first guy that came along, without making an effort to seek me out.

The pain I'm feeling can't be described. I wish I'd go to sleep and never wake up. It's not even the betrayal that's ripping me to shreds. It's seeing the image of her daughter. The bitch carried a child and never once mentioned her. What kind of mother does that?

I could never forgive her for this. I don't even know if I'll get to a point where I want to. As soon as my two years are up here in South Carolina I'm getting the fuck away from this place. Kat can stay here and rot for all I care. She'd ruined my life, and now there's nothing left to fight for.

I was a fool for loving someone with my whole heart. I should have known that I'd get burned. Now I'm lost, without a damn way to break free of this agony. Loving her was always my downfall. I guess I'd just never hit rock bottom until now.

The next time I spoke to my parents wasn't until a few weeks had gone by. Thankfully I was able to get out of bed without an excruciating headache from stress. My father answered the phone, and immediately I thought of the whole family, Kat included.

"Brooks, is that you? How's the weather in the south?"

"It's warm. Some days have gotten pretty hot, but it doesn't compare to where I was before. How are you and mom doing?"

"Good. Mom's out with some friends. I'll be sure to tell her you called. So, are you settled finally? Is the paperwork submitted for your surgery?"

"Pretty much. I'm still waiting for that appointment with the specialist. So far so good."

"Have you been able to track Katy down yet?"

I sat there for a second wondering why he'd say that. I'd never mentioned her to him before. "Why would you ask me that?"

"Son, it doesn't take a genius to figure out you'd go where she was near. Is she okay?"

"I haven't seen her," I lied. "Wherever she is, she doesn't want to be found. Let's just leave it that way, okay? I've got enough on my plate."

He cleared his throat, and I could tell that my comment had left him more curious.

"Brooks, is there something you're not telling me?"

"No." I responded quickly. "All is good. I was only calling to check in. When I get word about my hand appointment you'll be the first to know."

"Okay, son. Take care then."

"You too."

That night I was fighting demons that I couldn't defeat. There was no hope left in my future, and with that knowledge, it left me susceptible to rehash every single enduring word she'd written on paper. I found myself back at a bar, drinking until I couldn't feel it anymore. The utter disgust I felt for Kat had no end. I wanted her to admit to what she'd done, so I could figure out how to make sense of it all. There had to be a better explanation than she wanted to hurt me. I couldn't allow myself to believe the woman I once knew was gone.

That next morning I had to run an errand off base. In a military vehicle, I drove past her house, parking further away so I couldn't be detected. Like every day, she'd come outside to hang clothes. The little blonde child ran around playing in a kiddie pool nearby.

Once Kat was done with her chores, she sat down next to the little pool and played with the child. The blonde, curly-haired toddler, laughed and screamed with excitement. I'd never seen Kat so attentive before. Even from the distance I stood, I could tell she was in love with that child. That's when it really hit. It was obvious that her decisions were never about her, but more for the child. Kat must have been running and the man she was with was the first person to offer her support. She probably never planned on getting pregnant, but once she had there was no going back.

Perhaps in some ways she did love me. Maybe me being away let us have some sort of kindred romance. The moment she got word that I was coming home everything changed. She knew I'd find out the truth, so she stopped being available. Kat had cut ties with me because she knew I wouldn't like what I found when I finally got to her.

Then I started blaming myself again. If only I'd stayed instead joining the Army, maybe we would have had that chance.

It was too late.

I got in the vehicle and began to drive away.

May 7th
I've made a decision to let things go. I can't change who she's become, and there's no way I'm going to be a home wrecker. I have morals, and even though I'd crossed boundaries

in the past, this was different. She'd committed herself to someone else. I even feel bad about the letters that she's written me because I know her husband couldn't have been okay with some of the things she was saying to me.

I'm always going to love Kat. She's the only one for me. I'm content with knowing there's nothing I can do to change that. I was born to be with that woman. Maybe in our next life we'll have a chance at love again. I'm not going to wish for her to get a divorce. I don't want to share her with other people. I know that type of life would never make me happy. I wanted all of her, or nothing at all.

I pray that one day we can be friends again, but for now, I need time to cope. I'm a strong guy. I've been afraid of a lot of things, but this was something I couldn't stop from happening. I'd lost the love of my life, once and for all. She was happy, and it was enough for me to step aside. It was the least I could do after making her wait so long for me to come home. Maybe one day I'll find someone to share my life with. Sure, they won't be my soul-mate, but I could learn to appreciate the love they have for me, because being alone like this feels as if I'm living in my own personal hell, with no way to exit.

Chapter 27

By the first of July I was doing a little better. I happened to enjoy my new job, and for the most part, staying busy. There wasn't a day that went by where I didn't think of Kat, but I was learning to handle it in a positive way. She'd know by now that I was home safe, and I could only hope that she'd reach out to my parents so they'd be able to meet her little girl. I knew something that important would mean the world to them. They'd spoil her to no end, and Kat would finally be able to stop worrying that they were still upset. To be honest, I don't know if they were ever mad at her. Something told me they knew all along that the marriage to my brother was a huge mistake. It didn't matter anymore. Kat was married to someone else. They were happy, and I was moving forward with my life.

Because of my injury, and traditions in the town nearest to base, I was signed up to be a part of the Independence Day parade. It was an easy gig. All I had to do was sit on the back of a truck and wave with my good arm. Since I'd recently been working with a therapist, my wrist and arm were killing me. It had gotten so bad in the past couple days that they put it in a splint while I was up during the day. Only at night could I take it out.

After helping out as much as I was able, I climbed down the back and prepared to do my part. To the crowd of people, I was a hero. Little did they know I was just a guy who was desperately trying to find my place in a world that I no longer associated with.

I don't know why, but the whole time I stared out into the crowd, searching for the sight of Kat. I didn't care if she was with her husband. I just wanted to see her there, smiling and happy, because somehow that gave me the courage to keep forging forward.

When the parade was over we all hopped off the truck to commence with the people. I was making my way to get a drink when I spotted her in the crowd. It was just for a second, and apparently that's all it took. Down she fell to the ground, and all I could do was stare. Her husband fell to her side, followed by a crowd of spectators. Before I knew it I was being pushed to the side. I walked in another direction and stood next to a tree to make sure she was okay. The last thing I needed was to make a scene.

Once she sat up and started looking around I knew that was my cue to get out of there. I wasn't ready to be face to face with her. I still didn't know if I'd ever be.

I panicked, unable to accept that we'd been that close and not said a single word to each other. Another thing I wondered about was why she'd passed out? Why would that be her reaction to seeing me? I'd told her I was coming home to be with her. She knew I was back in the states, yet she appeared to have seen a ghost, or someone she feared. It made me feel like shit.

Three days later, I was sitting in my office looking over documents for new recruits that would be coming in to train. For the life of me I couldn't keep my focus on anything. I kept replaying seeing Kat at the parade, and how she'd reacted when our eyes met.

The phone rang, causing me to jump clear out of my seat. I pushed the button to answer it. "Valentine?"

"Sir, this is Matthews at the front gate. I have a woman out here claiming she needs to see you. She's says it's an emergency."

I tried to keep my composure, knowing only one woman knew where to find me. "Did she give a name?"

"Yeah, she said her name is Katy Michaels."

I rubbed my face with both hands, trying to consider my options. It wasn't like I had the gull to send her away. More than anything we needed to hash this out. Once and for all I longed to have closure.

"Send her through."

I'd had years to think about what I'd say if I saw her again, yet in this instant I couldn't come up with one thing. My heart was thumping so hard that I swore it was going to explode. If that wasn't bad enough, my throat felt as if it were closing. I took a sip of water before standing up and putting my hat on, hoping I could use it to shield myself from getting lost in those eyes that I loved so much.

It was one-hundred and seventy four steps to the parking lot. I know this because I counted them to keep my mind off what was about to happen. As the patter of her car pulled into a parking spot, I stepped out to greet her.

As impossible as it was to grasp, I could feel a tightening in my throat again, this time because I was fighting back my emotions. It was important to stay strong. She couldn't know she'd broke me.

Right away I could tell she was refusing to look in my direction. I stood on the curb, clenching my jaw trying to come to grips with the situation. Before I knew what I was doing, I found myself opening the passenger side door and climbing in. Right away I could smell her shampoo. It took me a few seconds to look in her direction. She was peering out the window, refusing to turn my way.

"Kat, look at me." The silence was torture.

It was hard for me to watch her turn to face me in slow motion. Her eyes said it all, even before my name escaped her lips. "Brooks."

I couldn't help from touching her, wiping those tears away that were falling from her eyes. "Don't cry. I can't handle it."

She scrunched up her face and cried harder. "I just got your letter. The last one you sent. It must have gotten lost."

I placed my fingers over her lips. Just for a second I wanted to avoid thinking she could be lying to me. The more I thought about it, the angrier I felt. "Like the letters you wrote to me, telling me you were married with a kid?"

Kat hid her face, placing it against her steering wheel. I'd hit a nerve, and as much as I felt the need to hurt her, I knew I didn't have it in me.

"I'm so sorry, Brooks. I didn't have the heart to tell you. I never expected that you'd still love me and when I found out you did, nothing else mattered except for you and me."

I was in shock. What did all this mean?

"Kat, do you have any idea what I had to do to get stationed near you? It was a pain in the ass and involved a lot of ass kissing. I figured that it didn't matter as long as I had you. We could get married and live on or off a base somewhere, and maybe even have a couple of kids. Do you have any idea how it felt to pull up at your house and see you with them? At first I couldn't believe it. I thought maybe you were living with friends. Then when that cop came and told me that you and your husband were concerned, I knew my fears were true."

"I'm sorry. You don't understand what happened to me."

This time I was the one looking away. I refused to let her see me upset. "How long have you been married, Kat?"

"Two years," she replied in a whisper.

I twisted my body to face hers, unable to come to grips with the fact that she'd been with this person for two whole years. I felt like an idiot. "Jesus Christ. Did you even mean the things you said to me, or were they all just bullshit?"

"Everything I said was the truth and you know it!" She defended.

I gazed out the passenger window again. I had to keep hiding my face. She knew me too well. "I wish I could believe that."

It shocked me when I felt her hand grazing mine. I looked in her direction immediately, catching her eyes with mine. It was important to change the subject before I did or said something I'd regret later. "I can feel your touch. It's gotten worse. The feeling comes and goes. If it keeps up I'm going to fail my next PT-test and then I'll be up shit's creek." Focusing on my injury was the best I could come up with.

Kat wasn't going to let it go. She ignored my comment. "You're the only man that I've ever truly loved, Brooks. Look at me and tell me that I'm lying."

She gave me that look; the one I couldn't refuse. "It changes nothing. I won't be a home wrecker. You never really belonged to Branch, but the man you're married to doesn't deserve to get his heart ripped out. If he loves you half as much as I do, that's what will happen. I can't live with myself for doing that. As much as it hurts me to say this, I've got to walk away from you, for good this time."

Kat sat there crying, and I did nothing to stop her. If she only knew how many nights I'd cried myself to sleep, how many months I'd prayed to be with her again. If she could only be in my shoes for a day she'd know why this was impossible for me to handle.

With a car full of silence there was only one thing left to do. Before I lost it in front of her, I had to walk away. Before I managed to step out, I could feel the burning in my eyes. I turned back one more time, displaying years of pent up anguish all over my face. It was so hard to push the words out of my mouth, but I did my best. "Take care of yourself, Kat. Be a good mother and wife. Give them the love that we have and you'll be happy. I know you will."

I heard her getting out of the car and coming at me. She didn't give me time to turn around before she had a hold of my uniform.

"Don't you dare walk away from me. I won't let you say goodbye this time."

Since I didn't want to make a scene, I pulled her inside until we were standing in my office. From there I paced around the room, waiting for whatever else she thought she had to say to me.

Finally I sat down at my desk and watched her. She grabbed a few tissues and started wiping her face. "Please don't do this. Don't push me away." She was sobbing so bad. "I can't live without you. I don't even want to."

I leaned over my desk, making sure she was hearing me clearly. "Listen to yourself. You have a child. How can you say that without me you don't want to live? Do you know what I would give to have a wife and a child? After everything I've seen, all I want is to care for the people I love."

"You don't understand." She shook her head, seeming confused.

I stood, but didn't leave from behind the desk. I was angry, so freaking angry. "Then tell me. Give me one reason why I shouldn't watch you drive home to your family and never look back."

"I can't. You'll never forgive me. I've ruined everything. I'm so sorry, Brooks. Please don't say goodbye. Don't give up on us."

I had to put my head down. It was too much for me. "Kat, I can't do this with you. I'm already going to hear shit for you coming here. This is a serious place and I have a damn job to do. This isn't high school anymore. I can't deal with the drama and I won't be involved with a married woman. Please if you have nothing else to say then you have to go."

"What about our love?" Her question struck a nerve, probably the last one I had.

"Our love has never been our problem."

Just when I thought there was nothing left to say, Kat's next words sent me to my knees.

"She's yours, Brooks."

"What?" Was this some joke? Was she willing to say anything to keep me from making her leave?

"My daughter. My husband isn't the father, Brooks, you are."

Chapter 28

No. This wasn't possible. Her words echoed off the walls, causing me to hear them more than once. I couldn't be the father. There was no way. Unable to accept her confession as the truth, I wanted more of an explanation. "Come again?"

Kat was bawling in her hands. I recognized this type of expression from her. It was genuine, but I wasn't sure if it was because she was telling me a deep secret, or feeling horrible about it. "She's yours."

"Why would you say that to me? We spent one night together in a hotel room." It made no sense. If she was anyone's child it would have been my brother's. For her to pin this on me made me want to send her out the door.

She cleaned her face with a tissue while answering me. "Because I hadn't been with Branch since before I had my last cycle. My doctor, who gave me the exact date of conception, also verified it. She's yours, Brooks."

She dug into her purse, pulling out a phone. At first I wondered if she was breaking out a calendar to show me more proof, but what she showed instead said it all. "See for yourself."

I jerked the phone from her grasp and began looking down at the photo. The resemblance was uncanny. This child was my blood. I couldn't deny it. In that moment I knew she was telling me the truth. Had it been Branch's child she would have gone home. She kept this a secret for one reason alone.

This child was mine.

"Her name is Brooklyn Michaela Valentine. I named her after you."

I couldn't handle what was happening inside of my body. Not only had this woman ripped out my heart, but she stuck it back in and squished it in the palm on her hand. She'd kept this from me. We'd been in contact for months and she'd never mentioned this child. I would have had more reason to stay positive. I would have done everything in my power to get to them sooner. This was unacceptable! I couldn't deal with her sitting across from me. I'd never been so mad at someone in my whole life. She'd betrayed me in a way that I never thought possible. It was time for this meeting to end. "Kat, I think you need to leave. Please, just fucking go. Get out of here!" I was adamant and to the point. This conversation was done, and so were we.

"Don't you want to hear about her?" I couldn't believe she was asking that. Did she think I was kicking her out of my office because I couldn't accept that I had a child? This woman was clearly insane.

I could feel the hot tears rushing down my face, but did nothing to wipe them away. She needed to see how much this was killing me. She needed to know that I would probably never be able to get past this. I wanted to hate her even though I knew it was never possible. "How could you keep this from me and our family? God, how could you do this to me? She's got to be two by now. You're telling me that I've had a child for two years and never known? You were pregnant for nine months and never thought to get in touch with me? I would have taken care of you. I would have wanted to know and you should be ashamed for not telling me."

She fell to her knees in front of me, breaking down more. I watched as she covered her face in shame, but felt nothing to console her. She didn't deserve it. This woman had single handedly ruined me to no end. She'd taken everything that I cherished and tossed it away like a dirty rag. I was done talking. The sooner she was gone the sooner I could figure out what would come next.

I threw her phone down in front of her. "Get out of my face before I say something I'll regret."

Kat ran out, saying nothing else. I was sure people in the building saw her, but I wasn't about to walk out into the hallway and face them. I knew I had to keep my composure above all. I had to set an example. Trainees couldn't see their superior weak.

For the next hour I sat at my desk crying like a baby. Nothing that entered my mind could alleviate the emptiness I felt in my heart. I thought about that little girl and all the memories that were stolen from me. I imagine her growing up not knowing me, and it was torturous. I couldn't begin to understand how I was going to explain this to my parents. They deserved to know as much as I did.

I have no idea what fueled me to do it, but before I could rationalize with my decision I was driving to Kat's house. Our conversation wasn't done. There was so much more to figure out. If she thought I was going to step aside and not want to be a part of my child's life she was wrong.

The fact that I'd sent her away only left me with more questions than I had answers to. From this moment on I was going to be a part of that child's life.

When I pulled into the driveway I recognized that Kat's husband was pulling in behind me. As angry as I was, it didn't even occur to me that he might not have known we'd been in contact. It didn't take a genius to see the pain in his own eyes when we came face to face.

Without a single thought I held out my hand as he walked over to my truck. "Hi, my name is Brooks, Brooks Valentine."

He gave me a once-over before extending his hand and shaking mine. "I had a feeling this was going to happen."

"Sorry to just show up. To be honest with you, I don't even know what made me come. I... I saw Kat a little while ago."

Before I could fully explain he answered for me. "I guess she told you everything, otherwise I don't see why you'd be here, knocking on our door. So what's next? You're here, but why? Are you going to take them away from me?"

I couldn't understand why he was asking me that. Had Kat told him that she'd leave him now that she knew I was alive? "I'm not here for that."

"Yeah, maybe not yet," he replied.

Once inside of the house it was apparent he was freaking out. I could tell he was upset, but wasn't sure if it was with me or Kat. "She didn't tell me to come."

"I get it, man. If it were my kid I'd do the same thing. That little girl is pretty special. I've done my best for the both of them."

"I appreciate that, but I'm not here to cause trouble." I started to give him reassurance, but we both noticed a car pulling into the driveway. My stomach knotted up when I heard footsteps coming up the porch stairs. Her husband pointed to the kitchen chair. "Have a seat. I'm sure you're going to need to."

I sat down and watched him doing the same across from me. It was quite obvious this man was not okay with my visit though I didn't care. I'd been kept away from my child for two years. I'd missed out on every first. I deserved to know her, and I wasn't leaving until I did.

While I watched the child standing right in front of me, staring at me with my same eyes, I heard Kat's husband speaking.

"Brooks was here when I pulled up. He told me about your visit today and I thought it seemed right that we all get everything out in the open."

God it was so difficult to contain my emotions. She was beautiful, perfect, and from that instant I knew she was mine. Her smile was the prettiest thing I'd ever seen in my life. I was captivated by her, unable to look away. "Is it okay if I say hello?"

"She's your daughter, too."

I got down on my knees in front of her, trying my best not to cry and freak her out. Just before I said hello, I watched Kat's husband fly out of the room. This was too much for him to handle. I didn't want to be in his shoes. I couldn't even begin to understand what this must be like for him. He loved this little girl, and I was a threat.

"Hi, pretty girl," I said with a shaky voice.

It took her a few seconds to decide if she could trust me. Then she reached her hand up an touched my face. I felt her palm rubbing over my cheek; her soft skin coming in contact with mine for the first time.

It was all too much to take. This was my baby. This little stranger was my flesh and blood. How could Kat keep her from me? I began to break down in front of the both of them. It was all too much for me to grasp.

I pulled the little girl into my arms and held her there close to me, smelling her hair and memorizing it in my mind. She wasn't only perfect, but in a matter of seconds I'd experienced a kind of love that was new and unconditional. Our immediate connection left me speechless. I wasn't just hurt, I was also overwhelmed with happiness. Never again would I be alone. This child was a part of me, and I would never deny that. From this moment on, I was always going to be there for her, no matter what I had to do to make it happen.

At some point Kat got down on her knees and touched my back, but I refused to give her my attention. She'd taken too much. "I know you'll never forgive me, Brooks. I never meant to hurt you, I swear." I could hear her crying. I wanted to care, but my grudge wouldn't allow it.

When I finally gained enough courage to face her I held my little girl close to my chest. "How could you keep her from me? Why, Kat?"

It was excruciating. My throat burned as I continued to weep. I knew the child was probably freaking out, but I refused to let her down. I was afraid if I let her go, she'd run away.

Kat left the room. I looked up to watch her disappearing. I then heard a door shutting and knew she was probably addressing her husband. For the life of me I couldn't even imagine how this was going to play out. Kat had a lot to explain, and it wasn't going to be easy. She'd made a mess of things. I could hear them arguing in the other room. It was obvious that he hadn't been told she was coming to see me. Kat was pleading, which only made me feel like she loved him. I was interfering in what her husband thought was their perfect family.

I let the child slide out of my arms and rubbed her face. "Don't worry little one," I whispered. "Nothing is going to keep us apart again. I promise you. I just want a chance to be your daddy." More tears trickled from my eyes. "You're the best thing that's ever happened to me, Brooklyn Valentine."

Saying her name was so surreal. It was as if I was dreaming. Nothing could have felt better than knowing she was my child. Although it had started out terrible, this day was the best of my life. I had a daughter, and already she'd brought joy to my life. I'd either died and gone to heaven, or had been given another chance at a happy life. Either way, I would put everything I had into giving this little girl everything her heart desired. I'd be the best daddy, and she'd never know what pain felt like, because I'd spend every waking minute keeping her safe.

Chapter 29

It was obvious that Kat and her husband were having it out. He kept raising his voice, making me want to keep Brooklyn occupied so she wouldn't get upset. We fetched some of her toys and began playing together on the floor. I still couldn't get over how easy it was being around her. Nothing about this made me feel uncomfortable. She was a gift from heaven. Her bright blue eyes were exactly like mine, and when she smiled I saw myself through them. She didn't know who I was. The child was too young to understand something as complex as that.

Time slipped by so quickly. Before I knew it two hours had gone by. Kat and her husband had taken their conversation outside, leaving me alone with Brooklyn. She didn't seem to notice they weren't around. I kept playing with her, making her smile and giggle. She liked me, which only caused me to fall in love with her more. She showed me more toys, and even her room, before leading me back into the kitchen to play with her dolls again.

I heard Kat come back inside the house. She was sniffling, letting me know she'd been upset. I still wasn't going to feel sorry for her, not after everything. I needed to be mad.

What she couldn't understand was that I knew I wouldn't hate her forever. It was stupid to try to convince myself of that. Kat was my soul mate. Even in the worst of times, my heart belonged to her. Yes, she'd hurt me. In this moment I was inconceivably grasping for ways to remain calm. This situation wasn't easy, not for any of us. Our lives were all about to change. From now on I was going to be a part of my child's life. She had to have known that when she told me about her. Maybe it hadn't gone as she'd planned, but I now knew the truth, and nothing was going to keep me from pursuing it.

I could tell the child was getting tired. She put her head down on the kitchen floor and pretended to pat her baby to sleep. Since I knew nothing about children, I picked her up and carried her into the living room. She clung to me as I sat down in a chair and began rocking her. I patted her back the way she was doing to her baby. Her little eyes became heavy, and I knew in a matter of seconds she'd be asleep.

While I sat there kissing her on the top of the head, trying so hard to come to grips with everything, I saw Kat watching me. I wasn't facing her, but could see her reflection in the window across from me. She was crying while witnessing me interacting with our child. The moment was bittersweet, also something she needed to see. I wanted her to know what she'd kept from me, and how hurt I was because of it.

When Brooklyn fell asleep, I found Kat in the kitchen sitting at the table. She was still crying quietly. I did feel bad for intruding. Maybe if I had waited she wouldn't have been fighting with her husband. "I'm sorry if I caused you problems, Kat. When you pulled away earlier, I couldn't stop thinking about her. I had to see her, and I wasn't even thinking that I would be walking into what I did. He didn't even know I was alive. My God, he looked like he was staring at a damn ghost."

She stared at her hands as she replied. "I'm not mad at you for coming. I don't even think Bobby's mad. He's just scared."

I crossed my arms. "Scared of what?"

"He's scared of losing B. He was there for me when I found out I was pregnant. He married me so that I could be on his insurance. I suppose he's been in love with me since then, but it wasn't until recently that we really started living as a married couple. Now, out of nowhere, you're in the picture and no matter how he plays this out in his head he loses."

"Why would he think that? I told him that all I wanted was to have a relationship with my daughter. I stressed to him that I meant your marriage no harm. My word is the truth, Kat." It appalled me that this guy thought I'd swoop in and steal her away. Yeah, I was still in love with her, but I knew being with her was out of the question.

She wiped her face and sniffled more. I couldn't look into her eyes and not feel bad for her. After she'd told me that her husband married her to take care of her and our daughter, I had a new respect for him. It takes a lot for a man to step up like that. "I know, but he doesn't know you like I do."

"Look, I'm not here to discuss your marriage. I'm here because I have a right to see my child whenever I want. I have a right to introduce her to my family." I pointed at her, determined to get my point across. "Let me get something clear with you right now. You will not keep me from her ever again. Do you understand me?"

She nodded.

"I can't believe you did this to me. My God, why? Why would you write me those letters, professing your undying love and devotion to me, when all the while you're hiding my child from me? How could you ever think that I would be alright with that?"

She curled her face and looked away. Apparently the truth was too much for her to handle. It was too damn bad. I wasn't going to let up until I had answers. "I don't know. I don't know why I couldn't tell you. After the first letter, I wanted to. I even told myself that if a second one came I was going to tell you all about her. Then you wrote me back and when I got it all I could think about was being with you again. I knew if I told you about Bobby and B it would change everything and so I got scared. The longer it went, the more scared I became until finally the letters stopped coming. Brooks, you have to believe me. I wanted you to know. I've always wanted you to know."

I ran my hands through my hair while trying to keep my cool. "It doesn't even matter now, does it? We can't go back. What's done is done."

She raised her shoulders and sighed. "Yeah. I'm the devil and you wish you never grew up loving me, right?"

"I never said that. Don't even make this about you."

"It is about me though. It's about me and my mistakes. It's about me holding onto some kind of false hope that someday we could ride off into the sunset with our daughter and live happily ever after."

All I could do was shake my head. This was impossible. "That's never going to happen, Kat, not anymore."

Kat brought her legs up to her chest and put her head down on her knees. "I know."

For a few minutes we sat there in silence. I didn't know what else to say to her. I couldn't change the past, and neither could she. We were both faced with a future. The chain of events that had brought us to this point was from years of miscommunication. We had to fix this because now there was a child involved.

Our child.

Since it was clear she had nothing left to say, I took it upon myself to say goodbye. "I better get going. I need to check in." I grabbed my keys out of my pocket. "I've got a lot of figuring out to do, but I'm coming by here once a day to see Brooklyn. You can choose to be here, or arrange to meet me somewhere that I can spend time alone with her. The choice is up to you."

When I started to walk toward the door she ran after me. "Brooks, wait."

I needed to get out of there. Holding it together in front of her was becoming harder as the time passed. I required space; time to take it all in. "Kat, don't ask me for anything right now. You can't just throw all this on me and expect us to go back to being the way we were. I'm really biting my tongue from saying what's on my mind. The last thing I want to do is hurt you. I probably have every right to, but I'd like to think I'm better than that. Besides, I'd never want you to feel the betrayal that you've made me feel. So, let's just call it a night and we'll see if tomorrow it gets easier."

She closed her eyes, peering down at the floor. "For what it's worth, I think she knows you're important to her. I could see it when you were holding her. She's young, Brooks. She'll never be able to remember a time when you weren't in her life."

I let out an air-filled laugh, feeling so betrayed. If she thought for a second this would make me feel better, she was dead wrong. "She may not remember, but I will. For nearly seven hundred days she's been here on this earth and I never knew she existed."

Then she became defensive. "You were in another country. Even if you knew, what were you going to do? Would you have escaped the country just to get court marshaled and ordered back? Think about it, Brooks. How hard would it have been for you knowing that I left town with only the clothes on my back? I didn't know anyone here and then found out I was carrying the child of a man who wasn't going to return for years. Even if I told you, what would it have changed? You missed contact with her since you got here, which has only been a couple of months, in which if I knew you were here, I would have come to you. So tell me, Brooks. Look at me and tell me how all of this is my fault. You left me too, you know. You left me before we even had a chance. No matter if I would have stayed in that hotel room with you, I would have still watched you leave for Afghanistan and that would have been even harder to do. You think I did all of this to spite you. I did it because I knew that either way I was going to lose you."

I got up in her face, like I did when were kids. "Don't go there. You kept the secret from me."

"We weren't even talking!" She reiterated.

"Because you walked out on me, on us." I wasn't at fault.

"Because you were too much of a pussy to admit that you were in love with me the whole time."

The room was silent. This hurt me. "Kat, you knew how I felt," I whispered.

She shook her head, denying it. "No. I didn't." Her hands went up in the air. "We've both made mistakes and maybe mine were worse. I can't change the past. I can't change that I spent years with your brother. I can't change the fact that I ran away from what we had, and I certainly can't change having our daughter and finding someone to take care of us when you weren't around. You didn't have to join the military, Brooks. You could have fought for us too."

I clenched my jaw and tightened my mouth. This was making me frustrated. "I need to leave."

As I started walking toward my truck she spoke again. "You were always good at walking away."

This pissed me off. I hadn't run from her. I ran because she wanted someone else. "I refuse to do this with you tonight, Kat. I'm mad and I need to take some time to calm down. I have a shift in the morning, but I can be here around three. Have my daughter dressed and ready to go."

"You're not taking her without me." Was she going to try to control me?

I put my hands in the air. "Great! Why don't you invite your husband so we can be one big happy family?"

"I don't know why I ever loved you!"

Her words made me laugh. She was full of shit. "I feel the same way," I lied.

I made it halfway down the driveway before my words started to haunt me. I couldn't do this with Kat. I couldn't tell her things to make myself feel better. We had to move forward, instead of dwelling on what we couldn't change.

I backed up my truck and got out, walking until we were face to face. "Take it back."

Her hands went to her hips as she held her ground. "No!"

I scratched my head, giving myself a second to think of what to say. "You see, I can't go to bed mad, so I'm not leaving until you take it back."

She crossed her arms and huffed. "I guess you're going to be standing here for a while then."

"You know, I could be a real dick right now if I wanted to be."

"Who said you aren't already?" Her cocked eyebrow made me want to smile. I missed this about her. I missed everything about her.

"Some things never change, I see."

"What's that supposed to mean?"

"You can't lie to my face. You never could."

Finally she surrendered. "Fine! I don't wish I never loved you. Are you happy now?"

That was enough for me to walk away. Above anything else, Kat was back in my life, and we had a child together. For the next fifty years she'd be stuck dealing with me whether she wanted to or not. "Our daughter is beautiful, Kat, just like I always knew our kids would be. Have her ready tomorrow. I'll be here at three thirty, and we're going out, with or without you."

My drive back to the base was thought consuming. I had a reason to live again.

Two reasons.

Kat and Brooklyn.

Chapter 30

It was difficult to sleep when I was so wired about meeting my daughter. I laid there all night staring up at the ceiling, wondering what I should do next. I was going to need to find a bigger place that I could bring her to. Eventually she'd stay overnight with me, so she'd need her own room. I'd have to get toys, and even clothes. I'd have to learn how to change diapers, and what little girls needed. I'd have to get special soaps, and shampoo that didn't burn her eyes. I'd need a car seat, and probably one of those strollers.

I needed to know when she was born, and what she'd want for her birthday. All of these ideas were popping in my head at once. It was both amazing and scary at the same time.

When the sun came up, I realized I'd spent most of the night worried. It was harder to go to my office when all I wanted to do was see my little girl again. Already I missed her.

While at my desk, I called my parents house. I don't know what I was planning to say because it happened so quick. I guess my conscious was making decisions for me. As soon as my mom got on the line I stuttered to find words to tell her what had happened. Instead of spilling the beans over a phone call, I decided it was best if I invited them to come visit. When we were all together, I'd let them meet their grand child. I'm sure they were going to have a ton of questions, mostly for Kat. I just needed to get her on board with the idea.

Later, I checked the internet for apartments and small houses. I talked to my commander about possibly moving into a bigger place on base and finally explained why. He gave me good advice, having been a dad himself. He even seemed to be sympathetic when I explained my whole situation.

By noon I was ready to explode. I kept playing with my keys, anxious to get in my truck and head over to see my girl. I wondered if I should have brought a gift this time, or maybe that was too much. I didn't want to seem like I was buying my way in.

By three twenty I was sitting in their driveway. Kat's husband Bobby came outside to greet me. "Sorry about last night. I won't barge in again. This transition needs to be more organized."

"I agree. I may have overreacted last night."

"I'm not here to cause problems in your marriage. I just want to know my daughter." I could tell this got to him; the fact that I'd called her mine. It was hard to put myself in his shoes. He'd been the only dad that child had known. Now I'd come into the picture and expected to have the title. It must have been killing him.

"I appreciate that." He looked away for a second. "Come on in. Katy's been sleeping for a couple hours. She had a rough night after you left. None of this has been easy for her."

"I know the feeling."

He led me inside to find B watching a show on television. She was dancing around not even paying any attention to us. "I'll go get her up."

It wasn't until a commercial came on that she turned to see me sitting there.

She wobbled from side to side, smiling, and then ran over and jumped on my lap. "Hey, pretty girl. Whoa. Careful." I held onto her as she started climbing up to remove my hat.

"Out." She pointed to the door then climbed down to show me something.

I followed her seeing she was looking at her swing set. "You want to go there?"

"Go. Go."

I picked up her and carried her outside. When I sat her down she ran over to the swing and looked in my direction. I lifted her in it and started pushing. She held onto the sides and smiled as the wind hit her face. Each time she laughed, so did I. She had that effect on me.

I heard the porch door closing and knew someone had come outside, but paid them no attention. I was too busy with my little girl to care about anything else. In fact, I could have spent my whole evening swinging her and been completely content. She was already everything to me, and I wanted her to know it.

"You're so pretty," I said as I continued pushing her higher.

Finally I heard the grass crunching behind me. One quick look showed me it was Kat. Her eyes were still swollen. I could tell she was struggling with everything that had transpired between us. "Hey. Sorry about that. I didn't get much sleep last night."

I laughed sarcastically. "You think I could sleep? Kat, I just found out that I have a kid.

Every aspect of my life is about to change. Sleep is the last thing that's on my mind."

For a second she stood next to me without saying anything. She just kept watching what I was doing. "So would it be easier if I drove since I have the car seat in my car already?"

I halted the swing and began to lift Brooklyn out. "Yeah if you don't mind."

When we got inside the car I sat her in the safety seat and felt overwhelmed. There was too much going on to know what went where. "I might need your help. I've never done this before."

Kat laughed at me as if anyone could have figured it out. "There's a lot of things you're going to have to learn." We both got into the front seats before Kat questioned me. "So where are we going?"

"Is there a park nearby?" I knew Brooklyn liked to swing, but other than that I was lost. She was right. I had a lot to learn.

"There are several. If you really want to see B smile, we should take her to the indoor play park. She gets a kick out of climbing through the tunnels and going down the slides."

It sounded like a plan, one that I could enjoy and maybe take her to when it was just the two of us. While Kat drove, I turned and talked to our daughter. It was a little uncomfortable being so close to her. For so long I'd wanted to hold her in my arms. For the past two days we'd been together, yet I hadn't hugged her once. I wasn't sure if I was okay with that. On one hand, I was angry as hell, on the other, I just wanted her in my life.

I think it was obvious I hadn't been around children when we walked inside of the play park. The sound of kids screaming as they ran around unattended made me want to hide. I cringe every time one would run by grabbing onto my pants, or stepping on my boots. They were like little terrorists, using their size to attack the larger enemy. Every bone in my body wanted to grab my little girl and protect her from their germ-filled hands.

Kat reached for our daughter, taking her out of my arms. "Come on sweet girl. You want to go play?"

"Mama, slide. I go slide."

I smiled when she spoke even though I was genuinely worried for her safety. "Have fun, little bug." I liked the sound of it.

"Bug? You nicknamed our daughter already?"

I shrugged and looked over at her, grinning cheek to cheek. She brought that out in me. In fact, It was hard to remember the last time something had made me so happy. "I couldn't help it. She's my little B."

My little girl made friends with two others quickly. She followed them around the play set, talking up a storm. I couldn't take my eyes off of her. She was the most beautiful child in the building by far, but probably the prettiest I'd ever seen in my life. She belonged on commercials with her chubby cheeks and little dimples. I was in awe of her.

When I realized we were sitting there so close, I knew we needed to talk. I couldn't avoid Kat, and she couldn't do the same to me. There were important issue that needed to be handled. "So, I had a lot to think about when I left last night. I think the first thing that needs to be addressed is my parents. Look, Kat, I don't care about my brother, but Mom and Dad need to meet her. I get that you're going to be mad, but I asked them to come visit next weekend. I hope you don't already have plans."

She seemed to take it pretty well. I watched her body language, trying to figure out what she was going to say so I could prepare myself. "I guess I'll talk to Bobby and see if we can drop her off to you. Are you able to baby proof your house? Do you even live in a house or an apartment?"

"I live on base for now. There's family housing available, and I filled out the forms while I was on shift this morning. If everything goes the way it should, I may be able to move

316

into something in the next seven days. I had to explain my situation to my commanding officer, but given the importance, he said he can pull some strings."

"So, you'd have a whole house?" Was she surprised that I could wipe my own ass by myself? What kind of question was that? Did she not think I could provide for my daughter?

"It's like a duplex. Two small houses connected. Some are one bedroom and some go up to three. I can also live off base, provided I can find something affordable and close. I'm not going to rush into anything. My parents won't care what my living conditions look like." That wasn't true. They'd care, but be fine if I was happy.

Without giving it a single thought Kat shocked me with her solution. "They can come to my house. Bobby still owns another house, so we'll go there for the weekend. The house is already baby proofed and B will be comfortable."

"Wow. That's pretty generous of you. Are you doing this to kiss my ass?" I wanted to know how far she would go to get on my good side again. It was plain as day that she missed me in her life. I knew it because I felt the same way. As hard as I tried to stay mad at her, my heart was taking over, and that could only lead us down a road that neither of us were prepared for.

"Is it working?" She questioned.

At first I laughed, shaking my head at her presumption. Then our eyes met, and nothing could have prepared me for the vibes she was giving off.

I smiled at her while staring into her eyes. "I'm still mad, but some of the things you said last night were true. Knowing you were pregnant and alone would have been torture for me. It doesn't make what you did right, but I don't know if I could have handled not being able to get to you."

It was the best feeling to have my own daughter come up and take my hand. "Pay wit me."

I followed her like a lost puppy. Climbing and jumping through things I had no business being in. I didn't care. The employees saw my fatigues and let it go. They weren't about to tell a soldier he couldn't be with his child.

After she found her friends again, my little bug went off to play in smaller tubes. I found Kat sitting on the same bench as before. "Is she always so playful?"

"Unless she's in grumpy mood. Then she won't want anything to do with you."

What happened next wasn't on purpose. All I was trying to do was adjust the way I was sitting. Accidentally I placed my hand on top of hers and electricity rushed through me, awakening the dormant places that had been holding out so long for her. Our eyes met again and this time I knew she was feeling it too.

I tugged my hand away as fast as possible. "Sorry."

Kat peered forward. "Yeah, so that was weird."

I cleared my throat, trying to figure out what to say next. "Your husband seems nice. Does he make you happy?"

"He'd do anything for me." I wished it weren't true. I wanted her to say he was a loser, so that I had a reason to still want her.

"So, you're happy? Well, before all this happened I mean."

I couldn't stop staring at her as I awaited her reply. She captivated me, just like she always could. It was effortless, the connection between us. "Yeah, I guess. We've had our problems. Bobby had an accident at work and his legs were both broken. It's taken him a long time to be able to get himself mobile again."

"I guess I just want to know if he gives you everything you need, because for all the years that I've been away, I somehow believed that I was the only person that could be all that you wanted."

When our daughter ran by chasing a little boy it made me chuckle. "Do you remember how I used to follow you like that?"

"I remember chasing you." Her answer made me beam.

"Kat, all of this feels like some sort of out of body experience to me. I've got a two-year-old daughter and you're married to someone else. I feel like at any second I'm going to wake up and it will have all been a wonderful dream."

Without removing her eyes from mine, she spoke. All I wanted to do was reach over and touch her lips. I wanted to remember what it felt like to touch her again. "It's real. I've been living this life for almost three years now. I can assure you that you're not going to wake up."

I leaned in close, so that I couldn't be heard by anyone else. "Then I just need to know one thing."

"What?"

"You're not going to like it. It's just really been bothering me." It was probably a terrible conversation to have in a play park, but I hadn't been given a rule book.

"Say it."

"Did you ever consider having an abortion?" I put my hand up to keep her from prematurely answering. "I'm asking because you were all alone. You knew I wasn't coming home for years and that you'd have to raise the child yourself. I keep trying to make sense of everything. I won't be mad if you did. Looking at what we'd created was the most fulfilling kind of feelings I've ever experienced, but I get that you were alone and scared. So tell me, Kat. How did you know you were going to be okay?"

She responded so quickly that I knew it was never an option for her. "I never considered terminating the pregnancy, Brooks." She glanced at our child for a second. "Because no matter where you were, I knew I had a piece of you growing inside of me. Giving that up was never a question." Our fixed eyes made the hair stand up on my arms. It was intense. "That night we spent together in that hotel room was the second best night of my life."

Her words meant the world to me. She couldn't know how worried I'd been that she'd regretted the night we spent together. "What was your first?"

"The day I gave birth to your daughter."

That did me in. That moment when the truth crossed her lips I was done for. I peered down at the floor, reached over and put my hand on her knee, knowing damn well I was crossing a line. "I can't stop loving you, Kat," I whispered.

I'd said it and she'd heard me. When I turned to look into her eyes again I was taken back by all the emotions overwhelming me.

This woman was my everything. I existed because of her.

Kat sat there stunned that I'd been so open about it. Maybe she was shocked that after I discovered her secret, I still had such strong feelings for her. That's honestly how I knew it was real. Kat was never an infatuation for me. It had been love from the very beginning; the kind that doesn't ever go away.

Chapter 31

It was so easy catching up with Kat, so long as we avoided discussing our own feelings. That topic was off limits even though I had to fight from expressing them on several occasions. It was hard being so close to her and not wanting to touch her.

Kat made it easier. When things felt like they were becoming intense she would change the subject. If anyone could tame my beastly parts it was her. She knew exactly how to lock them up and threaten them if they wanted to come out. To keep our conversations mundane we'd bring up silly things, or talk about old times.

She told me about her friends, church, and even a little about her marriage. I refused to let my guard down because I knew I'd start suggesting things that were inappropriate. Even though I wasn't going to lie about them, I didn't want to cause trouble for Kat. She seemed to have a good marriage, and I was no home wrecker, even if I thought she was mine in the first place.

Little B wanted chicken nuggets and fries, and I was determined to give her whatever her pretty little heart desired. We set out to have a nice supper together. The whole time I kept smiling because we were eating like a family. While I kept our daughter out of the high chair to be next to me, Kat made sure she was on her best behavior, by promising ice cream as a reward.

Seeing her as a mother was something I'd never taken the time to imagine. She was so good at it, almost like it was natural. I knew she'd had two years of experience, but her patience was impressive, especially since neither of us had ever been around small children before.

At one point she kept checking her watch. I asked Kat if we were taking too long, but she insisted that everything was fine. Every once in a while we'd catch each other gazing. I was so happy to be around them that I wasn't worried about anyone seeing us that might know her. We weren't doing anything wrong, but having a meal with our child. At some point, it wasn't going to be a secret who I was to them.

Our little girl couldn't make it through her meal without starting to doze. I paid the check and helped get her in the car before we started on our way back to her house. B feel asleep shortly after being buckled in. Even while she slept I found her stunning.

The closer we got to Kat's house, the more things were bothering me. There was a lot I needed to get off my chest, and I couldn't do it with people around. I pulled over on the side of the road and threw the vehicle in park. "What is it?" She asked.

"You know, I kept your letters, even after I moved back home and found out you had a family. I don't know why, but I couldn't come to terms with throwing them away, because it felt like I was throwing away our love." I brushed the back of my hand across her cheek while looking at her. "I don't know what I'm supposed to be feeling Kat, but when I'm with you, I feel like nothing has changed between us. Now we have a little girl. I mean, Jesus Christ, we made a baby together. She's so freaking perfect, too. I look at her and I see both of us. I can't be angry with you because all I wanted for so long was to be a part of your life again. I get that you're married, and he makes you happy. I can respect that. I won't push or ask you for something that you can't give me, but I have to know the truth. I have to know if what you said to me in all those letters was true. Do I still have your heart, or did you already give it to someone else? When you look at me do you see me as a threat or is it something entirely different? Kat, I can't see you every single day and not want to touch you. It's been one and I'm already freaking out because I'm having to take you home. Just tell me to back off."

She reached over and put her hand on my arm. I could tell she was in deep thought. Her eyes closed, and I half expected her to lean forward and kiss me. "I'm not afraid of you Brooks. I know you'd never hurt me. You love her already, I can see it in your eyes. I've watched you holding her and falling for her. Somehow she already knows you're special."

"You're avoiding my question."

"You don't want the truth."

I looked away, feeling as if she'd given her heart away. It hurt to imagine. "I think you just said it."

I knew it was time to take her home. I couldn't sit there and wish for something that was never going to come true. I didn't speak again until we reached the house. "So tomorrow, can I come by the same time?"

"Yeah. It's Sunday. We usually go to church, but we're back before one. You can come over anytime after that." She was very rehearsed, almost professional as she spoke to me.

"And you're going to tell Bobby about my parents coming?" I didn't want another fight happening because of me. This time it wouldn't be my fault since she'd offered.

"Yes, but just so you know, the house is mine. I had it built when I was separated from Bobby. It was part of my trust money. I own it free and clear."

I was happy for her. Her parents would have wanted that. "I should have known you'd spend it wisely. Your mom and dad would be happy about that."

"I think so too. They'd want B to have a home that she loved. I always loved where we lived. The only hard part was watching another child moving in after they were gone. Hopefully B won't have to deal with something so tragic."

I agreed, "Yeah. You don't have to worry about me going anywhere. Due to my injury, I'm no use in the field. All I do nowadays is train recruits on procedures. I feel more like a school teacher than a soldier."

"You're safe. That's all I care about." It felt nice to hear she cared.

She looked away, probably so I couldn't read her like I was constantly trying to do. "It's going to be nice seeing you again every day. I really missed you."

She touched my arm again. "I missed you, too."

It was hard to pull in the driveway knowing that I was saying goodbye. A part of me wanted to take them hostage and keep them for myself in some undisclosed location. I know it sounded crazy, but my mind wasn't really on a sane level.

After I managed to unhook my little girl, I hugged her close to my body, kissing her on the head. "I love you, bug."

Kat was quiet as I handed my sleeping beauty over to her. It was hard knowing they were going inside with her husband. It should have been me, and I think she knew it too. I couldn't put my finger on it, but I swore something was off about her. I kept chalking it up to us having had a nice night together, but she was giving off vibes that she didn't want to go inside and deal with her husband. I wondered if he'd said something about this whole situation that rubbed her the wrong way. Knowing Kat like I did, I figured she'd tell me if it was important enough to be concerned about.

I looked toward her while wishing I was still holding my daughter. Our eyes met one more time, and I couldn't help from keeping them fixed there. God, I wanted to kiss her. I wanted to be the one that she called when she was having a bad day, and the shoulder she cried on when she just couldn't take anymore stress.

I didn't mean to dislike her husband, but he was taking my place. He was doing my job, and I'm not just talking about in the bedroom. He had every bit of her that counted, well every bit except one thing, and as the words came out of her mouth I suddenly knew why she seemed so worried about going inside.

"I meant every word that I wrote in those letters, Brooks. I could never completely give my heart away, not when it was with you the whole time." Kat's last statement to me wasn't just a shocker. It had left me wondering what I could do to make it all possible for us. She still loved me, so much that she'd just admitted her husband didn't have that part of her, because it belonged to me.

I stood there wondering what I should do or say. Obviously we were in a complicated situation. She was married by law. I'd promised the man that I wouldn't interfere in their marriage, yet every part of me wanted to. I didn't know how to handle it.

I watched her walk inside before getting into my truck. Even after I'd pulled out of the driveway my mind was still on those words. I considered myself a strong man, but it took more willpower than I had to not turn back around and take what was mine.

As a kid, I'd always had to share. Doing so caused me to lose the one thing in life I wanted for myself. I'd been down this road before, and it had ended badly. While driving I wondered if my mistake was fighting for her, or doing nothing at all.

To say I was high on life would have been an understatement. I was in love with two girls, one of which I helped create. Thinking about them made me smile. I felt alive, and overwhelmed with optimism. My future would always consist of my daughter. Even if I couldn't be with Kat the way I wanted, nothing would prevent me from spending every second with my little bug, not even her husband. That child had my name, and I knew there was no way Kat would allow him to put a stop to my visitations. Still, I felt like the next topic we talked about was going to have to be custody. I didn't want a big court battle, but I felt as if I needed to have it documented. If this guy felt threatened, there was no telling what he'd do to keep me away. The worst part of it all was the fact that he needed to feel that way, because it was clear after one day I was definitely a threat, even to myself.

I knew it was wrong, but I still wanted her for myself. Married or not.

I wouldn't cross any lines, but that didn't mean I wasn't thinking about it.

Chapter 32

The next morning I was high on life. I'd been up for a couple hours, and my whistling was beginning to get on everyone's nerves. They couldn't understand what it felt like to be this close to heaven. I was so excited about spending the whole afternoon with my girls. This time I was going to take them on a tour of the base. I wanted Kat to know that B would be safe when she was with me overnight. If I needed help, I'd have it. This was all going to be okay.

When my phone started to ring in my pocket I put it up to my ear before answering.

"Sergeant Valentine speaking."

I heard her laughing right away. Apparently she got a kick out of me being professional. "Hey, it's me, Katy."

"You don't have to say your name. I don't have a slew of women calling me on this number." I didn't mean it to be anything more than a joke, but when the line remained quiet I wondered if she was considering that I did.

"Oh. Well, I'm calling to tell you that today won't be good to come over. Bobby made plans, and I didn't know about it."

This was terrible news. My day was ruined. How was I going to be able to make it another day without them?

"Man, I got off early in hopes to spend extra time there." I paused and tried to be nice about it. "It's cool. I'll figure out something else to do. I guess I can always start looking for places. My roommate in the barracks isn't going to want me bringing a kid to spend the night."

"I'm sorry, Brooks. I don't want you to feel like I'm keeping her from you. I'd never do that."

"It's fine. I know you wouldn't keep her from me." Kat sounded weird. It got me wondering if something else was going on.

"So, I better get going. It's early and I need to get B ready for Sunday school."

"Can you take a picture and send it to this number? I'd love to be able to show the guys." I was hoping the picture would be one with her in it too. Married or not, she was still the mother of my child. Our child. God, I loved the sound of it.

"Sure."

"So, I guess I need to hang up now?" I could have spent the whole day talking to her like teenagers do.

"What do you do on your days off?" Her question made me really worry. She didn't want to stop talking, which could only mean one of two things. Either she missed me already, or someone was putting her up to cancelling our play date.

I decided to give her something to be jealous about, only because I loved hearing her react. Yeah, it was wrong. She needed to stay focused on her husband, but I knew what buttons to push, and still felt like I had some pent up anger lingering toward her. I mean, she did keep my child from me. Making her jealous was a good payback because I knew how mad she'd get at me for doing it. That also meant more phone time for me while she tried to figure out if I was telling the truth or not. "I hook up with random chicks that love a man in a uniform." Then I realized just how naughty I was being. It was important for me to be a friend to her, not get my jollies over her making her freak out. We weren't teenagers anymore. I had to act like a grown-up would. "I'm kidding, Kat. Although, there are women that would pretty much do anything for a man in fatigues, I only have eyes for one girl."

"Stop it, Brooks. Today is not a good day to joke around." She was so short, almost rude. I'd hit a nerve.

"Sorry. Are you alright? You seem kind of snappy. Did your being with me last night cause problems with you and your husband? Was it what you said last night?"

The line got quiet. I almost started to ask if she was still on the other end of the call. "Talk to me. Am I overstepping? If I'm causing you problems, we can make other arrangements. I mean, I'll miss being able to see you, but I understand."

"I'm fine." That answer was way too short.

"I know it's been a while, but I'm pretty sure there's something you're not telling me."

I waited for her to tell the truth, but she refused by simply pretending I hadn't asked.

"Would it be okay if we just talked tomorrow? I've got to go get ready for church."

"Yeah, sure. I'll call you in the morning."

It was pretty upsetting for me to end the call when all I wanted to do was hold on for as long as possible.

I'd no sooner got up to refill my coffee and spoke to petty officer about paperwork when my cell phone started ringing in my office. I rushed inside to pick it up, noticing the same number calling again.

I answered it formally to get a laugh out of her.

"Sergeant Valentine."

Kat was crying as she spoke my name. "Brooks."

"Kat? What's wrong?"

Her voice was so shaky. Right away I was worried something was terribly wrong. My mind went back to when Mullins was explaining how he woke up and his daughter was dead in the bed beside him. I didn't know anything about SIDS, but wondered if this call was going to be the nail in my coffin. I couldn't handle losing what I just been given.

Kat's response left me relieved, but also concerned at the same time. "If something happens to me, I want you to take her far away from here."

"What are you talking about?" She needed to explain what was going on.

Before she was able to explain I heard Bobby in the background. "Is that him? You think he can save you?"

I was on high-alert, searching the desk for my keys when Kat answered him. "Please don't hurt me."

I heard her crying, begging him to let go of her hair. I knocked an entire cup of coffee onto the floor as I fetched my key ring and darted for the exit while keeping the phone up to my ear to hear what was going on. The whole time I kept repeating that I was coming.

Kat continued to beg him to stop. Her cries only made me drive faster. When I got to her he was going to be sorry. No man should ever put a hand on a woman, but the fact that it was Kat, my Kat, made me want to use all of my trained skills on him. "Bobby, please. I didn't do anything wrong. You don't want to hurt me, I know you don't."

In the background I could hear him starting to cry though I didn't let my foot off the gas pedal.

I heard shuffling next, and then the sound of our daughter, who was right in the middle of it. "Mama, I scared."

Bobby's voice was close again. "We need to talk."

"Not while you're acting like this," Kat responded.

There was a loud noise before he spoke again, raising his voice so I was able to hear it without straining. "You see what you make me do? That pretty boy comes anywhere near you and you're goin' to be the one to pay, you hear me, Katy?"

That was it. I was going to kill him with my bare hands, just as soon as I knew my girls were never going to be near him again. He'd lost his privileges as far as I was concerned. If Kat wanted to deal with that kind of shit she was going to have to fight me in court because I'd die before I let my child grow up in that sort of environment.

Then the line went dead.

I flew down the highway, praying to God that my girls were okay. While my mind was in a million places, I wondered how many times he'd done this sort of thing to her. I wanted to know if he'd ever abused her before I came into the picture. Was he reacting on rage from me being alive? Was this all because Brooklyn's real father was stepping into her life?

The worst part of this was the fact that there was nothing he could do. That child was mine, and there was no way I'd stand back and let someone else raise her. From what I'd just heard on the phone, there was no possible way I'd ever feel comfortable with her being alone with him again. Call me old fashioned, or even over-protective, but it wasn't happening with my child. I didn't care what I had to do to make sure of it.

By the time I pulled up at Kat's house a police cruiser was in the driveway. Bobby was outside talking to the officer while Kat was obviously somewhere in the house. I didn't even look in his direction as I made my way up the stairs to go inside. For all I knew he could have come after me, not that he'd be able to do much. I could take a man down with my eyes closed. Just because I had an injured hand and arm didn't mean I'd lose a fight. There were tactics I'd been taught to do that would send a person to their knees. One punch to the throat could end his life.

Before walking through the door, I turned back to look at him. It was obvious he was hurting. I wanted to feel bad for the man, but I couldn't. He'd crossed a line; one I'd never be able to forgive.

Once the door was shut behind me, I pulled her close to me, holding her at the shoulders. "How long has he been doing this to you? Is this because of me?" I was so angry, and above all concerned for them.

Kat sat down on the couch and started to cry. "No. It's not you. It happened before. That's why we separated. He got help, and I didn't let him come back until after he had his accident. Things were better for a long time, but now he's so jealous and I don't know how to make him believe that there's nothing going on between us. He thinks I've been sleeping with you."

I stood there clenching my jaw while B ran over and clung to my legs. I picked her up to make sure she was okay. "Has he ever touched her?"

Kat shook her head but avoided eye contact with me. "No. Never. I don't know that he would. Bobby only takes out his anger on me."

I pointed right at her, making sure she was paying attention "He won't lay a damn hand on you again, Kat. I can guarantee you that."

"You can't get involved, Brooks. It makes things worse."

I kneeled down in front of her, with our daughter still attached to my lap. "Don't you get it? I'm already involved. You might be married to him on paper, but that doesn't make you his."

"He said if I ran to you he'd hurt me."

I stood up. "Pack a bag for each of you. You're coming with me tonight and we'll figure out what to do in the morning."

Kat just sat there. "I can't do that. This is my mess."

"She's my daughter, Kat. I might not have been around her that much, but she's my responsibility. I will kill him if he tries to hurt either one of you again."

She finally got off the couch. "That's exactly why I don't want you helping. I can't let you put yourself on the line for me. I've done enough harm to you. My marriage problems are something I have to deal with on my own. I shouldn't have even called you."

"But you did. You called me because you knew I'd show up. Pack a damn bag now. I'm not leaving here without you. Bobby knows a lot of people in this town. He'll be released in a few hours and where do you think he'll come looking first. Is this the first time you've had him arrested?"

She began crying even harder than before. "Yes."

"Then he's going to be more pissed." I peered down at my daughter, noticing she was paying close attention to my actions. "Tell Mama that she needs to listen to me."

"Yisten, Mama."

Kat couldn't argue. She knew I wasn't giving her another choice. We were leaving, and they weren't coming back until he was out of the picture.

Chapter 33

The whole time she was packing bags I kept watching out the window, making sure Bobby hadn't gotten a chance to call one of his friends to come intervene. It wouldn't have mattered. They wouldn't get past me, nor would they be able to talk Kat out of this decision. She was running on autopilot, because like it or not, she knew this was the end result. No man should ever lay a hand on a woman. Even if her mind wasn't made up, she knew I'd never let her live under such conditions. Before I'd been content to accept that she was married and committed to another man. It was difficult, but I had values. Now things had changed. No longer did I care about that legal binding document. He lost that privilege the moment he put his hands on her. There was going to be no forgiveness, or take backs.

After helping her switch over the car seat, and tossing their bags in the back, we were off to find them a safe place to sleep for the night. I had duty in the morning, so it was important to be close to base, since I didn't plan on leaving them alone for the rest of the night.

Kat was pretty quiet in the truck, and I didn't want to overstep anymore than I already had. She obviously needed time to let it all sink in. I had to consider that she'd spent the past two years with this guy. She had feelings for him. They'd shared a bed together.

As much as the thought made me cringe, it was reality. I hadn't been a saint myself. She did what she thought was right at the time. I could have let it eat me up inside or accept that it was in the past. After everything I'd been through, all I wanted was to be a part of my girl's lives.

The closest hotel to the base was one of the big chain names. Kat seemed shocked that I was taking her to such a nice hotel. I needed them to be comfortable. There was no telling how long she'd have to stay there. The cost wasn't even as bad as I expected since I got a military discount.

Once inside of the room, I watched her looking around outside. We turned on cartoons for little B. "Is this your favorite, baby?"

"I yike bunny." She pointed to the screen as a man in a rabbit costume hopped around. I rolled my eyes but acted just as excited when I turned to face her.

Out of the corner of my eye, I watched Kat. She was a nervous wreck. When she went into the bathroom I worried that she was getting sick.

"Brooks, can you come in here for a minute?"

I rushed in the bathroom, worried she felt dizzy or something worse.

I found her holding the back of her head. "What's wrong?"

"Look at my head and tell me how bad it is."

I looked down and moved her fingers to the side to get a better idea of the extent of the injury. Anger filled me when I imagined it all playing out. "Did he do this to you?"

She looked at me in the mirror reflection with tear-filled eyes. "Yes."

I wet a rag and started cleaning the area to get a better idea of how deep the gash was. "You're going to need at least one stitch. I can run on base and get a kit if you'd rather me do it here."

She turned around to face me, and right away I could tell she was embarrassed. "I'm so sorry I got you into this."

I winced and shook my head. "Just stop with the apologies. We've both got shit that we wish we could take back. I don't care what you've done. All I care about is giving our daughter a good life. Whether we're together or not, we're still a team. We're always going to be a team, from now on. Do you understand?"

She twisted to lean her weight on the vanity. "I hear you loud and clear."

"Good. I'm going to run over to the base. I'll be back in a half hour to get that head of yours cleaned up. Do you need me to pick up anything? How about milk for B? Will she need anything special?"

B was still sitting perfectly on the bed, completely absorbed in the children's program. "Hey, sweetie. Do you want something to eat? Are you hungry?"

"Can you find her a can of fruit or something like that at your commissary?"

He smiled. "Does she like bananas and apples? We've got plenty of them."

"Yeah. She loves them."

"I'll get some milk and fruit and bring it back with me. Sit tight. I'll be back soon."

I was only in a hurry because I wanted to get back to them. Leaving them alone was never the plan. They were my responsibility now whether the law stated it or not.

Kat caught me before I could leave. "Brooks, wait!"

"Thanks for this." I wish she knew that she didn't need to thank me. This was my purpose in life. Taking care of her was one thing I knew how to do right.

"I'll be back. Take a nice bath and get that wound cleaned. I don't want any bacteria in it when I stitch it up."

When the elevator doors closed I saw her watching me. As soon as I got outside I lost it. I beat my hand on my steering wheel while driving the short distance to base. I wanted to kill him for hurting her. Seeing her wound, the blood, and the way she cringed when I touched it, only gave me more reason to seek him out and get retribution. He was the enemy now, and I'd been trained to take care of that type of person.

It was obvious that I was losing my composure. When I reached my room I took one look at my friend and knew it was important to calm down. "What's up with you?" He asked.

"I don't have time to explain. Toss me that bag. I'm going to be staying somewhere else tonight."

"Did something happen, Brooks? Are you in trouble?"

I shook my head while packing the bag with my kit and then some clothes. "I'm fine. It's my daughter and her mother. Her husband used her as a punching bag. Apparently it's been going on for while. This time I put a stop to it."

"Jesus, is she okay?"

"She's got a nice sized gash in her head. I'm going to do my best to stitch it myself. She doesn't want to leave the hotel to go to a hospital."

"If you need anything you've got my number. It sounds like you're knee deep in drama. Didn't you just find out about this kid the other day?"

I turned to face him, nodding at the same time. "Yeah. It's a long story; one too long to explain tonight. All you need to know is that Kat and I have a long history. We grew up together, under the same roof actually. There isn't anything I wouldn't do to protect her. I need to jet. I'll check back in the morning. I've got duty."

"Alright, man. See you then."

I was able to grab everything that B would need if she were to get hungry or want a drink before heading back to the hotel. In all honesty it felt so good to be on my way to spend the night with them. I wasn't thinking about it on some sexual level. This was about spending time with my girls, keeping them safe, and reminding them that I'd never let anything bad happen.

When I entered the room again, I saw B on the bed. She'd fallen asleep to her show and was still in the same position as when I left her. I stood there for a second taking in how cute she was. Cuddling up next to her was something I'd cherish. I still couldn't believe we'd made something so perfect.

I could hear Kat sniffling in the bathroom. The sound of water splashing let me know she'd taken my advice and gotten a hot bath. I cracked open the door and heard her adjusting. "It's just me."

She'd tried to put rags over herself to prevent me from looking at her naked body. I found it cute.

"Do you mind?" She asked.

"No, I don't mind at all. It's nothing I haven't seen before." That was the truth. I'd memorized every inch of her a long time ago.

She threw a wet rag at my face. I caught it in the air. "Go away, you perv!"

I left the room laughing at her. At least she seemed in better spirits.

While Kat got herself out of the tub, I crawled on the bed next to my daughter and watched her sleeping so peaceful, as if she had nothing in the world to worry about. I wanted her whole life to be like this; innocent and sweet. I stared at her blonde hair and those long eyelashes. Her cheeks were so full, and I could see a hint of a dimple even as her face seemed relaxed. It was amazing to me how two people could make something so perfect. She had my heart from the first moment, but now I knew she had a lot more than that. I loved Kat. It was real and true. It always had been, but this child, she owned me. In such a short amount of time she'd become my whole world. When I woke up in the morning her face was the first I saw. Kat had been right to keep the truth from me because I would have attempted to swim across the ocean to be with them. Nothing would have stopped me.

When Kat walked out of the bathroom in only a towel, she immediately caught my attention. I tried so hard to only stare at her face, but it was quite impossible, given the situation.

"Did you rob the base?" She asked while pointing to my bags.

I kept staring, like a peeping Tom. "I needed to be able to change in the morning before my shift."

"You're staying?" Did she really just ask me that?

She ducked down and started rummaging through her luggage for something to put on. A part of me wanted to tell her clothes weren't important, but there was a time and a place and this wasn't one of them. I fetched a shirt out of my bag since I knew it was the last thing I'd stuck in there. "Here, just put this on. I don't sleep with it on anyway."

I think I saw her smile, just a for second. "Thanks."

Kat went into the bathroom to change, leaving me on the bed wondering why she couldn't just do it front of me. I mean, she had nothing to hide. We'd bathe together when we were little, and since then I'd seen everything she had to offer.

While she was in the bathroom she spoke. "So, are you sure you know how to stitch?"

"Yeah, I learned it in basic. I need you to get under the light and let me look at it. I may need to clip a piece of hair to be able to get a clean stitch." I grabbed my kit and some whiskey out of my bag and watched her look down at me. "You're probably going to want to drink this."

"Seriously? I'll get drunk." It was extremely difficult to focus on anything but her in that t-shirt.

"I'll keep you from stripping and handing out your number to strangers. Just take a few swigs and lay on your stomach."

I could tell when I first touched her with the needle that she was in pain. I hate being the one to hurt her, but this was necessary. She needed to get sewn up to prevent infection.

When I was finished I rolled her over and kissed her forehead. "All fixed."

She smiled, probably because she was glad it was over. "Thanks."

We were both still sitting on the same bed. In this moment I felt like I needed some things answered. "Bobby knew you were still in love with me, didn't he?"

She never looked away when she answered, making her words even more powerful. "Yeah, he did."

This was another reason why I wasn't going anywhere.

Chapter 34

I couldn't believe she'd told her husband how she felt about me. It was no wonder he felt so threatened when I was around. "Kat, you really told him you loved me?"

"It was never a secret. He knew it when he met me. He was the person that held me when I cried about you. He was there for me when I had B, knowing that I didn't love him. He asked me to marry me and said that he knew I wasn't over you. After some time I came to love Bobby, but he'll never be you. I thought I learned that after the Branch fiasco, but

352

obviously I can't learn from my mistakes, because here I am married to another man that I'm trying to convince myself to fall in love with."

I knew she'd struggled. We both had. It was hard to imagine my pain and think of hers.

"I'm not the saint you picture me to be, Kat. I've seen and done things that I'm not proud of. Living in another country was hard. Sometimes I needed the comfort of a woman. It never meant much to me, but sometimes it helped with my sleep problems. You keep punishing yourself for the things you've done, but I don't see those things are all that bad. You ran from the family because you thought you tore us all apart. Don't you see that it wasn't you? It was me. I did it. I was the one that took you to my bed that night. It was selfish, and could have been done the right way, years before. I wanted to hurt Branch. I wanted to shove your love for me right in his face, because after all that time, I was tired of him having what should have been mine all along. I knew that being with you would ruin your engagement and I went for it out of spite."

This conversation was getting deep. I was imagining it going to other places, but kept telling myself that it was way too soon to assume she'd even be okay with it.

"I suppose this all could have been avoided if we knew how to communicate with each other." She didn't know how right she was. Not a day went by where I didn't regret my decisions.

I laughed at my stupidity. "Yeah. Probably."

I took her hand and kissed it, gently, becoming overwhelmed by the simplest touch. Immediately she responded to it. "Brooks, what do you want to happen now? I mean, once I figure out how to get a separation and file for divorce, which I am sure I'm doing, what do you want to happen? Can we be best friends again after all this time?" There it was. She'd used the friend word. I couldn't take it. I'd waited far too long to have all of her, and it was time she knew exactly where I stood.

I got closer, placing my arm to be around her shoulder. Our eyes were fixed on each other. "Kat, I can't be your friend. I'm sorry, but I can't be that person anymore." She burst into tears. I took her chin and lifted it so she'd look at me again. "What are you crying for?"

"I don't know. I guess I keep feeling like even after everything we've been through, we could run off and live happily ever after. It's stupid, I know. I thought that after the past few days we'd never want to let each other go again."

It was hard to hide the smile forming on my face because it was huge. "I don't want to be your friend because I need more than that. Open your eyes woman. I want to be your everything. I always have."

Kat's arms came around my back while her head plopped down on my chest. "Why didn't you just say that? I thought you didn't want anything to do with me."

"Jesus. I'm alone in a hotel with you and our daughter. Can you name one other place in the world I'd rather be?" I kissed her head and kept my face there. "I'll wait as long as it takes to get things sorted out with Bobby. As of right now, whose name is on the birth certificate as B's father?"

"You."

That was beyond shocking, yet another reason why the guy was freaking out. All along he'd known there was nothing stopping me from being a part of my child's life. "That's good to know."

"I told you that I never kept it a secret from anyone here."

Just then B woke up, looking around the room as if she was scared. "Mama."

I watched Kat hold her arms out. Our daughter made her way over and climbed on top of her. We were all three so close together. In spite of the situation, I was in heaven. This was what I'd survived to see. This was what I fought so hard to come home to.

"B do you know who this is?" Kat asked.

She nodded.

"Do you know his name?"

"Books."

We both laughed. "Sweetie, Brooks is your daddy."

B was confused. Her face curled up like she was about to cry. It broke my heart. "No. He not."

I wouldn't let this break me. I had her whole life to convince her of who I was. "Come here, kiddo. Let me show you something."

I carried her into the bathroom and stood her up on the vanity. First I pointed to Kat in the mirror, then myself, and finally her. "Mommy, Daddy, and B."

She laughed at us, pointed to herself, and said "B", then to Kat. "Mama." When she looked over at me it was obvious she was trying to figure it all out. Then she poked me in the eye while looking back in the mirror at herself. "Mine."

I couldn't believe she recognized me as having the same color eyes as her. I guess she'd known that neither Kat nor Bobby resembled her the way I did. I tried hard to not get choked up. After all, she was only a toddler. By morning she'd forget that we had the same colored eyes. "You're mine, little bug. I'm your daddy."

"Daddy?" B was obviously wondering what was going on. I wasn't even sure she knew what a daddy was.

I did my best to smile and look at Kat. "It's going to take her a while to get used to it."

"She needs to know the truth though." Her words were like music for my soul. This was so real. I still couldn't grasp it all.

B rested her head against my chest. I felt like she was giving me reassurance even though I knew she didn't understand. "How about we take it day by day and let B figure it out herself? I'm not going anywhere, Kat. We're going to raise her together whether you want to stay friends or get married. It's up to you."

Kat wrapped her arms around the both of us. "I don't deserve this," she whispered.

"You're getting it anyway, so shut up and be happy. You're going to have a lot of bad days coming your way. No matter what, I'll be there." It was a promise I intended to keep.

As the hours passed I enjoyed spending alone time with both of my girls, but mostly B. I got her set up on my iPad so she could enjoy her favorite shows without commercials. We laid there together like lifelong friends while Kat sat watching. Every once in a while I'd look over and see her smiling as if we were captivating.

After we ordered room service Kat's phone began ringing. My stomach knotted up because I had a good feeling I knew who was going to be on the other end of the call. "Just answer it, Kat. He can't hurt you."

Kat rolled her eyes before putting it on speaker. "Hello?"

"Really, Katy? This is how you're going to fuckin' be? I'm tellin' you right now, you better be home when I get there."

She closed her eyes while responding to his madness. "It's my house and you're not welcome there anymore. I want you out, Bobby. I've taken pictures of what you did to me this time, and I even had to get a stitch in my head. I'm done with you hurting me for things I didn't do."

"Don't even go there. You're with him right now, aren't ya?"

"That's none of your business. I want a divorce, and I'm not changing my mind. I never should have given you a second chance. I should have known you wouldn't change."

"Bitch, I ain't givin' you a divorce, and I sure as hell ain't lettin' you take that little girl from me."

"You don't have a choice, Bobby. She's not yours. If I want to keep her from you I can, and you know it's true. She's got her daddy's name on that birth certificate. Now, if I were you, I'd think long and hard about what you say to me from here on out. I'd like to eventually be able to come to a visitation agreement with you, provided that you go back to anger management and get help. If you try to harm me, in any way, my offer is off the table. I'll make sure you never see her again."

"This ain't over!" The click let us know he's hung up. I didn't want to mention that he wasn't going to have visitation, not anymore. Kat needed to calm down before we got into that discussion.

When it looked like she was about to puke I took both of her hands into mine. "Come here." I pulled her into a hug. "You're safe, Kat. I've got you."

She put her arms behind my back and clung to me for support. "Please don't ever let go."

It was obvious the call had her shaken up. All I was able to do was be there when she needed me. I'd do whatever she needed, because whether she wanted it or not, I was in this with her. Nothing would tear us apart.

While Kat sat back down, I started reading a book to B. I didn't want her seeing her mother so freaked out. It was probably silly, but I'd change my voice to sound like different characters. My daughter giggled each time, making me happy to continue. "Again," she requested.

I reached over with one arm, keeping a tight hold on Kat, while I read the story over and over to B. I was getting so used to calling her that. I liked it, but not as much as being able to bond with her this way, while keeping Kat from losing her shit.

After nearly reading the book until my eyes burned, I stood to stretch. B began jumping on the bed, almost falling off several times. "Don't do that. You're going to hurt yourself, bug. How about we go for a ride and let Mama get some rest?"

She shook her head. "Bye byes."

I got her seated in a chair with wheels, kissed Kat on the head, and pushed B out of the door. Right before it closed I gave Kat strict orders. "Take a nap. I'm going to tire her out and hit the snack machine. I'll bring you up a soda."

I honestly didn't know if she'd listen to me, but it was obvious she was exhausted. While we rode the elevator and explored the hotel, I worried about Kat. I wondered if she was rethinking her decision to leave Bobby. I thought about how indecisive she'd always been in the past. As much as it would hurt me, I knew I had to prepare for the worst, just in case it became my reality. I wanted to believe that all this time she was mine to keep, but it hadn't even been twenty-four hours.

What Kat needed to understand was that I wasn't going to give up this time. Nope, I planned on sticking around, being the best father my child could have.

B pointed to the vending machine. "Candy!" She knew how to say that word clearly.

"Daddy's going to get you whatever you want." I hadn't realized I called myself that until she turned around and looked at me. She said nothing while staring into my eyes. I wondered if I should address it or leave it be. Finally after a few seconds I pointed to the machine. "Okay, tell me what you want."

She pointed to at least five things. I kept shoving dollars in, hoping I pushed the right buttons. It wasn't like she understood the word patience.

By the time I was done I had almost one of everything in the machine. "You're mother is going to kill me for buying all this junk, kiddo."

She clapped her hands as if she was amused by my statement. I got a kick out of being with her. It was so funny because I'd never let myself think that I could have a child. It had been some distant fantasy. Now that she was in my life, I couldn't imagine a different path, and I didn't want one either.

Chapter 35

"Hey Mama. We're back," I announced as we came back into the room with all sorts of goodies.

Kat sat up in the bed and smiled though I could tell she'd been crying again. "I see that. Did you get everything they had?"

"We didn't know which one you'd want." I scattered all the items on the bed in front of her, watching B's excited to the vast selection.

Kat covered her mouth, giggling. "We'll never be able to eat all of this, and she'll never go to sleep."

I tickled B until she screamed and then gave her a second to calm down. "Again," she requested. I repeated the process, loving the way it sounded to hear her laughing and happy.

Kat opened the package of peanut butter cups and took a bite. "This is so good."

"Two matching cups, but you only get one." I opened my mouth so she could feed me while I was preoccupied. What I said to her had meaning. A long time ago, back in high school, I'd written her a little note to go with her candy. I wondered if she'd remember, but from the look on her face I could tell she had.

"What's wrong?"

"Do you remember when we were in school and you left the peanut butter cups for me?" Obviously! That's why I made the comment. Was she seriously just figuring this all out?

"One cup," I corrected.

"Was that note some cryptic way of you telling me to choose you?"

DUH!

"Maybe," I answered while still giving B all my attention.

She shoved me. "Why couldn't you just say it to me, instead of leaving me messages that made no sense?"

I had to laugh. She should have been able to figure me out back then. It would have saved us all this grief. "Because I wanted you to choose on your own, not because I persuaded it.

Little hints along the way couldn't hurt. Not that it ever helped anyway. You were too damn stubborn to think that what you were doing was wrong, or who I should say?"

"Brooks! Cut it out."

Kat got up and walked to the bathroom. I liked seeing her wearing my shirt. It was another reminder that she was so close to being all mine, finally after so long.

I heard her talking to herself when I stood up to check on her. "Jesus woman, you're lucky he doesn't go running the other direction." Outside of the room I began laughing. She obviously didn't realize how thin the walls were.

I didn't hear her approaching and was shocked when she opened the door to find me standing there spying. "I think you're beautiful."

Her shocked face let me know that she had no clue I was listening. "I think all that sugar is going to your head."

I allowed her to walk by me without another snarky comment, but that didn't mean I wasn't thinking of one.

Kat covered B up, who seemed to be calm even though she'd eaten some chips. "Love you, B," she whispered as she kissed her.

I made my way to the opposite bed. Watching them together was so comforting. They weren't the only ones who needed to feel protected. Being with them allowed me to know what it felt like to be fulfilled. I didn't care where we lived, or what we did to make money, as long as we were together.

Since I recognized it as being time to go to bed, I removed my shirt and got under the covers. It was obvious Kat was going to sleep with B, and as jealous as it made me, I felt content knowing they were an arm's length away.

When she stood up and gave me a weird look I couldn't figure her out. "What's wrong?"

She looked down at my shirt she was wearing and then back to me. "Shut up."

She was nervous. I didn't know why. "Kat, get comfortable and get in bed. I'm not going to make fun of you if that's what you think." She was crazy. Maybe her awful husband made her feel ugly. I hated him more for damaging my perfect girl.

She got all defensive. "It's not that."

She shimmied off her shorts and then took her bra off without lifting the t-shirt. It was so weird. I didn't get why she was hiding what I'd obviously seen before. I mean, the child in the bed next to her was proof of that. It had been a while since I'd seen her naked, but a body like hers wasn't easily forgotten. "Since when did you get shy?"

"Would you stop?" I liked getting under her skin, especially when it was over something so silly. She was so cute, yet vulnerable at the same time. It made me continue to smile even though it was clearly supposed to be a serious moment.

Even after she climbed into the other bed I continued laughing at her. She tossed a pillow at me as if it was going to get me to stop.

"Sorry, I saw this going a little differently," I joked.

"I'm not sleeping with you, Brooks. I just left my husband." She was so serious about it. I didn't have the heart to tell her I was only teasing.

She would assume that from me. I guess in some ways, she should have. It was taking everything in me to not invite her into my arms. "I never asked you, did I?"

"Whatever." She started to turn to face the opposite direction, like I annoyed her. I kept staring, waiting for her to make another smart remark. After a few seconds I realized she had no plans to face me again.

"Look at me, woman."

Her dirty look only made me want to tease her more. It was obvious I'd gotten under her skin. "What?"

I brought my feet up and sat on the edge of my bed facing her. Thinking nothing of it, Kat froze, staring at my naked chest. At first I thought she'd just realized I taken off my shirt. Then it hit me. I'd had it for so long that it was just a part of me.

I looked down at my tattoo and touched it. The K was obviously for Kat, and I'd had it placed there for a reason. "Oh, this. I should probably explain. I guess I got it so long ago that I forgot you've never seen it."

"When? Is that... Did you..." She couldn't get her words out. Her eyes were stuck on that one area.

I sighed before replying. "Kat, my heart belongs to you. It's not a secret. I got this done when I first went to Afghanistan. We'd just shared that night in the hotel room, and even though you'd left me I still loved you the same. I guess some people would call me stupid, but I just knew you were the one. I was going to put it over my heart. Instead, I put it here," I pointed to the area, "Because the moment you walked out of my life I felt like I couldn't breathe."

Her hand came up and covered her face as she sat there in shock. "I don't know what to say."

I looked down at the tattoo, and then over toward our daughter. "Now, looking at what we made that night melts my heart even more."

Kat had to peer away. She now knew that I'd carried so much of her with me every day. "Brooks." Her whisper was so slow, like she was falling out of consciousness.

"Come here," I ordered.

She shook her head, refusing me. "I can't." I respected her decision, but refused to let it be her final answer.

I reached over and placed my hand gently on her leg. "Close your eyes."

Once I got her to stand, I pulled her over to my bed. She halted me, opening her eyes to see how close we were. "I can't do this, Brooks. It's wrong."

I grabbed the edge of my t-shirt and pulled her in the rest of the way until our lips were touching. "I'm not stealing from him when you were never his to begin with. You didn't belong to Branch and you sure as hell don't belong to Bobby. A piece of paper isn't love. Close your eyes and tell me you don't feel it again? Tell me that you haven't thought of that night we spent together every single day since it happened? If you don't want this, then back up and go to sleep."

I didn't move my mouth from grazing over hers. I could feel her body shaking. It was just as intense for me. I'd kept this all bottled up, and now, being in this room with her, I couldn't keep from touching her. She couldn't imagine what it was like for me to sleep in a tiny bed for two years, wishing I was wherever she was, holding her all through the night. Dreams of her is what kept me going. I'd thought about this moment so many times. I couldn't wait any longer. My patience was running thin. She needed to be in my bed.

"I'm scared," she whispered.

I stood up, staring down at her while I tugged my own t-shirt over her head. She kept her eyes fixed on mine while I backed us up onto my bed.

There was only a pair of underwear keeping her from being completely naked. I didn't look down because honestly I didn't need to. I'd memorized every inch of her years ago. Kissing her would have been easy, though I didn't allow it to happen, not yet. I took my time, leading her under the covers with me, pulling her against my chest. She was still trembling, reminding how fragile this moment was between us. Years of pent up emotions were brewing between us. Words weren't needed because we both knew what the other was feeling.

I held her tight in my arms, silently promising myself that I'd never let her slip away again. I wanted to keep her safe, to protect her from the ugliness and give her a reason to smile again, each and every day for the rest of our lives. Just like when we were kids, I held her close, giving her the comfort she needed to get by another day.

While she lightly stroked my chest, I pressed my lips against her head. "Don't be scared, Kat. If you fall, I'll catch you. I always have and I always will. Except, this time I'm never going to let you go."

I could see where this was leading. It didn't take a fool to figure it out. I wasn't sure if I'd be able to stop her if she initiated it. All it would take was a kiss, and I'd be giving her all of me. I tried to stay calm under the covers with her so close. It was impossible, and she knew it too. This wasn't a game we were playing. In my heart she was mine. I really didn't care about a piece of paper. She should have known that. For Christ sakes, I slept with her the night before she was supposed to marry my brother. There was obviously no limits when it came to being with her.

I just hoped that when it did happen, she stuck around, because nothing could hurt more than losing both of them. I wanted to believe that this was our forever, but I was still petrified it wouldn't be.

Chapter 36

For a while Kat laid against my chest, playing with my dog-tags. She kept tracing my name, saying nothing in the quiet of the room. I rubbed her back, offering her time to think about everything going on in her life. I wondered what she was thinking about. I considered asking her, but knew when she was ready she'd talk about it.

There was a lot of things that hadn't been addressed. At some point she was going to want to know about every detail of my life when we were apart. I wondered if I should tell her about

Mullins, Anderson, and even Spence. They'd been my friends when I felt the most alone.

It wasn't like I didn't want to know about Kat's life. I knew she had friends that I hadn't met. She talked highly of them in some of her letters. She was a member of a church and even volunteered as the Sunday school teacher.

We'd both grown and experienced things that made us who we were. At some point we'd have to tell each other everything. For now I was more worried about getting through one day at a time. Bobby would be out of jail by morning, and with that I knew I'd have to figure out where they'd be safe from him.

Kat was probably going to want to take matters into her own hands, but this time she wasn't going to have a choice. My mind was made up. I loved her, and I was going to make sure she knew the depths of it while I did everything in my power to keep her protected.

I knew my coming back into her life was a huge game-changer. It wasn't only an adjustment for me. Every aspect of her life was about to change. My prayers had been answered even if it wasn't how I expected them to be. I'd never wish for her to be abused by her husband. I didn't even ask God to help me break them up. I'd only prayed that one day I'd be able to hold her again. It was never about the sex with Kat. I felt my happiness when she was in my arms.

While the tension in the room increased, I was left to control the growing urgency between my legs. Time had made it impossible to control. I needed her, so much that I was afraid to ask, because I knew I wouldn't be able to handle it if she rejected me.

I'd wanted her for so long. Now we were here, in a hotel room, with our daughter sleeping on the bed beside us. I'd lived every moment for this, and even though I was desperately trying to hold onto some composure, every single inch she moved made it unbearable. That's why when she looked up into my eyes I had to lick my lips. I didn't mean it in a sexual way, but looking at her mouth and remembering what it felt like to kiss her left me needing what I knew I shouldn't ask for, at least not yet.

All of a sudden everything around us disappeared. I stared deeply into her eyes, feeling the power of our connection leading us without effort.

"I love you." The words were so softly spoken when they came from her mouth. They were still so powerful; enough to break me.

I adjusted myself on the bed to be able to place my hands on either side of her face. I needed her to show me how much because dammit I'd waited forever for it. "You were worth the wait." Nothing could have prepared me for what it would feel like to kiss her for the first time after so long. I'd been staring at her lips for days, patiently waiting to have the chance to taste them again.

Our kiss, so powerful, paved the path for what was to come, both of us knowing there was no turning back. Kat and I both knew where we were headed. I didn't have the power to stop her, not when her touch was like an electric jolt to my heart.

In that moment she wasn't married, and we hadn't spent the past two years apart. We were lost in each other, right back to where we left off in that hotel room where we made B.

While our tongues mingled so perfectly together, I felt her hands coursing over my skin, pulling me closer. Her hunger for me was ravenous, and I wasted no time reassuring her of any doubts she might be experiencing. My hand slipped down between her legs, feeling the fabric of the other thing standing from me being able to feel her warm pussy in my hand.

I kept rubbing her, appreciating the fact that she was rocking her body at the same time. I took ahold of her ass, pulling her on top of me. The blanket and sheet slipped down, revealing her naked breasts for me to see. She wasn't being shy anymore. No, Kat was ready to bare it all. I could see it in her eyes and feel it in the way she was rocking those hips.

She leaned forward, bringing her lips to mine again, letting me suck on them before tracing my tongue over hers. She teased me with that tongue, licking mine and then pulling away. I pulled her closer, kissing her deeply. My intentions were obvious.

When Kat pulled away to catch her breath, I gave her a second to reconsider. It was going to be impossible for me to stop if this continued. I ran my hand up her hips, tracing her skin when I reached one of her breasts. Kat's eyes closed as she leaned back, preparing for me to kiss her there.

Out of the corner of my eye I spotted something that caused me to freeze in place. "Uh-oh."

My little girl was sitting up in the bed next to us, looking sad. Kat covered her exposed body up and held her arms out for her to join us. At first I tried to readjust myself, considering I was in a stiff predicament under the sheets. She headed to her mother in the beginning. Then, just as I realized I'd settled down, she climbed over and rested her body on my chest, placing her head down against my skin. I wrapped my arms around her and kissed the top of her head. Never in my life had I ever felt so needed. It was the most picture-perfect moment.

I couldn't control what happened next, even if I tried to be big, bad, and strong. I was falling apart, but not from being sad. I found meaning to life. I found my purpose. In all the times that I wanted to end my life, in all the moments that I was ready to give up on myself, I was so grateful that hadn't happened. I had more to live for than I ever could have imagined. My broken heart was finally beating again. I was healing, holding on to hope, finally, after so long of fighting for a reason.

This little girl was saving my life even if she'd never be able to understand how. She was my reason for existing. She was my everything. My heart didn't just belong to Kat anymore. She was going to have to share it with our daughter.

Burning hot tears fell from my eyes. I couldn't keep it all bottled up any longer. I was loved. My daughter was going to love me forever. It was all too much to accept without being emotional.

I held her tighter when Kat saw what was happening. I couldn't let her go, not when she was so comfortable being there. Kat rested her head next to me and cried too. I suppose someone watching would have thought we were being silly. To us, it was probably one of the most precious memories we'd shared. This trumped being naked in bed next to Kat. It was euphoria in the purest form.

Kat eventually reached her arm over and held both of us. We were a family, and I couldn't help wonder if she'd done this with Bobby. I'd missed out on so many things. I think a part of me will always ache thinking about it. It hurt knowing I'd never see her taking her first steps, or saying her first word. I would never be able to bond with her as an infant, or see the first time she showed her dimples to the world. I'd been robbed of it all.

It wasn't Kat's fault. Even if I knew, I was on the other side of the world. It wasn't like the military let us come and go as we pleased. I wouldn't have been able to watch her grow through a satellite connection. I certainly wouldn't have been able to keep my focus out on missions when I was worried about them at home.

Like it or not, she'd done the right thing; at least what she thought was right at the time.

Our opposite hands laced together as we continued laying there. I slid closer and wrapped an arm around the both of them. "This feels so right," I whispered while noticing she was dozing off. "I never thought I'd have this."

She squeezed my hand. "Me either."

For a while I watched my girls sleeping. I was afraid to close my eyes because I kept thinking when I woke up they'd be gone. I held onto B tightly, holding her close to my heart. I listened to her breathing while silently thanking God for her.

I thought about our future, and where we'd be in a few years. I pictured coming home from work and seeing them waiting for me. I thought about holidays, where my parents would come to visit. It was all so reachable. Sure, we had hurdles to get over, but we were a team now.

No, we were a family.

I knew it was too soon to discuss, but my parents were scheduled to come visit. They were about to meet our little surprise. At first they'd be shocked, but there wasn't a worry about her being accepted. They'd fall in love, just as fast as I had. There was nothing they couldn't love about her. She was absolutely darling.

I kept kissing her, looking over and seeing Kat fast asleep next to us. More tears came and went. It seemed like just when I thought I couldn't be happier something else made me weak again. I wasn't worried about Kat seeing me this way. I didn't have to hold back when it came to her. She knew me, sometimes better than I knew myself. I wanted to share this with her, just like I wanted her to be able to do the same with me.

While I laid there still choked up with emotion, I felt myself falling asleep. Since I knew I had to work I didn't fight it. This was the most comfortable I'd been in years. It was obvious that sleep time was going to prove to be my favorite from this night on.

Chapter 37

I don't know how long I was asleep before a little body was spinning around in the bed, kicking her feet until she found comfort again. I tried to remain still to prevent her from waking. Kat needed her sleep, probably more than I did.

While awake, I thought about being at work and having them here in the hotel. I wondered if there was a way I could get off work early. My superior officer was a nice guy. He had a family of his own. I was sure if I explained everything to him he'd give me extra time to be with them. At this point, I knew I had to make some serious decisions. My injury to my hand was going to help with that. There was a good chance I wasn't going to be cleared for duty. I could still teach, if that's what I wanted to do. If someone would have asked me a week ago, I would have said that life was good. Now everything had changed. I wanted out of the military, because it meant that I was free to have a life with Kat, without being married to my career.

My decisions were going to have to be rushed because time was of the essence. My girls needed stability, and I'd figure out a way to make it happen, even if I had to send them back home to D.C. to make sure they got it.

B was restless again, kicking around on the bed. When she readjusted I watched Kat open her eyes. She noticed that I was awake almost immediately. Her smile was contagious, while her intentions tempted me, causing me to react immediately, once I'd caught on to what she was insinuating. Where her body had been, sat a pillow. I watched her, still topless, walk over to the other bed and climb on top.

With little effort I slid off the mattress and tucked the covers so B couldn't wiggle around. By the time I made it to Kat she'd already scooted over to give me room. I pulled her back to rest on my chest, instantly getting sweaty as I did it.

I brought my chin down and kissed her shoulder. Just as I suspected that she was only going back to sleep, she moved enough to get me curious. I whispered sweet words in her ear. "I love you so much, Kat."

After my comment, it was quite obvious that we weren't going back to sleep, not yet at least. Kat wasn't asking me to stop either. I could tell we were on the same page. It was as if we were picking up exactly where we left off before B woke. This time I was prepared. I longed to be with her this way, because let's face it, I'd waited entirely too many years to feel her body again.

My hands traveled up her abdomen until they were right under her nipples. I peered down over her shoulder and saw them exposed, beckoning to be touched. As I became aware of what was growing between my legs, Kat shimmied her body back, making it known that she was fully aware.

She turned her body around, staring me right in the eyes. I leaned closer, pressing my lips against hers. As she pulled away she spoke softly, asking me for something I'd never been able to refuse her. "Make love to me, Brooks."

I had to be sure. "You said we couldn't."

Damn if she didn't lean forward and tease my lips with her tongue. "Don't you want me?" She whispered.

"Don't be stupid, Kat. You don't know how hard it is for me to hold back from what I really want. I just can't have you walking out on me like before. There's too much at stake here. If waiting will help you stick to your decision, it's worth it to me." In my defense I was saying what I figured to be the right thing. There was nothing I wanted more than to make love to her.

When she answered I knew she meant it. Her eyes never left mine, and I could have sworn that she was almost smiling. "All I want is us, forever. I won't be changing my mind or abandoning you. If you think we should wait, I'll respect your decision, but we're here, naked in this room. You love me and I love you. I've made a ton of mistakes, but there's one thing that I've done right in my life, and that's loving you. Brooks, look at me and tell me that you think I'm going to let you go again. Look over at that little girl who loves you after knowing you for only a few days and tell me that I'd be so heartless as to take her away from you."

I couldn't do that. I knew she wouldn't hurt me in that way, not ever again.

"Point taken. You can't blame me for being scared, Kat. I've lost you so many times, and I know that if it happened again, this time it would end me. I couldn't live with knowing that you and B were out there and I couldn't be with you. That's why I want everything to be right this time."

I pulled her closer, making sure we were skin to skin as we discussed this. I wanted to remind her what was waiting just below the blankets.

Kat seemed even more determined to convince me that this was real.

"I'll wait for you, Brooks, just like you waited for me."

I was her puppet, just waiting to be controlled. She could do whatever she wanted to me as long as she didn't leave this bed. "Yeah, I'm not real sure waiting is the best decision." I rubbed my erection against her smooth thigh. "I figure I've got two choices. I can go in the bathroom and take care of this myself, like I've gotten pretty used to doing, or I can be with the woman that I've waited almost three years to be with again."

"Seems like a really *hard* decision." The way she said it made me chuckle.

There was no doubt in my mind that we were about to get it on. I was all giddy just imagining where to touch first. "Yeah." I ran her hand over my crotch. "What do you think?"

When I let go of her hand, she didn't stop touching me. In fact, she dug down inside of the elastic band of my boxers and ran her fingers over my hardness. "I think that if you don't make love to me, I'm going to have to beg." She was massaging me, watching my eyes close. "Do you think about that night as much as I do? I want to feel it again; that connection that took us to places neither of us knew existed."

If she kept talking I was going to explode. I didn't need to think about that night because we had new memories to make. We belonged together, and I was going to remind her of it, once again in a hotel room.

We kissed again, this time letting our lips and tongue tantalize one another. The more we did it, the harder it was to stop. I was so hungry for her kiss that I reached to make it happen. "If I told you how much I've thought about you, I may scare you away. It's borderline stalking."

Kat's next sultry kiss was loaded with carnal desire. Her boundaries were way past us. Nothing could stop this from happening, not unless the building caught fire. Then I'd take them to safety before getting back to where we left off.

Feeling her tugging at my boxers only made me want them off faster. I hopped from the bed and shoved them down, climbing back on to a lower position. Her underwear was standing between me and that enchanting area of hers. I kissed the fabric, admiring the way her body jumped at my impassioned touch. I explored her with my fingers, sliding back the fabric to see her vibrant pussy, tempting me to taste it. I looked up at Kat as I rubbed her clit for the first time, smiling as her body bucked in response. I peered down, watching her cunt as I rubbed it, and how her lips separated when I spread them apart. I blew on that area, watching and waiting for it to react. She was so warm, and I couldn't wait to place my mouth down there to taste her again. My mouth watered as I continued to scope out the area, touching it with my thumb and watching her whole body shake.

I felt like an animal, ready to ravage her until she was left fulfilled, yet begging for more.

First I needed to remove those panties. I couldn't have anything in the way when I dove down and passionately licked over her delectable cunt. I would savor every juicy inch, making sure there wasn't any spot left unattended.

I stared at her as she exposed herself to me, bringing me back to the last time I'd been this hungry. My tongue drug over my lips as I narrowed in on the prize, dragging my hands over all the places I was prepared to lick. Just being this close to her was making me emotional again. Before I could devour every inch of this woman I needed an extra bit of reassurance. "Kat, promise me that this is forever. Tell me that when I wake up in the morning, you're still going to be in my arms. Assure me that this time is different."

I'd never seen such honesty radiating off of someone before. "I'm never leaving you again. Wherever you go, I'm going to be by your side. I want this, Brooks. It's all I've ever wanted. We're a family, and nobody can ever take that away from us."

She brought her lips to mine, making me forget the task I was so set on minutes before. I slid my fingers inside of her while torrid kisses led me to enter her. I couldn't hold out with foreplay, not this time. I was too horny; too provoked. "The first time's going to be fast, but after that, I'll be able to go all night."

She purred out her reply, letting me know she was just as turned on. I pulled her to be perfectly positioned with me. Her petite body was easy to maneuver. "We have forever, so time isn't going to be a problem."

I finally had her where I'd wanted her for so long. It was impossible to control everything that was running through my mind. I wasn't worried about the repercussions of this, or how much harder it would be for me to control my anger when I had to face her husband. I wasn't thinking about anything but us. I was going to push until she fell into everything I had to offer her. We were far from perfect, but close enough to be able to taste it.

Chapter 38

I'd tried to tell myself that she was gone. For years I felt like I'd never have a chance to be with her again. Now she was in my arms, asking me to make love to her. She had all of me, still, after so long. When she cried, I'd be there to wipe away her tears. I'd be the man she could count on, just like when we were kids.

Finally we were here together. She'd made up her mind, and I felt confident that she meant it. With every touch from her fingers I got chills. Her lips were like sweet candy; the kind that leaves one wanting more. I craved every inch of her skin, knowing that after this first encounter I'd be able to focus more to give it to her.

There was no victim in this room. We weren't doing this to feel better about anything. Us being together like this was about something much deeper. Just like the times before, I was losing my grip on reality. Only she could do this to me. Only Kat could make the world feel like it was spinning out of control. I was losing myself in her again, and this time I wasn't afraid.

Each time our eyes met I felt a surge shooting straight to my cock. I needed to be inside of her, immediately, before my arousal became painful.

We kissed several times before I lifted her onto my lap, sitting up for a better position. I didn't trust that this would make me last longer. Hell, I knew I'd be a puddle of nothing as soon as I slipped inside. Her eagerness was apparent. Even as engorged as I was beneath her, I could feel her juiced lips rubbing over me.

She held onto me tight, seeing what I was about to do even before I made the move. It was insane how synced we were to one another. I could close my eyes and make love to her without effort, or guidance.

Then it happened. She wiggled until I was there, sliding easily inside of her welcoming entrance. She was so wet, so salacious. We rocked together, both moving slow as we tried desperately to handle what was happening after so long.

For Kat, the reality of me not being dead was causing this to be super intense, while my own fears were controlling my movements, preventing me letting a single one get the best of me. I was no superhero, but I wanted to be hers.

Beads of sweat ran down my face and I held her close to me, allowing her to stay in control. My eyes remained open. I couldn't close them when I wanted to remain alert for this whole occasion. I didn't want to live or breathe unless I could feel her next to me each and every day for the rest of my life. Years of pain was dissipating as she rocked her naked body overtop of mine. Her tight walls surrounded me with pleasure, making me strain to stay coherent. All of these emotions were accompanied by lust. I was starved for this woman, unable to imagine how many times it would take to have my fill.

It was obvious that I was close. My hands held Kat's shoulders, silently praying she'd get the hint and slow up. Eventually I had to surrender myself over to her. I could feel it happening, my pent up release filling her. I clung to her body holding her close while I lost control. My heart started to beat in my head, I was desperate for air. Then finally I was done, lethargic, and satiated.

We were far from being done, but Kat gave me time to recuperate. Little did she know that I had plans for our next encounter. Just because this first time was more about me didn't mean she wouldn't be generously awarded.

We laid there together on the bed, panting and grasping for air to fill our empty lungs. Our hands were laced together, and I wasn't even about to let her go.

I held her close, but appreciated the way she traced her fingers against my tattoo. As if she needed another reminder, I felt it important to keep giving her one.

"No regrets, Kat."

"No regrets."

It was so late, and I had every intention of giving her a second round of my undivided attention, but sleep seemed to get the best of me. I tried to fight it, only to feel my eyelids winning the battle.

I only woke up because I noticed she was gone. Of course right away I feared she'd packed up and left me there, that's how scared I was of losing her. It wasn't until I sat up and looked over at the other bed that I realized everything was just as it was before. B was sound asleep, and the sound of the bathroom fan let me know where Kat was. I stood and put my boxers on, just in case the little one were to wake up. I didn't want to scare her with my private parts. Daddy or not, I wasn't ready for that situation where I had to explain why I looked different than her mother.

I cracked the bathroom door open to find Kat standing in front of the mirror. She had her head down and was clearly freaking out about something. At first I worried that she regretted sleeping with me. Maybe I should have waited. Yes, of course I should have held out. What was wrong with me?

"You alright? You better not be in here crying, thinking of a way to escape." I said it like I was joking, but was really trying to feel her out.

When she didn't answer at first I made a sound with my mouth.

"I told you, I'm not going anywhere. I came in here to get cleaned up, that's all."

I hugged her body and kissed her softly. She wasn't in here to clean up. Something was up with her. I wanted the truth. "I know you better than you know yourself. What is it, Kat?"

She handed me a calendar, making me wonder what the hell it meant. It was the middle of the night. My mind wasn't on technical things. I couldn't figure out her secret way of communicating. Then it finally hit me.

"Are you kidding me?" I ran my hand through my hair once it finally hit me. Apparently we couldn't fornicate without the risk of becoming pregnant. "Again?"

She put her hands up as if it was very possible. "So I'm thinking that if we stay together, we may need a school bus to cart all the kids in."

I pulled her back into my arms, reassuring her that no matter what we'd figure it out. In all honesty I'd be happy if she ended up pregnant. If she thought I was going to use protection with her she had another thing coming. There was nothing keeping me from having all of her, not even another kid. "Don't freak out yet, Kat. It's not like it's a definite. You've got enough to worry about. I refuse to wear a rubber with you. I never have and I never will."

She jerked out of my arms and looked up at me. "Jesus, what if I got pregnant back then?" I knew she was referring to when we were in high school.

I threw up my hands, trying to figure out how to word this so she wouldn't be pissed. "Hold up. In my defense both times I went into your room it wasn't to have sex with you. You begged me for it."

She answered like it embarrassed her. "I didn't know it was you!"

I cornered her, making sure she was paying close attention. "You wanted it to be me, Kat. Deep down you had to question why it was different."

"How do you know it was?" Oh yeah, she went there.

I laughed before I could reply. "Because there ain't no way my brother can make you cum like I can."

She blushed. It was quite obvious too.

"Am I right?"

Her smile was cute, like she knew admitting to it was like saying she liked being bad. "Yes. You're right. Although, I didn't think it was you. I just thought he was being sensitive of my feelings."

"Did you ever pretend he was me?"

"Stop, Brooks. Being with Branch was a mistake. He cost us a lot, and I don't want to think about a single second I wasted on him."

I took her hand in mine and kissed it softly. "I'm kidding with you. We were kids, Kat. Do you know how scared I was to face you the morning after I'd been in your room? I thought for sure you'd mention it to Branch and he'd come and try to kick my ass."

She giggled. "I did mention it. Both times I thanked him for being so good to me. He seemed weird, but never said a thing. When I think about it, I see how awful that was."

This left me in hysterics. How could my brother have been so stupid? "What a loser. He had his head so far up his own ass that he didn't know you were making love to me across the hall."

She squeezed my hands. "Can we go back to worrying that I've been impregnated for the second time in a hotel room? How could I have let something so important slip from my mind?"

I traced my lips over her forehead. "We were preoccupied, making up for lost time. And no, we're not going to worry about that. We're going to keep making love and when you get pregnant, I'll be able to experience everything I missed the first time."

"Brooks, I need to get a divorce first. Don't you think we're rushing? We can't just forget about everything else."

"I've waited to be with you for over twenty years. This isn't rushing. Kat, everything is going to be fine. Who gets pregnant two times in a row after one time being together? It's pretty impossible." In my defense I'm pretty sure I cut class during this discussion. I had no idea how any of this scientific stuff worked, other than what I'd learned out on my own. Kat was a mother. She knew exactly what she was talking about.

"Whatever."

I tickled her where I knew she couldn't take it, just to change the subject. I needed her to get back in that bed so I could start round two. "You're a worry wart."

Kat froze in place, causing me to lean down and kiss the top of her nose. "My girl."

"We need to go slow, Brooks, not for us, but for the sake of everyone around us that won't understand."

"We have a kid together. She's almost two. I think they can figure it out. Besides, I really don't give a shit what people think or say. All I care about is being with you and B. The rest of the world can kiss my white ass."

Kat couldn't contain her reaction to my comment. A giggle escaped her puffy lips. "It is pretty white."

"You've been looking?" I liked knowing she was checking me out.

She slapped me there, lightly. "I missed you so much."

When she said it all the jokes were put to the side. I needed to be serious for a second. "I missed you too, Kat. You'll never have to miss me again because we're never going to be apart again. I promise."

I did something I didn't want to do, but knew it was important to show her I could be considerate, above everything else. I put my shirt over her head and lowered it to cover her back up. We kissed slowly, making it last even though it wasn't going to lead to anything else, at least not then. "Thank you," she said while staring into my eyes.

"Never thank me for taking care of you. I was put on this earth to do it and you know it, too."

A little later while she was in my arms falling asleep I found myself laughing out loud. "You know, if you're pregnant after one time, then I have super sperm. I bet we could make a fortune selling it on the black market like they do kidneys. Can you imagine how rich we'd be?"

She never moved from her comfortable position when she responded. "You'd have a million kids."

"Yeah, well there is that. I guess it's a bad idea, huh?"

She laughed and slapped my chest. "I'm glad I don't love you for your brains."

"No, you love me for my white ass, apparently."

The longer we spent together, the more it felt like old times. I never wanted this to end. We were just getting started. When I fell asleep, I knew I'd never be rested enough to work, but a little was better than nothing. At least I knew I could come back to them and hold her in my arms again. It was something I'd never been able to do.

Chapter 39

I don't know why I set an alarm, because I woke up every day without it. I quickly turned it off and got dressed, trying not to wake either of the females sleeping, one of which was in my bed, taunting me to climb back under the covers. She faced me with tired eyes as I whispered. "I've got to go into work. Will you be okay here until I get back?"

"Are we staying here another night?" She asked.

"You're not going home. Listen, when I get back, I'll go with you to the courthouse to file for the protective order. We can see about getting an attorney if you want to get a jump on it." I knew I was pushing, and maybe she wanted some time to settle down, but I wasn't about to let it slip her mind. I'd slept with a married woman. It was something I always told myself I'd never do. Of course, the woman had been Kat, and technically I felt as if she belonged to me. It still bothered me.

The cutest little girl caught our attention. Her big beaming eyes were taking us both in. "Me go bye bye's?"

I sat down on the bed next to her. "I have to go to work, bug, but I'll be back later and we can play."

"We can pay?" I loved how excited she was about that.

I pretended to be as happy as she was. "Maybe we can go swimming."

"In da pool?" She got ecstatic.

"Yeah, baby, in the pool." I picked her up and kissed her. "I love you."

While Kat got up to put a dry diaper on B, I finished getting my boots on. It sucked that it was so hot outside and I had sweat my ass off all day, but there wasn't a shorts option. "If you need anything, you call. I'm right down the road. I love you."

I kissed her twice, making sure I savored each one. "Love you, too."

I'd no sooner reached the door when I came back into the room, stealing one more chaste kiss. "That was just in case you plan on leaving me again. Just know, I will come hunt you down. I have government resources this time."

She pushed me out the door. "Will you stop it? You're stuck with us now."

"See you girls later."

It was pretty difficult leaving them in the hotel all alone. Even though I knew they were just down the road, it was still too far. I wondered if Kat would need money for anything. I thought about her crying, and B not understanding what was wrong.

Before I got caught up and didn't have a way out I knew I'd have to pay a visit to my superior. I knocked on his door, hoping he had time to talk. "Valentine, come on in."

I saluted him. "Sir, permission to speak freely?"

"Have a seat."

"I'm coming to you first with this information, because time is of the essence, sir."

"Is this about your surgery?" He asked.

"No. It's about my family. I'm going to need some time off."

"When would you need this to happen? We have forms to fill out for leave requests. They're located down the hall..."

I cut him off, making his brown raise. I'm sure he wasn't prepared for me to be so rude. "It's an emergency, sir. I can't wait to have it approved."

"Listen son, I've got a meeting in a few minutes, but I'll be done in two hours. Can it wait that long?"

"Yes, sir." I stood up. "I'll come back then."

When I walked out I half expected to get yelled at though it never happened.

Next I called my parents. Since they were due to come visit I wanted to make sure they hadn't booked any flights yet. Our plans were about to change.

"Hello?"

"Mom, it's Brooks. How are you?"

"I'm good. We're excited to come visit."

"Listen, about that, I'm coming to you instead. I've got some leave available and thought I'd come home."

"That would be wonderful. I can't wait to tell your father."

"Expect me in a couple days. I have a big surprise for you. I'll see you then. I love you."

"Love you too."

Since I had that part taken care of, all I had to do was convince Kat it was a good idea.

An hour had gone by before I couldn't take it any longer. I dialed Kat's number, wanting nothing more than to hear her voice. "Hello?"

"Hey, I'm just calling to check on my girls."

I could hear the television playing in the background. Kat took a few seconds before she spoke again. "I listened to my messages."

I could hear that she was upset. I wished I could make all of this easier for her. "I imagine he's pissed about now. He knows you're with me and he ain't going to lay a hand on you ever again."

"Pretty much."

"Listen, I have a plan to keep you both safe. I'm meeting with my commanding officer in an hour to see if I can take a few days off. I'm due, so it shouldn't be an issue. Considering the circumstances, I doubt he'll have a problem. He's got a family, so he knows how important you are to me."

"Am I going to like your plan?" I wasn't going to give her a choice.

"Do you trust me?"

"With my life." That was good news because she wasn't going to like my idea at all.

"Kat, I'm going to keep you safe. I need to go. Stay inside until I get back. I love you."

"That will never get old."

"It better not. I've been practicing it in front of a mirror since I was twelve."

When the call ended I felt better. I knew they were safe, and that I'd be with them as soon as I could. Fingers crossed, I'd be able to take time off. My next training course wasn't coming in for a while and I already had my plans in order. There was no reason why I'd have to stay on base.

I'd no sooner come out of the meeting to request leave, with good news, when my phone began to ring. I pulled the vibrating device out of my pocket and put it up to my ear. "Sergeant Valentine."

"Brooks, he's here at the hotel. B and I are in the elevator. I hit the emergency stop button. He's going to hurt me. You've got to call the police. Tell them he's going to hurt me."

"I'm coming." Just then I saw my superior officer heading in my direction.

Kat was still on the other end of the call. "No! I don't want you hurt. Please, stay there."

"Kat, I'm coming and you're not going to stop me. Whatever you do, don't let that elevator start moving. You hang tight. I'll be there in less than five minutes."

"I'm calling the police."

"What's going on, Valentine?"

"Her husband found her. He's there at the hotel. She and my daughter are in the elevator with it stopped. I've got to get out of here."

He followed me, hopping in the truck before I could stop him. "You might need some backup." He suggested as I pulled out of the parking spot.

"Has your life always been like this?"

I scrunched up my face. "No, sir. This is the first time I've had to deal with abusive husbands."

He laughed at my comment. "We'll get them out of harm's way. Once they're safe you can bring them to the base. We'll find a place for them."

"Thank you, sir." In all honesty it was hard to appreciate what he was saying. I was too concerned about Kat and Brooklyn. They meant everything to me. I kept picturing the worst.

When I made it inside of the hotel, I saw her husband standing outside of the elevators. He took one look at me and backed up, turning his attention to the fact that I'd showed up. "Of course the bitch called you. Let me tell you something, they're both coming home with me. There's nothin' you can do about it. I knew she was here with you. I tracked her with my phone. It wasn't hard to find her when she was this close to the military barracks."

His threats meant nothing to me. Before I could shove him out of my face my superior put his hands between us. "Back up soldier. I'll take care of this."

"What are you going to do old man?" Bobby wasn't letting the sarge scare him.

Then I watched him change his tune. "Are you familiar with the penalty for assaulting a soldier? How do you think a judge is going to handle you fighting with someone who had earned a purple heart for his services overseas? You don't want to do this, son. I can guarantee that it won't end well for you."

Bobby threw his hands in the air, at the same time two police officers walked into the lobby. Right away my sarge let them know what was going on, while I made my way over to the elevator.

It took the mechanic a few minutes to get it moving again. As soon as the doors opened I saw her scared face. I didn't have to ask if she was okay, because I knew she would be, both of them would. "We're going to make a statement and get some papers drawn up. Are you alright with that?"

I led Kat over to my boss. "Kat, this is my commanding officer, Ferris."

He shook her hand. "It's great to meet you, ma'am." He turned his attention to B. "You must be little Brooklyn. You sure do look like your daddy."

It made me so happy to hear that. I knew she did, but it still felt amazing.

B got up in my arms and let me hug her. I was so glad she wasn't acting scared. "You need to go give a statement to the officer. I'm going to go up and get our things. I'll meet you down here in a few minutes."

Kat nodded and followed my sarge over to where the police stood. She didn't have to worry about Bobby. They'd already put him in a car and locked the doors.

The officers would help her get a protective order. It was a good start, but probably not enough to keep him away forever. We'd have to go to court for that to happen.

When I met her back in the lobby with all of our things, she only had one question. "What now?"

"We go back to the base. I've got to fill out some forms and then we're going on a road trip."

"A road trip?" She didn't like the sound of it. I could already tell.

"Yeah. I'll explain later." I stopped walking before we made it outside. "Give me your phone."

She looked shocked when I took it and broke it in two pieces. "The thing about cell phones is that they can be traced by anyone. Bobby had an app on his phone that told him where you were. The second you turned your phone back on, all he had to do was follow the damn arrow."

I could tell she felt stupid, but I didn't blame her. Everything happened too fast to consider he was that manipulative.

We all rode back to the base together. When the sarge got out of the truck, Kat shook his hand. "Thank you, sir."

"It was my pleasure, ma'am."

It wasn't until we were inside my room packing that she really started pushing about our trip. "So where are we going? Am I not allowed to know? Is there something you aren't telling me?"

I picked B up just in case Kat planned on wrestling me to the ground to change my mind. "We're going to my parent's house, and before you say anything you need to understand that your safety is the most important thing to me. I've got seven days before I need to report back, so I can promise you that it's not forever."

It was quite obvious that she was in shock. She stood there looking as if she were about to puke. This was going to be a long road trip.

Chapter 40

We'd been driving for a while in silence. It was obvious that she wasn't happy with me about my decision to go home. What Kat couldn't grasp was the fact that my parents loved her just the same as they always had. If she hadn't been so hard-headed in the first place she never would have married that asshole we were trying to get away from. "I'm getting hungry. Do you want to stop and eat soon?"

She wouldn't even look in my direction. "I feel like I'm going to puke. Just get something for you and B."

It was beginning to get dark out. B was steady dozing, in the back, while Kat continued giving me the silent treatment. I reached over and put my hand on her thigh. "Kat, you can't be mad at me forever, you know."

"Yes, I can." She shoved my hand away.

"You're being a baby. We were going to let my parents visit next week anyway. Stop acting like you don't love me anymore because I know it's not true."

She was adamant about making me pay for not telling her where we were going at first. "I can't believe you're making me do this."

When I couldn't take it anymore I pulled the vehicle over and placed it in park. "Look at me."

"No!" She stared out at an open field.

I ran my hand back up her thigh, taunting her. "Kat, look at me."

The pissed look on her face was priceless. I wished I had my phone out to take a picture to make fun of it later. "What?"

"They miss you. Hell, they miss us. I left too, you know? This isn't easy for me, but they deserve to know that little girl in the backseat. They weren't in the dark about my feelings, Kat. They knew how I felt and they probably knew how you felt. We were kids, who wore our feelings on our sleeves. I'm betting they weren't as surprised as you think that we ended up in bed, several times. After all, it is where you belonged anyway."

She huffed and puffed, but finally gave in. "I'm still mad."

I tapped her little nose. "No you're not. You're scared, but you're not mad."

"I don't think I like that you know what I'm thinking. A girl's got a right to some private thoughts."

"Get used to it. It's never going to change."

Kat sighed, but finally seemed to calm down. A few minutes later she made a good suggestion. "I think we should stop for the night and drive the rest of the way in the morning. We didn't sleep good last night, and could both use the rest before we see your parents."

"I don't know if that's a good idea. I mean, when we go to hotels, you get pregnant. It's scary." I laughed at my own convoluted joke.

She smacked me hard on the leg. "I should have never said anything to you."

"You know it's funny."

"What's going to be funny is when I don't get my period in two weeks. Then I'm going to watch you cry."

I looked right at her, making sure she was paying close attention. "I won't be crying out of fear, beautiful. They'll be tears of joy for me. So, are we stopping at a hotel, or are you scared?"

She covered her face. I recognized that I was getting on her nerves. For one reason or another I found comfort in us being this way. It was the reason I fell in love with her so long ago.

"I'm not scared of you!"

"You should be. I'll steal your heart and you'll never get it back," I promised.

"I gave it to you years ago, and I don't want it back," she replied.

I took her hand and held it against my lips. She couldn't know how amazing this was for me. "No matter what happens when we get there tomorrow, we're a team. If something bad is said, which I don't see happening, we'll leave together, as a family. I promise."

"I just don't want to see the look of disappointment on their faces. I'm already feeling that about myself. Being reminded of it only makes things worse."

"I guarantee that when we walk in there, and they take a look at that princess in the back seat, everything will change. Look at how she's affected me."

In a few short days, I felt like everything in my life had changed. Kat couldn't argue with the truth. She knew as well as I did that they were crazy if they didn't love our daughter. "I hope you're right."

I walked across the lot to reserve a room for us while Kat went into the restaurant to change B. She said she was too soaked to wait. When we met again I had the key in my hand. "I got us a room. Since you're scared of getting knocked up, I took a room with one twin bed. We can all share, right?"

She raised her brow, shaking her head the whole time. "You can sleep on the floor, I suppose."

"I'm just playing. I got a honeymoon suite with a vibrating bed. Bug's going to love it."

She shook her head and kept looking at the menu while I played peek-a-boo with B.

After we grabbed a bite to eat, we headed over to the hotel. The first thing we did was got B situated with some of her toys. Her schedule was all messed up and Kat was freaking out over it. The more comfortable the child was the better she would sleep.

I took it upon myself to get a hot shower. It had been a long day, and I needed to wash as much if it away as I could. I didn't see a problem with coming out of the bathroom in only a towel, but the look on Kat's face made me rethink that decision. She may as well have been drooling. I watched her taking me in while smiling cheek to cheek. I knew what was on her mind, and it didn't involve clothing.

I started to look for my boxers in my bag when my daughter walked over and looked at me curiously. I still had a towel on, but I could tell she was intrigued. "Hey, bug. What are you doing over here?"

"Pincess." She handed me a little princess doll.

"Where's her prince?"

She located the male prince and made them kiss. We all began to laugh at how she understood that gesture. "You may look like Daddy, but you act like Mama," I said as I kissed her nose.

B jumped into my lap and touched my nose. "Nose."

I touched her nose back. "B."

When she went to do it again, she paused. Kat climbed up behind her and whispered, "Who is that?"

B smiled. "Daddy."

It was another pivotal moment for me. She was mine in every way, and she even knew it. My whole life flashed before my eyes, only to bring me back to this monumental event. All the pain was worth it to have her in my life. Words couldn't begin to describe the happiness this child brought me. I was in awe of her.

"Say it again, B. Who am I?"

She giggled. "Daddy."

I kept asking her, hoping she'd never change her mind. After a while I could tell Kat was ready to put ear plugs in. I was getting a little annoying, probably purposely pushing her buttons.

B didn't fall asleep right away. It could have been the chocolate I fed her while her mother wasn't looking. We talked until her little eyes got heavy. Once I knew she was comfortable I made my way over to the other bed. I wrapped my arms around Kat's small body. "Are you excited about tomorrow?"

She turned to face me. "Seriously? My stomach is all knotted up."

I knew I had to leave it alone. I couldn't risk her freaking out anymore about it. She had enough on her plate with her psycho husband. Since it was important that every aspect of her life was taken care of I decided to ask about her personal property. "Do you have anyone that can run by and check on things at your house?"

"Yeah. I can call my old boss at the diner I waitressed at. She never really liked Bobby much, so he won't be able to influence her into thinking I'm a piece of shit."

"A waitress sounds like a hot job for you. Woman, what else are you hiding from me?"

Kat giggled. "I wasn't an exotic dancer if that's what you're thinking. There's no way dirty men are going to see me naked."

"I'd pay an arm and a leg to see you dance naked." I teased her with my eyebrows, moving them up and down with excitement.

She gave me a sarcastic look. "If I could dance, I'd do it for free, but we both know I have two left feet."

"Well, we're in luck, because I have two right feet."

She attempted to push me away, but failed horribly. "How about we get some rest?"

"How about you take off that Army shirt and we have a repeat of last night first?"

I was surprised when she didn't argue about it. Kat sat up and lifted the shirt over her head. Then she wriggled out of her panties. Completely naked in front of me, I prepared to devour her.

"This is never going to get old."

She climbed on my lap, pulling me forward by my dog tags until our lips were touching. "Tell me you love me and I'll give you that dance."

"I love you, beautiful. Now, stand up and show me what you've got."

I threw my arms behind my head and waited for my show to begin, all the while knowing she really couldn't dance a lick. It was going to be the sexiest catastrophe known to man, and I was going to love every single minute of it.

Chapter 41

I'd been lying in bed with her for about twenty minutes before I decided I wasn't going to be able to sleep unless I took care of a certain problem. While she seemed to be sleeping, I slid down under the covers, kissing her skin at the base of her pussy. Her body reacted, and I knew she was fully aware of what was about to happen. My thumb traced her little bud, bringing her to life. I listen to a soft moan escaping her lips while my tongue flicked her clit. Even though it was hot under the covers, I wasn't about to let my daughter catch me doing this. I'd never forgive myself. I kept going, sucking and lapping her up, until her knees came up around me. She dug her hands into my hair, keeping my mouth close to the task. The taste of her, the favor of her essence made me crazy. I wanted to bring her to new heights, repeatedly. One finger slid inside of her channel, immediately becoming saturated with her sultry musk. I couldn't stop. I had to continue until I felt her losing control, and in that moment I'd know without a doubt that I was the best she'd ever had. I wanted to be the only person in Kat's life to make her cum this way.

I sucked her clit in hard, holding it between my teeth while pulling back. I moved my head, rubbing my chin over her pussy, while I still thrust my finger in and out of her. Her walls began to close, sending my finger out again. I drove it back in, pulling my face away only to lick over it some more. Then I felt her, shaking, no seizing beneath me. I made my way up to her mouth, savoring the way she accepted my kisses.

"I'm never washing my face again," I teased.

"You're so sick."

"Love sick. That's what I am."

"Just go to sleep, Brooks. We have a long way to drive in the morning."

"Fine. I love you long time. Just remember that while you're getting your rest. I'll be right here when you wake up."

Later, after Kat fell asleep in my arms, I remained awake. I'd been up thinking for hours, trying to find a solution to her worries. She was so concerned about my parents and Brooklyn. I knew there had to be some way to make the transition easier for everyone involved. That's when it hit me. I knew what to say, all I had to do was run it by her first. "Kat, wake up."

She squinted when she opened her eyes. After checking the clock she seemed pretty annoyed. "Go away. I'm sleeping. It's not even morning," she whispered.

"I have an idea that might make you feel better. Come on, wake up. The sun will be up soon. Don't you want to know what it is?"

She leaned her head on her hand, like it was the only thing keeping it upward. "Fine, talk."

I could see that she was falling back asleep, but didn't care.

"You're all upset over me not knowing about Brooklyn. You think that they're going to flip out on you or something. I think I have a solution. What if we told them that I knew the whole time? I haven't been home and they suspect there is a lot of reasons why I'm remaining at a distance. It would only make sense that part of it was because of the baby. If we told them that you didn't want Branch to know, they'll believe us."

She yawned, but looked right at me anyway. "Brooks, the only problem with your story is the part where I run off and get married to a stranger. How are we going to even begin to explain that?"

"We won't tell them that either. They don't need to know. Look, we all make mistakes. Last week I felt like my whole life was worthless. I thought you'd moved on and started a family with someone else. I wanted to bury myself ten feet in the ground and never look back. I don't care about the details of when or who. All I care about is us. Wouldn't it be nice to have a family to visit on the holidays? It's better for them to know her when she's small. That way she'll never remember a time when they weren't a part of her life."

She shrugged. "Of course, it would be wonderful, but I think you're assuming that they'll forgive me. I hurt them, Brooks. Just because you've forgiven me doesn't mean they will."

"Kat, I love you and I love B. I don't care if it's been four days or four years. Nothing is going to change for me. Don't you get it? You've given me everything and you still think that you're this horrible person. You've always been a part of my family and you know it. Family forgives."

"I *am* a horrible person." She just kept blaming herself as if I hadn't been a part of the reason she left her life behind. "Brooks, I ran away from everything, had a child that you never knew about, and let another man, who beat me on occasion, raise her. What part of that is forgivable?"

I pressed my hand over her mouth, so she couldn't say anymore. "All of it. It's true, but you also assumed that we were through. Then you thought I died. If something ever did happen to me, I'd want you to find happiness. Besides, after seeing you for five minutes, I knew you were still in love with me. After that, I didn't care so much. Granted, I was pretty pissed that first night."

It was rough knowing that Kat assumed I was dead. I don't know how long she would have gone on living like that, perhaps the rest of her life. That made me so sad because I knew we'd all be missing out on little Brooklyn.

"I could spend the rest of my life apologizing to you and it will never be enough. What if we don't work out? What then?" Was that a real question? Was she serious?

"First of all, I've already forgiven you, at least for the Brooklyn part. Now, me being a guy, I can see where you'd think that Bobby was a good catch. He seems nice on the outside and given your circumstance, I can understand how him offering to take care of you was a good idea. What I don't understand is how you could let someone physically hurt you more than once. That is what bothers me. It's the only thing that I can't let go of, especially since I've spent my whole life looking out for you."

"I'm weak. Losing you broke me. Knowing what we could have been shattered my soul. Once I knew I'd made a horrible mistake, I just ran. I didn't stop driving until I was sure that I wouldn't be found. Facing any of you would have been impossible. I thought I had things under control, but I started getting sick and then I discovered I was pregnant. I know my decisions were prompted by desperation. I'll admit to that. I'll also admit that after time, I developed feelings for Bobby; feelings that may or may not have blinded me from a lot of things. The problem with falling for someone else was that I knew I was letting you go. When I thought you'd died, I snapped. I think a part of me died with you that day even though you obviously weren't dead. I gave up hoping and settled for what I already had. Was

423

it a mistake? Probably. At the time, I didn't have many options."

"Not until I showed up," I added.

I took her hand into mine and laced them together.

"When I found out you were alive, I didn't even tell him. I ran right to you. I had to see you, to touch you and know that it was real. You can't imagine what I went through. I was miserable. It was hard to even take care of B. My heart hurt for her never being able to know you. I couldn't let go because I wanted to believe that someday we'd be together. I'll always run to you, Brooks. It's why I know that this time is different. Our time apart taught me that my life is nothing unless you're in it. B needs her real father, not a replacement. She needs to grow up understanding what real love feels like. I will do anything to make what I did up to you and prove that no matter where I was, or who I was doing it with, I never gave anyone my whole heart. I fell in love with you when we were children and it's never gone away."

"Me too."

She shook her head, like she wasn't satisfied. "No, I think I even remember the exact moment. We were all three in the tub together. I guess we were around five. I'd asked my mother if she'd stop making me take baths with you two because Branch made fun of me all the time. Remember he used to point at me and laugh because I was different?"

I had to smile. It was fun thinking back to those days. "Yeah, I remember. He only picked on you because he liked you."

"Don't take up for him." She slapped me lightly on the chest. "Anyway, this one time he said I was ugly. It made me cry. You pushed him against the faucet and it cut his back. He got out crying and ran and told on you. Then you looked right at me, as innocent as it probably was, and told me-"

I cut her off. "You're pretty to me. That's what I said, wasn't it?"

She seemed shocked that I remembered.

"Well, you were always pretty, until you hit puberty. Then you became beautiful."

I could tell I'd earned brownie points.

"I don't deserve you," she said against my lips.

Being this close to her was so sensual. Everything about her body screamed for my attention. It was hard to stay focused.

"You know, Kat, I told my Mom once that I was in love with you. I think we were around ten and we'd all three been up in the tree house playing. You had those Barbie's up there and Branch kept throwing them out and making you climb down and get them. About the third time he did it, I grabbed his arm and yanked it until he cried. I remember him running to tell on me and when Mom asked me why I did it, I looked right up at her and said 'because I love her'. I think my mom always knew that it had never gone away. She even suspected something the night of our first kiss, or maybe my brother ran in and tattled about what we were doing. She kept giving me an evil eye all night, silently accusing me of something. Maybe I just felt like we'd done something naughty. At any rate, she knew how I felt about you. So did my dad. He pulled me aside when you started dating Branch. He told me that there were plenty of other girls out there for me. He didn't get that I didn't want any other girls. It's the reason I started bringing random girls home. Part of it was because I thought you'd get jealous and want me instead of Branch. The other part was because they both pulled me aside and asked me if I was okay with you being with him. I couldn't admit that I wasn't. Mom made a huge deal trying to keep me occupied while you were doing your own things and making out with Branch. Finally, I knew they wouldn't stop until I showed them that I didn't care. It wasn't always an act. Some of those girls were fun." I began to chuckle quietly while I waited for her to respond.

"I guess I deserve that."

"Stop. Kat, no matter who I was with, in my eyes, they were always you. Besides, I wasn't innocent. I lost my virginity to a girl who didn't even know it was me. You could hate me forever for that one alone, but I went and did it twice, because I couldn't say no to you. I couldn't go and get Branch when I knew I could be what you wanted. I used to dream that halfway into it you'd say you knew it was me the whole time. I was pretty messed up."

"You know, the first time, it was only my second time. It's probably why Branch didn't even understand what I was talking about. I wasn't running around sleeping with your brother. It took me a long time to do that. Maybe I always knew that it wasn't right."

"Damn, if I'd have known that I probably would have told you, seeing as I know I was better. I watched a lot of porn while you were out with my brother. You can learn so much if you turn the volume down and fast forward through the story part." It was so easy to be honest with her. I couldn't help share every detail about myself.

"Eww, don't tell me that."

"You should see the collection we had overseas. It gets real lonely."

"I wish we could go back."

"Don't," I said as I pressed my lips on the top of her head. "We're here now. All of that bullshit that we've gone through has only made what we have stronger. I'm not living in the past, Kat. It's time to move forward. I'll be by your side if you want to divorce Bobby. If you're not ready…"

"Not ready? It should have never happened. I think everyone is forgetting that I didn't marry him because I wanted to. I married him because I was out of options. Bobby was good to me for the most part, but I will definitely be divorcing him, the sooner the better."

"Just checking. So, about the plan. Will you go along with it?"

She looked me straight in the eyes. "I'll do whatever you want me to, Brooks."

Hmm, that was the wrong thing to say to a horny man. "Don't tell me that. I'll start making lists."

Just as Kat reached below the covers to check me out, we heard a sound coming from the other bed. There she was, our little girl, awake and curious. "There's my girl. Come up here. Let's get Mama."

While we wrestled and played I could tell Kat was still thinking about seeing my parents and introducing them to our little girl. I wasn't though. I knew they'd love her and be grateful to have Kat back in their lives again. It was just going to take a little push on my part to make sure it happened. When we all went back to sleep I was optimistic about our trip, but only time would tell if it helped or hurt us.

Chapter 42

When I woke up bright and early to someone smacking me in the face, I had to smile, because I knew who the culprit was. "Good morning, sunshine," I whispered to keep from waking up her mother.

B touched my nose. "Daddy."

"Let's change your diaper and go get mama some coffee. She needs her sleep."

I'd never changed a diaper in my life, so I paid close attention to the one I was taking off, in order to be able to put the clean one on. At first I felt like I was invading her privacy. I mean, she was a little girl, and I was a grown man. While she laid there smiling at me, I finally understood that this was a normal natural thing any father would do. I had to get used to it because from now on I was going to be pitching in. It was surprising when B helped me fasten the diaper. She grabbed her dress out of the bag and swung it around. It took me a second to figure out the buttons, but finally she was dressed.

As soon as I threw on a pair of pants and a shirt we were out the door, searching for some coffee to wake mama up with. Kat was never a morning person though our daughter seemed to be the happiest as soon as she woke up. I saw many future moments together between the two of us.

After we got two cups of coffee, and a fresh apple juice for B, we went back into our hotel room. Kat was already sitting up in the bed, probably wondering where the two of us had gone off to. She smiled when she saw what I was carrying. "Wow, I could get used to this. Oh my gosh," she noticed B was dressed. "You did that?"

"She helped."

Kat covered her face. "You're the sweetest."

"Anything for my girl. I wanted you to be in good mood when you woke up. Plus, my little bug needed some juice for the ride."

We stayed until Kat could get dressed and then got back on the road. I couldn't remember ever being so excited to go home, but I'd also never had everything I wanted within an arms reach.

Little B had no idea what she was getting ready to enter into. She couldn't know that she was about to meet two people that would cherish her every move.

She was about to be spoiled, and I couldn't wait to watch it happen.

Kat on the other hand needed a stiff drink. She was a ball of nerves while I drove, and as we pulled onto the street I thought she was going to vomit.

"We're in this together, Kat," I reminder her as we pulled up.

I helped get B out of the vehicle while I waited for her mother to follow. I half expected to have to carry her the rest of the way since she was being so stubborn. She looked right at me as I put B down and knocked on the door. I watched her taking a step backward and grabbed her hand before she was able to chicken out.

The door opened, and all eyes were on us. My mother pulled Kat into her arms. This was insanely beautiful to watch. It was like everything she'd been scared of was being lifted away. "Katy, oh my God. I can't believe it's really you." They both began crying, not letting go of each other. Then my mother gasped. She slowly removed her hold on Kat and looked up at our little girl. Never once had she noticed that I was holding a child. B clung to the string on my hoodie, hiding her face from the person she didn't know yet.

"Mom, I think you should let us in."

She backed up while staring at our daughter. Once we got into the foyer, B turned and began looking around. That's when she knew, without a doubt, that this little girl was my child. "I'd like you to meet my daughter, Brooklyn."

My mom lost it, covering her mouth as she began to bawl. I walked up and hugged her. When she pulled away, she just kept looking at her, crying. B swatted at her face. "No cry."

It was hard to see my mom so shocked. It broke my heart to know she hadn't ever met her before. I guess I wasn't even thinking that I'd just met her too. "Hi. I'm your grandma, Brooklyn."

"We call her B, so she doesn't get confused when she hears my name," I explained.

My mom turned her attention to back to Kat. She was so distraught, and I understood why. Everything was coming around full-circle, and although it was something she needed to get through, it still didn't make it easy. "I'm so sorry." She managed to get out.

Then my dad walked into the room. He was looking down at his camera. "Sorry, I just needed to replace the batteries." He looked up and saw us standing there, two women in tears, me with a big smile, and a child completely confused.

"Hey, Dad. Long time no see." I was trying to break the ice though I don't think it worked.

It was apparent he didn't know what to say. The poor man just kept looking at us, as if he were in some kind of dream. "Look, we know we have a lot of explaining to do. Can we get settled for a while first? B needs a fresh diaper and I know she's probably starving."

My mom took over as if she knew exactly what to do. "I've already made a turkey, and Dad got those sweet rolls you both love."

I stopped her. "Mom. Breathe. I know it's a lot to take in, but we'll be here for a week, so how about we take a breather, go unpack and meet you in the dining room?"

She nodded. "Okay."

B wanted to get down. I wasn't about to fight her. I knew she wanted to explore. There were a lot of cool things around the house to get into. She looked up at my mom and started swinging her body from side to side.

My mom bent down to her level. "Do you want something to drink?"

"Chocate mulk." My little bug knew exactly what she wanted, and she also used her cuteness to make sure she got it.

I watched the woman that raised me smile while tears still ran down her cheeks. "Well, okay. Let's go see if we can find some of that." She looked up at Kat. "Is it okay? I can change her if it helps?"

Kat handed her the diaper bag. "Sure. Thank you."

It was nice to see my dad walk over and pull Kat into a hug. I could tell they were both so happy to see her, with or without our huge surprise. "Welcome home, Katy."

Kat was still a mess as she clung to the man. "I miss you. I missed you so much."

When I knew she wasn't going to let go, I took it upon myself to remind her that we had plenty of time. "Let's go up and get settled."

One thing I hadn't pegged on was my dad tearing up. I couldn't remember ever seeing it happen. "We really missed you. Both of you."

I shook his hand out of respect. "I'm sorry it's been so long, Dad. We just needed time."

By the time we reached the steps I could tell Kat was a little relieved. I took her hand in mine and smiled. "Yours or mine?"

She shrugged. "Yours?"

While she sat down on my bed, I crouched in front of her. "How are you doing?"

"They don't hate me."

I put my hands on her knees. "I know you're freaking out. Close your eyes and breathe, Kat."

She did as she was told, taking a few deep breaths.

"Is it better?"

I didn't stand up until I knew she was okay. "We should probably put B in your room. I bet Dad even has some of those things in the attic so she won't fall out of bed."

"How can you be so calm about this?" She acted as if I had super powers. Didn't she know that this was like a dream to me? I had everyone I loved in the same house. My life was damn near perfect. Nothing could take that away from me.

"Because they can't change anything. We're here and B's here. It is what it is. It's also the same reason that I came after you that first night. I couldn't change what's happened, but I sure as hell could change the future."

"You told me that we'd never be together."

I laughed and shook my head. "I said that so you'd push me away. If you were happy then I wasn't going to ruin it for you."

"You're unbelievable."

"I'd like to think I'm generous."

"Not fighting for me is stupid, plain and simple."

"It's a good thing I didn't have to. You came to your senses faster than I thought you would."

One kiss turned into a heated moment. Before I could stop her, Kat's hand was running up inside of my shirt. My desire to toss her down on the bed and have my way was leading me to forget we weren't alone. I pulled away. "We need to go downstairs."

She cupped me between the legs. "Are you sure?"

I had to readjust my shorts, so it wasn't noticeable that I'd gotten turned on.

Kat teased me by licking over her lips. I pointed right at her. "Stop it. You can have your way with me later. Right now we need to go downstairs and clear the air. You're clearly stalling."

We shared one more kiss, a slow and passion-filled one at that. "I love you, Brooks," She said as she opened her eyes.

"Not as much as I love you, Kat."

Stepping into the kitchen was like being back in time, with the exception of little B, sitting on a chair with a phonebook underneath her butt. She had turkey in her hand and continued swinging her legs when we came into the room. "Grab the mayonnaise when you walk by the refrigerator, will ya?" Once we were all sitting at the table, I could tell they were waiting for answers.

All of a sudden, out of left field, Kat just started explaining how Brooklyn was my child. "She's Brooks' daughter. When I found out I was pregnant I had them check on the date of conception several times. I wasn't with Branch at all the whole month of December. Brooklyn was born September 11th if you need to check on the math."

I placed my hand on her knee to try to calm her. "Now that you know, can we talk about something else?"

It was obvious Kat realized she was a little nervous. She reiterated again. "Sorry. I know you were going to ask and I also know that Brooks and Branch have identical DNA. Anyone would want to know."

My mom reached over the table and smiled. "Katy, we weren't going to ask."

"I don't understand. You'd just believe me?" She had a point. Why wouldn't they question the paternity? We were about to find out.

My dad cut in. "We assumed Branch told you. When he proposed to you, we told him to tell you."

"Tell her what?" I wanted to know what the big secret was.

"Branch can't have kids. He was born with a tumor on his testicle and they had to go in and cut out part of the tube that sends the semen into the penis. He's sterile," my mom explained.

Kat seemed like she'd seen a ghost. "He knew I wanted children."

I could tell she felt betrayed, but we both knew he would have done anything he could to keep us apart. In that moment I began laughing uncontrollably. "That bastard. I can't believe the levels he stooped to keep us apart. You're telling us that he knew he couldn't have kids?"

"That's exactly what we're telling you, son," My dad reassured us.

I started making my plate while smiling huge. "This day just keeps getting better."

Kat kicked me under the table, only making the whole moment more funny. Didn't she understand that we won anyway? We were together, and nothing was going to change that, especially not my brother.

"Sorry, we were just worried that you'd think we were lying to keep Branch from B."

My dad folded his hands and looked toward Kat as he spoke. "I'm feeling a bit disturbed myself, Katy. It seems there's a lot of things that Branch did that we weren't aware of. If we would have known, we never would have let you accept his proposal."

Then my mother cut in. "Of course not. Katy, we knew how Brooks felt about you. I never could understand what made you pick Branch. I mean, I love both of my sons, but they're very different. I should have said something back then, I suppose."

Kat remained as calm as she could. "Brooks and I have decided that we're not going to dwell on what's already been done. We can't change any of it. We just want to move forward, with our daughter and our future." When she looked at me I knew we were on the same page, finally, after so long.

It only took me a second to give all my attention to little B. I shoved food in my mouth and opened it to show her. She mocked me and began giggling.

"I can see that some things haven't changed." My mother joined in.

"How about we start over?" Kat added.

"Katy, you're home. As much as I would have loved to be a part of your life for the past two and half years, I understand why you felt like you had to leave. I'm not going to lie. That morning you left was a day I don't like thinking about, but aside from sending everyone home with their gifts, it wasn't so bad. Walt and I were worried what would happen when you finally saw Brooks again. My mother used to tell me that absence makes the heart grow fonder. You two grew up in the same house. It wasn't hard to believe at all."

"I didn't want to hurt anyone. I left because I couldn't bear to see your faces. I thought you'd hate me."

"We were angry that we let it go as far as it did. Branch hasn't always been forthcoming, but he made it a point to shove everything about the two of you in his brother's face. We accept blame for allowing it to happen. The fact that you two found each other again, just proves that it's right."

I squeezed her leg as I spoke. "She thought you were going to make her sleep in the tree house."

"We might make you sleep there, but not Katy, and certainly not little Brooklyn, who's obviously named after her father." My mom was in heaven. When I saw her peer over at my

441

beautiful daughter I knew why. It wasn't just my dreams coming true, but also her own. She had her family back, and I felt overwhelmed with comfort.

Chapter 43

The rest of our first day consisted of a bunch of catching up. My parents were captivated by their granddaughter, and I had to admit that she was pretty crazy about them too. For me, it was surreal. I felt so at home, being there with them. It was as if I could picture our lives there with them, and B knowing she'd always have them to turn to. That's when I really started thinking about the future. I knew Kat had just built a house, and as much as I didn't want to take her away from it, I wondered if she'd ever be willing to move again?

My life now revolved around them. I wanted us both to be comfortable without worry. Since I'd never settled down since joining the military, I had a pretty big savings. I also had money that was supposed to go to my college that I'd never used. With all that sitting in a bank drawing interest I knew I'd be able to buy a larger home, possibly closer to my parents.

It wasn't until I walked outside to grab something out of my truck when I noticed the for sale sign on Kat's old house. It was obvious what I wanted to do. I just needed to make sure she'd be okay with it.

A little later my dad and I went up in the attic to try to find bed rails. Once we were up there, in the intense heat, I started looking around. My dad sat down as if it wasn't blistering hot. "Do you want to talk about it?"

"About what?" I asked.

"Well, the girls for one. The fact that you have a daughter. Any of it?"

"I'm happy, dad. That's all I care about. I want to spend the rest of my life providing for my girls."

"Did you really know about Brooklyn this whole time?"

I couldn't lie to my dad, not when he knew me so well. I sat down on a bin across from him, and prepared to tell him the truth, until I noticed the bedrails in plain sight. "Look, there they are."

"Brooks, I need to know you're okay. I mean, I know you're happy. You obviously have everything you've ever wanted. I'm worried about how it came to be."

I turned and looked the man right in the eyes. "Dad, it's hot as hell up here. When I tell you I'm fine, I mean it. Kat and B are my life. I'm not just happy, I'm ecstatic, I'm elated, I'm overjoyed."

He patted my shoulder. "I'm glad to hear it. I know your mom is going to be gone half the time from now on."

"What do you mean?" I asked as we started to pull the bedrails out.

"She's not going to want to be so far away from her granddaughter."

I smiled. "Yeah. I hate going to work and leaving them. If I could stay at home and live in a bubble I would. Hey, do you know anything about the house next door?"

"Why? Are you in the market?"

"I might be."

"I'll get you the information."

"Just do me a favor and don't mention it to Kat."

"Why, are you afraid she won't want to move. You know your mother and I don't blame her for leaving."

"It's not that, dad. I want it to be a surprise."

"Wow, you're going all out."

"I've got a family to consider now. I'm pretty sure I'm not going to be returning to full duty. My hand is too messed up. If things go as I suspect, I might be looking for a job outside of the military. Since I have security clearance, I'd be better searching for something around this area. It's still too soon to be sure, but I'm just trying to stay on top of it."

"Whatever you need us to do, we'll be there. Even if you need to stay here for a while. This house has been so quiet. It would be great to have it full of people again."

After we got the railings put in Kat's old room, we joined the women downstairs. I caught them in mid conversation and stood in the other room to eavesdrop.

I heard my mom's voice first. "Don't let that get to you. I think you both needed the time apart. I don't mean that like you're assuming. What I mean is that you needed the time to figure out your feelings. Between the two of us, I think you probably always knew. You've favored Brooks since the three of you were babies."

Kat sounded like she laughed. "I never really thought about it. When we were kids we all three loved each other. It was so innocent back then."

"Honey, we all grow up. We make mistakes and we learn from them. I wish that you all didn't have to hurt each other so much, but everyone's happy now. Even Branch seems content with his life."

"He won't be happy to know I'm here. I'm sure I'm the last person he and Melissa ever want to see again." That may have been true, but we were going to have to face them. My parents wouldn't take no for answer, not if they thought they could have us all back together again.

"Katy, it's none of my business, but maybe it would do you all some good to work things out."

"I don't know. I can't make a decision like that without Brooks."

I thought about joining in on the conversation, but decided to let it go. I didn't want Kat getting mad at me if I agreed with my mom.

A while later, right after B's bath, my dad I started removing the plastic on the rails so we could put them on the bed. My mom helped get B dressed while Kat reached in her bag and grabbed a book. "B, do you want Mama or Daddy to read it?"

"Daddy and Mama."

It made me so happy to hear her call me that. I almost forgot that she needed me to read the story.

Kat took the lead and then let me finish the book. It was cool how B started to doze off after the first few pages. She did get a kick out of how I read with excitement.

After our daughter was asleep, we met my parents downstairs. They were sipping on wine and offered us some right away.

"We've been talking while you were putting B down. Listen, I know you'll both have a hard time with it, but we want to have your brother and Melissa over before you leave. We're a family, all of us. So much time has passed and we never know when something could happen." My mom wasn't going to drop it. She was adamant about having my brother come for a visit.

"Okay," Kat replied.

I turned my attention to her, shocked. "Wait, did you just say okay?"

"Yeah. We can handle Branch and even my ex best-friend Melissa. Some more of this wine might be necessary though."

Everyone in the room began to crack up.

We stayed up for a while after that, talking and catching up. When my parents would ask questions that made Kat uncomfortable, I'd take over, giving them enough information to keep them satisfied. I was sure there were gaps they were trying to fill in their minds, but they seemed content with whatever I fed them.

Kat went up to bed first, leaving me to say good night to my parents. I wanted them to know how much I appreciated everything they were doing. Surprisingly I hadn't even thought about Bobby or the fact that we still had all of that mess to deal with.

When I entered my bedroom I didn't see Kat anywhere. It was obvious she'd gone through my bag. Clothes were strewn all around it. I pulled off my shorts and climbed into my bed, figuring Kat would come to bed when she was ready. I never expected her to come jumping out of the closet, wearing nothing but my camo jacket and boots.

When I realized what she was doing I put my hands behind my head and prepared for a show. The jacket was unbuttoned, leaving little to the imagination. I licked my lips as I watched her sauntering in my direction.

At first it was sexy. I was preparing for it to get even hotter when her knees hit the mattress. Unfortunately, that's not what happened.

Kat lost her balance, tumbling down to the floor. By the time I leaned over to see what had happened, she was holding her knee. It was obvious she'd had a little too many glasses of wine with my parents. While signs of blood were obvious on her knees, she sat there laughing at herself.

"Are you alright?"

"I feel like an idiot. This was supposed to be sexy."

I gave her a once-over "Trust me, Kat, you're extremely sexy. Maybe next time you can go without the boots." I pulled them off one at a time and helped her back up. Next I removed the large jacket, leaving her naked in front of me.

"You really think I'm sexy?" She asked.

I leaned forward and kissed her sultry lips slowly. "I can't wait to get you in the pool tomorrow."

She smirked. "How about we go swimming right now?"

I was thinking about it, that's for sure. "Don't tempt me with your nakedness, woman. I'm weak when it comes to you."

"You make me happy." She latched onto my arms to hold herself up.

I took her by the hand and led her to my bed. "We can swim tomorrow."

She sat straight up. "Can we make love now?"

I couldn't help from laughing at her. She was so cute this way. "You want to make love with my parents downstairs and our daughter across the hall?"

"Is this a trick question?"

I walked my fingers from her belly button to one of her breasts. Then flicked the tip, causing her to jump. "Can you be quiet?"

She snickered. "Probably not."

I was chuckling, but stopped to whisper in her ear. "If you can be really quiet, I'll make love with you. Can you be quiet, beautiful?"

She nodded.

I knew right where to kiss to send her into a frenzy. "Close your eyes."

I took my time, kissing her tenderly down there. I took my chin and rubbed my stubble over her whole pussy. She was already reacting the way I expected her to. I used one hand to spread her open and lowered my mouth to begin licking her. I sucked her clit into my mouth at the same time as two fingers slid inside of her. I loved making her feel this way. She was bucking against my face, suddenly screaming out when I brought her satisfaction.

Kat sat straight up, covering her mouth. I knew how embarrassed she was, hoping that when she slept it off she'd forget it happened, but I never would. As wrong as it was, I felt empowered.

I wiped off my face before kissing her. "You suck at keeping quiet."

"I couldn't help it. I'm never going downstairs."

I rubbed her between the legs, implying what was still to come. "You're going to have to put a sock in your mouth because I'm not even halfway finished."

She kicked off the covers and snickered as I came in for another kiss. "I'll be quiet this time."

"I don't care how loud you get. Do you have any idea how long I've wanted to do this is my bedroom with you?"

She slapped me lightly on the back. "You're funny."

"You're mine, Kat. You're finally all mine."

Chapter 44

I hadn't had my mother's breakfast in years, and damn did it smell good downstairs. Unlike me, Kat was freaking out about facing my parents after making sure the whole neighborhood heard her getting off before going to bed.

"I told you, I'll tell you again. I'm not going down there. I'm never showing my face again," Kat whispered.

"I hate to break it to you, but our daughter's been kidnapped by her grandmother. There's no telling what they're getting into. In fact, I think I remember her saying something about sugar and running around naked to be free."

Kat hopped off the bed and started looking around for her clothes. "You're an ass. I happen to know your mom would never do that."

"Then why are you so worried?" I asked.

She growled and went into the bathroom to brush her teeth. I met her in there, remembering having to wait for my turn when we were kids. While she was staring into the mirror I hip checked her, shoving her over so I could use it. She smacked my ass and pushed me out of her way. "I was in first."

I got on my tippy toes and looked over her. In the mirror I could see her checking out my naked chest. "You better cut it out. If my mom sees you giving me that eye it's going to remind her of those noises you made last night. I'm pretty sure she's going to have to pray for you at church. It's possible she might assume we were into some kinky shit."

While I enjoyed getting to her, Kat took a wet washcloth and smacked me on the side. "Shut up, Brooks."

I took her hand. "Come on. You don't need to get dolled up for our family. They've already seen you at your worst."

I knew she was reluctant, but Kat followed me down the stairs. I couldn't help notice she was wearing another one of my army shirts. In all honesty it made me terribly horny. At least I knew I'd be able to remove it later.

I made Kat a cup of coffee first, handing it over to her. "Just how you like it."

She seemed amused that I knew how she liked it.

"Did you two sleep well?" My mother asked.

I kept filling my plate with food while I responded to her question. "Go ahead and ask the burning question. I'm sure you all heard Kat. Apparently we need to watch giving her wine because she takes all of her clothes off and hides in my closet."

They started to laugh.

"Oh, it gets better. She put on my boots and jacket and thought that she was going to be sexy. After two steps she fell down face first. After that, we slept pretty good, right Kat?" I looked over and noticed how embarrassed she was. She was going to pay me back, and I couldn't wait for it to happen.

Kat tried to remain composed. "I'm okay if anyone is concerned."

My mom's next comment was obviously something Kat wasn't thrilled about.

"So I sent Branch an email this morning asking them to come to dinner Friday night. I'm waiting to hear back, but they both get off early during the week, since they live on the other side of the bridge, but work over here. The traffic gets so bad on the weekends that sometimes they get stuck in it for hours. I let them know that there is plenty of room for them to stay the night and go home on Saturday."

While my mom kept talking I teased my little girl by sticking my tongue through a large pancake. She giggled, so I kept doing it.

"Brooks Michael, don't teach her that!" My mom meant business when she went after my middle name.

"I've decided that since I'm a parent now I can make my own rules. If B wants to play with her food she can as long as she still eats it."

Kat didn't correct me.

"So, we were talking last night, and Mom and I want to know if the two of you have any plans yet? Are you going to finally get married?"

I could tell Kat wasn't in any shape to answer that. "We're not in a hurry to do it." I began. "I mean, I've been gone a long time. We've just found each other again. We're happy the way things are, and when the time is right, I suppose we'll get that piece of paper. For now I've got everything I want already."

I don't know if they could sense it wasn't a topic in which Kat and I had discussed yet, but they dropped it after my explanation.

When breakfast was over my parents took B to introduce her to some friends. That meant Kat, and I had the whole house to ourselves. "Get your suit on and meet me out back." It wasn't a request. I expected her to want to join me.

"It's ten in the morning. You want to go swimming now?"

"We're home alone and there's a pool outside. If you don't feel like changing then take off your clothes and come as you are. The choice is yours."

She gave me one of her looks as if she was too good to be naked outdoors. "We have neighbors."

"Actually, my beautiful lady, there's nobody living in your old house. Dad told me last night. Since the pool is on that side, you're out of excuses." I pulled her close, traipsing my lips over hers. All the while I watched as her eyes became heavy. I was seducing her, and she knew it.

In the middle of the kitchen, for anyone to walk in and see, I felt my shorts being tugged down. The next thing I knew Kat was on her knees, taking my full dick in her hand. She was on a mission of her own, and I wasn't about to stop her.

Her lips licked the tip of my cock before taking the whole thing deep in her mouth. My head immediately fell back. I was losing myself with every single rock of her head. The sounds of her sloshing saliva around for lubrication only made the gliding of her thrusts feel more intense. I couldn't help from groaning because it felt too damn good not to.

Kat was going all out, forcing herself to take me as far as she could. She used her other hand to jerk me off, causing a chain reaction to happen deep inside of me. I was about to lose it, my mind a puddle of mush. That's why I had to stop her. I couldn't waste it when we had this much time to kill.

"Hold up, Kat. Let's go upstairs."

She flipped "I have a better idea." She pulled me along until we were standing beneath the tree house. I smacked her butt, climbing each step with only one purpose in mind.

Once we were under the cover of our childhood clubhouse, I pulled her into my arms. My lips were on her while I wasted no time undressing her. Kat didn't have to work hard to remove my shorts and then boxers. We were on the same page, with one common reward to thrive for.

Our making out became so intense that we both sank to the floor, her body straddling on top of mine. I kept my hands on her hands, teasing her with how turned on I already was. In retrospect she had just given me a blowjob in my parents kitchen, which was obviously sexy as hell.

The small area served as a giant sauna. Beads of sweat ran down our skin, tasting like salt as we licked each other's throats. I was so ready to fill her, to make love where it all started.

I shoved Kat's body back to suck a nipple into my mouth. There was nothing romantic about this encounter once we got started. I craved to be inside of her; to give her everything I had to offer in this world, and then even more. "Please, Brooks," she begged.

"Please, what? Tell me, Kat. I want to hear you say it." She could have shouted it from the rooftops, and I would have obliged.

"I want you so bad," she cried out.

I teased her with my fingers first, feeling her tight walls accepting my strides in and out of her. "I can't get enough of this pussy. Tell me it's mine. Say it, Kat."

I could tell I was getting her off. She bit down on her lips and threw her head back, succumbing to her own desire. "This pussy is yours, Brooks. I'm yours."

I rubbed her clit, hard enough where I knew she wouldn't be able to stop what was happening to her. It gave me such pleasure to bring her this type of pleasure. "Oh yeah, that's it."

The next time our lips met I was sliding inside of her. She didn't need to recover from the finger play. That had been the appetizer, and this was the main course. I entered her easily, using her own juices to guide the way. When I realized it was feeling too good, it was apparent I'd have to slow down. "Stand up and turn around."

Kat turned and put her hands up above the window frame. I positioned myself behind her before entering. In the yard behind us a man was mowing the lawn. Kat said nothing as I began fucking her right there, where he could have seen at any moment. I reached forward, pinching her nipples and holding them in place while rocking my stiff erection in and out repeatedly. Then I reached between her legs, giving her little clit some undivided attention. I shoved her against the glass, pushing her tits on the hard surface. It fogged up where her face was close, only reminding me of the temperature inside the small area.

Kat cried out again, fueling my own release. My knees became weak, almost buckling. The more she cried the tighter her walls became. "That's it, Kat. Smother me with that pussy."

She screamed so loud I bet that neighbor could hear. It was so awesome. When we were done I turned her around, shoving my lips against hers. I entered her again, almost forcing my way in between her legs again. She was still trying to recover, but I couldn't hold it. The harder I pushed the more she accepted. I couldn't stop. It was quite literally the hottest sexual experience to date.

I kissed her once I was able to catch my breath. "God, I love you."

She was quite comfortable leaning against my soaked body. "I love you, too."

Chapter 45

We'd been at my parent's house for days, and I don't think any of us had ever been happier. Kat's problems seemed like a distant memory, and our time together was only proving how our time apart had made our love stronger.

The best part of every day was waking up seeing my little girl. Her smile made me weak, and when she called me her daddy I felt like the luckiest man in the world.

By the time Friday came around I could tell Kat was beginning to worry about Branch and Melissa's visit. The last time either of us had seen them was the night before Kat was supposed to wed Branch. I could imagine she had a lot of things she wanted to say to him, but wondered if it was the same for him. I hadn't spoken to my brother in the years I'd been away. Sure, he'd sent cards, but I had no interest in being his buddy. He'd cost me too much. Now that I had it back, I didn't know what to say to him.

"Kat, how long are you going to sit there? That bathing suit isn't going to put itself on, and if I have to stare at you in that towel for much longer, we're going to have a bigger and much harder problem." I pointed to my genitals as I walked over and kissed her head. "Look, I know you're nervous. It's one night and then they'll be gone."

"Am I allowed to hurt him?"

I laughed while grabbing the top to her two-piece and started putting it on her. "For the sake of my parents, let's try to be on our best behavior. When they go to leave tomorrow, you can run out and do whatever you want to both of them. I'll cover you."

She seemed please with that idea. "I don't know what I'd do without you. In one week you've changed my whole life. How is this even possible?"

"You weren't the only one who was miserable. If you'd seen the things that I've seen, you wouldn't want to live in the past either. Kat, we have a daughter now. I'm trying not to lose my man-card here, but I want us to work. When we go home, we're together. We'll have a lot to deal with, but we'll do it as a team. People aren't going to understand. They're not going to like that you're kicking your husband out and moving me in, but that's exactly what's going to happen. I'm not letting either of you out of my sight. The moment he laid a hand on you was when I lost respect for him. My daughter will not go anywhere near him and he can thank himself for that."

"It's still hard to believe."

I got down on my knees to assist her in putting on the bottoms. "No, it's not. Tell me this - when I came back the first time for the wedding, how long did it take you to realize that you were with the wrong brother?"

I could tell she didn't have to think hard about it. "You know the answer."

"Humor me, woman."

"I supposed I knew it even before I saw you. I remember standing there watching for you to get out of a cab in your fatigues. My heart was racing and I couldn't calm myself down. Then when I saw you for the first time, it was like the whole room disappeared except for me and you. Fighting those feelings was impossible for me. I knew I was making a mistake, but I couldn't figure a way out of it."

I stood back up and pulled her against me. "I was on the airplane with this old couple. They kept thanking me for risking my life for my country. About halfway through the elderly lady asked if I was married. I sat there with two strangers, and told them all about the girl I'd loved my whole life, and how she was marrying my twin brother." I shook my head and chuckled. "I was so messed up in my head that day. I'd thought about what I wanted to say to you a million times. It was shocking when that old woman, who'd been married for more than half her life, told me I had to stop the wedding. She said I'd never forgive myself if I didn't tell you how I really felt. When I got out of the cab and saw you standing there, I knew I was going after you. Something inside of me snapped. There was no way I could let you go through with it without telling you everything. I didn't do it to get you into my bed. That part happened on its own. Obviously, in making love to you that night, we made the most beautiful little girl. I could tell you that we're together because of her, but it would be a lie. I wanted you back the minute I saw you on the army base, I just needed to be mad first. I felt so betrayed and hurt. For my whole life I'd thought

Branch was keeping us apart. Then I found out you were married to someone else."

Kat put her arms around my neck. "Can I be honest about something?"

I nodded. I was prepared for anything she had to say. It wasn't like I had to worry about her not wanting to be with me. She'd run out of reasons to shut me out. We needed each other.

"I could lie and tell you that I would have been faithful in my marriage, to be honorable. The thing is, the second I knew you were alive was when I knew for certain that I was fighting a losing battle with my heart. If you'd have come on to me in those first five seconds, with my husband standing right there, I don't think I could have pushed you away. I felt like it was a miracle; like you'd come back from the dead to save me from myself."

For a few seconds we just sat there staring at each other. It was like we didn't need to say words to know what the other was thinking. As intense as it felt the doorbell snapped us both back to reality.

Kat put a dress on over her swimsuit.

B was coming at us, running full-force. I picked her up and spun her around. I could tell Kat was a nervous wreck, but at least our little one didn't have a care in the world. She was so high on life that one couldn't help from smiling when they got around her.

Kat was pretty comedic as we waited for them to come into the living room. I could hear them talking to my parents, knowing at any second my twin would round the corner. I didn't know what she was thinking, but she climbed on top of me and started kissing me. I literally had to push her off. "You're being bad."

She was grinning until they appeared. Then I watched her silliness vanish.

I stood up first, making sure Kat was behind me. In all honesty I wasn't sure if she was going to pounce. I knew, probably more than me, that she had major issues with all of his lies. The fact that he'd hid being sterile was just the icing on the cake. She was livid. He'd cost us so much time apart. For me, I didn't care anymore. I'd do anything to be with Kat even if that included waiting for her to divorce a husband she didn't love. Yeah, all of it derived from my brother's actions, but I couldn't exactly divorce him.

When I first looked at my brother I wanted to laugh. In the years that I'd been away he'd changed. He looked older, but thin, while I'd grown strong. If I would have thrown a punch he may have died. That's how much of a difference there was.

B came running out from around the corner and everyone looked at her. She froze when she saw me and then another man that looked pretty similar. Branch didn't have to say anything because the shock was written on his face. He took off his glasses and peered down at my beautiful daughter. "You've got to be kidding me?"

"Her name is Brooklyn after her father." Kat's tone left nothing to the imagination. She was rubbing it in big time.

Branch looked down and scratched his head. When he looked back at Kat, he held out his arms. "I think we're here to make amends, Katy."

She didn't respond to his gesture.

Melissa seemed just as shell-shocked. Everyone stood there silent for a few seconds. Then B went running toward my mom. "Mom-mom, yook."

She pointed to Branch.

My mom scooped her up. "B, this is your uncle. His name is Branch. Can you say Branch?"

"Banch."

Branch laughed, and then he did something that neither of us would have expected. He held his arms out for her. "Hey, little cutie. Come here and say hi."

She peeked over my mom's shoulder to look at me. I smiled and motioned that it was okay. We watched her, being taken into Branch's arms. He hugged her with more love and affection than I'd ever seen him have. I put my arm around Kat and kissed her on the top of the head. My brother, who was still in awe over her, finally looked in our direction. "She's beautiful."

B made it all easier. Melissa and Branch were captivated by her, and she seemed just as interested in them.

Kat finally spoke to her old friend. "It's been a long time, Mel."

They then hugged. "I missed you so much, Katy." It was nice to see her relaxing. I knew this was something she'd really been upset about.

"I missed you, too. Obviously a lot has happened."

"It's nice to see you, Branch," Kat stated while looking at my brother. It was weird how I didn't feel threatened at all. The truth was finally out. I had my girl, and nothing would take her away from me.

"I don't get a hug?" He asked.

Kat was brutally honest. "I'm not ready for that yet."

Branch let out an air-filled laugh. "It's okay. I guess we all need to warm up to each other."

"Yeah, something like that."

I pinched Kat on her back. "Don't mind her. She's gotten bitter in her old age. I think it has something to do with motherhood."

"Am I the only one here that thinks this is completely insane?" Kat was losing her cool while I cracked jokes.

Branch laughed. "It's only weird if we make it that way, Katy. Look, we've all moved on now and clearly it's for the best. Whatever you have against me needs to be worked out. We were a family before, and we're even more of a family now. Look, Mel and I are getting married. You've got a kid that I don't think any of us knew about. You're obviously with my brother now. We wouldn't have come today if we knew it was going to make you so mad. If it makes you happy, we can leave."

Kat looked around the room at everyone who clearly loved her. She seemed conflicted. Then I saw that look I recognized too well. Before I could stop her she said what was on her mind. "You're right. I'm sorry. I'm sorry for what I did. I'm sorry for lying about my feelings. I'm sorry for hurting everyone in this room, especially Brooks. All of this could have been avoided if none of you ever loved me." When she was finished she hauled ass upstairs.

"Are you going to go after her?" Branch asked me.

"She's not mad at me. Just give her a second to calm down. This is a lot for her."

"What about you?" He asked. "You have a freaking kid. What's up with that?"

I looked over at my daughter. "Yeah, about that. Before you get all excited for me, I think you may want to know when she was conceived."

It took him a second. "No way? You've got to be joking."

"I'm not."

"Who found who?" He wondered.

"She wrote me first. Then I wrote her back. Then I wrote some more. Then I moved to South Carolina."

Branch held up his hand. "Okay, I get the gist."

"I think you should go up and check on her." My suggestion made Branch seem uncomfortable.

"Is she going to stab me with something?"

"Maybe."

He whispered something to Melissa before heading for the stairs. "If she gives me a black eye I'm going to be pissed."

"You deserve it," I said before his body disappeared up the steps.

One way or another Kat was about to get a dose of Branch. They needed to have it out, once and for all. If he said something to piss her off I knew she could handle herself.

Chapter 46

Okay, I lied about being cool about Branch confronting her. After a few seconds I ran up the steps, standing outside of my bedroom door so I could hear what they were saying. I wanted to be there when she cut him to pieces for keeping us apart.

"Brooks is probably going to beat my ass for what I'm about to say to you, but I think it's time you and I got some things out in the open."

It was too soon to clench my fists together. I took a deep breath and remained calm.

"Fine. Say what's on your mind. I know you're dying to." Her response was flip and short. I smiled thinking about the look on her face.

"Some things never change, do they, Katy?"

"What do you mean by that?" Oh yeah, she was defensive. It was about to get good.

"I mean your attitude when it comes to you being in the wrong." Branch was testing her, that's for sure. He knew what buttons to push.

"You just reminded me of why we aren't together. You think the whole world revolves around you, like you should be worshipped." Her words made me cover my mouth to prevent them from hearing me laugh.

"We aren't together because you fucked my brother the night before we were to be married, or have you forgotten that? I'm sure you haven't because judging from my calculations that would have been the night you conceived that pretty little girl downstairs. I still can't believe it. I can't believe that you ran away and had his child without telling anyone. How could you do that? Did you do it to get back at me? You did, didn't you? You wanted me to pay so badly that you cost my parents years without their only grandchild. Tell me I'm wrong. Give me some other reason why you couldn't come home?"

Before I was able to go in there and attack my brother, I heard Kat defending us. "Don't you dare act like you're innocent. All of this is your fault, Branch. You kept us apart. You lied to me to make me think he never loved me. How could you do that to me? Why?"

"Because I wanted you for myself, that's why. No matter what we were doing, he was always your favorite. I hated how you looked at him. We were supposed to be the same. You think I didn't notice the way he always defended you? He promised me that we'd never fight, but yet he had to sneak behind my back when it came to you."

He was being bitter about me sneaking to be with her, but I had every right to.

"Are you talking about our first kiss?" She asked.

"You're damn right I am. He had to have more, even after we'd made a pact."

"We were twelve you big idiot. How can you look at yourself in the mirror, knowing that you're an adult and you act like a child?"

"Don't judge me, Katy. Go judge Mr. Perfect downstairs that at any time could have stopped you the night you were together. He could have pushed you away and told you he felt nothing. He was in the wrong. It's like you're blind when it comes to him. I don't even get why."

"Don't you dare turn this around. He's the victim and you hate that. You can't stand that you did all of this. You can't stand that after all of it, he still got me. Let me just tell you something. I don't care how long we were together, or what you did to try to make me happy. You could never be him, Branch. No matter how much you tried. You're too different. You care about yourself while he puts himself last."

I stopped laughing because her words confirmed it all. She wasn't just telling him how she felt. She was driving the dagger into his chest. Kat wanted Branch to apologize, and it seemed like she wasn't going to stop until he did.

"You're right. That's why I did what I did. It's why I told you he didn't want you and it's why I told him to back off. I knew he'd listen because he always cared about everyone else. Once I had you I knew he wouldn't want my sloppy seconds."

Her next statement shocked me. I couldn't believe she was being so bold. "That's where you're wrong, Branch. I bet you didn't know he lost his virginity to me in that room right across the hall. You see, on the anniversary of when my parents died, I thought it was you that would come into my room and comfort me. I thought it was you holding me because that's what a boyfriend was supposed to do. Little did I know that it was Brooks. He made love to me only days after our first time together, and then on the same day the next year. Both times it wasn't like anything I'd ever felt before."

He'd read my letter. Her statement wasn't a secret, but her knowing was. "What? You knew?"

"No. I didn't know at first. We were together twice, and he never told me. I can't blame him. Though, at first, I wanted to kill him."

"God, I can't believe this."

"I couldn't believe it either. More than that, I couldn't believe that the man I was planning on marrying had conned me into loving him. Did you really think that I'd be happy and that Brooks would never tell me the truth?"

"He gave me his word that I could have you." That's not entirely true. It wasn't like he was making it out to be.

"He told me no that night. That night at the hotel, you were so drunk. You said some horrible things and Brooks just wanted me to feel better. He found me on the roof crying, and everything happened so fast. I know you could never understand and that you'll probably hate me forever, but I've never felt something so powerful as when I'm close to him. It doesn't matter how long we're apart, or what's standing in our way, it's always there. Branch, I'm so sorry that I hurt you. I left because I couldn't face you that next morning. I couldn't look you in the eyes and tell you that I was in love with your brother. I felt so ashamed. The thing is, you knew it all along. You'd been keeping us apart because you knew what we had, didn't you? Do you have any idea what I've gone through because of all of this? I ran away from the only family I have left. I had a child that I couldn't tell anyone about, because I thought they all hated me, including your brother. I moved to a town with nothing but the clothes in my suitcase. You could have prevented all of this. Brooks didn't have to miss the birth of his daughter."

I was ready to walk away. There wasn't anything Kat could say that I didn't already know. Plus I didn't want her coming out and seeing me standing there.

"How did you know she was his?"

"I did the math, and the doctors gave me a three day window of when I conceived. Then we learned you were sterile, which by the way, thanks for that. Another lie that you went along with to get me to marry you."

"Okay. I get the damn point. I was a shitty brother and a lying boyfriend. It doesn't change that fact that you were only with me because you thought he didn't want you. I was your fucking consolation prize, so yeah, I lied. I didn't want either of you to be happy, so I did what I had to do. I gave you everything you wanted, and you still ran to him. All you had to do was be faithful for one night and you couldn't. You had to be with him. Let me know something, Katy. Would you have still married me if I hadn't caught you with him?"

Her answer, that probably hurt him, made me so happy. "No. I think I knew I wasn't going to marry you the moment he walked through the door. Branch, if you ever loved me, in any way, you'd know that I wasn't with Brooks because I wanted to hurt you. I was with Brooks because I couldn't stop myself. Every bone in my body calls for him. When he touches me it's electric. We both loved you and it was the only reason that I walked away from you and from him."

It was clear my brother was getting upset. His voice had changed, and his answers were taking longer. "I did love you, Katy. It wasn't the right kind of love, but it was real. I can't live like this anymore. I've got a good life and Melissa's a great woman. I love her, and I know we'll be happy. She's okay with having to adopt and I don't keep secrets from her. Except for one."

"One?"

"For so long I've told her that I hated you. I wanted you to be miserable and poor. Then I saw your daughter, and I realized what I'd taken from you. You don't have to remind me of what I did. Knowing that I can't have children has been difficult for me to come to grips with. Seeing that Brooks had a child is when it really hit me. You're right, Katy. I kept you apart, and it's my fault you ran away from Brooks. I'm sorry he wasn't there for you. I'm sorry none of us were, because family is supposed to stick together, no matter what. It's time I admit it out loud. I want you to be happy with my brother, because he's loved you for as long as I can remember and I'm sorry for keeping you apart. I suppose I deserved to hear about him sneaking in your room. He always was your hero."

She laughed. "He still is. I thought he'd hate me for keeping my pregnancy from him, but he didn't."

My brother's next words allowed me to walk away. We were all going to be okay now. There was nothing left to worry about.

"Can we please be a family again? I'd really like to get to know my niece, and Melissa misses you. She thinks you hate her."

I found Kat a little later after they'd both come back downstairs with the rest of us. Before she could tell me what they talked about I kissed her softly. "Do you feel better?"

"Yeah, I actually think I do."

"So I'm your hero, huh?"

"You were listening?"

"I'd like to call it protecting," I said sarcastically.

"Well, as you could hear, I had it handled."

"Yeah, you sure did. I'm proud of you, Kat."

"Thanks. That means a lot."

Chapter 47

After everyone seemed to chill out, especially Kat and Branch, I felt like it was a good time to run out to the store with my dad. Even though they had arm floats for B, I thought a swim ring would be better, so she could float around on her own and feel independent, while still being safe. She also needed another bathing suit, from rubbing her butt on the concrete her other one had gotten nasty in the rear.

It was nice driving through the familiar community with my dad, reminiscing about my childhood, and places I'd been.

"You don't talk about overseas much," he mentioned as we sat at a red light.

"There's nothing good to say about it. I watched a lot of people die. It sticks with you even when you leave. I was one of the lucky ones, dad. A couple of my friends weren't so fortunate."

"I figured. You know, your mom and I watch a lot of news about what's going on over there. It was rough knowing we couldn't do anything to help you."

"Yeah, about that. I'm sorry I didn't write. When I was away I wasn't myself. I had demons that kept me from expressing myself. I didn't have anything good to say. I still don't. I love this country, but what I've experienced will haunt me. I'm just glad I have Brooklyn because even on my worst days I know I can look at her and smile."

"She's beautiful, son. She's by far the best thing that's ever happened to this family. We understand why Katy stayed away. I just want you to know how glad we are that you're both back. I hope you consider moving closer, otherwise I can see your mom looking at real estate a little more south."

I let out an air-filled laugh. "It's nice down there, but I think in due time maybe we could settle back here, where we both grew up. Brooklyn would benefit. I have a feeling I'm going to like taking her to museums and other significant places around the area when she's old enough to appreciate it."

We pulled into the mall parking lot, but never got out of the car. "Is everything okay between the two of you, Brooks? I see that you're both overjoyed to be together, but I get this feeling like there's something you're not telling us. Is she pregnant again? Are you having money trouble?"

"You and I both know Kat is good on money. In fact, we're both doing well as far as that goes. There's nothing you need to worry about, dad. My little family is perfect."

"Maybe I'm just overreacting because it's been so long."

I put my hand on my dad's shoulder and looked him directly in the eyes. "My little girl needs us to hurry back so she can swim. Let's go try to pick out something Kat and Mom will approve of."

By the time we arrived back at the house we'd been gone for nearly an hour. Nothing had changed. Branch and Melissa had become obsessed with my daughter. I found them both on the floor playing dolls as if they'd turned themselves into toddlers. Kat was sitting on the couch behind them, seemingly interested in the whole interaction.

B saw me and came running. "Daddy!"

I happily picked her up into my arms, kissing her sweet cheek. "Hey, pretty girl. Daddy missed you."

"Me go to pool," she asked.

I knelt down and opened the bag that contained her new suit and swim ring. "Look what I got you?"

She grabbed the suit and spun around. "Put it on. Put it on."

It delighted me to have this bond with my own child. I loved her so much that I couldn't contain the happiness that radiated off of me when she was near. "Let's go upstairs and get your swim pants on first. Mom-mom won't be happy if you poop in her pool."

Kat had mentioned that she was trying desperately to potty train her. On some days she did well, but with all this excitement she'd been right back to needing a diaper all the time again. I wasn't worried about it. With my help we'd make it happen.

I caught Kat staring off into the distance. She assured me that she was only thinking about her own father, but I wondered if she was telling me truth. Don't get me wrong, I didn't think Kat had a habit of lying to me. The circumstance with Bobby rubbed me the wrong way, so if she was worried about that she'd keep it to herself. I gave her a kiss before turning all of my attention to our beautiful little girl.

She kept repeating the same words again, reminding me that she was waiting. "Put it on. Put it on."

I scooped her up. "Let's go get pretty and show everyone that Daddy knows how to shop."

Her little red bikini with ruffles was the cutest thing on her. I let her wear my glasses for her big reveal. I could tell immediately that Kat was pleased with my selection. "Yook at me. I pwetty," B announced.

My mom acted extremely excited, getting a reaction out of our sweet girl. She giggled and came running back to me, letting me scoop her back up. I brought her over to Kat. "What do you think? Is she not the cutest kid ever?"

"She is. You did good."

I started spinning my little beauty queen around in circles. "B, let's go out and learn how to swim."

When I pulled out her float and began blowing it up, B seemed memorized by its growth. I held onto the nozzle and reached it over for her to try. "You blow on it." She tried, getting more slobber than air. The slobber didn't bother me. That DNA was mine. I placed the float attachment back in my mouth without wiping it. Even though it didn't make me cringe, I saw Kat out of the corner of my eye scrunching up her face. Apparently she didn't have a stomach of steel. At any rate, I wasn't ashamed. I'd share anything with my little girl, and I wanted her to know it.

I pulled off my glasses and her flip-flops before I hopped into the pool. Then I held out my arms for her. She jumped right to me, letting out a scream when her body hit the cool water. She trusted me, and it was something I'd cherish for the rest of my days.

In less than a week's time I had everything I wanted. It was so overwhelming at times that I had to keep reminding myself that it was real.

Enjoying my time in the pool with Brooklyn while my brother watched, only made it all more entertaining. Though I felt bad about him being sterile, a part of me wanted to rub it in his face at the family I now had, after he'd stopped at nothing to prevent it. Plus, I think a part of me was still worried he could have been the father. Doctors have been known to make mistakes. Pinpointing the exact time of conception had to be difficult. Now I knew for sure, without a single doubt, she was mine. No matter what B would always be my flesh and blood. Perhaps Branch saw it that way too. If he were to have a child the same chromosomes would have been shared.

My daughter laughing captured my train of thought. "Again, Daddy. Again." I was spinning her around in the float, getting a kick out of how she acted when I stopped and watched her little head trying to catch up.

"How about you jump in? Do you want to do that?"

She nodded. I immediately lifted her out of the ring and stood her on the edge of the pool wall. "Okay, don't jump until I say go, B. You got it?"

She shimmied her little body from side to side. "Otay."

I held out my arms, appreciating the fact that she trusted me so completely. "One-two-three-go!" Like a bird taking flight for the first time, I watched my little girl jumping into my arms. I caught her easily, pulling her against my body. "You did so good. Daddy's so proud of your bravery."

She obviously had no clue what I was talking about, albeit I was too proud to explain it to her. I think she knew I was ecstatic.

After the first time, little bug jumped into my arms nearly thirty more times. We worked on her kicking until her short legs became too tired to keep going. While standing in the shallow end of my parent's in ground pool, her still in my arms, she fell asleep. I kept her there, close to my heart, while talking to my brother and Melissa about their life.

They didn't have anything that interested me. Branch worked in an office building. He had to wear suits every day. The thought made me cringe. Sure, my fatigues were uncomfortable in the summer, but at least I didn't look like a penguin.

I was pretty sad when Kat insisted I take B inside for a nap. I could have held her all day even though I realized she was pretty pruned up from being in the water so long.

Since I was tired out myself, I decided to just lay down with my daughter. Kat helped get her in a dry diaper while I changed my own clothes. Then she gave me a kiss before I climbed in bed next to B. She stirred, looking around and then curling up against my chest. Kat gave me a sarcastic head shake. "She has you wrapped around her little finger."

"Apparently it runs in the family. She must learn those skills from her mother," I teased.

Her smile was contagious. "Maybe."

"You could always come join us," I asked in a whisper.

"I'm going to help your mom with dinner. I'll come check on you in a bit."

Before she could leave the room I called her name, patting B on the backside so she'd settle back to sleep. "Kat, wait. How are you doing – with all this Branch and Melissa business?"

She held onto the door when she answered. "It's weird. I guess I need to get used to it. They probably feel the same way about us."

"I'm sure."

"I like seeing you so happy, Brooks. I still keep thinking about when I assumed you were dead. Sometimes this still feels like it's a dream."

I kept my arms around my daughter, kissing her on the head before I replied. "I'd come back from the dead for this, Kat. Nothing could keep me away."

I saw tears in her eyes as she grinned. "That's why I love you so much, Brooks. I know you would."

When she left the room I took a few minutes to think about how far we'd come. The little girl in my arms was worth every bad day because it was all in order to lead me back to this. If I was dead, then this was my heaven. Only a marriage certificate with her mother could make this any sweeter.

Chapter 48

Dinner out at the pool was pretty relaxing. Actually, every meal with my parents had been great. I wasn't used to family sittings, but I sure did like them.

It was pretty obvious my brother was infatuated with Brooklyn. He wouldn't stop talking to her and being playful. Even though she hadn't admitted it, I knew Kat noticed too.

Once we were settled in for the night, with my brother right across the hall after deciding to stay, Kat seemed upset again.

I pulled my shirt over my head to prepare for bed, noticing Kat staring me down again, particularly on my tattoo. I gave her a mischievous grin. "If I would have known that you'd be so into it, I would have sent pictures with my letters." I climbed on the bed, perching my head on her thigh. "What are you in here thinking about?"

Kat peered down at her hands. "I don't know. Life, I guess. It's just hard to believe that I'm here, with you, in your bed. It's surreal, you know? Us being together and everyone being okay with it?"

I laced our fingers together, reminding her that she wasn't alone. "To be honest with you even if they had a problem it wouldn't change us. We'd still be together, Kat."

"I love how you just know what you want, Brooks. I want you to know that I looked up what I need to do to get a divorce. It should be easy since we don't have children or belongings together. Bobby can walk away with his home and business while I keep my house and all of my money."

"He doesn't have access to those accounts?"

"No. I put them in Brooklyn's name as soon as she was born. Only she and I will be able to draw money out of them. Bobby doesn't even know how much I have left. He thinks I used almost all of it on the house."

I was shocked and curious at the same time. "How much did they leave you?"

Kat seemed to get a kick out of me asking. "Eight-hundred fifty four thousand-two hundred thirty dollars and fourteen cents was how much I got when I was able to finally access the account. I memorized the amount because at the time, I was so hard up and needed it. The house cost me three hundred grand. I gave my friends that helped me twenty five grand and I bought everything new for inside the home too."

This was hilarious to me. "You have half a million dollars hidden from your husband and he never knew?" It led me to believe that she never fully trusted him.

She flashed me a guilty look. "Yeah. I wanted Brooklyn to have the best life. I knew that after I built the house, I wouldn't have to work to afford a mortgage. I could be home with her, where I wanted to be."

"I can see where he wouldn't even ask. Look, you know I don't care about that money. Your parent's house and the life insurance was for you anyway. That money isn't for me or for your husband. I just have one question for you."

"Anything."

"When can I move in because me living on the base isn't exactly going to work for me when my girls have that nice big house and I can't be with them?"

"I told you already that you're going to live with me. I thought you knew that I meant now."

I leaned up in her face. "I'm teasing you. Do you really think I'd spend one night without the two of you? I've literally been to Hell. I'm in this for the long haul, woman. There's pretty much nothing you can do about it, either. I hate to break it to you, but you're stuck with this forever." I motioned over my body.

Kat cackled. "I'm pretty sure I can live with that."

I pulled her on top of me. "You sure I'm what you want? I mean, there's no going back this time. We're either in it together, or it can't happen." My face became conflicted. "I can't lose you again, Kat, not now that I finally have you."

"You won't," She assured me. "We're in this together."

I flipped us over, never taking my eyes off her. "I'm going to go get a shower. It's late, so nobody would notice if we were in there together."

"I'd love to get a shower with you." This was pretty exciting for me. I expected her to be against it with so many people in the house.

It wasn't until we were in the bathroom, trying to be quiet, when I got the best idea in my head. "I think it's time to pay back my brother for all the nights I knew you two were together. What do you say? Do you feel like expressing yourself a little louder than usual?"

I picture her scolding me, not agreeing to do it right away. Her reply was uncoached, but absolutely the best ever. "Oh, yes. Give it to me, Brooks."

It was difficult to keep a straight face when Kat was playing along. It was also quite hard to play around when she was removing all of her clothes.

I stood still, taking in every aspect of her body. From her curvy hips, to that supple ass, I was getting turned on quickly. The only thing missing was my hands all over her skin.

She turned around and began doing the same thing to me, licking her lips and acting pleased with my stature. "You were just eyeing me up, weren't you?" I questioned her intent.

Her hands went in the air as if I was about to arrest her. If only she was standing in front of a car because I would have bent her over and taken full advantage of it. "Guilty. Maybe you should punish me." She cocked one leg up on the tub. "Maybe you should spank me."

I thought I was going to choke on my own saliva. Not only was she taunting me, but Kat was speaking loud enough that my brother and Melissa, who were in the next room, could clearly hear. I didn't know whether to laugh or go for it.

The palm of my hand made contact with her ass followed by the sound of a slap. Right away I felt bad about it, wondering if she'd be pissed. "Sorry. I always wanted to do that. Don't be mad."

She backhanded me on the shoulder, but not that hard. "Jerk. That hurt." Kat stated as she rubbed her sore butt cheek. "Okay, I probably should have said I was playing around. I'm not mad at all, but you do know that you're going to kiss every inch of that cheek until the burn goes away, and then you're going to wash me, until you're ready to burst from the buildup."

I ran my lips around her face, avoiding her lips at all costs. "It will be my pleasure, but when I'm done, I'm taking you back to bed and fucking you all night long."

I started by washing her hair. The hot soapy water fell down from her long locks, lathering up the hard erection standing behind her. While taking my time to run my slippery hands all over her appendages, Kat looked me right in the eyes. There was nothing I wouldn't do for this woman, and because of that I knew there was a time and a place to joke around, and another to be serious. Though the mood had changed, I intended to make good on the bedroom promise, as soon as we were done in the shower.

Kat leaned her head against the shower wall, while I kissed her, running my lips down her wet body. I spun her around, focusing on her ass and thighs. Once I was in a sitting position with her facing the opposite direction I remain focused on making this moment unforgettable. I traced my mouth against the skin where her ass and thighs met. Her body began to shake, only showing me that I was getting to her.

I teased her rear entrance, taking my finger and sliding over it. I spread her legs apart farther, scooting in so my face was close enough to tease her there. I could tell she was losing control already, getting pampered in places she wasn't used to being touched. I sucked on her there, right where her little asshole sat. Little noises escaped her as she remained leaning against the hard tile. When she was ready to collapse I turned off the water. This was only the beginning. Once I had her in bed she'd be mine for the taking.

Wrapped in towels, Kat and I stepped out of the bathroom, only to find Branch standing there with his arms crossed.

"Hey, can you guys keep it down? Mel's got a headache."

I looked right at my brother. "You may want to shove some paper in her ears, because we're just getting started, bro." I didn't wait for his reply. I wouldn't have cared what he said anyway. There was only one focus on my mind, and it wasn't being quiet. She'd awakened the animal in me and I was about to fill her with it.

"I can't believe you said that," she said while I tugged the towel off of her body.

"It wasn't a lie, beautiful. Knowing it's bothering him makes me want to go at it all night. I don't think either of you thought about how thin these walls are. I could hear everything and Branch knew it. It's time he gets paid back."

She glanced at my arm. "How's it feeling?"

I shrugged. "It's manageable, why?"

She stuck her arms around my neck and jumped. "Because I also have reasons for wanting to piss him off."

Every touch of her hands, kiss from her lips, and emotions she fed me were satiating my desire to pleasure her. It was as if the harder I tried to satisfy her first, she was doing the same to me. Our synced bodies rocked back and forth on my bed, sharing a rhythm. From my head to my feet had goose bumps, and each time I felt her tongue touching mine I swore the room was spinning.

Kat's hair flew in my face as she began vigorously swaying her body around. We'd been going at it for a while though I knew I was close to being finished. There was only so much of her I could take without losing control. When I felt her cumming for the second time I let it happen, succumbing to the utter relief she brought me.

For almost an hour we'd been at it, and if I still had the energy I would have wanted more. Although someone else had other ideas about us spending time together. When I went out to use the restroom I peeked inside of B's room and saw her sitting up. She smiled before I could duck out unseen. "Hi princess."

"Daddy, I want mama."

"Well let's go get her."

I picked her up and carried her into the room. Kat scooted over making room for the two of us to join her. B nestled her body in between us and went right back to sleep, while I kept staring into the eyes of my soul mate, wondering what I'd done to deserve such a perfect life.

Chapter 49

I wasn't sure if it was the sex, but Kat woke up so happy. She headed downstairs while I insisted on helping B get beautiful before breakfast. She was picking clothes out of her suitcase that didn't go together and handing them to me. "What's daddy supposed to do with two pairs of pants? You can't wear both of these."

She giggled when I stuck one on her head. "No daddy. You wear."

I took the tiny pants and held them up to one leg. "They won't fit me, B. How about you try them?" She gave me her leg and helped me get them up. "Oh don't they look fancy?"

B peered down at her pants, rubbing her hands on them while smiling. "Where's mom-mom?"

"She's downstairs, princess. Let's find a shirt that matches and we'll go find her."

I turned when I heard someone coming in to the room. All of a sudden Kat's happy demeanor had changed. She looked like she'd seen a ghost.

When I turned back to look at our daughter she was attempting to put a bikini top over her head. "Hey, you going swimming already?" Kat asked.

I laughed. "She woke me up asking to jump in the pool. You know me, I give her anything she wants." Kat knew I was kidding. We'd both agreed that B had to eat before swimming.

"I need to talk to you about something. I'm kind of freaking out, right now." That was obvious.

I reached over and touched her arm. "What is it?"

Kat sat on the bed explaining how Melissa had left her messages and she'd went on to check them, finding her voicemail completely emptied. She told me that only one other person knew her password, and that's why she was freaking out. He knew she wasn't at home, and possibly where we'd gone.

I didn't want to alarm her anymore than she already was. We'd been in D.C. for almost a week with no calls. After going to jail I assumed he'd learned his lesson. It wasn't like I'd let him anywhere near my girls.

"What are we going to do if we go home and he's trashed the inside of the house? I won't be able to prove it's him. His fingerprints are all over the place." Kat began to cry and all I could do was hold her. I didn't know what to say. If she didn't calm down, my parents were going to wonder what was going on. Kat didn't want anyone to know about Bobby, or the fact that she was married to him, and neither did I. We were finally in a good place. I couldn't have him destroy that for us.

"Kat, he can't hurt us. He's there and we're here. When we leave tomorrow night, we'll worry about it. If he's done something, we can figure out what to do when we're there. Please don't let him ruin our last day together. Mom and Dad want to see us smiling today, like we don't have a care in the world. Focus on

Branch and Melissa. Talk about their wedding like you're excited for them. Do whatever it takes to keep your mind off of that asshole, okay?"

"Asshole." B giggled, like she knew it was a bad word.

"Daddy's sorry. Don't say that. It's bad!" Oh shit. I should have known. Kat didn't seem amused.

"Asshole."

Kat covered her face with both hands. "Oh my God. What else?"

"Asshole." B giggled.

I couldn't help but smile at the situation. It was funny hearing a cute little girl saying bad words. Kat scolded me. "Don't laugh at her. If we make a big deal about it, she'll keep saying it. Let's just go downstairs and ignore her."

I picked her up. "Let's go eat breakfast. Are you hungry, bug?"

"Asshole, Daddy."

"For what it's worth, she learned it from you." Kat noted while leading us down the steps.

"Yeah. Live and learn."

As soon as bug saw food she was done using her new potty mouth. My mom greeted her and she all but jumped out of my arms to get to her. I noticed Kat saying something to

Melissa, but was too busy making sure B was managed first.

Just like the day before, my family planned to cook out on the grill. Branch and I rode to the grocery store while the girls were cleaning up breakfast, and my dad vacuumed the pool. We got about a block from the house before my brother said anything. "Are you planning on having a birthday party for B? Melissa was talking about maybe traveling to South Carolina."

Kat and I hadn't discussed that far. "Her birthday is September 11th. I'm sure Kat's planning something. It's the first one I'll be able to celebrate with them."

"I can't believe you didn't get to see her when she was first born. I feel like an asshole. Katy really ripped me a new ass last night. I deserved it too. Brooks, I didn't know this is how our lives would turn out. I would have been a good husband to her. I hope you know that. It wasn't all a game to me. I loved her too."

"Kat and I have made a pact that we weren't going to let the past dictate our future. We're happy and together. B has her mom and dad in her life. At the end of the day it's all I care about. Besides, you didn't make me join the military. I did that on my own. My tour in Afghanistan was part of the job. Even if we were together, I wouldn't have been there for B's birth. I'll regret it for the rest of my life, but I know it's the only time she'll ever have to be without me. I don't plan on missing anything else."

"How come you're not engaged yet? I'm sure Kat's itching."

"She's fine. Trust me."

"Whatever. It's your business anyway. I've got my own woman to worry about."

"So, about the whole sterile thing." I had to bring it up. It had been bothering me since I found out. "How does Melissa feel about it?"

"We have options. We talked about her being inseminated, or adopting. Right now we're content I think. Mel's planning the wedding, so she's happy she gets to keep her figure. We'll figure it out when the time comes."

I could tell the topic got to Branch. He was obviously living with demons of his own. "I'm sorry that happened to you. I don't even remember it."

"You wouldn't. You were too far up Kat's ass to pay attention to me. I'm pretty sure you spent the night at her parent's house when I had the surgery. I know you were together."

"Weren't we always? She was our best friend, you know."

"Some things don't change, bro. It seems like Kat still feels that way about you. Sometimes I wonder if she ever loved me."

"This conversation is weird. We need to change the subject before you're using the steaks we're about to buy to relieve a black eye."

Branch chuckled. "It's not like that. I have no interest in your girlfriend. I swear. I'd like to think of Kat as my sister, of it's okay with you?" I almost made a comment about them sleeping together, but decided it was best if I closed the door on the whole conversation. "Look, Branch. I'm trying to keep it all in the past. I'm pissed at you. I might be that way for the rest of my life, but you're still my brother. It's obvious you care about my daughter, that means a lot. Let's take baby steps to repairing our relationship."

He agreed before we walked into the grocery store. On the way home we talked about sports, which we both shared a common interest in.

The girls were drinking tea out by the pool when we arrived back at the house.

I hurried to put my suit on so that I could join them for an afternoon swim.

It was obvious Kat was happy to see me back. I'd only been gone for about thirty minutes, and in that time I had to admit I missed her. This was all still so exciting for me. It wasn't just about being a couple, or even having a beautiful daughter. It was the whole life we were going to have together. I was on cloud nine, and nothing could bring me down.

We floated around the pool together, both of them wrapped around each arm. I could hear my brother and Melissa talking about their wedding plans, but paid them no attention. I was too captivated by my own little family.

A little while later we had burgers and salad out on the patio. B was trying to manipulate me back in the pool, and she was pretty close to getting her way. I conned her into eating more in an effort to wait longer before spending more time in the water.

It didn't take her long to empty her plate. I didn't make her ask again. We got back in the pool while I let Kat relax and chat with the women. In all honesty I thought nothing of her walking in the house after my mom. I figured she'd come right back out. Seconds turned into minutes, making me start to wonder if she was okay. At first I thought she was playing a joke on me, trying to get me alone to be freaky again. I slipped into the house to find her, only to come back out after not seeing her anywhere.

"Mom, do you know what Kat's doing?" I asked.

"Someone came to the door asking for her. I supposed they're still talking."

Right away my heart dropped. I yelled for them to watch B while I rushed into the house. When I didn't find her downstairs I ran to my room, finding a huge tear in my sheets, and some of her things gone from the room.

That's when I knew for sure who'd been knocking on the door. He's listened to her messages and looked up my parent's address. We weren't hard to find. They'd lived in the house since we were born.

I hurried outside to catch the back of a truck peeling around the corner. At first I started running after it, soon realizing there was no way I could catch up. Kat's husband had taken her from me, and I didn't know what he was going to do next.

When I opened the front door my dad was standing there waiting. "What's going on?" I pushed past him, searching for truck keys. "We need to hurry. He's going to hurt her."

"Who, Katy? What are you talking about, son?"

I didn't have time to stand there and explain what was going on. "Her husband. He's come to take her from us. She's in danger. Please, I'll explain it all later. Just help me find her."

When we rushed out of the house I didn't know what to say or do. All I could think about was finding Kat and bringing her home safely. This all felt like a terrible nightmare.

Chapter 50

I didn't even know where I was going. All I could hope was that he had every intention of driving her back to South Carolina. I was prepared to stop at every single hotel, restaurant, or gas station until I found them.

I tried to focus on Kat, like I could somehow sense her whereabouts. While I concentrated on the road my dad continued badgering me for answers. "What do you mean when you say her husband has her?"

"She's married, dad. Kat got married when she found out she was pregnant. She was alone and scared. There was someone there who offered to take care of them, so she agreed."

"Why would he hurt her? Did she run out on him to be with you?"

"No, it's not like that." I was disgusted with the situation. "He beats her. They married as friends, but it was never enough for him. When I came into the picture he went crazy. He wanted her to stop seeing me, and when she refused he busted her head open."

I turned a corner and jumped on the main highway. "Where would he take her? Is this guy a danger to Brooklyn?"

"Dad, I don't know where they're going. We need to call the police. There's a restraining order against him."

My dad pulled his phone out of his pocket and connected with the police. He told them we were on route 495 headed toward the 95 north. I gave him the description of Bobby's truck, but at the exact moment I knew we didn't need their help looking. Flipped upside down, in the center of the road, surrounded by other involved vehicles, sat his wrecked vehicle. Smoke was coming from the engine area, and I could clearly see two people inside seeming to be dead still.

"No, no no!" I slammed on my brakes and took off toward the truck, praying to God she'd be okay. "Kat. Kat, can you hear me?" She was unconscious. Blood was dripping from her head. The truck was too smashed to see Bobby on the opposite side, not that I cared whether he lived or died. My only concern was getting her out of there. "Kat, please wake up, baby. Open your eyes."

I pulled with all of my might to get the door to budge, but it had been welded together with the frame as it slid across the pavement. In the distance I could hear sirens, and the sound of my dad's voice.

Everything happened so fast after that. Two ambulances pulled in, and the paramedics shoved us aside to start attending to the injured. They worked to pull Kat from the wreckage. The whole time it was happening I stood there watching and praying she had a pulse. I knew that if they covered her up there was no hope, but if they got her secured properly she was still hanging on.

In those moments I thought about our perfect life, our little girl, and all the dreams that might not get to happen. I imagined raising my daughter alone, and how I'd never be able to cope with knowing I had a part in Kat's death. I imagined the loss of her, how it would affect me, and of course little B. When I say I couldn't live without her, I meant it. I'd been down that road, even knowing she was alive still. There was no way in hell I could live out my life knowing she was dead.

When I saw them strapping her to a stretcher I fell to my knees. There were no obvious signs of life, but I knew there was hope. I ran toward the ambulance. "Is she going to make it?" I had to know.

"Sir, do you know this person?"

I nodded. "She's my girlfriend. Please let me go with you."

My dad approached us. "Give me the keys. I'll go pick up everyone at the house and meet you at the hospital."

"Please hurry, dad. She needs us all there." When I looked at my dad I could see nothing but fear. He knew if Kat died, he'd lose me forever. There was no way I'd ever be able to celebrate life. I'd be no good to my daughter because her mother's death would end me.

I'd been in bad places before. I'd feared that I wouldn't live to see another day. I'd watched fellow soldiers get burned and shot. I'd seen my best friend blown to pieces in front of me, but nothing compared to the anguish I was suffering from. This was so brutal I couldn't snap out of it.

We had so many memories to make together. Our future was just over the horizon. We were so close to having it all. How could this be happening to us?

Why?

Hadn't we suffered enough?

If there was a God, why wasn't he looking out for us? Why weren't her parents watching over her?

This wasn't even about my sudden lack of faith. It was about not believing that anything could help the situation. The idea of losing her left me so vulnerable and petrified.

"We'll be right behind you, Brooks. I promise." My dad ran off toward my truck, leaving me there to deal with the paramedics. I kept asking them questions. Begging them to give me her vitals.

They pretended I didn't exist, going so far as to prevent me from riding in the vehicle with her. I had to go with Bobby instead. He'd become conscious and was screaming profanities as they lifted him into the second ambulance. Even though he was strapped down for safety, he continued trying to swing his arms around to hit me.

Silently, I sat there listening to the men calling in Kat's suspected injuries, and then Bobby's. When he said head trauma I wanted to throw up. A brain injury is major. If Kat had a skull fracture or worse it could mean long-term memory loss.

I began letting my mind wander again, imagining her waking up and not knowing us.

I'd spent every single second of my life loving her, but there was a chance she wouldn't know me, or our beautiful daughter.

No matter how hard I tried, I couldn't put the bad thoughts out of my mind. It was as if I was only able to envision the terrible, instead of remaining hopeful. My throat burned, and I was sure that tears were falling down my face, yet I didn't bother wiping them away. I was completely numb on the outside because I was being ripped apart on the inside.

Bobby kept yelling at me on the way. I heard the paramedic mention alcohol on his breath and hoped he was in big trouble for what he'd done. The whole time we were riding in the back he was steady trying to swing at me. "I'm going to fuckin' kill you. You'll never see her when I get done with my plans. If I can't have her neither will you."

"I'll fucking kill you!" I jumped up and threw myself at his helpless body. "You won't ever lay a hand on her again."

The paramedic shoved himself between us. "Knock it off!"

I felt so disgusted being in the same vehicle with this man, but I knew it would get me to the hospital sooner than waiting for my dad and family. They'd have to sit through the wreckage traffic. It would take them hours.

When we arrived, I stood back and let the paramedics wheel both patients inside. I tried to go with them into the room they took Kat, but was led by a nurse to a lounge area. "You don't understand. That's my wife," I lied.

"Sir, we understand you're with them."

"Her. I'm with the female. Not the male victim," I corrected.

"As soon as she's examined and her injuries are determined I'll be back out to get you. Until then, please let us do our jobs."

Instead of sitting like I'd been told, I stood there, waiting for that door to come back open. I needed to know something; anything!

I paced.

I knocked.

I rang bells.

I paced some more.

Anything was better than sitting and waiting. The longer it took, the worse I imagined it to be. I was losing hope fast if I had any left at all.

When they refused to answer the door I began beating on it, screaming at the top of my lungs for someone to help me. The people who were waiting quietly got up and left the room. A few minutes later my family arrived, crowding in to see if I knew anything.

Then I saw my daughter, and I lost it. I'd never cried so hard in my life, and it didn't stop there.

"None of you get it. She's here because of Branch. It's his fucking fault."

"Brooks, watch your mouth." My mother was not happy with me. I knew they were all worried.

I was holding onto my chest, finding it hard to catch my breath. "You don't get it. This could have all been avoided. He beats her. She's married to a man who abuses her. Don't you get it? I was trying to save her; to give them both a new life. I was trying to get them away from him. He doesn't deserve to be anywhere near my daughter or Kat. He doesn't deserve anything!" I picked up a chair and proceeded to throw it at the door. Branch and my dad got a hold of me as soon as a nurse was exiting.

Security was called, and I was led to a small holding area. While sitting there, begging him to help me out, a doctor came into the room. "I hear you're giving my nurses quite a show."

"I just want answers. My girlfriend's been in an accident. They won't tell me anything."

"She's unconscious. We're running tests to make sure her head is okay. We need to reset her hip because it's been dislocated. You've got to calm down. I don't want to have to contact the authorities because we have a man going rogue in our hospital. I can't let you in the room with your girlfriend until you can manage your temper."

"I'm sorry, doc, but you've got my whole future back in that room. I'm afraid I can't calm down until I get to see her. My heart is beating out of my chest. It literally hurts. I feel like I'm going to pass out. I can't calm down. I won't."

"Have you suffered from anxiety before?"

"What? No never."

He got on his little phone and made a call. A few seconds later he sat down on a chair in front of me. "What do you do for a living, sir?"

"I'm a Sergeant in the United States Army."

"Really?" He sounded surprised.

"A few months ago I got back from doing a tour in Afghanistan. The only reason I survived is because of that woman you have in the back."

"Are you allergic to any medications?"

"Huh?"

"I'm going to give you something to help you calm down."

"I don't need anything," I argued.

When our eyes met I knew I didn't have a choice. I'd pissed too many people off. "I'm not allergic to anything."

"I'll let your family know where they can find you. A nurse will be by to give you something to relax. Have you had anything to drink today?"

"No, sir."

"As soon as I know more about your girlfriend I'll come find you."

A few moments later a nurse came in. She triaged me from a small laptop and handed me a cup of water with one tiny pill.

"What is it?"

"Lorazepam. It's a low dose."

"What the hell is it for again?" I wasn't taking medicine. I wasn't even the damn patient.

"It's for anxiety, panic attacks. Trust me, you'll feel better almost immediately."

I thought about all the time overseas where I'd witness mass destruction, and how I could have used something to help me calm down. In this case, like those, my temper was getting the best of me.

I popped the pill in my mouth, hoping it would alleviate some of the pain I was suffering from. Instead I started to feel drowsy. The last thing I remember was walking back into the waiting room with my family and sitting down in a chair.

Chapter 51

"Brooks, wake up," my dad said as he continued shaking me. I sat up straight and looked around the room, finding that the rest of my family weren't anywhere around.

"What happened?"

"You've been asleep for several hours. Whatever that nurse gave you knocked you right out. She's come out to check on you every hour. She even took your vitals once."

"I'm not used to taking any sort of medication. It must have been super powered.

What's going on? Where is everyone? Did they leave for the night?"

All of a sudden a little girl came climbing up into my lap. "Daddy, I go bye byes?"

I took a second to hug her against my chest. I remembered how badly I was freaking out, and the things that were taunting my mind. Initially I thought I wouldn't be able to raise my little girl if we lost Kat, but holding her in my arms reminded me of how special she was. Nothing, not even death, could keep this child away from me.

While still keeping her close I looked up at my dad. "Tell me she's okay."

He smiled. "She just woke up. They were worried at first about head trauma, but she's improving. They reset her hip and she's pretty banged up." He paused for a second. "Brooks there's something else you should hear before you go in there."

I gave him a curious stare. "What?"

"Mr. Parsons didn't make it."

"Come again?" He'd been alert the last time I saw him. In fact, we were fighting. How could he have died?

"He had bleeding on the brain. Apparently he lost consciousness after they brought him in. He died during surgery."

As much as I wanted to be sad that someone had lost their life, I couldn't feel bad for him. He'd almost killed the mother of my child out of selfishness. "So it's over? He can't hurt her anymore?"

"Brooks, the man lost his life."

"He beat Kat, dad. He beat our Katy. I've killed people for less reasons." When the words came out of my mouth I watched my father freeze in place. There were some things he obviously didn't want to know about me.

He turned away. "We should go check on Kat. I'm sure she wants to see both of you."

Before he finished speaking I was already heading toward the doors I wasn't able to get through before. My father buzzed the ringer once, and they came open, giving us entrance. I followed him back to the room, finding my whole family standing there. Branch was backing up when he spotted me entering. I watched my mother do the same thing, giving me and my daughter the space we required.

"There she is, bug. Just like you said. Tell Mama hi."

"Hi, Mama."

Kat's response was weak. I could feel the same strain to my own body seeing her in such pain. I wished I could take it all away. "Hi, baby."

I reached down and took her hand into mine. The tears in my eyes couldn't be controlled. This was too intense. "Don't you ever do that to us again. My heart can't take it."

Kat cried softly. "I'm so sorry. I just wanted to get him away. I didn't mean to cause the accident."

"What do you mean? Bobby was intoxicated; way over the legal limit. He shouldn't have even been conscious." I was pissed. I'd been in the ambulance with him. I'd smelled the alcohol and seen how belligerent he was acting. There was no way this was her fault.

"I hit him in the face with the bottle of bourbon. He was hurting me and threatening me, saying he was going to take B away. I just wanted him to let me go. I wanted it to stop."

"You stopped it alright and almost died doing it. You weren't even wearing a seatbelt," Branch added from behind me. It was strange seeing my brother so torn up. I think in so many ways he really did blame himself for all this. Perhaps it was partly his fault. The chain of events happened because he'd been selfish. For now, all I cared about was having Kat in my life.

"I've got this, bro. Why don't you take Mom for a walk and give us a minute?" I needed to be alone with Kat. I wanted her to know how stubborn she'd been for thinking she could handle him on her own. Had she come running out back I would've protected her, but I knew she was more worried about disappointing the family with the brutal truth of her being married, to a monster at that.

I pulled up a chair once they were gone, sitting closely to Kat's hospital bed.

"You know I'm mad, right?"

She attempted to shrug. I could tell she was upset with herself. "I had my reasons, Brooks. I didn't want him in your parent's house."

I hated even thinking about the moment I realized she was gone. "Kat, I got out of that pool and B jumped back in. I had to retrieve her before I could get a towel and come inside to look for you. I don't know what I was thinking, but I never assumed that Bobby had driven all that way to kidnap you."

"I'm sorry," she cried. "I didn't know what to do. All I could think of was getting him away from you and B. I knew she was safe, no matter what happened to me."

"Listen to yourself. What about me, Kat? Did you ever consider how you being gone would affect me? Did you even think that being without you again would kill me? We're a team, remember? No more lies or secrets. You promised."

She shook her head as if that wasn't enough. "I did what I had to do whether you believe me or not. I wanted you to save me, but

I didn't have time to think about it. I had to get him away from our family."

"He could have killed you, Kat. Tell me something. Did those marks on your face and arms come from him, or the accident?"

Kat sobbed more, giving me the answer without saying anything. He'd hit her again, and if he wasn't in the morgue, I'd be in that room strangling him myself. I hated considering my actions volatile, but nothing was going to prevent me from protecting my girls. "Please don't hate me," she whispered.

I squeezed her hand, trying to cope with my own emotions. Tears were falling down my face, but only because I was too wired to convince myself that she was going to be fine. "Have you ever felt so happy that you're almost wondering when something bad is going to happen?"

She moved her head up and down.

"Then you know what it was like to pull up to that accident and know that I could have prevented it."

"It wasn't your fault," she argued.

I looked down at our daughter and then back up to Kat. "It doesn't even matter anymore. He won't be bothering you again."

"Did he get arrested? Is he going to jail?"

"He didn't make it, Kat. He passed on during surgery."

Her monitors started beeping, and from the look on her face I could tell she was freaking out. What I couldn't bring myself to understand was why? Why would she care if he was gone? Our problems were over. He couldn't hurt her, threaten her, or stand in our way of being married. His death literally solved all of it. In that very moment I realized she wasn't on the same page as me.

It crushed me.

The idea of her caring about someone who caused her pain was unimaginably difficult. I couldn't rationalize with it. "Please don't this, Kat. Don't shut me out."

"I want to be alone." She pulled her hand out of mine.

I touched her leg, hoping she wouldn't push that away as well. "I'm not leaving this room. I'm never leaving you again."

"Brooks, don't you see how toxic we are? Someone is dead because of us. He didn't start out as a violent man. Bobby took care of me. He gave me a home, and loved me, even when he knew I could never feel the same way about him. I know you don't understand this, but I did love him in some ways. For a while he was all I had. That man loved our daughter. He treated her like she was his own flesh and blood. People in town even believed it. He lived every day to make her happy. Go ahead and sit there imagining all the bad. I know you are. You didn't know him like I did. You'll never understand how it feels to know I had a hand in his death."

What could I say to that?

How on earth was I supposed to rationalize with how she was portraying the man? I didn't know him. She was right. I could only judge the parts I knew about, which were violent and erratic. "I'm sorry you feel this way. I wish I could take away the pain. Your heart is so much bigger than mine."

I couldn't stop crying like a pathetic baby. When she looked at me, I felt like she didn't even want me around. I was trying so hard to understand, to be compassionate, but all I came up with was the same result.

I hated him.

I was glad he was out of the picture.

Now I feared that instead of this helping us build a future, it was going to be a huge setback; one that could separate us once again.

Chapter 52

Several hours later, when visiting times were over, my family headed back to the house. I sat quietly in the chair next to the medical bed. It was hard to contain the feelings that I was trying to keep bottled up. This hurt me so much, feeling her slipping away, as if the past week hadn't meant anything at all. "Kat, please say something to me. I don't understand why you're doing this. He put your life in danger. You did what you thought you had to do."

"I ended his life."

"The accident ended his life."

"I caused the accident. I killed him."

"His drinking killed him, Kat." Why couldn't she see that? What was so special about him that made her throw away everything else?

"No. He used to tell me that all he ever wanted was for me to be happy. He didn't mean it like this, Brooks. I ruin everything I touch. I always have."

"That's your pain medicine talking."

Her next statement shocked me. I was so taken back by her change in demeanor that it took me a second to comprehend it all. "No. I'm a very selfish person that went after what I wanted, not even considering how drastic the consequences would be. I can't do this right now, Brooks."

The worst part of all this was the fact that I had to head back to South Carolina. My leave was over, and I was expected back to base. "If we don't talk now, it's going to have to be over the phone. I've got to head back to Fort Jackson first thing in the morning to report back for duty. Mom's going to take care of you and B until I can fly back next weekend."

I didn't know what she was thinking about when I said it. Kat looked away from me, silently sobbing to herself. I half expected her to tell me to walk out the door and never come back.

When she finally responded she was choked up. "So you'll call?"

I reached for her hand, wanting to give her reassurance. "Kat, we'll get through this. I promise. Don't you dare give up on us. I know what you're thinking. Don't do it. Please don't push me away."

I was basically saying goodbye to her, praying it would only be temporary. "I'm so sorry, Brooks. Please don't look at me like that."

I stood up and peered into her eyes, praying she'd understand how I wasn't willing to give up anything with her. "I love you with everything I have in me. I know what it's like feeling like you caused someone's death. I can see it all over your face. They train us to handle those situations, so when you're ready to talk about it, rationally, you pick up that phone and I'll be there." I kissed her lips before whispering into her ear. "I will never give up on you."

I had to leave the room, not because I wanted to get away from her, but because I wasn't able to control my need to break down completely. I waited until I reached the stairs before burying my face into my hands.

When I arrived at the house I didn't climb into my own bed to sleep. Instead I found comfort sleeping next to my little girl. It killed me knowing I had to leave, but I didn't have the resources to take her with me. While she nestled her warm body against mine I sat up watching her breathe. I played with a ringlet on her head, twisting it around my finger. Tears streamed down my face while I silently strained to acknowledge the fact that I was leaving them behind. Somehow, after being apart for two years, a five day separation seemed like too long to be away from them.

When she began to stir I rested my head down and pulled her close. She opened her eyes briefly and smiled. "Daddy."

"I'm here, baby. Daddy's never going to leave you again. I promise." I didn't mean that I wasn't heading back to South Carolina. I mean that once she was home, we'd be together forever. "I love you so much."

That night I cried myself to sleep, much like the night when I was a teenager and found out Kat had picked Branch over me. Mistake or not, it broke me. I swore I'd never feel that pain again, but it had repeated throughout my life, all surrounding around my love for Kat. Now it wasn't just my love for her that made all this so hard. My little girl had become my reason to smile. I was going to miss both of them so much.

That next morning I hugged my family goodbye, managing to keep it together until after I kissed my daughter and turned around. When I arrived at the hospital I wasn't much better.

Kat was eating her breakfast. She sat her fork down when I came into the room. "Hey, you."

"Hey." I leaned down to kiss her. "I wanted to come by before I left. I'm going to drive straight through."

"Will you call me when you arrive? I'll be worried."

"Of course. Don't fret. As soon as I'm on base I'll make sure to call. You'll be at Mom and Dad's by then. I heard him saying he was going to move some things around to fit the wheelchair. Your biggest obstacle will probably be our daughter. She's going to want a ride constantly."

Kat smiled. "I know you're mad at me right now, Brooks. You have every right to be. I wish I could change how I feel about this. I think I just need time. I've got to make calls, and arrangements. I'll be responsible for getting his body shipped home. I'm not looking forward to dealing with his family."

"Just keep in mind that you didn't do this to him. I don't give a shit what you think about it. He chose to come here and put your lives in danger. He chose to hurt you, over and over again. Nothing you say will change that."

Kat looked away. I knew she was upset with what I was saying, but I was getting sick of watching her blame herself for everything. People are responsible for their own actions. She didn't beg to be beaten, and she certainly didn't invite him to kidnap her from my parent's residence. "Brooks, please don't do this when you're getting ready to leave."

"Why? It's how I feel."

"What if something happens? What if this is our last conversation?"

Then I realized she was afraid of me driving. Of course, she'd just been in an accident. It was expected that she'd assume the worst. "Baby, I'm not going anywhere. When I get there I'm going to call and prove it to you. Nothing is going to keep us from having a future. You keep that in mind while we're apart."

She shook her head to agree. I could tell she was choking back her tears.

I kissed her one more time. "I've got to get on the road. I love you with all my heart. You better miss me."

When I left the room, I knew she wasn't okay. The longer I stayed the more I wished I didn't have to go at all. While Kat had things to do regarding Bobby, I had other plans that needed attention. Like it or not, I was going to move in with her. Her regret wasn't going to force me away.

Before leaving the area, I had one more stop. I'd managed to get in with the doctor at the Bethesda medical center to evaluate my injury. I wasn't in there for more than fifteen minutes and had enough information to know that I wasn't going to regain full use of my hand. My injury was permanent. I'd never be cleared to operate military issued weapons again.

The drive was difficult since I hadn't slept at all, and I got news that would basically end my career.

I stopped three times to get a fresh coffee. By the time I made it to base the sun had gone down. I pulled out my phone before exiting the vehicle.

My mom answered Kat's phone. "Hello?"

"Hey, mom. Is Kat around?"

"Are you there safe?"

"Yeah, I just pulled in." I yawned. "That drive is hard alone."

"I bet. Here she is."

"Hey you. I guess you're there."

"I am. I miss you already. Is that crazy?"

"No. They released me to go before lunch time. I've been sitting here wanting to call you all day. B misses you. I can tell. She keeps looking in your room and asking when you'll be back."

"If I could, I'd drive all night to get back to you."

"It's only a few days, Brooks."

"I know you're in good hands. Just take care of yourself so you can get home to me. We'll figure everything else out together."

"I hope you're right."

"Don't make me worry, Kat. I love you too much to hear you having doubts." She could deny it all she wanted. Something was different. She was holding back, and I hated it.

"I love you, Brooks. I always have and I always will, no matter what happens."

Her words made me feel sick to my stomach. I had to end the call before I got upset over it. "I love you too. I'm counting down the minutes until we're together again. I'll call you later to tell B good night."

When we hung up I carried my things into my room and plopped down on the bed. I was exhausted and couldn't wait to sleep. After setting my alarm to get up and call my daughter, I changed out of my fatigues and climbed under the covers, wishing I was back in my larger bed surrounded by my girls.

Chapter 53

Twenty-four hours after leaving Kat back in D.C., I was miserable. She couldn't realize how hard it was to be away from them. It was like giving a child a candy factory and then taking it away. I wanted my girls with me. I needed them.

It was so nice to get an early call displaying her number. I'd been sitting at my desk going through my phone looking at pictures from our week together. Each one made me smile a little more. Maybe I was partial because she was mine, but I swore I had the most beautiful little girl.

I answered professionally since I was at work. "Sergeant Valentine."

"Hey, it's me." I already knew it was.

"Are you okay?"

I wasn't upset for her calling. If I could have kept her on the phone all day I would have.

"Yeah. I'm fine."

"Kat, please tell me you're not calling to give me bad news. I'm having a terrible time being here when you're both there. I can't take much more this week."

Not only had I been missing them like crazy, but I'd been by her house, and from looking in the windows it was obvious she wasn't going to be happy when she got home. From the one room I could see, Bobby had paid the house a visit before going after her. Furniture was turned over and items were strewn all over the floor. I couldn't bring myself to tell her that, not yet at least.

"I'm not. I'm calling because I'm coming home. Your mom is going to drive us and stay with me. She wanted me to call and tell you that we'll be home late tonight."

I didn't know what to say. Above being highly excited, I was also worried. Why did my mom have to suggested her to call me? "She wanted you to call? So you weren't going to?"

"I didn't say that."

"Yeah. You didn't. So, do you want me to head over to your place when I get off?"

I needed to clear out as much mess as I could. If Kat walked into that mess she'd lose it. Her perfect house was now damaged, and I was determined to assess the full damage for myself. "Yes. There's a hidden key attached to a magnet underneath the fender to the riding mower. It's in the shed. That key opens the front and kitchen door. I have no idea what's there to eat, but help yourself. We'll call when we get close."

"I can't wait to see you. We're going to get through this, Kat."

She was quiet when she replied. "Okay."

Kat was withdrawing. If she thought she could push me away she had another thing coming. Nothing would stand in my way this time, especially not a dead guy. "Don't you dare give up on us. I know what you're doing."

"I'm not doing anything,"

"You're pushing me away because you think it's the right thing to do. You think you caused all of this to happen. Kat, you didn't make him put that bottle to his mouth. You didn't make him raise his hand to a woman. He did all of that himself. I know you feel guilty, but he could have chosen other paths. He didn't have to viciously hunt you down and you know it. If he found my parents address, he very well

538

could have gotten their phone number. Please, Kat, just think about it. We all know you'd never hurt someone intentionally. You did what you had to do to get free. You said it yourself."

"He's dead because of me. Nothing you say will change that. Now, I've got to come home and face all the people that loved him. They never believed he did those things to me, so they'll never understand that this was an accident."

"He was drunk. It was confirmed through blood tests. Those people can say whatever they want, but they can't deny the damn truth." I hated fighting with her, but didn't see an end to it. Kat couldn't let herself heal. Instead she was determined to keep punishing herself because she felt it was the right thing to do. I would convince her she was wrong. I just wasn't sure how to do it yet.

"I love you, so much," I whispered into the receiver.

"I love you, too." I could hear her sniffling on the other end of the call. It tormented me.

"I'll be there waiting for you tonight. We'll get through this together. I promise."

When the call ended, I was set on getting my workload done early so I could make my way over to Kat's place. Unfortunately, from being gone for a week, I had a pile to sift through. Hours went by before I was able to finish up. My intentions of getting to the house in time to clean up anything out of place was turning to crap.

I rolled in probably an hour before I expected them to arrive. Nothing could have prepared me for what I found inside. Things hadn't just been thrown around. The pungent smell of gasoline filled my nostrils. I opened all the windows and doors before searching for where it was coming from. When I found which room it was I almost wanted to throw up.

Gas cans were laying sideways on the carpet. I picked them up and carried them outside, hoping to alleviate some of the stench. When I came back in to reassess the damage I still couldn't believe my eyes. He'd set fire to their bed. A giant charred black spot was all that was left of the mattress.

In the corner I saw an extinguisher. He wanted her to know that he'd only burned this item. This was all intentional. It took everything I had in me to not break more shit because I was so irrefutably angry.

Since I knew I had to get some of the mess cleaned up, I started with what I could get out of the house. I threw away the bedding, placing it in garbage bags. I tossed out the area rugs, thinking maybe they still had remnants of gasoline on them. I closed the bedroom door to keep the smell confined to one room.

Then I looked around the rest of the house. Plates had been thrown in the kitchen, leaving shards of sharp porcelain everywhere. Curtains had been torn down. The couches were flipped. Tables were tipped over, and everything that had been on top of them. He'd trashed the entire house with the exception of B's room. I didn't know whether to even be grateful for it since he'd damaged so many other things.

Since I knew B was going to have to walk around the house, I began the task of picking up the shards, one by one. Though daunting, I felt the need to do everything I could to prevent from Kat freaking out, which I knew she was still going to do. One can only take so much before they reach a breaking point. This was clearly not going to go over well.

After nearly thirty minutes of picking up the larger pieces, I started looking for a vacuum. Before I turned it on I got a call from my dad.

"Hey, it's not a good time," I said as I answered.

"I was calling to see if the girls got there safely."

"Not yet, but I'm glad they haven't. Dad, her ex trashed the house. He set their bed on fire, destroyed her property. It's a damn mess. I don't know what to do."

"Have you tried cleaning some of it up?"

"Yeah, but it's not a one-man job. I've never seen anything like this."

"I can't believe she got involved with someone like that. I hate to say it, but I'm glad he's no longer going to be around to harm her. She doesn't need that kind of role model around Brooklyn."

"I wouldn't let him near her even if he was around. The only male influence my daughter needs is from her real family."

"Listen, Katy was a mess yesterday. She made a few calls to notify Bobby's family. I'm guessing it didn't go very well. Apparently they didn't know the side of him that you saw."

"I figured." It wasn't to help me though. "Listen, I better get off of here. I need to at least clear a path for when B gets in the house, otherwise she's going to have to be locked in her room."

"Do the best you can. Once they've arrived pull your mother aside and get her to help with replacing whatever is damaged. She'll know where to find everything, and how to have it delivered. You know there is a positive to this, Brooks."

"Oh yeah? What's that?"

"You'll have all new things that he didn't use. If I were you I'd buy a new bed anyway. In fact, it's the first thing I would replace."

We both chuckled. "Yeah, you're funny. I don't think Kat would be laughing though. I'm pretty sure this is only going to break her heart."

"Brooks, try not to push. Katy is a good girl. She's just having a rough time. I get why you're upset, but you've got to put yourself in her shoes. She obviously cared about him whether you want to hear it or not. They were married, son. This is something she's going to have to deal with for the rest of her life."

Of course my dad was right. It wasn't fair to blame Kat for being so irrational. For two years she'd given herself to Bobby. As much as that hurt me, I had to accept it, or else I'd never be able to handle the way people were going to look at us as a couple. "Let me know about the house next door. I think the sooner we get out of here the better."

"I'll call you tomorrow. Have your mother let me know they've arrived safely. Give Brooklyn a kiss from me."

"I will. Thanks, Dad. Thanks for everything."

"Just make sure you two keep coming around. It was a pleasure having everyone home again."

When we hung up I felt a little better. I just needed to prepare for Kat's arrival, and her upcoming nervous breakdown.

Chapter 54

I knew they'd be tired when they arrived, and Kat would be stiff from the long ride. From the moment the vehicle pulled up in the yard I started to worry. I looked behind me at the mess that I couldn't manage to make any better. It was going to be a long night.

When I heard the car doors opening I rushed to greet them. Kat seemed pleased to see me standing there waiting to pull her into my arms. "I missed you." We kissed first before she walked into the mayhem.

"Daddy. Me get out." B wanted to be freed from her car seat, and I couldn't wait to be the one to do it.

"There's Daddy's bug. Did you miss me?"

She took my hand immediately, making me feel like a million bucks.

I don't know how I expected her to react when she first set eyes on the place. A part of me wished I could have hired a crew to come in and just empty the place out. It certainly would have been better than it was. "I've been cleaning since I got here. I didn't want you to see it like this."

Kat covered her mouth as she walked from room to room, noting the damage.

When she was ready to open her bedroom door I pushed myself in the way. "Kat, let's get you settled first."

"What is it? What did he do?" She was already in tears, brought on by the shock of it all. I couldn't begin to imagine how betrayed she felt.

"You need to remember that this is just a house. Everything in here can be replaced."

"The fumes are still bad," I said before she could walk in and see the worst for herself.

"What has he done?"

"I already bagged the bedding and the fire extinguisher. I'm assuming this was all some sick message, considering he'd been prepared to put the fire out before it got out of hand. Like I said before, we can replace all of this. I can buy us a new bed tomorrow. With a couple cans of paint and some fresh carpet we can get the smell out of here and you'll never even be able to tell it ever happened."

She stood there, shocked, shaking her head. "Don't you get it? This is all my fault. Everything! He did all of this because of what I did to him - what we did to him."

I tried to grab her shoulder, but she shoved me away. "Please, Kat, you're not thinking clearly."

"My husband is dead because I broke his damn heart. We did this to him. It didn't have to be like this, Brooks. Stop acting like we're just going to be happy and move forward. There is no moving forward. I'll never forgive myself. I can't even begin to think about it."

My mother was in the other room with B, probably wondering what the hell was going on and all I could do was stand there watching my life turn to shit. Fear struck me as I began to contemplate what this detour meant for our relationship.

"Kat, don't make me leave. Please talk to me."

She closed her eyes when she spoke. "I won't ask you to leave. Your mother and our daughter are here."

"You just need time. That's what this is, right? We'll get through this?"

"Maybe. It's too much right now, Brooks. I'm not trying to hurt you and this isn't about our love. There will never be anyone but you. I know that. I need to sort things out in my head before I can do anything."

I hated it. I hated the idea of getting her back only to be shoved aside while she sorted things out. Why couldn't we do it all together? "So what am I supposed to do? Do I come here every day and pretend that it's okay to not be able to touch you? Do I avoid eye contact because looking at you is like shards of glass being driven into my eyes? I've waited for you, Kat. I've been so God damn patient. If I could take the pain away from you I would. I'd do anything to keep you from hurting, but I can't accept that we can't be together. I won't let you push me away this time. Do you hear me?"

I grabbed both of her arms, forcing her to give me her full attention. "Look at me, Kat. Look me in the eyes and swear to me that we're going to get through this."

"What if we don't?" I couldn't believe she was saying it. Her tears meant nothing to me because she was brutally damaging all hope we'd work this out. With each word I felt like a wall was being shoved up between us.

I started shaking her, trying to get her to snap out of it. She couldn't possibly think we were better off being separated. "Don't do this, again."

"Brooks, what if I can't move forward? Look at my house. A man is dead. Our love is like poison and everyone around us ends up getting hurt. How much more has to happen before you see that?"

That was it. I couldn't hear anymore of it. I had to walk away. I refused to let her see me upset. I didn't say goodbye to my mother, or even little B. I simply rushed out into the dark yard, jumped in my truck and drove away.

For a while I coasted down the side roads, blaring the music to hide my sadness. I was so close to having it all, only for it to be taken away from me again. What was it about our love that made things so difficult for us? Why couldn't we ever find a common ground and settle into it?

I didn't understand.

The longer I was away the more I missed her. I drove by the house several times seeing that the lights were still on. It killed me that she wasn't calling. She was angry, but so was I. Maybe it was best if I gave her time to calm down, even if it killed me to do it.

It was one in the morning before I pulled back into her driveway and parked my vehicle. I didn't get out, but instead crouched down and planned on sleeping it out. Just because she hadn't asked me to come back didn't mean I was going to give up. Not this time. I couldn't handle it. I refused to let Bobby's death ruin our chances at being a family. We had too much to be thankful for.

An hour later my cell phone started to ring. I jumped before seeing that it was her number calling me. "Kat, is that you?" I had to ask because it could have been my mother.

I could hear her sobbing on the other end of the call. "Yes. It's me."

"Please don't cry."

"I can't sleep. All I keep thinking about is being without you. I feel so sick over it. My head is all over the place. I feel like everything is my fault, but I also know that there's no possible way I could ever give up on us. I just feel so lost, Brooks."

This was such a relief to me. I couldn't bear it either.

"Babe, I'm not going anywhere. I promised you that no matter what happened I'd stick around, and I meant it. You've got a lot going on, but in time you're going to see the big picture. You're going to know without a doubt that we should be together. I know I get hardheaded about you. It's only because I've waited so long to start our life together. Now we've got a little girl to raise. As much as I hate that you've got baggage, it doesn't mean I'll give up. Nobody is going to come my way and take your place. You have my heart, Kat. You always have. Please calm down. I hate it when you're so upset."

"I know I love you and I know I'm supposed to be with you. That's never been my problem."

"Yeah, I know. I feel the same way."

"Will I see you tomorrow?" It was music to my ears.

"Do you want to see me?"

"Of course." My stomach started turning with excitement. Our time apart had helped her calm down.

I got out of the truck and walked up to the side door, opening it while I spoke. "How about now?"

Kat was smiling when our eyes met. "I thought you left?"

We both hung up our phones at the same time.

"I did. I drove around for a while and then came back, seeing as I had a feeling you were going to need me. I can see now that I was right."

"What if I didn't call?"

I shrugged. "I've slept in worse places than a truck. I would have gotten up and drove in to work. I wasn't leaving you three girls here alone. Since you obviously needed some space, I gave it to you."

"Your mom was nice. We talked for a bit. I told her about Bobby. I may have left out a few details, but she knows everything there is to know. I can't tell whether she hates me or not. I think I already hate myself enough for the both of us."

"She doesn't hate you. Didn't she tell you that you were her daughter, just a few days ago?"

"That was before she knew I was a lying, married, awful person."

"Do you hear yourself?"

"It's true."

"You lied because I asked you to. I told you to keep it from them because I thought it would be easier. I didn't know Bobby would show up, and if I had, we could have been prepared."

She pointed to the living room seats. "Will you come sit with me?"

"Will you let me?" I didn't want to overstep her boundaries.

"I'll always let you. Stop asking such stupid questions. You never have to ask me."

I kicked off my boots before sitting down next to her. "Come here." I put my arm around her and pulled her down against my chest. "Try to get some rest."

Our hands laced together as she got comfortable "Please don't go anywhere, Brooks."

"You are on top of me. I don't see how I could sneak out without you noticing."

"Will you tell me a story that I've never heard?"

"Let's see. Can it be about anything?"

She nodded. It felt great to have her in my arms. This was where she belonged.

"Before I left for boot camp, I asked Branch if he planned on marrying you someday. I don't know why I did it. I guess maybe I just needed that push to tell me that I was doing the right thing by leaving. At any rate, he told me that as long as I wanted you, he'd have you. Do you believe that cock sucker said that?"

She laughed. "Yeah. I do."

"Anyway, that's not the best part of the story. While he thought he'd damaged my ego, I laughed, thinking about the two times that I'd been with you that nobody knew about. Then I said the first thing that popped into my head. I asked him if he was alright with knowing that when you were with him if it bothered him that you pretended it was me." I cackled to myself. "You don't have to tell me if you ever did that, but it made me feel better saying it to him."

"I'm sure it pissed him off."

"Yeah. It didn't matter. I left, and he got to be with you. He got to live with you and spend countless hours in your presence while I was so far away from everyone."

"How did you get through it?" She asked.

"I thought of you. I drew pictures of you and wrote you letters that I never sent. I hooked up with other soldiers, but they weren't anything spectacular. To be honest, I stayed busy most of the time. It wasn't until I was in bed thinking of you that it got hard."

"It broke my heart when you left. I felt like I was being punished."

"My brother fooled us both. Don't let it get to you. We're together now, Kat."

"Please be patient with me, Brooks. I know I said I couldn't move forward, but I also can't lose you. I just feel like I ended his life. I feel responsible and I've got to work that out on my own. You understand, don't you?"

"You hurt me earlier. I keep letting myself fall harder for you each time. The thing is, when I do that and you push me away, it hurts worse. All I can tell you is that no matter how many times I've tried to not love you, it's never happened. So you can push me away. You can tell me you don't want to be with me, but I'm not going anywhere. I'll stalk you if I have to."

Kat giggled. "I told you where I hide the house key. You've been invited in."

"Good because I was planning on having a copy made in the morning."

"Promise?"

I peered down at her with a smile on my face. "Yes, I promise."

The next morning I awoke to find Kat still on top of me. I tried to scoot her off without waking her, but it was impossible. Her eyes flew open. "I need to go to work."

She grabbed my hand when I tried to step away. "Will you be back later?"

"You've got a hard day ahead of you. Are you sure that's what you want?"

She nodded.

"Woman, you're so confusing."

"Please?"

I leaned over and kissed her. "I'll see you later. I love you. Give B a kiss and tell her I'll be here after work."

"I don't know what I'd do without you in my life. No matter what happens, you're always there to protect me. Sometimes I think my parents made you that way, like they somehow connected us so I'd never be alone."

"I hate to break it to you, but I loved you way before they died and I promise that they didn't put any spells on me. It happened because I wanted it to. There's no other reason that I want to be there for you. No one makes me do it. I do it because it makes me happy. It makes me feel close to you, even when you're not paying attention."

I winked at her before stepping out of the room.

When I left for work, I felt better than I had the night before. We were going to get through this, no matter how many obstacles stood in the way.

Chapter 55

Since I knew Kat was spending her whole day making arrangements for Bobby's funeral and getting in touch with their mutual friends, I took it upon myself to work on my own little project.

With the help of my mom, who was left at the house still watching B, I was able to get the measurements for curtains, bedding, and even replacement area rugs. On my lunch hour, I went to the stores that my mother suggested and picked up replacements of all the things Bobby had ruined during his rampage.

It felt so good to pick out things for Kat. I wanted to give her the world, and this was just the beginning of it.

When I got back to base, I made a few more calls ordering a new bed. It was a special kind that I figured Kat would enjoy. I knew I certainly would.

After gathering a couple of my buddies, we headed over to the store to pick up everything else I needed, including the new mattress. Then, before we arrived, I called home to check on her.

"Hello?"

"You're crying? What's wrong?" I didn't like that she was having a hard time and hadn't reached out to me.

"I just got off the phone with Sarah."

"That bad?"

"Well, they all loved him. They could never believe the things that I said he did, and of course, I got blamed for everything that happened, including him coming to D.C. and losing his life. She even said that the whole town was going to hate me and I needed to prepare myself for it."

"Kat, listen to me. You've got to calm down."

"Sorry."

I wished I knew a better way to console her. "We're going to get through these next couple of days. Mom and I will be by your side the whole time. I don't give a shit what those people think of you. I know the real Katy; the one that cares about other people and leaves her life and everything behind because she's disappointed them. I know the girl that lost her parents and somehow grew up to be an amazing mother. And last but never least, I know the woman that loves someone with her whole heart, no matter how far away they might be. Please, try to calm down. I'll be there around four. I've got to stop and do something first."

"Brooks?"

"Yeah?"

She sniffled as she responded. "I don't deserve you."

"Yes, you do. Go take a hot bath. Close your eyes and think about B's smile. Think about how happy she is when you walk into the room. Think of things that make you happy. Just try to relax."

"I'll think about you, Brooks."

I can't even begin to explain how much of a relief it was to hear her saying that to me. "Without clothes. That always seems to change my mood."

I heard her attempt to laugh. "I'll try that."

"That's my girl. I'll see you in a bit."

Kat never expected me to show up with bags, and she certainly couldn't have known I'd bring a few guys to give me a hand. The look on her face was priceless. "Hey. Now before you freak out I just want to say that I did my best picking out something you'd like. If it's no good, we'll take it all back and pick out something else."

I put the bags down on the coffee table and kissed her. "You didn't have to buy me anything."

I'd already started walking back outside to get more. "If I'm going to be living here, then I need to pitch in."

When I came in again I noticed she was already going through the first set of items I'd brought in. She seemed so delighted, and I couldn't help but smile. Finally I'd done something right. "I can't believe you did all this. Did you take off early?"

"No. I ordered it all on the computer and it was ready when I got off. Mom suggested it."

Kat seemed pretty shocked. "This is pretty amazing. I can't believe you did this."

I sat down beside her and ran my hand over the soft part of her face. "I'd do anything to see you smile, Kat. Put your feet up and start opening packages. I've got to go back outside and help my buddies with something."

"Your buddies?"

We all took a corner and began carrying the heavy mattress in through the doorway, and then to the bedroom. I couldn't see Kat's face, but I was pretty sure she was shocked.

After we got that positioned, we then carried in a new area rug to take place of the ruined one. The whole time they were in the house I couldn't wait for them to leave so I could give all my attention to my girls.

I saw my friends out and thanked them, promising a case of beer to each for their assistance. Once I was back inside, I picked up Kat and carried her into the bedroom, sitting down on the soft mattress beneath her.

"So, how does it feel? The Internet said it's the most sold bed in America. The rug is even softer than the one we had to throw away. It matches all the new bedding. Mom picked them out based on what you had before."

The memory foam made me excited to sleep at night. I hoped she liked that kind of comfort. Her old mattress felt kind of hard. "It's great, but there's just one problem."

"What? Too soft? I know some people like a bed to be firm."

"No. It's too comfortable. I don't see how you're ever going to get any action when I fall asleep as soon as my back hits the bed."

I laughed before pulling her close to me. "Am I allowed to kiss you or are we still waiting?"

She closed her eyes and separated her lips just enough to tell me she was ready. "Waiting only prolongs the inevitable."

I kissed her slowly, running my wet lips over hers. "I don't think I have to worry about you falling asleep on me. I know ways to keep you alert and ready." Right as I began to run my hand between her legs the door came open and in popped B.

"Hey, Daddy will be outside in just a second. I need to talk to Mommy about something first. Go on with Mom-mom and I'll meet you there."

She hopped down and went looking for her grandmother. When Kat met my stare I think she saw the intent in my eyes. I wanted her.

She still kept me from touching her there. "What's wrong with you?" I questioned.

"Don't you dare do it. I need time, Brooks. I can't just spit on a grave that hasn't even been dug yet."

I just shook my head. Sure I was disappointed, but I was willing to wait. "Look, now I get that you're worried I'm going to push you, but I won't push for that. Kat, I will wedge myself so far into your life that you won't be able to get rid of me, but I wasn't going to ask you what you think I was. In fact, I wasn't going to ask you anything."

"Sorry. What was it?"

"While you were in the hospital, I stopped by and had my appointment with the medical board. It seems that my injuries are more severe than I thought. They're going to have to do surgery, and they're not real sure that they can fix the damage." I was lucky to be seen in Bethesda on such short notice, but after they'd examined my records they knew what the results would be. I think they also appreciated that they weren't going to have to fly me out there since I was already in the area.

I saw her looking down at the scars on my arm. "What does that mean?"

"Well, depending on a few factors, I may not be able to stay on active duty. I know I can't pass a normal physical evaluation. Without feeling in my hand and arm, I can't operate the machinery that I was trained to use."

"You said it didn't bother you."

"It doesn't. For the most part, I can't feel much of anything. I just assumed that it was alright. But I can tell that sometimes I lose the feeling and control over it."

She put her hand over her mouth. "Jesus, you picked me up before. You just carried a mattress. What were you thinking?"

I lifted my fingers up to run them over her lips. "I was thinking that I'd waited my whole life to be with you and hold a child that we shared together. When the opportunity was in front of me, I couldn't refuse it."

"So, it's our fault you may not be able to work?"

I shook my head. She was just being silly now. "Even if it was, I wouldn't be mad. I've got plans for us, Kat, and they don't involve the military. Getting out wouldn't be that bad. I could get a job and we'd be fine."

"I still can't believe that you want to be with me. So much has happened. If you were smart, you would have forgotten about me a long time ago."

"We're a family. I've doubted myself for many reasons in my life, but deciding to love you was never something I ever considered giving up. That probably makes me a fool. I really don't care what anyone thinks about it. We can be something beautiful together and that's all I need to know."

Kat smacked me lightly on the chest. "Stop doing that."

"What?" I played innocent.

"Making me love you even more."

"You say that like it's a bad thing." I quickly changed the subject. "I've got some paint outside. I'm going to need to paint the ceiling before we can get the sheets on the bed. I bought you the nice thick ones like we had growing up."

Kat rolled over as if she was going to spectate only. "I guess I'll just lay here and watch."

I kissed her on the nose before standing up. "Sounds good to me." Right before stepping out of the room I stopped to ask her something else. "So, did you get everything taken care of today?"

Kat leaned up on her elbows. "For the most part. The church is basically taking over and everyone pretty much made it clear that I wasn't going to be welcome. They all think I'm a terrible person. I know you don't see it, but maybe they're all right. How else could I feel so happy to start over with you, in the midst of a tragedy?"

I felt it necessary to walk back over where she was and kneel in front of her. "Kat, you're human and you're coping. If I wasn't here, life would be different, but I can't let what's happened come between us. I won't. Only you and Bobby know what happened in that truck. You can blame yourself for the rest of your life if that will help you cope. The fact is that, he forced you into that vehicle, after breaking a protective order and hunting you down, with every intention of harming you, or maybe even worse. Wake up and see what I see because nowhere does it say that defending yourself can be construed as murder. You were trying to survive in a dire situation, one where your life felt threatened. If they can't understand that, then screw them. They weren't your real friends anyway."

After gathering all the supplies, I went back into the bedroom. I hopped on the bed and looked at the ceiling close up. "I need to seal the spot. I checked earlier, and it didn't go through. He must have put out the flames as soon as they started to get high. One coat of this primer and couple coats of the paint should do the trick. If you hate it, I'll rip out the drywall and replace the whole area."

"You know how to do all that?"

"Do you think I just wear this uniform and walk around all day looking sexy?" She obviously did.

She laughed at me. "Of course not. I just didn't think they taught you stuff like this."

"Woman, you've got a lot to learn about the things I know." I bent down and touched the tip of her nose with a wet paintbrush.

Kat reached over and ran her hands up my shirt. She knew it would make me crazy. "I'm a more hands on kind of learner."

I sat the paint can down and hovered over her, prepared for whatever she had in mind. The painting could wait. "Let's get started then."

Chapter 56

The next couple days seemed like they had been before all hell broke loose. The house was finally put back together. I'd repaired any dings or holes that had been put in the walls. My mom had made sure every square inch was scrubbed clean. Kat was able to rest her hip knowing that we had everything taken care of for her. I had to admit that my mom being there during the day was a godsend. In the evenings she made dinner for when I was set to arrive home. I appreciated knowing that she was making sure Kat stayed off her feet, but also that B had someone to keep her occupied.

In the evenings I spent all of my time with the three of them. My most favorite part was when it got close to bed time. B would nestle her body up against mine while Kat always sat next to us. I'd put my arm around her and enjoy being this close to them at the same time.

As the days got closer to Bobby's service, I could sense Kat getting nervous. She wasn't snappy, but it was clear she had a lot on her mind.

During the day, I focused on getting my financials together for the realty company back in D.C., so that I could attempt to buy back Kat's parent's house. I still hadn't mentioned it to her, but knew without a single doubt, she'd appreciate it more than any other gift money could buy. It wasn't just her childhood home. It was where all of her special memories with her parents still remained.

I could picture us raising our family there. It seemed like the good choice to make, especially since my career options were about to change.

Lucky for me I had a great resume to provide, and with a couple military bases, NSA, and even the FBI within driving distance, I'd have a ton of options to apply for.

The night before Bobby's funeral, after I'd put B to bed and made sure my mom was comfortable in the cleaned up guest room, I climbed into bed next to Kat and pulled her in close. "Stop worrying about tomorrow, woman. It's just another day."

"That's easy for you to say. You don't have to go there and face all of them."

"I will. I'd be happy to accompany you."

She turned and gave me a questionable look. "Seriously? I can't show up to Bobby's funeral with you. It's wrong in so many ways."

"I'm the father of your child and your best friend. What's the big deal?"

"It's inappropriate, Brooks. I'm going alone. That's the end of this discussion. Let it be."

I ran my hand through a clump of her long brown hair. "You're feisty tonight. You're like a female lioness."

"Don't be funny. You're freaking me out about showing up. Brooks, you can't be there."

"Calm down. I won't come."

Kat wrapped her arms around me. "Don't get mad. I just can't handle anymore negative drama. I feel like tomorrow will finally close a lot of doors for me. I've lived here and made friends. Now I'm worried I don't have any left. It hurts."

"You're never alone, Kat."

"I know. It's the point though."

I kissed her nose and then her lips. "I love you. Everything I do is because of that."

"I know it is. That's why you're the man of my dreams, Brooks. You always know what I need. I love you for being you."

That night while she slept I tossed and turned, even with a new mattress. It wasn't that I was uncomfortable. I was worried about her getting into a situation and me not being there to save her. She wasn't going to like it, but I was going to show up at the funeral even if I had to hide it from her.

I'd borrowed my friend's car to ride to the funeral in. It had tinted windows, making it easy for me to be there without being seen. It wasn't hard to spot Kat's car as she pulled in. I watched her hobble out toward a group of people. After I knew she wasn't looking around for me, I pulled into a spot closer and cracked the window so I could hear what the people were saying to her. It hurt me so much that she was going there alone. I had a terrible feeling I couldn't shake. That's why I put on my military dress apparel and went even after she'd told me not to.

Right away I could hear hostility as the people addressed her.

"Hold up a minute. Where do you think you're goin', Katy?"

"Inside. Where else would I go?"

The man shook his head and pointed back toward the lot. "Yeah, I don't think that's a good idea. Do everyone a favor and just go home. We're all here to remember our friend, not sit in the same room with the person that ended his life."

I gripped the steering wheel while telling myself she could handle them.

"I have every right to be in there. He was my husband, and I loved him."

"You loved him?" The guy spit on the ground in front of her. If I hadn't seen it with my own eyes I wouldn't have believed it. "You loved him so much that you had him arrested for a crime he wasn't capable of doin'. You know that man never laid a hand on you, but yet you had him arrested for it, didn't ya?"

"You think I inflicted those bruises all of those times on myself?"

I kept reminding myself that she was prepared for this.

"It don't even matter what I think you're capable of. If that weren't bad enough, you took your daughter and ran off with your lover, so he couldn't even see her. All he wanted to do was work things out with you." At this point I was losing my cool. Kat didn't budge from where she stood though, so I remained in the car.

"No, he wanted to hurt me worse." She started crying, making me wonder if it was the right time to make an appearance. If she needed me, she wouldn't be mad that I'd come.

"Katy, do us all a favor and spare us the drama. Sarah's so upset because she brought you into Bobby's life. She doesn't need to see you here."

"Please, Dave. Please, just let me pay my respects. I have every right to say goodbye to him. You couldn't be more wrong about me. I swear, I would never want this for anyone, especially Bobby."

I watched the minister approach her. I expected him to help her inside. "Bobby told me things during our sessions. He had his own demons, but I've got to be respectful of my daughter. How about we meet later and you can say your goodbye's then?"

I was done listening to them tear her apart. I got out of the vehicle and headed right for them. "How about you get off that high horse and let the girl through? Isn't this the Lord's house? Where everyone is welcome?"

The first guy started to come at me. If he thought for a second he could take me, he was wrong. Kat grabbed the back of his jacket, while I stood there, showing him how much I wasn't threatened. "Get your boyfriend out of here,

Katy. My best friend is dead because of you. Leave now before someone gets hurt."

"Dave, please. We'll go. Please just stop this," she pleaded. I didn't get it. She was backing down because of this loser?

When the guy shoved Kat, I was done. I went right after him, taking him down with little effort. Kat took ahold of my arm before I could pound it against his face.

"Please stop. You need to leave, Brooks. Please, just go."

I stood and dusted off my clothes. "I came here for support because I knew they were going to treat you like shit."

She touched my hand. "I can handle them without you interfering. Just go before it gets worse."

I pulled away from her. She was insane if she thought this was okay with me. "You know what, I'm sick of trying."

I peeled wheels when I pulled away from the church. I was so angry at her for not letting me finish giving that man a beat down. He deserved to be hurt. I wasn't going to stand around and let him shove her like that.

What really burned me up was the fact that she felt like sending me away would solve her problems. Whether I was there or not, they were still going to treat her like shit, and she was prepared to let them.

When I got back to the house, I didn't really explain what was going on to my mother. I grabbed B and announced that we were going out for a little while. Once we reached the park I started to calm down. It didn't help that she was going on and on about a puppy that was running around.

"Daddy, I pet doggy."

"You can pet him. Be gentle."

"Daddy, I want puppy."

I watched the owners smile as B hugged the small vanilla Labrador. "You can't have that puppy. He belongs to these nice people."

She stuck out her bottom lips. The guy looked at me and laughed. "How do you say no to something that cute?"

I threw up my hands. "Clearly I don't."

B was sad when they walked away, making me wonder if we had room in our lives for a puppy. Then I stuck the thought aside, realizing we didn't even know where life was going to take us in the future.

For a while after that, I pushed her in a swing. She went down the slide several times allowing me to catch her at the bottom. When she began to yawn, I knew it was time to head home.

"Did you have fun, bug?"

"Yes, but I want puppy."

"I know you do. Maybe when you're bigger we can get one."

It was weird walking into the house with a cheery little girl and seeing two women crying. When I first saw them, I wondered if Kat was telling my mom how she couldn't take me being around anymore. Maybe I'd overstepped and caused her to change her mind.

"It's time I told you both the truth, because I can't sit here and watch you two fall apart, when you've got a real chance at happiness." I had no idea what my mother was talking about. What truth?

I whispered in B's ear to go turn on her cartoons in her bedroom. When she ran in that direction, I gave them my attention.

"Look, Mom, I appreciate you trying to help, but if it's all the same, I'm just going to head back to the barracks for the night." I didn't want to be told to leave.

Apparently my mom was in charge of whatever was happening.

"No, Brooks. You're going to come sit down next to Katy and listen to what I have to say."

When I refused to move, she pointed to the couch. "Now."

I had no idea what my mom was about to say to us, but when Kat took my hand, I realized it had nothing to do with the funeral. Something else was going on, and from the look on my mother's face I wasn't going to like it very much.

Chapter 57

My mom had obviously just started a conversation with Kat. From what I could make it out seemed as though she'd had inquired about something. I felt lost at first.

"Katy, I know why your mother went to visit your father that day."

I felt the need to protect Kat. "Do you honestly think this is going to solve anything that's going on now? Don't hurt her more with the past, Mom. Whatever it is, just leave it be."

Kat squeezed my arm. "No. I wanted to know since it happened. Please. Tell me why she was there."

My mother broke down right in front of us, hiding her face as she spoke. "I just want you to know that no matter what, I do love you like you're my daughter. I've never done it out of guilt."

I was at a loss for words, and obviously so was Kat. "What are you talking about?"

"We didn't know she was there. She told your dad that she had a PTA meeting at the school. We wanted to tell her, in fact that's why I was there."

Kat put her hands in the air. "What are you talking about? Where were you? Who were you with? I'm so lost."

I took her hand, feeling like I knew where this was going, finally, and if it was what I thought, things were about to get really depressing. "I think I know what you're going to say. Mom, please don't do this to Katy. Don't do this to our family."

"Your father has known since the night before they died. I told him first. We had decided to separate, and I walked next door to tell your father."

Kat kept looking down and then over at me, but I wasn't about to share what I'd suspected.

My mom cried harder. "Katy, I loved your father. I wanted to be with him, and I had ended things with Walt thinking that he wanted to be with me too."

I tightened my grip on Kat's hand, making sure she knew she wasn't in this alone. "Please don't tell me that you were having an affair with my father. He wouldn't. He loved my mom. I know he did."

I could tell she was about to go off the deep end. Kat had always pictured her parents as being the perfect people. My mom was now confirming a huge sin her father had committed. This wasn't going to help Kat understand the past. It was going to haunt her forever.

"I saw you kiss him and you told me that I was mistaken. I believed you. That's what I saw wasn't it? You lied right to my face." I felt it was important to bring it up in case she mentioned it.

"You both need to understand that we'd all been friends for so long. It just happened and we couldn't stop it. I tried to stop, I swear I did."

Kat was starting to lose her grip. I felt her body shaking beside me. "So she caught you? Is that what happened?"

"Yes," my mom sobbed. "We'd been having a heated argument, and I followed your dad into his bedroom. We could hear you three in the tree house and thought we were alone. He rejected me, Katy. You're father told me he couldn't do it. He said he wouldn't ever leave your mother."

"Then how did she catch you? She caught you talking about it?"

My mom got quiet, like it was too hard to talk about. "Mom, answer us. What did you do?"

She shook her head. "I was so hurt. I'd ended my marriage for him and he wouldn't leave her. So, out of desperation, I threw myself at him, begging for one last night together." She was quiet for a second. "And he didn't resist."

When Kat got up and ran into the bathroom I knew what was about to happen. I took it upon myself to scold my own mother.

"How could you do something like that? She trusted you. Dad trusted you." I was heading into the bathroom to check on Kat, who I was worried more about.

"Brooks, don't walk away. You need to hear everything."

B came into the bathroom with a doll in her hand. "Mama, boosh hair."

I watched Kat, with tears streaming down her cheeks, brushing a baby dolls hair. B didn't like seeing her mom so sad. "No cry."

I waited for B to run back out before addressing her mother. I leaned against the doorframe and listened as she spoke. "I can't listen to her."

"I know what you mean, but I need to know the whole story. This doesn't just involve you or my dad. It involves all of us, even Branch."

"I just had to bury Bobby, and now she's making things worse. I can't do it, Brooks. Find out what she has to say and then make her go. Buy her a ticket and send her home."

"Kat, this time I'm asking. I need you." She wasn't in this alone. It involved me too. My mom had secrets, and now that they'd been revealed I was having trouble accepting them.

I helped her stand up and watched as she began comforting me.

I felt like it was important to let her know where I stood. This would change nothing for me. "No matter what she has to say, however it affects us, it won't change anything for me. If you want space, I'll give it to you. If we can't move forward, I'll accept it."

Even though she didn't answer, Kat took my hand as we went back out into the living room to face my mother.

"Why was my mother in that building, Danica? I need to know."

"After she walked in on us, we didn't exactly have the words to explain. She put on a pretty face and told me to leave, without saying anything else. I think that hurt me more than anything; the fact that she refused to look at me. I felt so ashamed and regretted everything immediately. I don't know what they talked about, or how she managed to get through the night without anyone knowing. I went home and made dinner, just waiting for her to confront me. I even called you boys in early that night, in fear of having to leave and spend the night away from the house. Your father was a mess. I'd broken his heart, and he wasn't willing to accept that we were through. The thing is, I never stopped loving him. I just got so caught up in the affair."

It crushed me to think about my dad going through all of this. I couldn't imagine what it was like for him to have the woman he loved and his best friend sneaking around to be together. Kat squeezed my hand to remind me she was there, but it really wasn't helping much, not with this situation.

"The next morning he left for work and finally was able to call. He said that you were all going to be moving, and the house was going to be up for sale within the week. He told me that I was a mistake and that he'd spend the rest of his life making his mistake up to your mother."

She put her head down and cried harder. "That's the last time I heard from your father, but not the last time I heard from your mother."

My mom looked right at Kat. "Katy, that morning she drove you all to school, and none of you probably caught on that anything was wrong. She was going to meet your father so that they could talk."

"How do you know that? Because I know she wouldn't have called to tell you that."

"The school called me first, letting me know that I had to come get the boys. They asked if you'd be coming home with me, too. As angry as she was at me, I knew you were her first priority, so I called her. When she answered I could tell that it was bad. She didn't get on the line and start cussing me out, or accusing me of ruining your family. She was calm, almost like she knew what was happening and that they weren't going to make it. I'll never forget the words she said to me." She paused and kept her gaze on Kat. "Take care of Katy, Dani. Keep her safe and love her forever. Make sure Brooks never takes her for granted."

I think we both started crying at the same time. It was like we were living that moment again, but now with complete understanding of how it all came to be. "Shh," I whispered as I tried to console her.

I wanted to make this easier for Kat, but had no idea how. Her heart had been ripped in two the day she lost her parents. It was hard to remember her mother. I had a few instances where she made it a point to pull me aside and say something about Kat, but it was too long ago. I'd been through too much to remember back that far.

The fact that she knew I cared about her daughter back then made it all so real to me. I felt like somehow she knew we were supposed to end up together. Even as mad as she was at my mom, she could still picture Kat and I being together. I had so much adoration for the woman, and I hoped Kat did too. Her parents had met because they wanted to work things out. They died together, in each other's arms. They loved one another until their last moments.

After several minutes of sobbing, Kat wiped off her face and looked toward my mom. "Why now?"

"Don't you get it, Katy? You can't move forward with Brooks because you think you were responsible for Bobby's death. How do you think I felt, raising the daughter of the couple that I killed?"

God, I didn't want this to be the conversation that brought Kat back to me, but damn if it wasn't. She turned and looked at me with so much pent up sadness. I had no idea what to expect next.

My mom added one more thing. "Katy, you've got one life; one chance to make things right. It's taken me a long time to accept the things that I can't change. I've got to live with myself every day. I've got to look in the mirror and face those demons, but I do it, because I have you and the rest of our family. You see, out of something tragic, I learned to be better to myself and to the people around me. I worked things out with Walt and I've never loved anyone like I love him now. Seeing you making the same mistakes I made is killing me. I don't want you walking away from something you were always meant to have. Even your mother knew it. You two have been in love your whole lives. I've never seen something so beautiful in all of my life. I'm so sorry for what I've done. I don't expect you to ever forgive me, but please don't give up on each other. I know your parents are looking out for you. They brought you two back together. I have to believe that."

When my mom got up and left the room, it was difficult to come to grips with everything she'd said. For a while I sat silent, staring into Kat's eyes. She had some valid points, and even though I didn't agree with hashing it all out like she had, so close to Kat having attended a funeral, I knew why. We both did.

Now I just needed to know if it was going to make us, or break up the only family either of us had ever known.

Chapter 58

After all these years, the truth had been confirmed. Our parents were having an affair; one that led to her mother being in the Pentagon while the plane hit it. Like a row of dominos life had followed that path of destruction. I was speechless, and from the look on Kat's face she felt the same discontent. Even though I'd suspected it, I didn't know how I was supposed to look at my mother the same ever again. For my whole life, I'd assumed she and my dad were happy. They were such good parents. I wondered what went so terribly wrong that she fell into the arms of his best friend. Better yet, I wanted to know why Kat's dad didn't push her away.

Our families did everything together. It was almost sickening to imagine how right under our noses, they were sleeping together.

Then there was the fact that my mother chose to tell us when we were struggling. Was this her efforts to open our eyes to what was at stake? I didn't know about Kat, but I already knew what I wanted. There was no doubt in my mind that we'd get through this. My hardest struggle was having to wait it out. Perhaps this confession would bring us closer together. I was too in shock to consider anything else.

It was strange how after my mother left the room we sat there in silence. I couldn't find the words to express my feelings. I didn't want to overstep what Kat could be experiencing. She was the one who lost her parents. Mine were still fine.

Without saying a single word, she took my hand and led me into the bedroom. "Wait here," she requested.

I don't know where she went in those few minutes. I kept listening, wondering if she'd gone in to confront my mother some more. I half expected them to have words, but the house remained silent. When Kat came back in the room, I was still sitting on the bed with my hands on my knees. I kept my face narrowed on the floor because I was afraid to look in her eyes and witness her pain.

Kat got down on the floor and wedged herself between my legs. Our eyes met, and she reached up to wipe away a tear that was still lingering on my cheek.

"I'm so sorry about my mom, Kat. If I would have known-"

She put her finger up to my lips before I was able to finish what I wanted to tell her. "Shh, don't talk about it. Just listen to what I have to say."

"Do you know that there's not one single day in my life that I can remember where I didn't love you?"

I didn't know where this was going, but so far it seemed like it was in the right direction. A hint of hope filled me as I listened.

"Tell me something I don't know."

"I'm tired of fighting with you. I'm sick of all of it." She paused for a second, and in that amount of time I felt confused again. Her explanation was all over the place. I was going to get whiplash if it continued this way. "What your Mom told us may be unbelievable, but I get why she did it. For the first time, I understand what she's been trying to get through my hard head. It's like I'm seeing clearly, finally. Brooks, if you don't move all of your shit into this house soon, I'm going to go crazy. There's no reason you're still going to the base to change. B and I need you here. We can't be a family unless you're here with us, all the time. Your mom was right. I can't change my past, and I shouldn't ruin my future; our future. If it's still okay, I'm ready to fall completely into this with you. I've been ready my whole life, but I was just too scared of losing you. I'm not afraid anymore, Brooks. I'm not worried of what tomorrow might bring because I know you're going to be there. I know you'll protect me and love me like you've done our whole lives. God, I've wasted so much time. Are you even listening to me? Do you still want this? Say something?"

I was speechless, unable to move a single inch. Of course I heard her, I just couldn't begin to express how thankful I was.

I fell back onto the bed and began to laugh. I have no idea what made me do it. I supposed I was so delighted that I couldn't control what I was feeling. Tears streamed down my cheeks, not because I was sad. I was elated, flabbergasted, utterly overwhelmed.

Kat stood up and grabbed me, shaking me as if I'd gone mad.

"Are you okay? Is it the affair? Do you want to talk about it?" I found it more funny that she assumed something was wrong. Finally everything was right.

"I can't be mad about something that we had no control over. I've never been one to live in the past, not when I knew you were always my future."

"Come again?" It was silly that she needed me to repeat myself since I'd been telling her the same lines our whole lives.

"I said that you are my future and I've always known it, well felt is a better word."

When she leaned forward to kiss me, I pulled her against my body. In that moment I didn't want to let go. Unlike every other time we were together, I could feel her finally giving me all of her. It was as if she'd finally been given a reason to stop fighting the inevitable. Our future was set in stone. Nothing could steer us away, not anymore.

We kissed like teens making out for the first time without their parents being home. With each slip of her tongue, with every movement of my hands across her skin, I got excited. My palms were sweaty, and even though we were on the bed, I felt dizzy. This wasn't just a passionate embrace. It was taking everything in me to go slow when all I wanted to do was get her naked.

This was my Katy, my Kat. Every inch of her belonged to me. She owned my heart, my soul, and everything else I could give her. She wasn't just the mother of our daughter. She was going to carry all of our children. There wouldn't be a moment in our future where she would have to worry that I'd leave because it would never happen. Wherever I went, she'd be there at my side. I finally felt something that I'd waited my whole life to experience.

Secure and stable.

There was nothing but content pouring into each of our kisses, and I think she felt it as well. Our minds and bodies were in complete sync. It was beautiful, and in no time at all, I was undressing her. She helped me lift the white undershirt over her head. The two last things to go were her panties and bra.

Then Kat began unbuttoning my dress jacket. One by one the fabric loosened while she teased me with her wet lips. My t-shirt came off next, and as soon as it left my head, I felt her fingernails coursing up my naked chest.

I cupped her breasts, taking one nipple into my mouth and sucking on it. Kat leaned back, using her hands to unfasten my belt and then my pants. With little effort I shoved my boxers down, eager for what was to come afterwards.

While Kat removed her panties from her ankles, I directed her back onto the bed. She climbed on top of me, straddling my erection as if she needed no assistance to position it at her entrance.

I played with her hair, taking a few strands and covering her breasts with it. She looked so damn sexy. I couldn't help but to ask for a reminder. "Tell me you're mine."

She leaned down and teased me with her sultry lips once again. "I belong to you, I always have and I always will." She traced my tattoo, looking down as she finished. "And you belong to me."

I ran my hands on both sides of her arms and started moving her body into a steady pace. Kat tickled my chest with her nails, crossing over my nipples with the palms. Right away they were stimulated by her touch. She leaned forward licking each of them while leaving a trail of wet saliva when she pulled away.

I gasped and threw my head back, forcing myself to stay collected. Kat pulled away with an ornery grimace on her face. She knew she was making me crazy, and I didn't want it to stop.

Then, after our lips separated from another tongue-filled kiss, She leaned back, giving me ample space to reach down and feel her slickness. She was prepared and hungry for what was about to fill her. I took ahold of my stiff erection and taunted her there, making sure to spread her juices over her sensitive clit. Her body bucked before I thrust inside of her, filling her with so much more than a hard cock.

We'd been struggling, and this was an end to it all. This makeup session was all about getting over the hurdles and giving in to what we knew was right.

Our connected bodies converged, moving amidst a steady rhythm. I was lost in her, succumbing to the pure fact that this was all finally mine. With every grind, slip, and even halt, I was captivated by her body. Her essence beckoned me, satiating my hunger to have her in every way possible. She was what I'd wished for in my darkest of days. She was the last missing piece to my puzzle. I'd found my forever and knew for certain that she'd never slip away from me again. This pivotal moment in our relationship would stand out amongst the others. This was the night that everything significantly changed for us.

We made love: beautiful, debauched love, christening our new life and future. Her serious stare only intensified the moment as I filled her with intoxicating passion. Hot sweat rolled down the skin between her breasts as she continued riding me. I held onto her hip and used my other hand to gently rub her clit, guiding her body into a generous orgasm. As her walls tightened around me her release felt so fierce, like it contained years of pent up hostility. Rather than give her time to come down from her lustful high, I flipped us over.

Kat began stroking me, making me want to slip right back inside of her. I was on the brink of losing it, desperate to satisfy my salacious appetite. I teased her with my tongue, forcing her to fight to touch it with hers. Her inviting lips begged to be kissed, and I happily obliged.

"Don't make me stop, Brooks. We have all night."

I corrected her, "No, Kat, we have forever."

We flipped around again and I watched Kat sinking down between my legs. The idea of her tasting her own arousal on me sent me into a frenzy. I grabbed her body and pulled her up until her pussy was right in my face. From there I began my decent, licking and sucking until I felt her body spasming over mine.

After that I knew I was running out of time. I repositioned us, getting up on my knees to wrap her legs around my waist. There was no need to look down to enter her.

My pace was unhinged, provoked by my own desire to lose absolute control. I could feel my own rapture as I lost control over my actions, falling down when euphoria left me to explode inside of her.

Afterwards, I pulled her to lie on top of me. We kissed as she stroked my sensitive skin. I took her hand and kissed it gently. "I'll move my clothes in tomorrow."

Then I saw the smile I loved so much taking over her whole face.

Right before she started to fall asleep, I began laughing. Getting caught up in something she had said before.

"What's so funny?" She asked.

"I was just thinking how you said I wouldn't get any action on this bed."

She let out an air-filled laugh and reached between my legs. "We're just getting started."

Chapter 59
September 11ᵗʰ 2013

"I can't believe it's been twelve years," Kat said as we stood together looking down at her parent's headstones. B was running around Branch and Melissa with a small bouquet of yellow roses. Since it was also her birthday, she was dressed for the occasion.

I took Kat's hand and squeezed it reminding her that she'd never have to do this alone. "They'd be proud of you."

"I know they're watching over us. In my heart, I know they gave us B. Her being born on the same date they left me can't just be a coincidence."

"It's fate," We heard my mom say as she and my dad made there way over to us. "It has to be."

It took us a couple weeks to get over the shock of what my mother had told us. I still think there is a little animosity between she and Kat, not that they ever let anyone see it.

It took a call from my dad to help us see that we needed to put it all behind us. If he could forgive her, then so should we. For me, I was just angry she'd kept the truth from Kat, when I knew in the long run it had only helped her.

We all had skeletons in our closets and it wasn't right to judge.

My brother came up behind us and put his hands on both Kat's and my shoulder.

"I think it's time we go back to the house and have sour beef and dumplings. The past two years Mom refused to make them, because you weren't there, Katy. We had some craptastic chicken instead."

"In my defense, it was an award winning recipe," our mom added.

I turned my attention back to Kat. Not only was it already a special day for a couple reasons, but I had something else planned that I needed to tend to. It was a special surprise, one that required me to separate from my one and only for a little while. "I need to go get B's cake and pick up a surprise. Are you good riding with Mel back to the house in our car? Branch is going to drive me."

My mom had ordered a cake from a fancy treats shop in the heart of the city and they'd decorated the entire back yard in balloons, including some floating in the pool. B hadn't seen it yet, but Kat and I knew she was going to go crazy over it.

Since I'd recently been released from duty from the Army, I had been spending a lot of time job searching, amongst other things. Thankfully, I'd managed to get an offer I couldn't refuse. The only stipulation was that I'd have to relocate. With the help of my father, I'd also been looking at homes in the area, hoping we could move back to where it all began. It was obvious that Kat didn't want to live in a town where everyone treated her like crap. Personally, I hated it.

With having time off, it was easy to get caught up with my girls. B was the apple of my eye. I woke up every morning to her bright smile.

Buying her a ring was never in my plans. Unlike my brother, I knew what Kat wanted most in the world was to wear her mother's wedding ring. Since it had been stored safely at my parent's house for years, I knew exactly where to find it when I was ready to pop the question, and boy was I prepared. It was all part of a big surprise I had planned. With the help of my family I was pretty close to pulling it off. All I could hope for was that when I presented it to her, she'd say yes.

"Earth to Kat." She finally looked up from the gravesite to see me waving my hand in front of her. "Do I get a kiss goodbye, or are you going to stand there in your weird trance?"

She raised her brows and leaned in. "Sorry."

When a little peck wasn't enough, I held the back of her head, shoving my tongue in her mouth for added result.

Branch started making gagging sounds. "Can we go before I puke?"

Kat pulled away and wiped off her face while B came running in my direction. "Daddy, I go."

"Daddy's got to get you a surprise. Go home with Mama and I'll see you there. Okay?"

B stuck out her bottom lip. "No. I go with Daddy."

I kissed my little girl on the forehead and turned to Kat for some assistance at getting away. Ever since the first night I moved in she'd made it impossible to go anywhere without her.

Once I was in the car with my brother, I took a deep breath before pulling away from the parking spot. "I'm nervous."

"What for? You've been married to Katy in your mind since we were kids."

"What if she's not ready?"

"It's not like you're asking her to marry you today, Brooks. I'd be more worried about the other part of the surprise. I mean, you really went all out."

I smirked thinking about how hard my parents and the contractors I hired had worked to get the house next door ready for the big reveal. As soon as I saw that it was up for sale, I knew she was meant to have it. Luckily I managed to get a good deal on it, plus we'd have built in babysitters at our disposal one house over.

I think the biggest part of the surprise was going to be our daughter's room, which happened to be Kat's. I needed every detail to be perfect, but still wondered if I'd gone a little overboard. I mean, who buys a house to propose in?

"Don't fret. I'm sure she'll say yes. Apparently you're the man of her dreams."

I chuckled to myself after what he said. Branch and I had been getting along better in the past month or so. I think it helped that Melissa and Kat had buried the hatchet. They spoke almost daily. Little B really loved them, and I wasn't the type of brother to keep my family away from my daughter. She deserved to be loved by all of them.

Nearly twenty minutes after we left the cemetery, we pulled back up in front of the house. I carried the cake in, praying to God that all this wasn't going to blow up in face and be a disaster. The last thing I needed was to make Kat upset in any way though I was nervous how she would handle being back in that house again after so long.

"Katy, Katy, Katy. You're about to shit your shorts." Branch taunted Kat, purposely to get to me. I flipped him my middle finger.

My mom tossed a dish rag in his direction. "Cut it out. You aren't kids anymore. Let your brother have his moment for once."

When I walked up to Kat and extended my hand, it was obvious she knew something major was about to happen. "Come with me," I requested.

"Where are we going?" She asked.

"Close your eyes."

Just to make sure she didn't peek, I tied a handkerchief over her eyes to prevent her from seeing anything. "Seriously, what are you doing? Why can't you show me inside?"

I kept pulling her along, walking her out of the house. "I have some surprises for you. The first one is that I wanted to tell you that I got a job. It's a good one, Kat. I won't ever have to travel and I'll be home for dinner every night."

We came to a stop as we were facing the front of her childhood home. "The next surprise you may not like, but I want you to hear me out before you say anything. I've spent a lot of time and money on it, but if you don't like it, for any reason, I won't get angry. Branch said he'd take it off of our hands."

"Is it a car? Did you buy me a new car?"

I kept walking her toward the house, spinning her a few times to confuse her. Once we were standing at the threshold, I loosened the fabric from her eyes.

It only took Kat a few seconds to realize where we were. We walked inside, noticing right away how empty it was.

I didn't give her time to look around since I was already leading her up the stairs. "Where are we going? Did you ask the realtor if you could see this place? I don't understand."

"We're almost there. Keep walking."

When we reached her old bedroom, I put my body in front of her before opening the door. I'd had a painter come in and put butterflies on the walls and added Brooklyn's name in wooden blocks. We'd purchased furniture and rugs, matching the décor on the walls. To make the room suitable for our little princess, I'd gone all out and bought her a royal bed.

While she was taking it all in, I placed my hands on her shoulders.

"Kat, my job is here and so is our family. You don't have to run anymore, so I thought if it's okay with you, our daughter could grow up in the house that your parents built to raise you in. We can take old memories and make new ones with our own children. I know I took a huge leap, but I know you and I-"

She shoved her mouth against mine, preventing me from finishing. After a few minutes, I backed away. "So, it's okay that I already bought it?"

She nodded. "Yes, it's very okay. It's the most beautiful present, aside from B, of course."

I agreed. "Of course."

Kat walked up to the pink four-poster bed. "It's beautiful."

"This room was all Mom and Dad. They hired someone to come in and make it perfect. Do you think she'll like it?"

"She won't want to ever go home."

I could tell it had finally sunk in that we were going to have to move. Her other house would go for sale. "We can talk about it later."

"No. We'll sell it. I don't even care how much I get for it. There's not another house in the world that could mean as much as this one does to me. I don't even know what to say right now." I followed behind Kat as she made her way into her parent's old bedroom. For several minutes she stood there as if she were reminiscing about them. I finally wrapped my arms around her. "I think they're happy we're here, Kat. They're watching us, you know. I think they always have been." I spun her around to be facing me. "I never told anyone this, but there were so many times that I could have died, that I should have died. I swear someone was keeping me safe while I was out there. Now I know for sure, that it was them. I think they brought us back together."

"Thank you for waiting your whole life for me."

I wiped her tears away with my thumbs. "Maybe in our next life you won't make me wait so long," I joked.

"Let's enjoy this one first."

I waited until the bedroom filled with people to get down on one knee. It was important that everyone was around for this. "There's just one more thing, Kat." I popped open the old velvet box and watched her eyes light up. As we stood in her parent's room, I was proposing with the same ring her father had given to her mother.

"I'd very much like it if you had my name. What do you say, Kat? You think you might want to be my wife?"

She dropped to her knees and let me put the ring on her finger. She kept kissing me, all over my face. "Yes, of course."

I could count on my hand the moments in my life that mattered to me. This was one of my top events. I'd never forget the way it felt to have her accept my proposal, or to hold my daughter while we celebrated it.

A little later, downstairs in the kitchen, we popped open a bottle of wine and each held up glasses. "Here's to coming home."

In unison the rest of the family announced, "cheers."

Chapter 60
February 14th 2014

I'd already been up for hours, pacing around my parent's kitchen when my phone rang. She knew we couldn't see each other until she walked down the aisle, and I wasn't going to let her persuade me to sneak a peek. "Hey, babe. Don't you dare beg me to come over there. You know the rules."

"I'm calling on behalf of your daughter. She's up and insisting on being with you."

"I'm in the kitchen. If you promise to stay in bed, I'll come get her."

"I hate that you wake up before the sun rises."

I laughed as I walked out the door and followed the path to our kitchen entrance. "Do you miss me yet?"

I could hear her talking to our daughter, who had become quite impatient. "He's coming."

Little patters of feet could be heard as soon as I got inside.

"She's on her way down to you."

"Stay put until you hear me leave," I added.

"The answer is yes."

"To which question?" I'd forgotten already. My mind was in a million places. It hadn't helped that I'd stayed up late writing a message in a special card for her.

"Both. I will stay put, but also that I missed you. I hate knowing you're that close and I can't see you. How much harm can one kiss do?"

"I don't want to find out. In a few hours you'll be my wife, and then you can spend forever kissing me. Just so you know, I'll expect morning breath kisses, coffee kisses, and every other kind of kiss that you find gross. Now's the time to back out, Kat. When you say forever today, you better mean it."

"I'm ready to take the plunge. How about we just call the official right now, get him over here, and have them marry us so we can go back to bed for the rest of the day?"

"You didn't sleep either?"

I started walking up the stairs even though I knew I wasn't going to open the door. The last thing we needed was bad luck. "I couldn't get comfortable."

"Me either. Listen, its a couple more hours. Get all dolled up for me and meet me out back. I can't wait to see you, Kat. You're going to look so perfect."

"I'm going to look fat. You better say a prayer that this dress still fits me. I haven't tried it on for two weeks, and I swear I've gained ten more pounds."

"Being four months pregnant will do that, but just to be clear, you're not fat. You're beautiful." She was. I loved her little bump. "Imagine if you would have gotten pregnant over the summer. Then you'd be huge," I teased.

"Are you just going to stand at the door all morning torturing me?"

I tapped it twice before I replied. "I came up to tell you that I love you. I'll see you in bit."

Cold feet.

It was something I'd never have with Kat. She was mine and the piece of paper making it legal wasn't going to change anything.

I'd been wondering how I was going to sneak into our house without seeing her, but B made it the perfect excuse. Before we headed back to my parents, I tucked a card underneath of the package of peanut butter cups on the countertop.

She'd get a kick out of the card considering it was sentimental. Being that it was both our wedding day and Valentine's Day, a particular special day for someone that carried the name, I was more than excited to give it to her.

When Katy opened my card, she'd probably cry. The poor woman had been a babbling mess with her pregnancy hormones.

I smiled thinking back to the day we found out. On the first day of her missed period, I drove to the store and bought the test while she and B waited at home for me. I always got a kick out of seeing my daughter standing at the window, watching for me to pull in the driveway, especially since we'd moved into Kat's family home.

They'd met me at the door and the three of us rushed into the bathroom as if there were a tornado headed for the house.

Three minutes later we celebrated.

Our lives had changed for the better, especially since we'd moved. Kat smiled every day, making me feel like I was doing my job, keeping her happy and safe.

As far as our daughter, well let's just say that she was spoiled beyond belief and had become both of my parent's reasons for breathing.

Brooklyn wasn't just my daughter. Seeing what Kat and I brought into the world, and knowing that she helped bring us back together, made me the happiest man on the planet.

My brother was in the kitchen when we both walked inside. B spotted him and ran up to him, smacking into his legs. "Good morning, pretty girl. Uncle Branch has something for you."

He leaned down and handed her a stuffed bear holding a heart. When he squeezed it, it said 'I love you'.

B hugged it and brought it to show me. "Daddy, look."

"I see it. Go say thank you."

She hugged Branch and ran into the living room before we could tell her that nobody else was awake, and being that it was such a special day, I didn't care if she woke up the whole house.

While waiting for her to come back, Branch cleared his throat and got my attention. "I guess it's not necessary to ask if you're ready for today."

I raised my eyebrows and let out and air-filled laugh. "Yeah, I've been ready for this my whole life."

My brother looked down at his cup of coffee as he replied. "I shouldn't have been such a dick to you when we were kids."

I leaned across the counter and looked my brother in the eyes. "None of that matters anymore. She's mine forever, man."

Branch shook his head and laughed. "She always was."

I don't know why hearing him saying that got to me the way it did, but I felt myself getting choked up about it. Far be it from me to show my brother that he'd affected me, I quickly turned and refilled my cup. "You got that right." Inside though, I felt like Branch was finally able to accept that nothing could keep her from me, not time, not distance, and certainly not him.

The room filled with voices, and for the next couple of hours things were chaotic. Melissa and my mother headed next door to be with Kat, while I got everything ready, including myself.

Just like I'd promised her, I was standing there at the arbor waiting. Since it was winter, and the weather was unpredictable in D.C., we took precautions and rented a tent with heaters. One giant tent filled our two yards, and I had to admit that it was quite toasty when the plastic doors were closed.

The moment I saw her walking out of our back door, my knees started to get weak. She took a few steps and wrapped her arm inside of my father's. Even with her face covered by a tiny sheer veil, I could already tell she was stunning. Bug came running up the aisle, instead of walking. When she realized that she'd forgotten to throw out the flowers, she went back and tossed them going in both directions. The tiny crowd of neighbors and friends laughed, but then gave all of their attention to Kat.

When she was halfway to me, my lips began to quiver and my palms were getting sweaty. I wiped them on the side of my pants and hoped that nobody noticed.

The moment she was within reach, I had her hands in mine. The officiator knew us, and as the guests laughed, he shooed my dad to sit down and not to worry about the whole giving her away speech. I felt it necessary to address it, so I turned to the standing people. "She doesn't need to be given away since she's always been mine." I winked at them before turning my attention back to my beautiful bride.

She pulled one hand away and lifted the veil. That's when I saw her crying. Her hands were shaking as much as mine, but I didn't move my eyes away from hers. I mouthed the words, 'I love you', while the official started speaking.

Honestly, I don't even know what he was saying, because I was completely captivated by her beauty. We stood there, in some sort of trance as if nobody else existed.

Finally, I felt someone touch my arm. "Are you ready to exchange your vows?" Neither of us had noticed the person trying to get our attention.

I smiled and answered, "Yes. Yes, we are."

We'd discussed me going first, but Kat spoke before I could say anything. "This morning I woke up to a Valentine, from my Valentine."

Everyone attending laughed, and she waited for them to finish. "I had written down my vows and polished them a dozen times, but after I read what Brooks wrote to me in this card, I knew my vows could never come close. So, I'm going to read it to everyone and let you all see the real man I'm marrying today."

She waved to Melissa, and I watched as she approached us with the card in her hand.

Since I'd poured out my heart to her, I felt a little overwhelmed.

Kat opened it up and looked down, clearing her voice before she began.

"The outside says, 'To my wife on our first Valentine's Day as a married couple.' Then Brooks wrote his message on the inside."

"Dear Mrs. Valentine, my beautiful bride, mother of my children, my soul-mate and my very best friend,

I've loved you my whole life and perhaps even in lives before this one. There was no amount of time, distance, or even people that could ever change the way I feel about you. I've literally waited my entire life for this day. It's easy to say that I've never felt more complete than when you're in my arms. Every time I look at our little girl, or feel our baby moving around in your belly my heart melts, because it's just another anchor of our love for each other. You're mine forever, Kat. You don't need a ceremony to know that. No matter where life takes us, I'll be by your side, and when the good Lord comes at our last breath, I know we'll find each other again, because you are who I will always choose for that other peanut butter cup. I hope now you can finally know without a single doubt that I will hold you when you're sad, love you when you feel lonely, and protect you when you feel scared. I guess I don't have to ask you to be my Mrs. Valentine, because you already are and will be for every single moment of every single day, for as long as we both are breathing. Love, your husband, Mr. Valentine."

I wasn't really sure how much the crowd could understand through Kat's sobbing, but as I turned to look at them, most were shoving tissues into their faces. To avoid losing it completely, I looked back to Kat. Even as a babbling mess, she was still gorgeous. "There's nothing that I can say to you that you don't already know, Brooks. I've already given myself to you in every way. You give me comfort and support and your love is more than I could ever deserve. I'm in awe of you, and I thank God every day for giving us this life. I love you so much."

She couldn't say anymore, and she didn't need to. We could have stood there staring at each other all day. We were already married in my eyes.

I glanced at the guests and flashed a half-smile. "How about we make this official and get to the celebrating?"

"It gives me great pleasure to announce the marriage of Mr. and Mrs. Brooks Valentine." The officiator leaned in for only us to hear. "Go ahead and kiss her now, Brooks."

My lips were on Kat's before he finished his sentence. She was mine in the eyes of the whole world and I let her know exactly how happy I was about it in our embrace. At first people clapped. Then some whistled. Then my brother started making perverted remarks. When our kiss ended, half of the guests had gotten up and were already in line on the other side of the heated tent.

I wiped away her tears. "You're my wife."

She smiled and leaned her cheek against mine. "I know."

Bug came up and wrapped her arms around my legs. I acknowledged her by rubbing her head.

We couldn't stand there for the whole day, so I grabbed Kat's hand as we turned to face everyone, knowing that after they'd all gone home and went about their lives, we'd have forever to spend together. Knowing that made me the happiest man in the world.

Epilogue
July 17ᵗʰ 2014

"Promise me that you'll keep your phone turned on all day?" Kat asked while still sitting in our bed. I was busy trying to adjust my tie in the mirror, focused on a presentation I was giving in a few hours.

"I told you I won't turn it off." I spun around to face her. She had her hands sitting on top of her huge belly as if it was a snack tray. "Do you want me to reschedule the meeting?"

"No. It's fine. I just don't want you to miss anything."

"I won't. I promise. I'm ten minutes from the hospital. As soon as your contractions get within five minutes of each other I want you to call me." We'd been up half the night counting the time between each one, hoping they wouldn't last much longer. Kat was miserable. She'd organized the house three times since we moved in, and for the past week she'd been crying about everything. Just the night before she cried because B didn't want to eat her vegetables. It was insane.

"My bag is still in your car, right?"

I leaned over and kissed her. "Kat, calm down. We've got this. I have a nine o'clock presentation and then I'm coming home. I'm using my two weeks vacation as soon as you give me the order to report to the hospital."

"I don't want you to miss anything."

"I won't. I promise. Our son or daughter is going to see my face first. Stop worrying. Stay in bed and wait for me to get home."

Kat agreed and told me goodbye before I walked back downstairs. It was a good thing B was still asleep, otherwise I'd have to go through a whole ordeal with her before getting out the door. What my girls didn't understand was that the sooner I got to work, the earlier I could get back home. I wouldn't miss this delivery for the world.

Two blocks was as far as I got before I stopped the car and pulled over to the side of the road. The phone rang twice before she answered. "Did you forget something?"

I clenched my jaw and considered what I wanted to say. "What do you want for breakfast?"

"What? Is your mom asking?"

"No, I am. Do you want pancakes?"

"Brooks, why do you want to know? I thought you left."

While she spoke I turned the car around and started driving home. "I did. Now I'm coming back."

"What's wrong?"

"Kat, I'm not missing a single second of this. I want to be there for every contraction, every scream, and all of the pushing. Nothing is more important than that."

"What about the security presentation?"

"I'll email it to my boss and let him give it. We've already gone over the software several times. It's not a big deal."

I was already home before we ended our call. After kicking off my shoes, and changing into something more comfortable, I called work and let them know my wife was starting to go into labor. I forwarded my calls to my boss and emailed him the information he needed. My last stop was crawling into my warm bed with my beautiful, expecting wife. "I'm back."

"I can see that." She leaned over and closed her eyes. "How comfortable are you right now?" she asked.

"Why?"

"I have to pee and I need help getting out of this bed."

I'd never been so happy of a choice I'd made before, because when Kat stood up and soaked the floor I realized that coming home was the best decision I'd ever made. We both looked at each other in shock. "Tell me you peed yourself."

"I don't think that was pee, Brooks. My water just broke."

I smiled. "So the baby's coming today?"

"I guess so."

Standing in the door way was a very ornery toddler. She had a doll shoved up in her shirt. "I have a baby too."

I rolled my eyes and started undressing my wife from the waist down. "Go put your baby back to bed, B."

I couldn't let Kat go out soaked. After I helped put dry shorts on her, we sent B over to stay with my parents. She cried that she couldn't go with us, but that would have been a catastrophe.

While in the car, Kat started having heavier contractions. I tried to keep her focused on breathing, but apparently it hurt too much for her to concentrate. In all honesty I was scared for her. I had no idea what to expect even though I'd been reading books on childbirth since we discovered we were having another child.

"What can I do, babe? Tell me how to help?"

"Shut up and drive," she announced in a demonic voice.

I was in shock. I pushed on the gas pedal praying I'd get her there before the next contraction. Ten minutes later we were walking into the hospital and immediately led up to the maternity ward. She'd messaged her doctor, and called Melissa all while suffering from a second contraction in the car, while I clung to the steering wheel, feeling the worst fear of my entire life.

When we got into a room, they hooked Kat up to monitors and checked between her legs to see the progress. "As soon as the doctor gets here you'll probably be pushing. This baby wants to come out already. You're lucky."

I didn't feel lucky. I felt as if I were going to pass out. Kat took one look at me and pointed to the chair. "For someone who is trained for combat, you're looking pretty pathetic. Snap out of it, soldier. I need you to keep me strong."

I rubbed my face with my hands. "I'm freaking out. I just watched her look at your vagina and it's huge. I'm not talking like a little stretched. It's gigantic. I could almost stick my head in there."

Kat shook her head and rolled her eyes. "Brooks, seriously?" I threw up my hands. "Sorry, I didn't mean it that way. It's just so swollen. I hate seeing you in pain, and THAT has to hurt."

"I've done this before, and back then all I wanted was to have you by my side." She started crying. "Brooks, I need you here with me, really here, holding my hand and cheering me on. I've dreamed of this day since I found out I was pregnant with B. Please be my anchor. Help me bring our baby into this world."

I nodded and rested my lips against her head. "I'm sorry. I've seen all kinds of crazy things, but this is you. I'm afraid I can't handle seeing you like this. It's creeping me out."

At that exact moment, Kat had another huge contraction. She grabbed the railings on the bed and scrunched up her face. When I saw the determination in her eyes, I knew I had to stick it out. I wanted to witness this even if seeing her in pain made me uneasy. "I'm not going anywhere, Kat."

I grabbed her hand and held it as she squeezed, harder and harder. "We're in this together."

About thirty minutes later the doctor came in. I stood back and let him examine Kat. He ordered an epidural, and for part of the procedure I left the room. I'd already seen enough to make me want to pass out. Watching a giant needle go into my wife's back wasn't going to happen.

When I knew she'd been taken care of, I headed back inside to tend to her. Another hour went by before he checked on us again. She was ready to start pushing. In no time at all, our little bundle would be with us. Since we'd waited to find out the sex of the baby, I couldn't wait to make the call to announce if it was a girl or a boy. I didn't care what we had. Kat and I planned on having at least three kids, so if it was a girl we could always be hopeful that the next child was a boy. Either way I'd love them all the same.

I held onto my wife's hand as she pushed until her face turned red then relaxed. She had to keep doing it, over and over again, unlike the movies portray. Each time the baby's head would come out a little and then go back in. I was starting to wonder if maybe it just wasn't ready to be born. Then, like a slippery noodle, I watched it sliding out, head to feet.

In those moments, I don't remember being freaked out, or dizzy. All I saw was my beautiful child coming into this world. Then I was asked to cut the cord of my newborn son. After that, everything seemed like it was easy. I held him first before Kat. She'd insisted on it, claiming that it was only fair since she had B to herself for so long. I couldn't stop staring down at him. He was so tiny and fragile. I was in awe of him, feeling another unbreakable bond with Kat. I held him close for her to see. "We have a son."

"He's perfect, just like his daddy," she announced.

"You were so brave," I said as I leaned down to kiss her. "I love you so much."

"You were brave too, Brooks, after you stopped freaking out." I could tell it hurt her to laugh. The doctor was still fixing her up, making it difficult for her to get comfortable.

"You were right. It was worth it. I've never been so happy." Tears of joy streamed down my face while I stared down at my beautiful son.

"Are you sure about the name you picked?"

I nodded. "I am. Are you sure it's okay?"

Kat reached over and touched my shoulder. "Of course it's okay. I think it's a beautiful idea."

I ran one finger over his tiny hand. "Welcome to the world Trevor Michael. You're named after a brave soldier that daddy used to know. I'm sure he's looking down smiling today."

A little later, I heard the door opening and little feet running inside. Kat had been resting after nursing Trevor for the first time. He'd been back in my arms as soon as she was finished.

I put my finger over my lips to signal for B to be quiet. "Shh, the baby is sleeping."

She peeked at him and smiled. "Is that my brother?"

"Yes. Isn't he perfect?"

She nodded, but never took her eyes off him. I patted the seat beside me, noticing how my mother already had her camera out. She focused it toward us and snapped the first picture of me with my two children. Then gently I helped B hold her brother. Kat opened her eyes and looked over to see the sight for herself. It was that moment that I mouthed the words 'thank you' to her. She'd given me everything I could ever want, and I knew our life together was just beginning.

If someone would have asked me where I'd be on this day a few years back I would have probably answered them simply by saying dead. I thought I had nothing to left to live for. Through the hardships and the pain, I found my way back to her. Maybe I always knew I would. After all we'd been through, we finally had everything we could ever hope for, and even more.

If you enjoyed this story please leave a
review on the purchase site.
To contact the author:
www.jenniferfoor.com